# ASSISTANT TO THE BILLIONAIRE CEO

A HOT ROMANTIC COMEDY

JOLIE DAY

*Assistant to the Billionaire CEO* © Copyright 2023 Jolie Day

Copyright notice: All rights reserved under the International and Pan-American Copyright Conventions. No part of this book may be reproduced or transmitted in any form or by any means, electronic or mechanical, including photocopying, recording, or by any information storage and retrieval system, without permission in writing from the publisher, except in the case of brief quotation embodied in critical reviews and certain other noncommercial uses permitted by copyright law.

This is a work of fiction. Names, places, characters and incidents are either the product of the author's imagination or are used fictitiously, and any resemblance to any actual persons, living or dead, organizations, events or locales is entirely coincidental. The author acknowledges the trademarked status and trademark owners of various products referenced in this work of fiction. The publication/use of these trademarks is not authorized, associated with, or sponsored by the trademark owners.

Warning: This story contains mature themes and language.

Assistant to the Billionaire CEO; *Kiss a Billionaire* Series; Jolie Day

info@joliedayauthor.com

Cover Design: ARP Book Covers

**ISBN:** 9798391184164

**Imprint:** Independently published

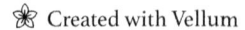

❋ Created with Vellum

# ABOUT THIS NOVEL

**She's my best friend's sister, and I'm her new boss.**

There are three things I expect from a good assistant:
Punctuality, honesty, and trustworthiness.

She says she's all that. Despite my reservations, I decide to give her a shot.

To my surprise, she's not the nerdy girl I knew when we were young.
She follows my every command.
She wins over our clients.
She charms her colleagues.
Including me.

Our one-on-one "meetings" are getting hotter—by the copy machine, in the archive room, on top of my desk.
We're putting on a show for the company security cameras, that's for sure.

I'm determined to make her mine.
Until I catch her in my office with her hand in my secret drawer.
I can't wait to hear what she has to say for herself.

Her job (and a happy ending for us) is on the line.

# 1

## ACE

IT STARTED GOING TITS-UP AT TALIA'S

"You weren't in love with her, were you?" my buddy Miles asked with a cocky grin on his face.

"Don't be stupid," I grumbled and directed my gaze toward Gracie, the bustling bartender a few yards away, hoping she'd spot me. She didn't. "She was an *assistant*." I emphasized the last word and noticed that Miles didn't follow immediately. It must have been the lead he had on me beer-wise because he wasn't usually that slow on the uptake. "Sex and work don't mix," I continued. "Besides, I'm not looking to get involved. But I do need a new assistant."

"Dude, getting an assistant is not that fucking hard," Miles argued, and next to him, Oliver nodded in agreement.

"Then you've probably never tried to find a trustworthy and not completely incompetent assistant. Agencies, headhunters—they all keep putting me off. I need an assistant now, not in three months. My paperwork is piling up, my calendar is about to explode—I don't get shit done."

Being back in New York was daunting in its own way—never mind the fact my personal life also needed a complete makeover. At least I had three people back in my life I trusted, even though they got on my nerves. Damon. Oliver. Miles.

Damon had been the first of the group to befriend me when we were in college. The guy was a straight-talking, strait-laced businessman—incredibly driven—with a love for bikes, not unlike me. Miles and Oliver were brothers. Oliver was what you'd best describe as the watchful, protective kind, and, well, Miles was just the same fun-loving dude he'd always been. A real jokester. Unfiltered and snarky.

It felt good to be with the boys again.

Back then, Talia's had been our favorite place to hang out: an old-school biker bar in the city, unchanged since it had reopened in the early '80s, with several pool tables in the back. The beer used to be too warm for my taste, and it still was—I guessed some things never changed—but we liked going there anyway.

"What about the smart lady who sat in during our last meeting?" Damon asked. "Why don't you get her more involved?"

"Mrs. Mills doesn't have the architectural background that's needed."

"Look on the bright side," Miles said. "At least you're not getting bent over your boss's desk by a delivery guy."

Oliver erupted into raucous laughter. He raised his fist to Miles, but Miles faked him out and then pulled his hand away. In return, Oliver put Miles in a headlock and roared, "Not this time, brother. Not this time." Even Damon smirked, which was saying something. The dude rarely smiled.

"Hey...*guys?*" a sugary-sweet voice asked from behind me. I swiveled in my seat, only to notice a face I didn't recognize, holding a tray. "Can I offer you boys a shot?"

Oliver turned his head. "It depends on who's offering."

"The company I work for is sponsoring it." The chick parted her red lips in a cheeky smile to reveal a mouthful of blindingly white teeth. "We're supposed to offer customers shots when we're not...*dancing.*" She threw a sassy wink at Oliver, then at Miles.

"*Dancing?*" Miles peered at the woman with a curious expression. "Since when does Talia's have strippers?"

"It's not *that* kind of dancing." She playfully slapped his arm, flipped her long ash-blonde ponytail over her shoulder, and rested her left hand on her hip. Her bright-green nail polish matched her green T-shirt perfectly. With her gaze, she directed our eyes from the top of her shirt to her tits, making each of us look down.

A white slogan sprawled across her curves in a thick Non-Serif:

*Get Hot for Some Shots*

The letter "O" in "Hot" was a fire emoji.

At first, I was certain that somewhere out there, a wannabe marketing executive had been mulling this little catchphrase over in his mind for weeks and was likely feeling immensely proud of it. Second, I asked myself how effective the slogan was—compared to the short-cut shirt that almost exposed her nipples.

"Strippers take off *all* of their clothes," the dancer explained, giving Miles another sultry wink. "*We* don't undress all the way…"

"You only undress a little bit?" Amusement swung in Miles's voice, meaning, "Girl, you're basically naked as it is."

"Yeah," she chirped. "It's a new thing the bar is trying out—you know, to get some new faces in here. So, are you boys going to have some shots, or are you a bunch of *chickens*?" She shifted her gaze and stared straight at me.

She hadn't addressed me because she thought *I* was a chicken. No. Clearly, she recognized the decision maker of the group.

"Sure, we'll have some shots," I decided, making up my mind on behalf of the four of us. "But right after we're done here, I need you to find our waitress and ask her how long a man has to wait for a refill around here. Our glasses have been empty for ages."

"I second that," Oliver added.

"Who's your waitress?"

"Gracie."

"Yeah, I'd be happy to, but first things first." The blonde girl whipped four shot glasses out of her apron pocket before withdrawing a small bottle of green liquid.

"That looks like poison," Damon grumbled, furrowing his brow.

"Oh, it is, big boy. It is," she sang and poured the green liquor into the first shot glass.

By the time she'd finished filling the fourth glass, she was batting her eyelashes at Damon, who was not giving into her attempts. She handed him the final shot, obviously making an effort to *lean* in, making it undeniably clear she wasn't wearing a bra—as if we all hadn't fucking noticed.

She wiped her fingers on the small apron, which was already showing traces of the sticky lime-colored concoction. "Enjoy, boys."

She stepped backward. It seemed like she was about to leave when she hesitated for a moment, looking back at Damon. "I hope you don't mind me asking, but could I have your number? I think I'd like to see you again. You know, hopefully somewhere more…romantic."

"I've got a girl, doll," Damon replied.

"You sure?" She looked disappointed. "I've heard you're a big player in the construction business."

"Says who?" he asked.

"One of the waitresses."

"Babe," Oliver jumped in, canting his head toward Damon, "if that guy was a property, he'd be a mansion made out of gold, situated on a beach made of ground-up pearls on Manalapan's coast."

She blinked twice. "Ehh…meaning?"

"Properties like him are *never* on the market."

"Oh." She shrugged. "Too bad." With one final glance, she pivoted on a heel and walked to another table.

"What's wrong with you?" Damon huffed as soon as she was out of sight. "Shut the fuck up."

"Yeah, bro. What the corny fuck was that?" Miles stared at his brother, shaking his head. "Are you drunk?"

"Nope, I'm driving," Oliver said with a "duh" face. "I was just trying to ease the situation. Make a joke. Make light of the awkward moment." He turned to Damon. "Dude. Didn't you fucking see how you crushed the girl's confidence with your brutal rejection? *I've got a girl*," he mocked him, imitating Damon's signature baritone. "You know the balls it takes to walk up to four big-ass guys? And the even *bigger* balls it takes to ask one of them out?"

"And your line helped exactly, how?" Damon asked, clearly pissed.

"Yeah, man, you made it worse," Miles said, grabbing his shot glass. "You embarrassed her even more by piling shit on top of shit."

"I did not."

The whole conversation had started to get on my damn nerves. "Cheers," I announced, raising my shot.

"Cheers." They lifted their glasses to mine. "Cheers!"

We all clinked and brought our drinks to our lips before we slammed them back down onto the wooden surface. The shot was good. Tasty.

The guys voiced their approval. Damon, Oliver, and Miles all worked in the same billion-dollar real estate company: Humphries Properties, built from the ground up by Miles and Oliver's father, Charles Henry. Humphries Properties was on the brink of acquiring my business, Windsor Architects. The deal would turn us into the biggest and most influential construction firm in the country, and I was determined to ensure there would be no more damn roadblocks.

Damon was my contact person. He was a soon-to-be partner at Humphries Properties and a decision maker in the acquisition. Not that he made me nervous by any means. We were best buddies. I was confident that if push came to shove, he'd vote in my favor.

Well. I was almost sure.

For one, Damon had a damn good poker face. But, I'd also been away from the flock for a long period of time. San Francisco and New York weren't exactly a stone's throw apart. Even though we'd stayed in touch throughout, this was business. It would be a lie to say that Damon was known to let his business persona overwhelm his private real-life personality at times. In fact, sometimes it was hard to distinguish Damon "the normal guy" from Damon "the adamant businessman" (his far more serious counterpart)—as if Damon "the normal guy" wasn't serious enough already.

"*You're* the one who needs to fucking relax," Oliver said to Damon, still on the same topic. "You scared her off."

"Nobody scared anybody off." Damon swiveled his gaze between the three of us. "A girl like her appreciates directness. I can only imagine what kind of shit she hears all day."

"Sorry, disagree." Oliver shook his head. "She looked crushed. She's probably crying her heart out as we speak. If you ask me, she's never coming back."

"She has to," Damon said, undeterred. "She needs to get these shot glasses."

Miles looked up and scanned the room. "Wait, hold on, Damon's right. She's coming."

We stared as the blonde ponytail girl returned to our table. For a moment, she seemed to wonder why we were staring at her. "Just back to collect the shot glasses, guys," she said. I gave her extra points for returning instead of sending another one of her green-shirt-wearing colleagues.

She turned to Oliver. "And sorry, I've got a question, but what's Manapan? None of the girls knew." She lifted her chin, directing our attention to Gracie and the other girls by the bar. Her blue eyes darted between Oliver, Miles, Damon, and me as she seemed to try to gauge our reactions. She was a daredevil in her own right. I appreciated a bold woman.

"Manalapan," Damon corrected her. "In Florida."

"Oh." She gulped, giving Damon a scrutinizing look and frowned. "Isn't he way too young to live in Florida? I thought only old people lived there."

"He has an ancient soul," I interjected and was rewarded with a grimace from Damon.

"Anyway, as he said," Oliver pointed to Damon, "he's not on the market." He crossed his arms over his chest. "None of us are."

"Actually." Miles arched an eyebrow at me. "Isn't Ace single right now?"

The blonde girl looked at me with a curious expression as she chewed on her gum.

I shook my head. "Sorry, I'm not looking for anything serious." I shifted my gaze to Miles and gave him a "What the fuck?" expression. He clearly knew I wasn't—

"I'm not looking for anything serious either," the girl chirped, interrupting my thoughts.

I let out an impatient sigh and faced her. "Yeah, no, sorry."

"You deaf? You heard the lady, man," Miles hissed at me. "She's not looking for anything serious either."

What the fuck? "Stay out of it," I said to him. Why was he being so pushy?

"You sure? No girlfriend? No relationship?" She leaned into me further, brushing my arm with her tits. "Absolutely no...fun?"

"No." I set my empty shot glass on her tray with a cold *clink*, possibly a bit too forcefully. It was a knee-jerk reaction, and not one I'd given any thought to, but it caused the girl to take a step back.

"That's okay," she squeaked. "I'll be over there if you need me." She gathered up the other three empty shot glasses, hastily set them onto her tray and hurried away.

"Dude, what the fuck was *that*?" Miles asked me. "That was the worst fucking rejection ever. Even more brutal than Damon's."

"Shut. Up. You're the one who got me into it."

"So?" he asked.

"So, I was just being honest."

"That's worse than being direct. It's pedantic. Dude. At least package it up differently if you can't help it. There's a difference between being *nicely* honest and being *fucking* honest."

I didn't answer. Since when was honesty a bad thing? As she sauntered in the direction of the bar, I allowed my eyes to linger on her. I should have felt something. Sure, she had gorgeous tits, thick hips, and legs, but I couldn't exactly admit any sparks were there. The old me wouldn't have minded a flirt or a hookup, even though she clearly didn't seem to be very picky when it came to the men she chose to spend time with.

"Back to business," Damon said, as we noticed Gracie hurriedly shuffling toward us with four more draft glasses full of—I could already tell—lukewarm beer.

Damon plucked a glass from Gracie's arms and placed it in front of him, then turned back to me. "Cards on the table. Are you still interested in the acquisition? Or have you changed your mind?"

"No," I answered curtly. "Why should I?" I'd let no wild horses stop

Humphries Properties from acquiring Windsor Architects. "Just because the server broke, files got lost, a few boxes got shipped to who knows where, and my former assistant shredded what she thought were 'duplicate papers' from the boxes that *did* arrive?" I tried to sound confident. Frankly, it was a huge mess, but nothing I couldn't handle—I just needed more time.

"Was that before or after she fucked that delivery guy on your desk?"

I gave him a hard stare.

"Jesus, what a clusterfuck." Miles raked a hand down his face. "Are we sure we wanna merge with this guy?" he asked, and they all chuckled.

I wasn't laughing. "I'm working on it."

"You better. You're not getting out of it," Damon said. "We've been stuck in the information exchange stage for too long already—nothing's happening. We sent you our info ages ago, and we need that information to start the valuation and synergies, before we send in the offer. You know that. You need to get your shit together. And quickly. Dad and the board are getting impatient. Two weeks—max."

"Four," I countered, unable to hide my irritation at his deadline. "That's the bare minimum." I had never been the type to give false promises or make excuses. Already, we were more than two weeks behind after moving to New York. While the recoup process with my teams between San Francisco and NYC was in full swing, putting together a convincing presentation was time consuming. "Humphries Properties benefits from the merger as much as I do." It didn't hurt to remind them that the deal was a two-way street and they wanted it just as much as I did.

"All right. Tell you what. You get your four weeks. On Monday morning in exactly one month, I want the papers on my desk, or the deal is off."

I wouldn't get more time from Damon, I knew that.

"Done," I agreed, and we shook on it. Even if the lost boxes were to show up again—unlikely—and even if I *did* find the ideal assistant within the next few days—equally unlikely—it was a damn close call.

Gracie handed me my beer, and I looked at her. "Keep them coming.

Let's say, get the next round to us in thirty minutes, sound good?" The place wasn't as crowded as it had been when we'd arrived. There was no reason for a delay. "Don't make us wait."

"Yes, *sir*," she sang, playfully placing her right hand to her temple, giving me a mock salute. "I'm sure a man like you isn't used to waiting for anything." She leaned in to grab Oliver's empty whiskey glass, giving him a "What's wrong with this guy?" look.

"Hey, Gracie. No worries," Miles replied before his brother had a chance to. "Tonight, he even kicked Damon from the dickface pedestal."

"I've got to piss," I announced, not giving a shit if it ruffled the guys' undershirts—they'd live. I'd gotten tired of the circular conversation and decided a walk to the urinals and a splash of fresh water might calm me down. "But I'm serious about that beer, Gracie."

"Yeah, I heard you the first time, tiger," Gracie said as I turned my back on them. "Lighten up. I've only got two hands."

Okay, I knew I was acting like an asshole. I'd been this way for quite some time. Trying to care was hard after everything I'd gone through. Perhaps some of my mood may have been self-inflicted, but nobody wanted to hear that after a breakup. Just pick up, move on, business as usual. But life wasn't that simple, and it seemed my personal shit had started to affect nearly every aspect of my life.

As I parted an ocean of patrons to make it to the other side of the bar, a scruffy biker dressed in tattered leathers sat slumped against the farthest wall, snoring loudly. It was impossible to remember the last time I'd had a good night's sleep. The empty bottle clasped in his limp fist spoke volumes. Poor guy. These days it took me a lot more, and only a small part of Allison and my breakup was responsible for my insomnia. I wasn't sad Allison and I hadn't worked out. No, I was pissed the fuck off. I also had enough self-awareness to know that my biggest issue was mostly offended vanity that hung over my head like a thundercloud. This feeling would soon evaporate, I was sure. Then sunshine and rainbows, and all that shit.

Time would tell.

"Where are you going, stranger?" A voice interrupted my train of thought.

Turning around, I was met by the blonde ponytail girl from earlier, staring at me eagerly. "I realize I didn't introduce myself to you earlier. I'm Emily, but my friends call me Emmie." She wiggled her hips from side to side like an excited puppy preparing to pounce. "You're Ace, right?"

"How do you know?"

"I overheard it earlier when you guys were talking."

"Thanks for the shots, Emmie. But I'm on my way to the bathroom, excuse me," I grumbled, pushing past her. I opened the Western saloon-style double doors that separated the men's room from the rest of the bar, and strode in, hoping I'd left her behind.

"Hold on," Emmie practically squealed. "I'll come with!"

She skipped into the bathroom beside me, matching my pace. Her hand touched my ass as she followed, and when I glanced at her over my shoulder to confirm it was an accident, she winked at me. The blonde ponytail now cascaded over her shoulders, bouncing around in the middle of her back. It wasn't the only thing that was bouncing around. My cock stirred, but not enough to make me succumb to temptation. Silently, I cursed Damon and the fact he had brought the merger to the table. Instead of a quickie, lost boxes and a faceless future assistant haunted my mind.

Emmie slinked closer to me like a wild cat stalking its prey, licking her lips. As she reached out to undo my pants, I gently grabbed her wrists.

To hell with the boys and their suggestion that I should be more polite in my rejections. Apparently, Emmie didn't want to understand that I wasn't in the mood for a dirty fuck in the restroom. "I don't think that's a good idea. *Seriously*," I growled, and this time—finally—it was enough for her to understand.

Her eyes widened as realization dawned, and she shrugged indifferently. "All right, cowboy. You know where to find me." My sympathy was limited. I wouldn't even have been her first choice—she'd put Damon first. I'd never been good at being number two, and I wouldn't start now.

## 2

## DAMON

"Don't forget about Ace's beer, doll," I said as Gracie handed Miles his drink. "Don't make him come looking for you to get it either. He's dealing with some shit."

"I won't," Gracie replied. "You know I won't. I was joking. I can tell something's bugging your friend. Nobody, not even Ace, can be that grumpy without a good reason." She nodded at me and smiled, causing her messy brown bun to flop around on top of her head.

"Appreciate it, Gracie."

"But he better cheer up soon, or Axel will kick his ass out." She grabbed an empty glass, gave me another smile, turned on her heel, and shuffled away from our table.

"I feel bad for Ace, man." Miles held his pale lager in one hand and rested it against his chest, like he was holding some kind of helpless baby animal. A few light beers and one shot were enough to make him tipsy. "Allison, that"—he made quote fingers—"'dream girl' of his, really did a fucking number on him. I've never seen him like this."

"It's damn normal. He thought he loved her." Oliver speared his fingers through his hair. "You can't blame him for feeling a little down."

"I'm concerned about him, too," I admitted. "But not for the same reasons."

"What do you mean?"

"Look, I don't want to speak ill of the guy while he's taking a piss, but doesn't this all seem just a little...*off*? The breakup. The sudden move to New York. The rush. Files got lost? Papers got shredded? Hello? Now he can't get the paperwork ready. Would he really be selling Windsor Architects to us if it was doing as well as he says it is?"

"Damon, hang on," Oliver said. "We've known Ace since college. He'd never screw us over. You know that." He took a swig of beer. "He's only selling 51 percent of it, and he still wants to be a director. Ace would never be stupid enough to make this position a condition if his company was built on sand."

"I know that. But something's not right."

"He's a stand-up fucking guy." Miles flashed a toothy grin at me. "Yeah, you need to chill, man. He's not the enemy."

"For fuck's sake, listen. I'm not saying he's a bad guy." I took my glasses off and pinched the bridge of my nose, trying to concentrate, despite the beer. "I'm saying that we need to do our homework. Your father will have our asses if this deal goes sideways and hurts the company."

"*Well.*" Miles glanced up at me. "He will have *your* ass. And not just your ass. Dad will fucking put you on the chopping block. He can't harm me and Oliver because, well...he'd have no heirs. But you, my friend, are fair game."

I took a swig of my beer. "Yeah. Thanks for that, Miles." I set my drink in front of me and put my glasses back on to glare at him.

"*What*? Just being direct. Honest."

Our table was rickety and wobbled at the slightest touch. Its poor construction had cost us more than one drink over the years, and I wasn't looking to risk losing another one.

"Hmm. Actually, I see your point, Damon," Oliver said, leaning forward, rubbing his chin. "I mean, I don't think Ace is up to something, but checking up on how Windsor Architects is doing would be normal procedure. Just like any other firm. We need to know whether everything checks out, if the company's financial reports confirm his claims—which they will, of course."

Behind him, a group of dancers in bright-green T-shirts started "dancing," circling around a table occupied by a group of burly bikers. Oliver lost his train of thought, glancing over his shoulder at the spectacle.

"*And* we need to know who he's doing business with," I said, attempting to draw his attention back to me. "Earlier tonight he mentioned drafting a blueprint for a mansion in Short Hills. Isn't Ecclestone Construction currently busy with a project in Short Hills? If it were any other suburb, I'd be less worried, but there's not a lot of construction that happens out there."

Ecclestone Construction, a billion-dollar firm led by CEO Edmund Ecclestone—the self-proclaimed "Construction King of New York"—was not only a thief, but an immoral deceiver. An online cartoon in the *New York Times* titled "*Après moi, le déluge*" (basically "devil-may-care") had made fun of the "Construction *Shark* of New York," hinting at money-laundering scams that had brought several reputable firms to their knees. The article with the cartoon, and its absurdly large mustache gracing Ecclestone's character, was removed twenty minutes later, unsurprisingly. Ecclestone had half of New York City in his pocket, and the colossal staff of lawyers he employed were doing their fucking jobs. Funnily enough, that and other claims going around hadn't hurt Ecclestone in the least—his empire was thriving, bigger than ever.

Oliver turned back to me and narrowed his eyes. "*What* did you say?"

"Ecclestone? Nah, man." Miles set his beer down mid-swig and shook his head. "Nah."

"Yeah. You're going too far." Oliver frowned and swallowed the last dregs of amber liquid from his glass. "There's no fucking way. Ace is an honest guy. He would *never,* not in a million years, associate with Ecclestone."

"I know, and I won't be any happier once we confirm that very point. But we've got to be sure," I insisted, leaning back. "We've got to do our due diligence."

"Hold on," Miles said, lifting his hand. "I've got an idea."

"What?"

For a moment it seemed like he was sifting through the drunken fog of his mind to find what he wanted to say. "Let's just ask him. When he gets back from the bathroom, we'll sit him down and say, 'Hey, dude. Are you bankrupt—or, worse—buddy-buddy with Edmund fucking Ecclestone, that shady son of a bitch?'"

"Are you serious?" I was quickly losing my patience and definitely not sober, but what Miles had suggested wouldn't have even made sense if I was flat-out drunk.

"Yeah, why not?" Miles appeared offended. "He's our bro. Why shouldn't we be *direct* and *honest* with him?"

"Because," I replied, growing irritated, "we have no way of guaranteeing that he'll be *direct* and *honest* with us, that's why."

"Hmm." Oliver inclined his head. "Damon's got a point. We better not mention anything to him."

"Of course we shouldn't." I gave a curt nod. "There's no point in pissing him off and screwing up the potential merger."

Oliver leaned back in his seat. "And a perfectly good friendship."

"That too," I agreed.

"Yeah. Whatever." Miles drank what was left of his beer. "*Fine*," he added when Oliver glared at him.

"I won't mention it either," Oliver confirmed, shifting to face me, "but I'm sure as hell not going to help you to dig up dirt on him."

"I don't expect you to," I said, as I noticed Ace making his way back toward the table out of the corner of my eye. "That's my job, anyway. I'll investigate his firm like I do with all of our high-risk cases. It's procedure. This one won't be special. I won't make it personal. I'll keep it objective."

"Ace, *heyheyhey*." Miles cut me off. "Bro! Did you have a nice dump?"

Ace shook his head. "I wasn't taking a dump." He hung his semi-formal black jacket on the back of his chair and quietly sat down. "Dick."

"Nobody pisses for ten minutes," Miles argued, chortling at his own words and flicking a beer cap at Ace. "You do look happier than when you left. Oh, I got it. Were you rubbing one out?"

"I was outside getting some fresh air." Ace lifted the beer glass in front of him and tilted its contents down his throat.

"Since when are you a fresh air fanatic?" Oliver narrowed his eyes suspiciously.

"Get out of my ass."

*Beep, beep.*

We all paused and stared at my cell.

It was lying face-up on the center of the table, since I'd ignored making it part of our "no phones during nights out" initiative. To my annoyance, its screen lit up and revealed a preview of a message from my baby sister, Stella.

It was a brief one.

**Stella:** Hey, Batman. Remember spending Halloween in Big Bend National Park...

The message itself wasn't problematic, but the photo that accompanied it was.

It depicted a much younger version of me, dressed up as the Dark Knight, a.k.a. Batman. Even worse, it showed a, let's say, rather unflattering version of my sister, wrapped in orange cloth—a failed attempt to dress up as a pumpkin. Her round, orange-painted face was perfectly framed by a pair of chunky tortoiseshell glasses and her braces glistened in whatever light source we'd posed in front of for the photo. She was making a funny face and crossing her eyes. It was the stupidest picture I'd ever seen of her. By a long shot. Not that I could talk. I didn't look any better.

Needless to say, I didn't feel the urge to get into that conversation. I was hopeful that in their drunken state, the guys hadn't registered any of it. In one smooth motion, I snatched my phone away, stowing it in my pants pocket.

Silence.

When I looked back up at them, all three were staring at me.

"Batman?" Ace asked.

"Dude." Miles grinned.

"So what?" I grumbled.

"The better question is: Who was the oddball?" Miles pointed out, crossing his eyes. The guys chuckled.

"Yeah, exactly." Oliver jumped in before I had a chance to wave it off. "The girl. Who was the pumpkin next to you? Your fugly neighbor?"

"My sister."

Everybody's face dropped. "Oh."

Miles and Oliver gave me sad "Fuck, sorry" eyes.

"She doesn't look like that anymore," I said, unsure why I felt the sudden need to explain myself. Maybe some weird sense of protection over my baby sister. Not that it mattered what my buddies thought of Stella's face or her costume choices.

They still stared at me. Ace gave me an "Oh, *really*, she doesn't look like that anymore?" look.

"She never looked like that," I corrected. "That was a failed attempt to look like an enchanting Jack-o-lantern."

All three of them stared at me.

Miles was the first to speak up. "No need to apologize, bro." He hiccupped and reached for his lager, only to realize it was empty. "Chill, bro. She's your sister, and we're cool with her. Never saw you hide your phone like that though. It's not like any of us are invested in her looks. Chill."

"Don't tell me to chill," I bit out. "I *am* fucking chill."

"How's she doing these days?" Ace asked.

"She just graduated from Princeton, actually," I said, glad for the change of subject. Despite my irritation, I couldn't hide the sense of pride welling up in my chest when I noted their appreciative nods. It was still hard for me to believe my sister had graduated. The guys raised their glasses (including Miles and Oliver with their empty ones) in excessive congratulatory gestures, clearly trying to make up for the earlier awkwardness.

"Good for her," Ace said. "And what degree?"

"Architecture."

"Really?" Miles said. "Architecture? Cool."

"Yeah. She's been applying for junior architect vacancies, but she hasn't had any luck so far."

"That's too bad. Junior architect, you say?" Oliver asked.

"Yeah. She's currently keeping herself busy with an unpaid internship at a smaller engineering firm, but not sure if she's really enjoying it. She spends her days assisting the CEO's assistant, helping with the calls, keeping things organized and prepared. She's good at it too, but she told me it isn't what she's passionate about. Anyway, her internship is almost over."

"If you ask me, she needs to get a foot in the door at an *architecture* firm," Miles suggested with a drunken smirk and nudged Oliver with his elbow.

Oliver returned the gesture, leaned in, and said in a conspiratorial tone, "Hey, don't we know a poor SOB with an architecture firm who just lost his assistant in a truly tragic accident?" He jerked his head in Ace's direction and winked at me.

# 3

# ACE

*Fuck* me. The first word that had popped into my head when the photo of Stella had flashed across Damon's cell was "nerd."

She couldn't have been much older than nineteen or twenty when the picture had been taken, and she radiated an *unprecedented* level of geekiness.

Those dorky glasses.

Those braces.

And those eyebrows, almost unibrows. Jesus Christ.

No wonder the guys didn't recognize her. Hell—*I* barely recognized her. She looked different, and not the good kind of different. Although it wasn't hard to tell she still had a curvy figure under her homemade pumpkin costume. Her hair was different too. It used to be mousy brown, but in the photo, it hung all over the place in weird orangey-colored ringlets. It looked frizzier than ever before.

The last time I'd seen Stella, she had just turned eighteen, and it'd been a hot afternoon in July. I was at the Copelands' home, hanging out with the guys. I was twenty-six at the time and busy wrapping up the last year of my Architecture Experience Program to become a licensed architect. Back then, I didn't think of much, except how much money I'd make—ready to grab life by its horns and pull off the grand plans I had for my new career.

I hadn't been wrong either—I had made a lot of money.

And a lot of mistakes.

Actually, a substantial number of mistakes. Some would even say a shit-ton. Not that it was uncommon for a startup. *You fly the plane as you're building it.*

Anyway, that day, I was sitting around the pool with Damon, Oliver, and Miles. We were all lounging around in our swimming trunks, having a couple of beers, and discussing what we thought our lives would be like.

We were dangling our feet into the pool's cool water when Stella came stumbling out onto the deck.

I barely recognized her.

Instead of her nerdy thick-rimmed black glasses, she wore fashionable white ones. It was a record-breaking summer filled with nothing but abnormally high temperatures and whining, so I wasn't too surprised to see Stella dressed in a bikini that was far skimpier than the baggy black swimwear she usually wore. No, this time, it was a tiny white number that contrasted well against her slightly sun-kissed skin.

Of course, I attempted to avert my gaze.

I lived by the "bro code," a silent set of rules that were all centered around one golden rule: Bros didn't kiss, date, or dip their dicks into other bros' sisters.

In fact, they didn't even look at them.

Trying to clear my mind, I tried to think of something else: a white motorcycle I'd set my eyes on—I mean…a black motorcycle I'd set my eyes on, when I heard a loud splash. I lifted my head just in time to notice one of the guys throwing a handful of frigid ice water at Stella. Her bikini turned see-through the second the water made contact with her skin. She shrieked and whipped a pool towel off a nearby chair, tightly wrapping it around her curvy body, and dropping her white sunglasses in the process.

Everyone laughed. Sure, it'd been funny. That shriek! I bet the whole neighborhood had heard it.

I, for my part, wished I could say that she'd wrapped the damn towel around herself fast enough.

She hadn't.

In the split second between someone throwing water and Stella reaching for the towel, I'd seen more than I was supposed to. Gorgeous, gloriously shaped tits. Her fully erect pink nipples practically blushed at me through her translucent bikini top, ready to be sucked. Of course, I looked downward to stop myself from making eye contact with them—only to be met with the alluringly clear outline of the "womanly charms" nestled between her thighs. She was fully waxed.

"I think I'm going to sunbathe for a while," was the first—and only—thing I said, before awkwardly teetering over to the closest lounger and slamming myself down onto it—stomach-first. The guys, mostly Miles, protested and teased me for leaving our beer circle to "toast myself," but I hadn't slipped away to catch a fucking tan. I'd made myself scarce to hide the one thing that eventually betrayed all young men: their own body's damn response to fucking physical perfection.

After all, the bro code prohibited me from even looking in Stella's direction.

Let alone at her wet tits and wet pussy lips.

I'd tried to justify the whole incident by telling myself that my stressed-out, caffeine-fueled mind was longing to give into my most basic urges because I'd denied them for a bit too long.

I had seen (and felt) plenty of other women naked. But this here, *she* —the curvy Stella in her transparent white bikini—had awakened something in me that had not stirred until then.

It was the first time the beast in me had opened its eyes, ready to hunt.

"Dude."

"Ace?" I heard someone call my name.

"Earth to Ace! Bro, hello?" Miles jeered loudly, slamming his palm against my back.

And with that, I found myself back in Talia's and yanked from my recollection of that hot afternoon in July.

Blinking to clear my thoughts, I took a swig of my beer, sweeping the rest of the cobweb-like memories of Stella in her bikini from my mind. "Hmm," I replied, nodding, unsure of what to say. I'd lost track of the conversation.

"So, are you going to hire Damon's sister or not?" Miles stared at me, eyebrows raised. "Man. What's there to think about? Didn't you hear? She did admin for Princeton's dean. Now she's assistant to the assistant, it means she gets shit done. Sounds like prime assistant material to me."

"There's no harm in giving her a shot." Oliver smiled sympathetically in Damon's direction as if to tell him, "I'm on your side, bro."

"You really don't have to offer Stella a job." Damon shook his head at us. "Might not be the best idea."

"*You* were the one who brought up that she was looking for a job," Miles said, his tone clearly teasing. "Sounded to me like you were covertly trying to line up a position for her at Windsor Architects. Am I right?"

"No, I wasn't, and stop pissing me off," Damon grumbled. "You guys asked how she was, and I answered."

I looked at my beer glass and wondered where the hell Gracie was with our next drinks. "Oliver and Miles are right. She sounds like the ideal candidate," I said. "Tell her to send over her résumé."

# 4

# DAMON

Once I stepped over the door's threshold and into the chilly night spring air, my glasses fogged up.

"See you, bro," Ace said as we exchanged quick bro-hugs.

"Remember to tell the pumpkin to send her résumé to Ace," Miles almost slurred. "And tell the pumpkin we say hi!" Miles waved as Oliver dragged him to his car. "See ya tomorrow."

A layer of pebbles crunched beneath the soles of my shoes as I made my way down the sidewalk toward my car. Under better circumstances, I would have ridden my motorcycle to the bar. Hell, we all would've arrived there in a cacophony of roaring engines if it hadn't been for the shitty weather. On a normal day, I'd drive home, light a fire in my living room's fireplace, and surrender to a cuddling session with Aria as we sprawled out on the couch in front of it. But today hadn't been an ordinary day. Aria, Oliver and Miles's sister, was in Europe on a "girls-only trip."

Before I knew it, I was winding my way up my private road on a ridiculously long driveway, wondering what nutcase had decided to make it the gold standard to spend what seemed like twenty minutes on a scenic drive from the road to their house. I parked my car under the *porte-cochère* in front of my front door and killed its engine. The outside world was eerily quiet as I got out. It didn't take much to make silence seem eerie when you were used to spending your time in rowdy biker bars or in corporate negotiations—which, believe it or not, were on occasion, the louder of the two.

Typically, I'd end the night with a glance in a folder or my laptop to read up on a current project, bourbon in hand. Today, I decided to end it with a glass of wine. I had a surplus of the blood red. Ace's parents lived next to a commercial vineyard in France's beautiful Burgundy region, where they'd moved to retire. In a show of generosity—or perhaps gratitude—they'd sent me a case of exquisite Musigny Pinot Noir Grand Cru straight from their neighbor's cellar, a gesture they repeated at least once a year. It wasn't the kind of alcoholic beverage I'd typically drink in public, bourbon was my drink of choice, and so it was reserved as my little guilty pleasure—something I preferably indulged in with Aria, simply for the sake of indulging.

However, instead of opening a bottle, I found myself fishing my cell phone out of my pocket.

Even though I'd dismissed Miles's suggestion to ask Ace outright about his connection to Ecclestone, something urged me to reconsider, concluding that it wasn't the worst idea he'd ever had. I wouldn't be able to live with myself if I didn't give Ace a chance.

My phone's clock read 2:13 a.m., but I dialed Ace's number, anyway.

*Tuut. Tuut.*

I held my cell up to my ear and listened to the monotonous dialing tone. Several rings in, I was about to give up and end the call when I heard a click on the other end of the line.

"Damon? That you?"

"Yeah, it's me."

"Everything all right?"

"Yeah. Sorry." I reclined on the couch. "I hope I didn't wake you."

"You didn't." Ace's voice sounded raspy, but not sleepy. "Are you just calling to check up on me, or is there a different reason you got me on the line in the early-morning hours?"

"You know me too well. I actually want to talk shop." I put my feet up, enjoying the warmth radiating from the fire. It was a chilly night outside, but you'd never know it from my spot on the couch.

"Shop? You mean business?"

"That's what I mean."

"You want to chat about business at a quarter past two in the morning?" I could practically hear him pulling his bed covers over his head. "Why didn't you say what you had to say earlier at Talia's? Slipped your mind?"

"Something like that. I thought it would be better to discuss it sooner rather than later," I explained.

"Okay, what's up?"

"Earlier tonight you mentioned that you were drafting blueprints for a mansion in Short Hills."

"Yeah. And?"

"Ecclestone is busy developing property in that area. I can't help but wonder whether you're working with him, or perhaps worked with him, and that's why you're looking to sell Windsor Architects."

I waited for Ace to reply. The silence was deafening.

"So, which one is it?" I pushed.

More silence.

"Are you high?" Ace finally said. "Did you take something?"

He sounded angry, likely for a good reason. I hadn't expected that he wouldn't be. Hell, I would be if someone asked me this. But, I needed an answer.

"No and no. What a bullshit question. I've never met the fucking guy. Do you really think so little of me?"

"You know I've got to do my job."

"Fuck your job," Ace said.

He abruptly ended the call, leaving me staring at my phone's blank screen. Well, I had my answer. I would call him back when the sun was up. He couldn't stay mad at me forever. He knew it was my due diligence to cross the T's and dot the I's.

Instinctively, I found myself dialing Miles's number next. The clock now read 2:18 a.m. Oliver would've gone to bed the minute he got home, but I knew that Miles was likely lounging around having his last beer, kind of like I was—sans the beer.

He answered immediately.

"Tsup, bro. You gonna come over for a drink?"

"What? Right now?"

"When else?" he replied happily.

"That's not why I'm calling," I said. "I just spoke to Ace. Asked him about Ecclestone."

"What the fuck, bro? Didn't we say we weren't gonna do exactly that?"

"I know, I know," I rumbled.

"So, what'd he say?"

"He called it a 'bullshit question.'"

"Well, there's your answer." I could hear him opening the fridge.

"Hang on. Before he denied it, there was an awkward pause. A long one. I don't think he knew what to tell me. It was like he was buying time to come up with an answer."

"Or maybe he fell asleep, man." Miles snorted, and I could hear him shuffling in the fridge. "It's almost two in the morning."

"Actually, it's well past two in the morning."

"Is it? Damn."

"I was thinking we could put Harris on him," I suggested, a sense of urgency shooting through my veins.

"No way, dude." Miles sounded shockingly more sober than he had seconds earlier. I heard the fridge door close. "Too late. If you put Harris on it now, Dad will find out about it. If Dad detects we set up a merger, and now we're having doubts? Man, he will be *pissed*. Shit has already leaked to the press—it will look shittier. You know how Dad is about our reputation."

"Better late than never."

"That's not how Dad thinks. And you know it."

"We don't know that Harris will definitely tell your father about it."

"Are you kidding me? He'll definitely tell him," he said. "But if your Spidey-sense rings true, then—"

"We're fucked."

There was a pause. "I've got an idea," Miles said.

"What?"

"Your sister. What was her name again?"

"Stella. What about her?"

"You need to ensure Stella gets that job at Ace's company..."

"Be...cause?" I asked, already guessing where this was going. "So she can spy on Ace? Are you fucking *nuts*?"

"Huh. Not what I was going to say, but that's fucking genius!" Miles sounded thrilled. I heard a beer can crack open. "Problem solved then. Talk to you later, bro."

"What? Wait. Don't hang up. What the fuck? What were you going to say?"

"Well, that *she* can ask him, get him to open up. Female sensitivity and shit. But your idea is better! *Way* better."

"What's *way better* about it? It's fucked up. Investigating a company is one thing, but *snooping* on our friend, via my sister—of all people—is something else entirely. Don't you get it? Stella is my blood. Not a fucking spy. I could never do that."

"Why not?" Miles's voice sounded calm. "We can't use Harris. Your own investigations will only get us so far. And time is running out. If Ace isn't doing anything wrong, then nobody will be hurt by it. And if he *is* hiding something, then he's no friend of ours. It's a win-win situation. Easy-peasy."

"Sending in my sister to fucking spy is not a fucking win-win situation. No matter the result."

"Bro, you're thinking about it the wrong way. She isn't *spying*. She's *paying attention*."

"Paying attention, huh?"

"Yeah, dude. We're not asking her to go through his drawers. She's just *keeping an eye out*. You know? Nobody will ever know. We merge, we're all happy. Done. Flawless idea."

"No. It's a shit idea. It's shady as fuck."

"But we've got to do our due diligence. It's procedure. Those were your words, Damon."

"I fucking know," I grumbled, annoyed.

"Like I said, no harm no foul, if Ace isn't hiding anything. And he isn't—we all agreed on that. She's not going to find shit. So fucking loosen up. I don't think asking Stella to 'keep an eye out' is shady at *all*. It's legitimate. She'll enjoy pretending to be a 'double agent.' She's a nerdy geek like that."

"Hey. That's my sister."

"Doesn't mean it's not true." Miles chuckled, and I couldn't even prove him wrong. It wasn't as if I hadn't presented proof of her geekiness just this very evening. I heard Miles take a swig of his beer. "Just think about it. It's fucking perfect."

"Fucking perfect," I grumbled, staring into the glowing red fire in front of me, sorrow filling my mind.

"Get her on board."

I should have gone to bed, not fucking called him. "All right. I'll ask her."

"Don't just ask her. Get her on board."

"You're wrong about one thing though: I don't think she's going to like it."

Miles ended the call, and I sank further into the couch.

*Double agent, my ass.*

The room spun around me. The cool air seeping in through unseen crevices chased the fire's heat around the space. Darkness enveloped me with one more worry. Precisely, how the *fuck* was I going to bring this shit up with Stella?

But first things first: she needed to get the job. Then, and only then, would I approach her—and not a second sooner.

The desire for a bottle of Pinot Noir was completely gone.

# 5

# STELLA

*S*itting up in bed, I looked over at the red alarm clock on my bedside table. It read 6:30 a.m. Superb! I loved early starts. Lazily, I stretched my arms upward and brought my frizzy hair into a messy bun.

This would be a perfect day.

I swung my legs off the bed. My humble but lovely apartment's well-worn wooden floor felt cold beneath my feet, and I bent over and stuck my arm under my bed, searching for my fluffy slippers. *Where did the darn things go?* My fingers brushed against their fuzzy surface, and I whipped them out, hastily wiggling my feet into them.

Time for a coffee. I'd planned to spend the day baking and the evening reading *Poirot Investigates* by detective novel queen, Agatha Christie. My favorite author in the world! Then I would re-read the short story "The Four Suspects," featuring Miss Jane Marple, Christie's most famous detective character. My late mother had introduced me to Miss Marple when I was a teen, and to this day, I felt closer to Mom and truly comforted when I picked up one of her books. The way the loveable old English spinster did everything in her power to solve those difficult cases was simply brilliant! She was astute and witty, and most of all, madly courageous in her spirit as an amateur detective helping to bring rightfulness to the world. How I admired her unwavering boldness. It was the opposite of me—I wasn't the bold and unwavering kind. I was the "quick to have a heart attack at any sticky situation" kind.

Oh, how I enjoyed the days I had to myself, the days when I wasn't working or worrying about finding work after my internship was over. The last applications I'd sent out hadn't yielded any results, and quite frankly, I was growing anxious. Very anxious. Maybe I should try to make éclairs before jumping back into job hunting. Baking relaxed me, and I loved the smell of fresh baking. Except for the last time. The last time I'd attempted the recipe, I'd nearly set my kitchen on fire. I wasn't the clumsy type, and usually all my baking attempts yielded success (and later ended up on my hips). So, not sure what went wrong there, but I was intent on making it work this time.

Full of enthusiasm, I set the pot on the stove, added the milk, water, sugar, and butter, and let the mixture heat up. Today would end on a fantastic note, I could feel it.

I was in the process of pouring the flour (all at once, just as the recipe noted) into the pot, when my cell phone rang. It vibrated in my pocket before I heard my Miss Marple theme song ringtone. The song was reaching its climax by the time I got it out. Oh, *damn*. With the choux pastry for the éclairs, the key was to stir the mass constantly once the flour was added. If I stopped now, I'd have to start all over again. But what if it was a call from a company I had applied to? Fumbling, flour all over my hands, I tried to swipe right to answer the call, but I was too late.

"Missed call: Brother *heart emoji*," my phone's screen flashed.

"Darn. Too late," I mumbled to myself, wiping my floury hands into a kitchen towel and pulling the pot off the stove before I really lay my kitchen in ashes this time. I dialed Damon's number and waited.

"Stella?" His raspy voice crackled through my phone's speaker.

"Oh! Hey, Batman. You sound awful. Are you okay? Are you sick or something?"

"I'm okay, don't worry about me," he said. "I was out with the guys last night. It was a rough night. Probably should've gone home earlier."

"Probably," I agreed. "But I'm glad you're okay. How are Miles and Oliver?"

"They're fine. Ace joined us too."

*Ace.* I cringed hearing the name, but didn't say anything about his presence. "To discuss the merger?" I asked instead. My brother couldn't shut up about it, and I was in the picture.

"Mostly just to have a few drinks. Listen, Ace was feeling a bit down because he...well, he had to fire his assistant. He's lost without her."

*Figures.*

"Why did he fire her if he can't get anything done without her?" I asked, maybe a tad too emotional, fiddling with a teaspoon I'd found on one of the kitchen's countertops.

There was a pause. I could hear Damon's news channel blaring in the background.

"I'd rather spare you the details," he finally replied.

"Oh. Is it something juicy?"

"Possibly."

"Tell me! Tell me!" I practically begged into the phone. "I'm dying to know." Damon knew how curious I was.

"That's not why I'm calling."

"No?" Of course he hadn't called me to tell me about Ace. I twirled the teaspoon around like a baton before dropping it on the floor. It landed with a loud clang.

"What was that?" Damon asked.

"Nothing." I scrambled to pick the spoon back up again.

"Anyway, let me get to the point. Ace needs a new assistant. I told him that your internship is almost over and that you're looking for a job, and he suggested that you should apply."

Oh.

"*He* suggested it?"

"Yeah."

"When? *Immediately?*" I asked.

I didn't have too many good memories of Ace, to say the least, and honestly, I'd doubted he'd remembered me—and *that* day. And by "doubted," I meant I hoped he had long forgotten it.

"Immediately. He wants your résumé," Damon said without hesitation. "Plus, it's an architecture firm. It's a starting point. You could make a career there."

Of course. Of all the companies, Windsor Architects had to have an opening for a position architect graduates would kill for.

Yes, I needed a job. Yes, I was desperate. But was I *that* desperate?

Darn it.

Yes. Yes, I was.

But was Ace as desperate as I was? It was more than unusual for an inexperienced person like me to even be considered for a position of trust as assistant to the CEO.

"You didn't somehow...force him to offer me a job?"

Damon snorted. "You don't have the job yet, sis. He wants to see your résumé," my brother reminded me. "Ace isn't someone who lets himself be talked into his business decisions. I told him about your qualifications and convinced him."

Oh. A warm feeling spread through my chest as I heard the pride in my big brother's voice.

Not gonna lie, I used to have a huge crush on Ace. He was *the* hottest guy in school, with his messy "fresh out of bed" hair and those incredible eyes. I'd never seen eyes like his. Every girl had a crush on him. Too bad he was such a douche. A jerk. A real asshole. And men like him never changed. They became worse. Like cheap wine that turned into a sour unappetizing gunk.

"Would I work for him directly?"

"Yes."

"Why doesn't he hire somebody more, you know, experienced?"

"It's impossible to find a good assistant with an architectural background in such a short time. You might have a shot."

"Not enough trustworthy and diligent people out there, huh? And the pay?"

"From what I've learned so far, Ace pays his employees well above industry standards."

Well, *that* surprised me.

What chance did I really have? Yes, Ace Windsor was a jerk face. A total dick.

But I needed a job. Soon. Now.

Was I ecstatic at the thought of working for the biggest douche on the planet? Hell no. Was I in the position to be picky? Not really. Also, it wasn't like I could say no to my brother for handing me this unexpected opportunity without at least thinking about it objectively—and without grudges. It would be good for my bank balance, that was for sure. Maybe it would be good for my growth too. You know, like an "if you make it in a bosshole's firm, you can make it anywhere" type situation.

Especially since it would mean that I didn't have to ask my brother to help with my rent, *again*. It was bad enough that I had asked Damon to help me "a little" during my studies and with my loans, furniture, and other stuff. I knew he'd give me anything, his last shirt if needed, but it was time to stand on my own two feet.

One thing was odd though. It didn't make any sense why Ace would want *me*—of all people—to work for him, let alone pay me to be anywhere near him eight-to-five, five days a week. He disliked me just as much as I disliked him. Sure, I was honest, hardworking, and reliable, and he would be getting a great assistant with me. Still, I wasn't naïve enough to believe he was offering the job because the years had softened his heart and turned him into a good guy. I was a realist, and was convinced he was the same asshat who was just doing my brother a favor.

A favor I'd ultimately pay for. The moment I'd walk in, he'd show me his ugly side, and boss me around. Yeah, you know what? Bring it on. I could handle a jerky grump any day of the week.

A hot jerky grump, nevertheless. But who knew, maybe he wasn't hot anymore. Guys changed. Typically, the college heartbreakers turned shockingly ugly, while some of the dorky-looking guys aged into attractive men (Matthew McConaughey...*swoon*, Johnny Depp...*meltmeltmelt*, Colin Farrell...*heaven have mercy*).

Most certainly, time had given Ace the hideous appearance he deserved.

Ultimately, I told myself that, if for whatever reason I couldn't handle the monster, I'd quit. Simple as that.

"I mean, if he personally suggested that I should apply, it would be rude if I didn't," I said, hating myself for the hint of excitement at the prospect of seeing Ace again. Only because of the job, that was. Not because of him as a man. I told myself it was just my curiosity getting the better of me, wanting to find out *exactly* how ugly he'd become after all these years.

"Definitely," Damon replied. "Get your résumé and a cover letter ready and email them to me. I'll pass them on to him." It seemed like Damon was really worried about Ace's ability to run his company without an experienced assistant at his side.

No worries. Stella Copeland would soon have that sorted out.

"Despite everything, you know you're the best brother ever, right?"

"I know," he teased.

"Love you." I made kissy sounds into the phone. "Bye, Muffin. Love you. *Mwah*."

"Bye, Pancake. Love you too."

I abandoned my dreams of crafting the perfect éclair the minute the call ended. Flying around my kitchen like Cinderella before the ball, I haphazardly stashed all of my baking supplies back into my small pantry and almost threw the almond milk back into the fridge.

After flying into the corner of my living room that I'd turned into my cute "dedicated home office," I opened my laptop. My sunflower screensaver lit up the otherwise poorly lit room.

I searched through my laptop's files. *Where is it?*

So far, I'd applied online by filling out application forms. I hadn't updated my résumé in ages, but this was Windsor. The lady who was facilitating my internship was one of my professors' friends and hadn't even asked to see it. After what felt like an eternity of panicked searching, I found the correct file. I had labeled it "My resume_final_final_real_final."

*Gotta remember to rename that before I send it over to Damon.* Imagine if I'd sent it off like that.

After some quiet contemplation, I started typing.

More specifically, I started listing my achievements during college that would interest a CEO in an architectural firm: how I'd been on the dean's list, how I'd acted as the dean's personal assistant, and how I'd attended every lecture and aced every test (jeez, such a geek). It didn't feel like a sufficient ode to the dedication I had shown toward my education, but it was honest—and likely a better choice than mentioning that I'd obsessed over Miss Marple so much that I'd even taken up knitting, gotten into bird watching, and became Captain of the Agatha Christie Book Club. It was embarrassing stuff, definitely not the kind of thing you'd want your future boss to see. Delete. Delete. Delete. I didn't want to risk him laughing his ass off at me. Once was more than enough.

Instead, I pointed out my love for detail, my organizational talent and appreciation of to-do lists and notes (I loved getting notes), as well as excellent communication skills. Communication was one of my strengths. I was quick on my feet, and typically, I had a witty line ready in most any situation, especially awkward ones. It was sort of my superpower. One that I could really use, because somehow, I kept getting into tricky situations.

When I was finally satisfied, I wrapped it all up with a longer section dedicated to what I'd learned during my internship as "strategic assistant to the CEO's Chief of Staff" at my current engineering company. This was the part that would be most interesting to Ace, so I made sure to make things sound extra fancy by highlighting my tasks as a "collaborative partner with high-level administrative support experience": organizing presentations for sales pitches, coordinating, and managing schedules, writing up analyses and research that would be helpful in preparations for upcoming mergers. Ha! If anything, he would love this part. Last but not least, I mentioned that I had experience at the front desk to show that I was a flexible team player who loved social interactions with customers and clients.

Okay. Yes. I knew I lacked the experience in years, but the truth was, I had learned a *ton* during my internship, especially after the CEO's assistant became pregnant and started to have severe morning sickness.

*That'll have to do.* I observed my handiwork, and despite everything, felt quite proud of it. I inserted a professionally taken photo of myself and saved it as a PDF.

Very good! Turning to the cover letter, I took a deep breath.

*Dear future boss*, I started. Then I gushed on and on about how much a job at Windsor Architects would mean to me, dedicating nearly two pages to what could only be described as being only an inch short of outright begging. I didn't want to seem desperate, but the truth of the matter was: Your girl was freakin' desperate.

It was almost noon by the time I started drafting my email to Damon. It said only what was necessary: "Here is my résumé and cover letter." I attached both documents after giving them professional names —I had many flaws, but luckily, being forgetful wasn't one of them— crossed my fingers and hit "Send."

Then waited.

And waited.

# 6
## STELLA

*After* one hour, I checked again.

This was silly. It would be a while before Damon forwarded my résumé to Ace, and who knew how long it would take him to review it? It could take several days, if not weeks. I should do something useful to keep myself busy.

If I had been less distracted, I may have decided to resume baking the éclairs I'd originally planned to make. But I was distracted. Very distracted. Ace, or rather the job opportunity at Ace's firm, had completely derailed my day.

So, I decided to occupy myself by choosing my potential interview outfit instead. Was I being overly optimistic? Yes. But I didn't see optimism as a character flaw. After gathering my thoughts—somewhat (and a few necessities)—I made my way back into my bedroom.

My favorite piece of furniture was a large antique wardrobe that stood against the wall opposite my bed. I'd inherited it from my dad and stored all of my clothes in it. My love for old furniture and anything that was a period piece I'd inherited from Dad. There was just something romantic about antiques. My huge collection of old books that were left to me by Mom sat on several wooden corner shelves right next to it. The wardrobe's double doors gave a loud squeak as I opened them. I peeked inside. The wooden shelves and hangers were filled with a heap of gray leggings, three pairs of blue jeans, a collection of cute summer dresses, some T-shirts and pullovers, and exactly three formal outfits. So far, I never needed more than that—the engineers I worked with weren't too concerned about the office's dress code.

I suspected I'd need more business attire, if Windsor Architects ended up hiring me.

The old wardrobe creaked as I leaned into it to reach my formal outfits. I laid them out on my bed and stared at them. They consisted of an emerald-green dress with mid-length sleeves, an elegant pantsuit, and a cream dress with black piping. I wondered what a potential boss would think of me in each of them, and then decided on the cream dress.

While pulling the wrinkled oversized white T-shirt I'd slept in over my head and almost bringing my glasses along while doing so, I kicked off my sweatpants and scooped the dress up into my arms. Quickly, I sashayed over to the full-length mirror that stood next to my wardrobe and started squeezing into it.

After a bit of a struggle, I managed to pull up its rigid zipper. It was very snug, but not uncomfortably so. My only hope was that it would look as good on me now as it had when I'd bought it. Slowly, almost hesitantly, I lifted my head to examine myself in the mirror.

Bad hair day, but okay. The dress hugged my curves, stretching taut across my breasts and round bottom, and cinching in at my waist. The color looked good on me. My frizzy brown hair *almost* seemed to have a hint of gold in it when contrasted with the dress's lighter color, and my dark-brown eyes looked even darker.

I smiled. *If he doesn't think I look good in this, and hire me on the spot, he's a lost cause.*

Satisfied with my outfit, I peered into my wardrobe to find a suitable pair of shoes. I decided on a pair of elegant sky-high cream pumps. They were my favorite for two reasons: first, they'd been a gift from my best friend from kindergarten, Bonnie. Bonnie was an operations agent at a huge firm, and I loved her more than anything. Second, they made me look taller. At just under five feet two, I was used to being the shortest person in the room. When I was wearing the pumps Bonnie had gifted me, I was closer to being average height and felt a bit more confident.

Bonnie would love it if I snapped a photo, and that's what I did, just to make her happy that I was putting her gift to good use. After unlocking my phone, I aimed it at the mirror, and made a funny face. Selfies were so awkward, but if anyone would appreciate it, it was Bonnie.

My message included the caption: "Do these look familiar?"

A moment later, my phone vibrated.

**Bonnie:** Yass, gurl! *Smiley with heart eyes emoji.*

**Bonnie:** Who are you all dressed up for?

**Me:** Prince Charming ;-)

**Bonnie:** Really? Who!?

**Me:** JK. I may have a job interview coming up. Do I look okay?

**Bonnie:** You're the whole package.

**Me:** You're too sweet. *Hug emoji.*

**Bonnie:** What place? *Heart emoji.*

**Me:** I'll let you know—IF I get invited to the interview.

Truth was, I wasn't really eager to tell Bonnie that it was Ace's place. She hated the "ace-hat" more than I did after she'd had to comfort me for several hours when I'd cried my eyes out to her about him not loving me back.

**Bonnie:** Good luck! We'll go from there. *Heart emoji.*

**Me:** Yes, thanks! XOXO

**Me:** *Heart emoji.*

After I tossed my cell phone onto one of my bed pillows, I unzipped my dress, and prepared to slip back into something more comfortable: a pair of gray leggings and a T-shirt. I was still busy wrestling the T-shirt over my head when I heard my phone vibrate again. *Bonnie's feeling chatty today.*

I stretched over my bed, picked it up, and unlocked its screen.

**Damon:** I've sent your résumé to Ace, Pumpkin Face.

**Me:** Thank you so much, Batman.

**Damon:** He should get back to you soon. Let me know if he doesn't.

**Me:** Okay.

**Me:** I'm dying to find out if I made the cut.

**Me:** Thanks for lining this up for me.

**Damon:** Anytime. Remember to let me know if he doesn't get back to you.

**Me:** *Nerd emoji.*

**Me:** *Hug emoji.*

**Me:** *Kiss emoji.*

*He better get back to me.* I flopped down onto my bed. Hugging one of my pillows, I started wondering whether Ace was reading my résumé right this second, perhaps even staring at the picture of me I'd selected.

My phone didn't vibrate again, and I shuffled out of the room, heading straight to my cozy home office. My laptop's fan was humming loudly. "Don't die on me there, little buddy," I whisper-begged as I plopped myself down onto the chair behind my desk. "It's not warm enough today for you to be making that racket, and I can't replace you if you succumb to heat stroke."

Before I could help myself, I had opened Google and typed "Ace Windsor" into the search bar.

Within seconds, Google regurgitated hundreds of pages related to "Ace Windsor." The search result at the top of the list was a link to Windsor Architects' website. After scanning through the first page, I clicked on a link at the top that read, "Meet our Team."

Ace's picture was the first thing that appeared as the new webpage started to load.

No. Impossible. That was *not* him.

Squinting, I adjusted my glasses.

The guy in the photo didn't look good. He looked hotter than hot. Burning. Those eyes. *Stunning. Piercing. Mesmerizing.*

Under the photo, it read, "Founder and CEO, Ace Windsor."

For a few seconds, I tried to calm my thundering heart. He was sporting a cheeky smile across a pair of rather handsome lips. His dirty-blond hair partially obscured one of his icy-blue eyes and stuck up rebelliously in the middle. It was like his eyes held all the stars in the universe and one look into them enchanted you for the rest of your life. And that jawline, girl, it was lick-worthy perfection. Ace was wearing a dark-blue tie, and a pastel-blue dress shirt that was particularly tight over his broad chest and muscular biceps. It was almost so tight that it was transparent in places, revealing an array of tattoos.

He was a ten without the buts. Maybe even more. No, definitely more. A thousand.

The "jerk" had aged well. He hadn't turned sour at all, that much was certain. Damn.

After scanning the "Recruiting" section and making sure that, yep, the CEO's assistant position was still open, and feeling intimidated as could be by the tasks and experience "preferably" required for that position, I calmed myself with the knowledge that I still had a chance because I held one "unique skill" that would set me apart from all the other applicants. The Damon card.

I navigated my way back to Google's search results and clicked on the second link from the top. It took me to an article about the "Infamous Billionaire Ace Windsor."

The bold headline read:

*Rumors Run Wild as Windsor Engagement is Called Off*

According to the article, Ace had been engaged to a woman named Allison Gardener. It contained a picture of them embracing each other on an ivory-white beach. Truth? She was spectacular. Long platinum-blonde hair meeting size zero. She could best have been described as spectacular perfection. *So that's still his type.* Not that I cared. The article didn't say why their engagement had been broken off. All possible scenarios that could cause a woman like her to leave a man like him rushed through my head, but honestly, only one plausible likelihood came to mind. He *was* a self-absorbed douchebag.

Obviously, he was still running around breaking women's hearts.

She had likely fallen into his trap. I needed to stay away from him—as far as I could, heart-wise.

The final website Google guided me to read:

*An Ace up his Sleeve: Ace Windsor Wins Triple Gold*

The article was nothing less than a worship of Ace and his performance on his college's swim team. They'd come first in several regional competitions. I wasn't too interested in his lap times, and I wasn't interested in the picture that accompanied them. Not at all. Specifically, the one with him standing bare-chested just in his swimming trunks. I clicked to enlarge it. Then zoomed in on his tattooed pecs and six pack. Then zoomed out a little bit again. Ace was posing with the rest of his team, his arms wrapped around his teammates' necks in a friendly victory hug. A hundred and ninety-four pounds' pure strength. His rippling washboard abs started from the "V" peeking out of his Speedo and ended under his bulging muscles. He could have upstaged a Greek god. I tried to force myself to look away, but I couldn't. Instead, I nonchalantly took another gulp of my water bottle and sat forward in my chair (while glancing back at the "V" disappearing into the speedos), feeling my cotton underwear dampen. "Stop it, Stella!" I practically scolded my own body. "OMG. You're not in high school anymore. You can't let him get you this excited."

Luckily, I *did* take my own advice. I did *not* find myself staring longingly at the photograph of Ace, and I did *not* imagine what it would be like to peek inside his trunks at you know what. Most of all, I did *not* wonder for even one second what it would be like to be touched by him, by his gorgeous, strong, manly hands. And to feel his undoubtedly big, long, thick you know what—you know where.

Just when my fantasies threatened to steal me away from the real world forever, my phone started ringing again.

My heart skipped a beat when I saw a number I didn't recognize flash across my screen.

It was him.

*Him.*

I answered my phone, a little light-headed and frazzled by all the "excitement," and loudly said, "Stella here! Hi there!" Maybe I sounded a *teensy* bit too overeager. A smidge?

"Am I speaking to Miss Copeland?" a stern female voice asked from the other end of the line.

Oh. *Not* him.

So. Awkward.

*You totally got this, girl. Just breathe.*

"This is she," I replied in a friendly (not high-pitched) voice, hiding my disappointment—and relief—that the caller wasn't him. "How can I help you?"

"I'm Glenda Meeks. I'm calling from Windsor Architects' administrative support. Our executive HR team has reviewed your application for the assistant position and would like to invite you to a formal interview the day after tomorrow at eleven o'clock."

Before I could stop myself, I squealed into the phone's speaker, "I-I-I...Thank you! Thank you!" It was the pent-up stress that burst free into sheer excitement. Yeah, that was a bit high-pitched. *And, we're back to awkward.*

"Miss *Copeland*," Glenda said, raising her voice above my own. "A modicum of professionalism, please."

Wow! What a cow. Surely she was a real Cerberus, a hellhound who monitored all contact with the boss—and reduced it to a minimum.

"Whoops. *Sorry*," I squeaked, my voice properly "shushed" back down to normal volume. "I'm just so excited. I studied architecture, and it has always been a dream of mine to—"

"Very well. See you the day after tomorrow then."

"Wait, one more question," I said before she could end the call.

First, there was silence, and it made me think that she'd hung up after all. "Yes. What is it?" Glenda sighed impatiently from the other end of the line.

"Will the CEO be interviewing me? Or will I be meeting with someone else?"

"Ha-ha...tsk-tsk." There was another mocking laugh. "It's *highly* unlikely that Mr. Windsor will meet with you himself. He's a very busy man with important matters to attend to."

"I see. It's just that—"

"Goodbye, Miss Copeland." Glenda clearly couldn't wait to end our call, and hung up. A Cerberus, as I had thought.

Hopefully, "being as unfriendly as humanly possible" wasn't part of the company culture that Ace cultivated. I rotated to face my laptop again and allowed my eyes to drift over the picture of him one last time.

I didn't know why, likely because of the rudeness of the caller, it triggered a certain memory—one I had been trying to repress.

It was the week after I'd turned eighteen. My brother had invited Ace, Miles, and Oliver over to our house, and they were lounging around the pool, drinking the beer from my dad's secret bar fridge stash. I'd had a crush on Ace from the first day I'd met him, and decided I'd try to catch his eye. To do so, I'd purchased a brand-new white bikini from a cute online boutique the previous week. It reminded me of something that Marilyn Monroe or Audrey Hepburn might wear. With all the suaveness and fashion sense of a wide-eyed teenager, I accessorized with a pair of super-glam thick-rimmed white sunglasses and a white sun hat. I thought I looked like a goddess—I know I must have looked like a hat on two (short) legs—but back then, I was aiming for "glamorous."

It was an unusually sweltering summer day, so my chosen outfit was ideal. It allowed the gentle breeze that danced through the air to caress my pale skin in passing. In my fantasies, I was a sun-kissed goddess with Aphrodite's body and a seductress's charm. (In reality, I spent way, way too much time with my nose stuck in my books to bronze my skin to a color that was more than half a shade darker than its pages.) I remember applying more makeup that afternoon than any eighteen-year-old had any business wearing (or anybody of any age really), de-frizzing and curling my hair for almost thirty minutes, and then emerging from my room to make my way outside.

I stepped out into the sunlight, ready for my "big reveal."

Ace's eyes met mine as I stepped onto the wooden deck that led up to the pool. I started strutting toward the group of boys, making an effort to keep my left hand on my hip and to sassily sway my hips from side to side. Just as I approached the water's edge and prepared myself to throw Ace a sassy wink with a blown kiss (one that I had practiced in front of the mirror all morning—cheeky sideways glance, slight smile but not too much, blow a kiss, then hold it like Marilyn Monroe, then a quick wink with the right eye, smile sassily, then turn away, *and*, mic drop). All I remembered was being in the middle of the "blowing a kiss" sequence when I heard my brother yelling, "Incoming!" and then flinging a *whole* bucket of ice-cold pool water at me. It splashed across my torso, soaking me to the bone. I was mortified. The shock of the freezing-cold water had me paralyzed from the neck down for a millisecond or two, mouth wide open. To my horror, once I managed to look down, I realized that my "bargain basket" online purchase was *not* water friendly after all. It had turned almost completely see-through, and you could see absolutely *everything* underneath. Faster than the speed of light, I whipped a white pool towel from a nearby chair and wrapped it around my essentially naked body before any of the boys could notice.

Luckily, nobody saw anything.

"You bully!" I remembered berating my brother. Never in all my life had I been so angry. I definitely hadn't anticipated that Damon would humiliate me in front of the boy of my dreams. It was so embarrassing. When I turned to storm back into the house, I saw Ace, Damon, Oliver, and Miles laughing their asses off. Ace. *I will never forget his face.* It was at that crushing moment that I realized he didn't feel the same for me. He didn't love me, not even a little. He was just like the others. A dick.

Later that night in bed, I came to the conclusion I'd never be the kind of girl that Ace Windsor could love—I simply wasn't his type. Not that it mattered anyway. From now on, he wasn't my type, either! I wasn't into jerk faces who made fun of fun-sized women. I would not love him anymore—*never* again.

From that day forward, he avoided me like a cat avoided a bath. It was like he had suddenly developed a severe allergy to my very existence, like I had suddenly become his Achilles' heel, a piece of gum stuck to the bottom of his shoe, a walking embodiment of his worst nightmare, and he couldn't escape fast enough.

After that, I made it a point to avoid him as well as I could. My move to study at Princeton helped. Not once did I stalk his socials or ask Damon about his whereabouts (for real, for real). I knew my brother kept in close contact over the years, especially when Ace moved states with his pretty girlfriend, but I refused any knowledge of him.

Today, I could only hope that Ace had forgotten all about the bikini incident. I'd be utterly mortified if my potential boss remembered how I had tried and failed to impress him in the most embarrassing way possible.

*Ring. Riiiing.*

My phone pulled me away from the humiliating memory I was replaying in my mind. I lifted it up. The screen read: "Brother *heart emoji*."

I held the phone up to my ear, ready to speak.

"Have you heard anything from Ace yet?" he asked without waiting for my greeting.

"Well, hello to you, too," I said. "Actually, I was just about to call you. I just heard back from Windsor Architects."

"You're not crying. I assume it's good news?"

"Like I would be crying," I said. (I totally would be.) "They invited me to an interview the day after tomorrow at eleven. The woman I spoke to said that Ace probably wouldn't be interviewing me personally though."

"CEOs don't typically conduct interviews. He has an empire to run. And in this case, why would he? He knows you. Don't take it personally."

"I won't," I assured him. "I'm sure I'll get more than enough opportunities to talk to him once they've hired me."

"I'm sure you will," Damon said. "Keep me updated on how it goes... and good luck." With that, he ended the call, leaving me alone with my thoughts again.

*I have the best brother ever.* He was *so* invested. I loved him. Who else could say that their big brother had gone out of his way to find them their dream job?

# 7

# STELLA

*Two days later, 9:35 a.m.*

My lucky day.

My life flashed before my eyes as I heard a loud *snap*. *Shit.* In my reflection, I saw myself standing in front of the full-length mirror in my room with one half of my beige dress's zipper in my hand. The other half was still attached.

*Shit, shit, shit.*

The zipper was only halfway up, and now I had no way to pull it up any further. It was now 9:38 a.m., and I had less than one and a half hours until my interview at Windsor Architects, an event I'd already decided would be Act One of my dream life. That seemed less likely to be the case as I stood staring at my own shocked reflection, sweating bullets.

Shaking my head, I picked up my cell from the bedside table. Bonnie's number was saved as my emergency contact.

The ringtone hit my ear as I waited for her to answer.

"Stella! Girl!" Bonnie's sugary voice came flooding through my phone's speaker. It had a melodious quality that reminded me of the Disney princesses I'd admired in my youth.

"*Bonnie.* I'm having a crisis. Something terrible has happened."

"Oh, no," she gasped. "What happened? Are you okay?"

"No. I'm dying...dying of frustration! I'm getting dressed for my interview, and the slider to my dress's zipper broke off. Do you think that's a bad omen?"

"No, just a bad slider or pull tab," she said, releasing a laugh.

"Well, I can't pull it up. I'm going to have to go half-dressed, because I can't pull it down either."

"I'm sure the person interviewing you would think it was hilarious," she replied. "Have you tried using a wire coat hanger to pull it up? If you can hook it through what's left of the zipper tab, you should be able to get the job done. It worked for me last time."

"I love you," I said more sincerely than I meant to. "Hold on, let me put you on speaker phone so both my hands are free."

"Okay. It's a bit tricky. You have to wiggle it into the sliding thingy."

I put my phone down on my bed and retrieved a wire coat hanger from the wardrobe. It took a good dose of athleticism (and gymnastic prowess) to hook it into the zipper's remains, but I managed to do it without pulling a muscle. One proper upward jerk (and more sweaty armpits) was all it took to pull the zipper up all the way.

"It worked!" I did a little happy dance around the room.

"Yay! I told you it would," Bonnie cheered. "Are you nervous about your interview?"

"No, I'm *perfectly* composed," I said, throwing the coat hanger I'd used across the room like a boomerang. It landed on Laundry Mountain without making a sound. "I'm the picture of poise and control—can't you tell?"

"Uh-huh, girl. I know you're being sarcastic, but the thing is, despite everything, I've never seen you shy away from a challenge."

"But I'm a nervous wreck."

"Roosevelt said that courage is not the absence of fear," she said, "but doing stuff even when you're scared shitless."

"Yep. I'm sure that's *exactly* what he said." I laughed. "I better get going. I've still got to do my hair and makeup."

"Your hair and makeup? Wow, you're really going all-out for this interview. I can't wait to hear how it went. But wait—what company is it? You were going to tell me if you got the interview. You got the interview."

I gulped. "Promise to not get mad."

"Girl, I'm not promising shit. Spill."

"Windsor Architects." I mumbled the words.

"What did you say? Wait. Did you say Windsor Architects...as in *Ace Windsor Architects*?"

"Uh-huh. Maybe."

"Girl. What the actual fuck? Seriously? You want to be *his* assistant? Cocky Ace's assistant? Please tell me you're kidding. Have you lost your mind? You seem to have forgotten the tears you shed for that ace-hole." I heard a loud sigh when I didn't say anything. "Now I *really* can't wait to hear how it went."

"I can't wait for it to be over either. Bye, Bonnie. Gotta run! Love you!"

"Let's hope he *doesn't* hire you. Love you, girl."

The room seemed markedly quieter without Bonnie's voice reverberating through it. Yes, she had a point, and yes, something was clearly wrong with me.

Mascara and lipstick were next on my to-do list. Makeup was non-negotiable when it came to job interviews. (It had nothing to do with Ace.) Also, I had this new lipstick that just looked phenomenal on me. After putting in my contacts, I quickly applied mascara with a few precise flicks of its round brush and finished off my "look" with a single layer of strawberry-red lipstick.

There I stood, examining myself in the mirror. It was understandable why some women made a habit of wearing makeup every day. Maybe I should, as well. Undeniably *hot*, that's how I looked, even if I did say so myself.

I left my hair hanging loose across my shoulders. Good hair day. *Jackpot*. Usually, when allowed to do as it pleased, my hair hung to the middle of my back in a frizzy sea of messy curls, but I didn't usually give it free rein to do so. Normally, I wore it in a large bun on top of my head or in a thick low ponytail to stop it from getting tangled, but I was willing to risk any number of tangles to make a good impression at Windsor Architects.

As I put on my coat, I texted Damon, hooked my handbag's handle in the crook of my arm, and boldly opened my apartment's door.
**Me:** I'm leaving now, dork.
**Me:** *Heart emoji.*
**Damon:** Good luck, nerdy birdy.

The sun was shining outside—it was a welcoming sight and I decided to take it as a good omen. The first warm smells of spring were starting to take hold of the morning air: fresh blossoms, dew, and churned earth.

*It'll be warm enough for summer dresses soon*, I thought excitedly as I made my way down toward the road that ran in front of my apartment building.

My cab was approaching, or what I hoped would be Jay in my cab. I counted my blessings as it decelerated, carefully coming to a stop next to me.

"At your service, mi'lady! Almost didn't recognize you without your glasses," Jay said in his distinctive British accent, leaning out of the cab's open driver-side window. "That lipstick, though...*phwwwhht*," he whistled.

I stepped over a puddle next to the curb, opened one of the cab's backdoors, and got in.

Jay was my new friend from yoga class who had moved to the States from Hackney Wick, east London, a few years ago, for love. Specifically for Zeke, a sassy and quirky pro-choice guy I'd met at their wedding only a few weeks ago. According to Jay, Zeke used to be a "a dog with two dicks"—translation: a man-whore—but completely became a one-man man after meeting him.

Jay turned down the exotic music he was playing as I made myself comfortable on the back seat. "Where to, love?" he asked, peering back at me.

"Third Avenue in Manhattan, please, darling," I replied, in a weak Brit accent attempt. "The building is on the corner of East 60th Street. And step on it."

"No problem, sweet cheeks," he countered with a surprisingly good but still wonky US accent, before he slipped back into his usual gentle Cockney twang. "Big meeting today? You look a bit on edge... Not gonna rob them, are ya?"

"Me? *Maybe*. Rob their senses that is," I corrected, chuckling at the suggestion and my own joke. "I'm just going to an interview."

"'*Just an interview?*' Nice one. It's your lucky day already then, innit? Never enough jobs in this bloody city. Zeke always says that, and he's bloody right."

"He's bloody right," I agreed, "but I'm about to get one."

"Yeah, you bloody are! Any music requests for the drive there, love?" He tapped at a pair of mini disco balls dangling from his rearview mirror. "Gift from Zeke." They cast glistening specks of light that zipped across the car's outdated interior like shooting stars through the night sky.

"Nope. Actually, I liked what you were playing when I got in. You can turn that back up again, please."

Jay smiled and nodded, adjusting the volume. "Excellent choice. Nice reminder of my honeymoon—me and Zeke wandering round Mumbai, that gorgeous Konkan Coast. Seems like longer than a month ago..." He pulled away from the curb and joined the rest of the traffic rushing toward New York's heart, subtly swearing and tapping on the horn at a female driver in a sports car who cut him off *and* who also proceeded to give Jay the bird. That was actually so funny to me that I had to hide my grin behind my hand, as Jay mumbled, "Yeah, yeah, same to you, daft cow. Some people don't belong on the road."

"They say that men are the worse drivers of the two genders though."

"You're 'avin a laugh! Bloody ridiculous, that is. Anyway..."—with his chin, he gestured to the player of the car—"So this tune here is a Hindu folk song about a troll who falls in love with a handsome priest. She tries to seduce him, but he's not having it. It's quite the story."

"Sounds like it," I said and listened intently. "Tell me—did the troll wear a beige dress?"

"A beige dress? Nah. Why? Reckon that might have worked?"

"Well, it better!"

He looked at me, and his eyes fell to my beige dress, and we both grinned. Jay started to spout off more stories about his honeymoon trip and the exotic food he and Zeke had eaten as I listened to the soothing music, with my head resting against the cab's window. Jay would never know how much I appreciated his attempt at distracting me.

The city rushed by like a Hollywood-style montage of sounds and colors, and it wasn't long before we crossed Manhattan Bridge. The digital clock in the cab's center console read 10:11 a.m.

"Should be there in just under twenty minutes," Jay announced, smiling back at me through the rearview mirror.

"That should leave me with more than enough time to get to the reception desk and calm down a bit—you know, before the execution," I said, evoking a chuckle from Jay.

"Nah, nah, nah, no talk like that. You are gonna smash this. Got pepper spray and a taser in the boot though, y'know... *just in case*..."

"Sounds great. I should keep a taser in my handbag in case my future boss tries something funny." Chuckling, I wrung my sweaty hands together as we reached the end of the bridge. Despite Jay's jokes, I could feel myself growing more and more anxious as we moved closer to my destination.

We had just crossed over onto East Broadway Street, heading past Chinatown, when I saw it. Traffic was jamming up, and we were slowing down, slowing until we were traveling no faster than your average tortoise.

"Oh, fuckin' 'ell, mate," Jay exclaimed. "Move it, you muppet!"

When I craned my neck, I could see what had happened over the roofs of the cars in front of us: a multi-lane accident obstructing one, two, three lanes. A huge food truck lay horizontally with hundreds of crates sprawled out across three lanes, with what looked like red and green apples rolling around everywhere, and a yellow convertible with its fold-down roof steaming against a tree trunk on the other side of the sidewalk. Two guys—the drivers I assumed—stood nearby, arguing loudly. Luckily, nobody seemed seriously injured.

I heard the low whine of an approaching police siren somewhere in the back. "How did that happen?" I asked, turning my head just in time to see it navigating its way through the rows of stationary cars.

"Well, I can tell you how—they're complete bloody pillocks, that's what the problem is. Look how mangled all that fruit is. I think you're going to need to call that lot you're supposed to be meeting. This shit can take forever to clean up—could be waiting here bloody ages."

"Oh, dang," I replied. "I'm supposed to be there no later than eleven. I can't show up late for a job interview. They'll never take me seriously."

For a moment, I just stared at Jay through his rearview mirror, trying not to panic.

"Well, I don't think you've got a lot of choice." He shrugged. "Sorry love, unfortunately not within my powers to magic all this crap away. Bloody wish it was…"

He was right, of course. There was just no way we could get there in time, and I started to search for my cell. "Dang, dang, dang. I need this job." The words had barely left my lips when I saw a flash of white in my peripheral vision. It was as if time itself slowed down to give me a moment to concoct a plan. A pizza delivery guy was zooming through traffic on a dirty white scooter, unfettered by the growing flock of cars. He was headed straight toward us. Without thinking twice, I whipped open the cab door and got out.

"Jesus Christ—what are you doing?" Jay's eyes widened as he realized what I was planning.

"Hey! Hey there! Please stop," I screamed and waved at the scooter.

Jay joined me. He got out of the cab and waved one of his hairy arms to get the delivery driver's attention. "Stop! Oi, over here, mate! *Stop!*"

For a moment, I was certain the white scooter would simply race past us. Just as I was preparing to resign myself to my fate, the vehicle slowed down and pulled up next to us.

"Were you gesturing at me?" the driver asked in a raspy voice, tilting his scooter to one side and placing his right foot on the pavement.

"Hey there, *yes*," I started. "So sorry for stopping you. But I need your help."

"What kind of help?" the delivery driver asked suspiciously. He was a younger guy, somewhere around twenty-two, with a patchy brown beard covering his cheeky face. He looked friendly enough. He raised one of his hands and leaned away from me. "But fair warning: I don't have any medical training if it's something like that—"

"No, no. It's nothing like that," I reassured him. "Can you give me a lift? It's just that I'm going to be late for an interview."

"An interview? For a job?"

"Yeah." I nodded. "A job that I really, really need."

"Where do you need to go?"

"You'd give me a lift? Oh, my gosh, thank you! I thought I was pushing my luck—"

"Hold up, Miss. I haven't agreed to anything yet. I've got to stick to my route. If where you're going is on my route, I'll take you there."

I told him the street and corner I needed to get to. "I can pay you. I have an extra twenty in cash on me. I'll give you twenty dollars if you can just get me there. You have no idea how much it would mean to me."

"Hop on! It's your lucky day. I'm headed that way anyway. I'll have you there before you can say 'interview.'"

"Make sure she gets there safe please, mate," Jay told him, as I pulled out my cell to pay the cab dues plus a sizable tip. Jay refused to accept, telling me that as always, Damon was covering all costs in my account, including tip—and so I fumbled my way up onto the scooter.

"Thanks!"

"No probs—you just get there and get that bloody job. Good luck, love."

Maybe it *was* my lucky day. The delivery man started the scooter's engine again before it spluttered to life, and we zipped forward. Within a matter of seconds, we were snaking through the traffic, drawing even closer to my final destination.

Just as he had promised, the scooter guy promptly delivered me to the address I had given him. "What time is it?" I asked as I scrambled to my feet and started digging through my handbag to retrieve the payment I'd promised him.

"Ten minutes past eleven," he replied.

"Shit."

"Hey, how about instead of paying me, you give me a kiss and your number?"

Huh? I wrapped my fingers around my purse and looked up at him, taken aback. "I'm sorry, but I'm not looking for a relationship right now. It's nothing personal." It was the truth. Sure, I could have used Bonnie's favorite technique and told him that I had a boyfriend to avoid the awkwardness, but I couldn't bring myself to lie. I waved a twenty-dollar bill at him and hoped he'd forgive me for turning him down.

"Okay, just your number then?"

"No…I'm sorry, I'm good." I started feeling a little uncomfortable.

"Just have dinner with me then? I'd let you choose the pizza place, you know."

"Don't get me wrong, I'm flattered, but I'm good. It wouldn't be fair of me to let you buy me dinner. Thank you, though, I appreciate it." I tried to deposit the twenty-dollar bill into his hand, but he pulled away.

"Keep your money, sweetheart," he replied with a mischievous smile. "No hard feelings. Just go in there and get the job."

"I'm going to try my best."

"Maybe I'll stop by in a week or two. Maybe you'll have changed your mind," he rasped and winked, and this time it gave me creepy vibes.

"*No*, plea—" I was unable to complete my sentence before he sped off, disappearing into Manhattan's buzzing streets.

W ell, this was it. *Better late than never*, I thought as I turned to face the looming building I'd been told to report to. The sun illuminated its large glass windows, casting an almost ethereal circle of light around it. The ground was covered in small white flowers that had fallen from a tree planted beside them. Two eastern bluebirds were sitting on one of the branches, looking down at me, chirping happily. Usually, I would have appreciated the sweet moment much longer, but I was too focused on my trembling legs as I climbed the handful of steps that led up to its imposing double doors. They swung open as I pushed my way through, revealing a receptionist seated at the other end of the huge bright foyer.

My stiletto heels clicked on the elegant ceramic floor as I approached her.

## 8

## STELLA

"**M**a'am, can I help you?" the receptionist asked, staring at my shoes. She, herself, looked flawless, from her blonde hair braided in a perfect ring, to her subtly shimmering dark-blue silk blouse. I was sure the rest of her appearance was impeccable, but since she was behind the reception desk, I couldn't see it.

"Sorry, so sorry," I instinctively began when I stood before her. "I'm late. I'm here to interview for the assistant vacancy."

The receptionist tilted her head. She seemed to be trying to determine whether I could be trusted or if I was a crazy person. "And your name is?" she asked coldly.

"Oh. Stella Copeland. I was supposed to be here at eleven, but there was an accident near Chinatown."

She glanced up at the clock. "You're late, Ms. Copeland. I see here on my list that our CEO Mr. Windsor has scheduled to see you personally at 11 a.m. sharp. I'm afraid I'm not supposed to let late interviewees in. Mr. Windsor sets exceedingly high standards for his employees, and neither he nor HR tolerate tardiness."

"Could you make an exception? Just this once?" I pleaded. "I'm usually very punctual."

"I don't think I can. I'm sorr—"

"Could you phone Mr. Windsor, please? I'd really appreciate it," I insisted. "Please tell him I'm Damon Copeland's sister."

She stared at me, motionless.

"It really wasn't my fault that I'm late."

"Very well," she said with a smug sigh. "But the chances that he'll be interested in seeing you really are minuscule." She picked up the office phone and punched a few numbers on its keypad. "Mr. Windsor, I'm sorry to disturb you," she said into its speaker. "There's a 'Miss Copeland' here to see you. She's *very* late for her interview, but she's insisting I phone you to find out whether you'd still like to meet with her, despite her apparent lack of time management skills. She asked me to mention that she's Damon Copeland's sister."

I couldn't hear what Ace was saying on the other end of the line, although I desperately wished I could.

Suddenly, her face fell. "Oh. Very well. Yes, Mr. Windsor. Of course, Mr. Windsor. I'll send her up," the receptionist said into the phone's speaker. She hung up slowly, as if to come to grips with how truly astonishing whatever she'd just heard was. Then she looked up at me. "Mr. Windsor says he will see you. Take the elevator to the 8th floor, and Mrs. Mills will show you the way. In case she isn't at her desk, head down the hallway to your left. The last door at the end of it leads into a conference room. It's next to Mr. Windsor's office. He will meet you there."

"Thank you, but I thought he wouldn't be personally interviewing me?"

"His schedule opened up this morning," she explained, then added a rather weak, "Good luck," which clearly meant she wasn't wishing me good luck at all. She pointed toward the elevator and motioned for me to hurry. I smiled at her and set off at a near jog.

A group of people were squeezing into the elevator by the time I reached it. I joined them and stood shoulder to shoulder with two well-dressed businessmen. "We're kind of like sardines in here, eh?" I joked, but no one reacted. *Tough audience.*

So, there I stood and took a deep breath, counted to five, and exhaled. It was an old breathing exercise my former yoga instructor taught me several months ago. He said that utilizing it would help me to calm my nerves during exam season. However, standing in the middle of Windsor Architect's elevator surrounded by all the well-dressed ladies and gentlemen, I feared it wasn't nearly potent enough to diminish my sweaty hands.

*Ping.*

When the elevator doors finally opened at the top floor, I bolted through them.

Gosh, my heart was drumming ninety miles a minute.

There was nobody there. The nearby receptionist's desk was empty. Where did the woman at the front desk say I needed to go? Was I on the correct floor?

*He is going to think I'm so scatterbrained*, I scolded myself, accelerating to a sprint that any track athlete would have been proud of, and zooming down the hallway to my left. The creamy-white wall color complimented the calming spaciousness. I just needed to pay attention to the door signs.

The hall was lined with office doors that had names and important-sounding titles clearly marked on each of them. One said, "Mrs. Mary Kettles: Senior Account Executive," another said, "Mr. Harvey Hardy: Head Engineer." I wondered if he was as fun as his name sounded. I also wondered if I'd ever have an office with my name on it. I could see it now. "Miss Stella Copeland: Head Architect."

What would Ace's sign say? "Mr. Ace Windsor: GWIC (Grumpzilla Who's in Charge)"? I was so busy fantasizing that I almost forgot where I was.

I continued my sprint.

*Inconveniently*, my armpits were sweating, and other places too. My boobs. Was the A/C even working up here? A bead of sweat started tracking a path down my lower back. *Gross.* I couldn't greet him all sweaty. Hopefully my deodorant was holding up.

What would be the best thing to say to him?

"Hi, Ace."

No. That didn't feel right.

"Hey, long time no see?"

Nah, worse.

"Hello, Ace, thanks for inviting me."

Better, that could work. Maybe a tad more formal. We'd never been "buddies."

"Good morning, Ace, thank you for inviting me to the interview."

That was it.

Professional. Perfect. On point.

"Oof," I grunted. It was like running into a wall, sweaty breasts first. A hint of expensive aftershave hit my nose. Cedar and sandalwood. Invigorating, fresh, and powerful. Before I knew what was happening, my sweaty butt was seated on the hardwood floor, and I was looking up. Luckily, my contacts had survived the collision.

I blinked.

Six-foot-four. Black tie. Impossible jawline. Dimples. Perfectly straight nose. The most kissable lips I had ever seen.

And...piercing icy-blue eyes that seemed to see right through your soul.

My breath hitched.

Ace. Windsor.

The air crackled. Time froze. All I was physically capable of was staring at him, speechless. For the first time in forever, I could not find any words. They were lost.

But they weren't the only things that were lost.

My big handbag had flown halfway across the hallway, and I'd lost a shoe in the fall too. My dress had definitely ridden up to reveal my legs. Millions of thoughts attacked my brain. The first was: Thank goodness I shaved my legs this morning. I quickly sat up, smiling awkwardly. I adjusted my dress and hooked my foot back into the stiletto I'd stumbled out of.

Why the *freaking* hell was he even hotter in person?

"Didn't your mom ever tell you not to tackle people in hallways?" he rumbled in a deep, stern baritone, and extended his hand toward me. I took it and allowed him to help me up. I was dumbstruck by how effortlessly he lifted me, as if I weighed less than a feather.

Ace nonchalantly strolled over to my handbag, picked it up, and returned to my side.

"Oh, my gosh," I blurted, finally finding my words. "Well, tackling CEOs is sort of my thing," I joked.

He didn't find my comment funny. He raised a stern eyebrow, and for whatever reason, his chiseled jaw looked even more herculean. "So, you decided to go all in?"

"Well, of course, since I was a little late," I continued, "I wanted to make up for it with a well-planned collision, head-on, you know, with the full intention to leave a lasting first impression." I smiled at him. I mean, at this point, I had nothing to lose.

"Well, it's not a first impression," he grumbled, not smiling back and not acknowledging my attempts at humor—jerk, that's what he was. He ran his hand through his blond hair, causing it to momentarily obscure his eyes in the sexiest way. "We've met before, although I think I last saw you when I was in college." He handed me my bag.

"That's right." I took the bag, refusing to get into any college-related memories, at the same time, unable to stop myself from staring at him.

He was taller than I remembered, and bigger, and more vigorous. The photos on the Internet hadn't even come close to his larger- and mightier-than-life persona. He was breathtakingly gorgeous. His well-muscled arms could barely be contained by the thin white cotton shirt he was wearing. I imagined the buttons across his chest beneath his tie were likely pulled taut by his bulging tattooed pecs. He had always been athletic, but now he looked formidable.

"I'm surprised you remember me," I said.

"How could I forget?" he rumbled, his piercing eyes connecting with mine.

A tingling I'd never felt before washed over me. Was he flirting with me? *No way.* Blood rushed to my cheeks, and my heart pounded against my ribcage like a wild animal trying to escape. Each breath I took made me more aware of the fact that I was tingling all over. *What's happening to me?* Panic started setting in. *He's going to notice something's wrong with me.*

*This man is an asshole*, I reminded myself. *Just a regular run-of-the-mill asshole. Act normal!*

"Are you okay?" he asked.

"Yes! Uh-huh, of course." I nodded quickly.

His icy-blue eyes sparkled like moonlight reflected off the ocean's surface. "You look a little flushed. Let's go to my office over there and have a seat. I'd hate for you to faint on me."

He led me into one of the rooms connected to the hallway. Its beautiful old wooden floor creaked as I stepped onto it.

"Excuse the floorboards." Ace gestured to the ground. "The interior designer reclaimed the planks from the *Titanic* film set. It's a good talking point during boring meetings, but they creak. I've been threatening to pull them up and redo the floor, but I haven't gotten around to it."

"You couldn't do that! They're worth a fortune."

"And noisy," he said matter-of-factly. He pointed at a brown leather chair on one side of the large oak desk in the center of the room. "Please, take a seat."

Obediently, I complied, neatly tucking my beige dress beneath me.

"Here, drink this," he said, handing me a glass of water. "I suppose I only have one question for you. Why do you want to be my assistant?"

## 9

## ACE

Sitting down in my chair, I leaned forward, and rested my hands on my table. She was more attractive than I had anticipated. I'd half-expected an "enchanting pumpkin" to show up for the interview, but it didn't. At least the photo on Damon's phone had proved that she didn't take herself too seriously. I had firm priorities for my staff. The last thing I needed was another pretty face or an apple-shiner crumbling under pressure—those were my exact thoughts as I listened to her rather boring ramble about her college achievements. I could tell she was nervous, and it was obvious that she was desperately trying to hide it, which in itself wasn't a bad thing. Getting this job seemed to be crucial to her—but something was off. She kept staring at me like I was a ghost from her past, which made little sense. Her chest rose and fell quickly as she regurgitated a speech, highlighting her skills gained during an internship that, according to her, had proved to be more effective than your typical training. I heard everything, despite being busy trying to make my mind up about her.

"And that's why I think I should be your assistant," she finally concluded, slightly winded from her lengthy speech.

She would break under any pressure, I surmised. She wasn't the right fit. What it ultimately boiled down to: she had almost no experience, even though she'd done her best to gloss over it to convince me otherwise. It was true: experience wasn't everything, but we were in a time crunch, and I needed someone who had built a certain portfolio to remain calm in stressful situations.

She wouldn't last.

It would be madness to hire her.

I knew that. *She* knew I knew that.

I owed Damon. He was my bro. If she weren't his sister, I wouldn't have asked for her résumé in the first place, much less demanded—after my HR department had dismissed her application with a depreciatory chuckle—for Glenda to call her in ASAP.

The move had caused a certain disarray, and if anything, we'd become masters of improvising. Many people were on edge. I was no exception. Until things were back to our smooth rhythm, we had to power through. Aside from renovating the building, setting up offices, hiring new staff, and taking care of day-to-day business, the merger was on top of my priority list. It was the one thing I'd been working toward over the last months, ever since Damon had brought it up. Back then, it seemed like an impulsive idea, but it turned out to be one I was growing to like more each passing day—albeit not for the obvious reasons. Sure, a fusion with Humphries Properties would mean more opportunities, more control, more power. It would turn us into the largest architecture firm in the country and relieve me from dealing with the corrupt deeds of the other major players breathing down my neck.

But that hadn't been my only motivation. For me, it was about more than just the money.

Time. That was what I wanted. To focus on the shit that really mattered to me. Tilly. My sister—my family. She had just moved in with me, and I craved time away from the office.

Timing was essential. The sooner my team and I got this merger in the bag, the better.

In short, I couldn't allow any more mistakes to slow us down. My new assistant needed to be on the up and up. We had four weeks. Four weeks to put together information that presented us in the best light regarding finances, history, and future.

"How do you feel about working overtime?" I decided on one last question, offering her a perfect way out. "I work late most nights and, ideally, I need an assistant that won't mind facilitating me during them."

"Oh," she said, still seeming to try to catch her breath. "I don't mind working overtime. I'm a bit of a night owl anyway."

"You? A night owl? I remember you being an early bird."

"Well, we haven't seen each other in quite some time. There's probably a lot you don't know about me."

"That's true," I conceded. "I think the last time I saw you, you had just turned eighteen."

"Yeah, true."

"Wasn't it at a pool party?"

"Ehh...sort of," she said, stiffening.

"Your brother had invited Miles, Oliver, and me over for a few beers. We were hanging out around the pool. Do you remember?"

"I...remember..." Her eyes widened and fixed on mine. Did she stop breathing?

"Yeah? And you wore a white bikini?" I pushed, arching an eyebrow. Maybe I was an asshole, but I was curious how she'd react to the memory. "Do you remember that?"

The way she looked at me reminded me of a deer caught in the headlights, and for a second, I regretted wasting more time by digging up the past. But again, it was a perfect out for her. She'd better take it. Stella turned a shade of bright red one rarely saw, and I was sure she'd storm out at any moment. Just like she had done that summer.

She caught her breath, saying, "I *did* wear a white bikini, and I was hoping *you* wouldn't remember it."

"Oh, I remember it," I said. "Someone splashed you with water just as you came out of the house."

She shook her head and breathed out. "My brother Damon did, yes. And my bikini turned see-through." I perked up. She was upfront, not trying to hide what had happened or brush over it. I appreciated truthfulness in people. In my line of work, it was hard to find. I listened intently to her, watching her shake her head, as if she were reliving the moment. "I grabbed a towel before anyone could see...and luckily, nobody did," she continued, "but still, it was the most embarrassing moment of my life. And then you laughed at me as I fled the scene."

"I wasn't laughing at you."

"Yes, you *were*," she insisted. "You don't have to deny it. It was ages ago."

"I wasn't laughing at you," I repeated calmly.

"Oh, really?" Stella sat across from me and frowned, clearly not believing a word I'd said.

For some reason, something inside of me was enjoying her reaction. I'd always despised ass-kissers or sheepish people, but the young woman in front of me clearly had a mind of her own, and she had no problem voicing it.

"It was ages ago, anyway," she said as she tried to compose herself, taking another drink of water. "Consider it ancient history. Let's just forget about it."

A breeze glided through the air, making its way into the room from an open window behind her. Her loose mahogany curls danced around her round face like they had a life of their own as a sweet mandarin orange smell enveloped me.

"Take a walk with me," I said on a spur-of-the-moment decision, and got to my feet. "I want to show you something."

"O-of course," she stuttered, pushing up from her seat. "Where are we going?"

"Follow me."

Once we were out in the hallway, I led her toward the conference room at the end. "We were supposed to meet in here, but after you nearly knocked yourself out, my office felt more personable," I said as we stepped into the room.

"I didn't nearly knock myself out," she corrected. "The floor nearly did."

Huh. Inside, I couldn't help but chuckle. All things aside, she was keen—bright even, with a ready tongue. She had proven that on numerous occasions today.

"This is what I brought you here to see." I led her to a large table in the conference room's farthest corner, with a model apartment building resting in its center. "This is Sky Gold Tower, one of our developments in Los Angeles. When it's done, it'll be the world's most expensive apartment building complex. It has a restaurant on the ground floor." I watched her approach and examine the model. "Naturally, it will have a bar stocked with the world's rarest liquors: several bottles of 1796 Lenox Madeira vodka that has been purified by filtering it through diamond shards, and crates full of whiskey bottles made from white gold and rubies. The top floor is dedicated to a penthouse with an indoor pool that stretches out onto a large balcony, becoming an infinity pool with the most spectacular view of Hollywood. Each apartment will be luxurious, with five or six bedrooms. Each bedroom will boast a large en suite, of course. What do you think?"

"I like it," Stella said and broke away from the model for a moment to look me straight in the eyes. I could tell she was still anxious, but now she held a confident smile. She knew I hadn't made up my mind whether or not to hire her. She was compulsively fidgeting with one of her curls, twisting it around her finger and tugging at it. "I mean, I'd prefer something a bit more...quaint, but that's just me," she added.

"My clientele doesn't do 'quaint.' Do you know why I'm showing this to you?"

"Well, of course. So I'd know what I'd be working on?" She poked the tip of the model building's roof. There was something fresh about the energy that radiated from her. Its intensity was tangible, almost like the kind you'd expect from the late afternoon sun during summer. I couldn't put my finger on it, and that irritated me.

"No. To show you the kind of company that Windsor Architects is. We are one of the top-five largest firms in the state. That means I can't afford to hire anyone who isn't up to our standards. Do you know how many projects we're working on, daughter firm in San Francisco included?"

"I don't know...let me guess. Fifteen, big ones. Twenty?" She paused and appeared to be thinking. The sunlight highlighted her frame as its rays cascaded through the building's windows. She wrinkled her forehead like she was busy doing some kind of complicated calculation. "Ooh! I'm guessing forty," she finally exclaimed.

After I told her the number that was much higher than the one she had suggested, I watched her eyes grow large. Turning, I glanced out of one of the conference room's windows where the traffic below was rushing by. "We're busy." I looked her in the eye to make sure she knew what "busy" meant—never-ending focus, working overtime, vigilance, and above all, going above and beyond the ordinary. "Plus, as I'm sure you're aware, we're in the process of merging with Humphries Properties. I need someone who's able to withstand stress, who's reliable, honest, *punctual* and mostly, trustworthy."

"That's *me*. I'm sure I'm the best candidate," she said, still feigning confidence, but I realized it had more to do with uncertainty about what my answer would be than with her self-assessment. It wasn't the typical boasting and bragging, and although she overestimated herself, I liked her confidence. It was promising.

"We shall see," I said, turning back around. "I've still got other applicants to interview before I make my decision."

"How many have you already interviewed?" she asked.

"Many."

"How many? More than twenty?"

"Fifteen."

"Then I guess I must be lucky number sixteen." She smiled.

"It was nice to see you again, Stella." I approached, offering her my hand. "We'll let you know the outcome of your application either way. You may return to the foyer."

"It was nice seeing you too, Ace." She took my hand, and I shook it. "I know you're a busy man. I'll wait for your call. I just know you'll end up choosing me."

"You do?"

"I do. Today's my lucky day, remember?" She beamed, letting go of my hand and flipping her curly brown hair over her shoulder. I watched as she turned and left the room, her hips swaying seductively with every step she took.

Just like they had on that summer day when she'd blown me that kiss.

# 10

# ACE

The end of the day came faster than it usually did. The late afternoon sun dangled lazily above the horizon as I packed my briefcase, shoving an assortment of documents and my laptop into it.

Mrs. Mills, the office manager and my receptionist, who now more or less acted as my fill-in assistant for the time being, came storming down the hallway as I closed my office door behind me. Her long skirt fluttered behind her like a banner as she rushed in my direction. She was a straightforward, lively, and incredibly vivid widow in her 60s, who had immediately jumped in to offer her help when she'd heard of the discrepancy. Even though she lacked the necessary architectural background, in her ad hoc stand-in, Mrs. Mills had proved to be invaluable in assisting me anywhere she could, including the paperwork needed for the acquisition.

"Mr. Windsor! Mr. Windsor," she exclaimed, a smile spreading across her face, deepening the heavy lines at the edges of her mouth and around her gray eyes. "Congratulations on landing the Children's hospital project with the new OBGYN clinic. We received written confirmation. Also, Mr. Garfield just agreed to a meeting. Seems like it's your lucky da-ay!"

"Thanks, Mrs. Mills."

"Oh, speaking of lucky day—how did your interview with that Copeland girl go? Was she as promising as you thought she'd be?"

Mrs. Mills had no problem matching my step as I strode toward the elevator that would take me to the underground parking lot where I'd left my Sián. "It went well," I said. "She seems competent enough."

"So, you're going to hire her?" Mrs. Mills' eyes were the size of saucers.

"We'll see." I pressed the silver button to summon the elevator and waited. Its doors slid open, but Mrs. Mills was still hovering at my side, waiting for my decision. "I'll see you tomorrow," I told her. "Good night, Mrs. Mills."

"You should tell that girl you're hiring her before she finds other employment," Mrs. Mills shouted after me as I stepped inside the elevator. The doors slid closed again, but I could still hear her. "Good assistants are hard to fiii-ind!"

∼

My Sián's leather seat felt smooth and familiar as I slid into the Lamborghini, and its steering wheel's curve fit into the palm of my hand like we were made for each other. The drive home was uneventful. In fact, I couldn't remember much about it—"highway hypnosis" was that the official term?—flying past the other cars without any recollection of doing so.

Making my way back through traffic, I continued to run a cost-profit analysis in my head. There weren't many memories of Damon's sister I could recall, but one stood out: I vividly remembered her having an almost unhealthy fascination with books. Back then, it seemed to me as if she had a book obsession. It was only later that I learned that she clung to those books because they had been her late mother's.

Despite having urgent projects to think through, I moved on from reminiscing about Stella Copeland's reading habits and recalled an event where she'd rescued an injured pigeon from the side of the road. I hadn't personally witnessed it, but Damon had recounted the tale to us.

Apparently, the Copeland family had been en route to Disney in Florida when young Stella witnessed the truck in front of them speeding over a bird that had found itself sitting in the middle of the road. According to Damon, she forced their parents to pull over and dashed across the busy highway to retrieve it.

Instead of riding rides and eating Disney delicacies, she spent their Disney vacation cooped up in the hotel room, where she'd smuggled the pigeon, nursing it back to health. At least nobody could blame her for not having kindness, humility, or empathy, and a big heart for birds. The latter in particular was not a qualification for the job as my personal assistant, but the fact she had gotten both her parents and big brother to bend to her will was different. It seemed like Stella Copeland had been assertive even as a young girl.

My apartment on the Upper East Side had designated underground parking, much like Windsor Architects offered. Once I parked my car in the spot that bore a sign: "Penthouse Apt," it was a short walk from there to the elevator that would take me straight up to my floor, after I punched in the security code.

"There you are," Tilly squealed as soon as I opened the front door and strolled through. My sister had been living with me since my nephew's birth three weeks ago. Teddy, as he had affectionately been named by her, resembled a chubbier version of my father, but had Tilly and my mother's soft blue eyes.

Both of my parents had moved to France to retire a few months after Tilly and I had gone off to college. My mother said that there was more to do there for two retirees than there was in the States, but I didn't think that was quite true. If anything, my mother moved to France for the wine. She had always been a self-proclaimed "wine mom"—the kind of woman who had a selection of red, white, and rosé for guests to choose from at every birthday party and special occasion, just so she wouldn't have to drink alone. My mother wasn't an alcoholic—"hedonist" was probably a more accurate description. After all, France had the longest history of winemaking. The most expensive bottle of wine ever sold at auction was a seventy-three-year-old bottle of French Burgundy, fetching a whopping $558,000.

Regardless of their motives, their move to "the continent" meant that Tilly and I were left alone in the US. It wasn't anything that came as a surprise to me, not really. Tilly took it somewhat harder than I did. To me, they were pretty much keeping their promise that they had tried to help us come to terms with as teenagers, and to this day, I admired their eagerness to fulfill their dreams and spend their time in a way they had always wanted to. Maybe Tilly hoped they would change their mind or return. They didn't. Tilly and I didn't have any other immediate family. In many ways, I knew my sister felt that I was all she had left, and as such, I had vowed to protect and care for her and her newborn son. Teddy's father, an unemployed "musician" from California, where Tilly had lived for several months until recently, hadn't acknowledged his birth—the son of a bitch, although Tilly didn't seem to miss him in the least. I decided I'd be Teddy's father figure, at least until Tilly found someone to fill that role.

In any case, it was nice not having to come home to an empty apartment, and I was looking forward to actually being able to spend quality time with them once the merger was set in stone.

"Sorry I'm late," I replied, hanging my silver-gray coat from a coat rack next to the door. Tilly stood up from the cream-colored leather couch, walked over and wrapped her arms around my neck, kissing my cheek. I hugged her back. "How has little Teddy been? Have you had a good day?"

"He slept the afternoon away." She smiled, picking up a glass of grape juice from the coffee table on her way back to the couch. The maroon liquid in her hand caught the light like a ruby. "You want one?"

"No thanks. I'll have the other grape juice. Is it normal that he sleeps so much?"

"My new doctor, Dr. Maxwell—a handsome devil, I'm telling you—said he'll spend a lot of time sleeping during the first month." She sat back down and tucked her legs underneath her.

"Handsome devil?"

She made swoony eyes. "Yeah, too bad he's only my replacement until my regular doctor is back from her vacation. Stop looking at me like that, I'm not interested in him. Only because I met someone. No, do *not* ask. No reveal yet. Back to Dr. Maxwell. He also said I should enjoy the peace and quiet while I have it, so that's what I'm doing."

"Makes sense. Who did you meet?"

"I said *do not ask*. You're not ready for that discussion yet. Stop disturbing my peace and quiet."

"Peace and quiet," I growled, annoyed, but calmed myself with the knowledge that my sister would tell me eventually. She could never keep news to herself for too long. "Speaking of peace and quiet. Remember what Mom said about you? When you were a baby?"

"That I spent half the time crying and the other half pooping? That?"

"*That*."

"That's what she said about *you*."

"No, she didn't," I countered. "It's you."

"At least I didn't disassemble Dad's answering machine. And his printer. And his remote control. On the *same* day," she said and playfully stuck her tongue out at me.

The memory made me grin. "I've never seen him that angry before."

"Me neither. Except for when you smashed that old bottle of wine. What was it? A Château Lafite Rothschild?"

"Hey, it wasn't my fault. It rolled off the table."

"Because you kicked your soccer ball against it."

"That was an accident."

"And disassembling the gadgets was an accident, too?"

"Sort of. I wanted to see how they worked." I walked over to the wine rack next to my living room and chose a perfectly tempered bottle of Chardonnay. "I thought I'd be able to put them back together again when I was done."

"But you couldn't. And neither could Dad. Actually, I think that's the day you became the asshat you are today—the day you realized you could get away with stuff."

"Me? An asshat? I don't know what you're talking about." Retrieving a wineglass from my open-plan kitchen, I made my way back over to the couch with the wine bottle tucked under my arm. I sat down next to her and poured the rich yellow liquid into a glass. "I didn't get away with anything. I was grounded for a month, and Dad made me pay for the repairs. And for the record: I'm the fucking best brother ever."

"You are." She grinned, taking a sip of her juice. "But you're a bit of an asshat too. Like most men are. I love you anyway though."

I wrapped my free arm around her shoulder and placed a kiss on her forehead. "I love you too."

"So, what are we having for dinner?"

# 11

# STELLA

*W*hile I listened to the news, I used a tiny rake to tidy up the loose soil in the pot around my bonsai tree. "A storm's on the way, and it's a big 'un!" the weatherman bellowed. "It should hit us by Monday morning. Be sure to keep your raincoats with you, folks! You're gonna need them."

I stood up, walked over to my small television, and turned it off. A storm. Sounded like lazy foreshadowing. I'd probably find out I wasn't hired soon.

It had been 142 hours since my interview with Ace. Over 142 hours of anxious waiting. With each passing hour, I was growing more and more worried that I hadn't gotten the job. Before I knew it, I was back to trying to find ways to distract myself. My newly acquired bonsai tree was one of them. The day after the interview, I got around to attempting to make éclairs again and burned them. (I got "a little" distracted by the dozen *Business Insider* magazines I scoured in search of more gossip on Ace Windsor. No luck.) The second day, I binge-watched old Agatha Christie movies. Since then, I'd gotten back into knitting, and had even re-started bird watching in my landlord's garden. I was busier than ever, but I couldn't get Ace Windsor out of my mind.

*Rrrr. Rrrr.*

My cell phone vibrated. Pulling it out of my jeans' pocket, I unlocked its screen. It was a message from Bonnie.

**Bonnie:** Hey, girl. So, how did your interview go? Heard back yet?

**Me:** Not yet. I'm trying to stay positive, but I think they may have decided to go with someone else. *Sad face emoji.*

**Bonnie:** Hey, don't be sad. Remember, he's a *jack-ace*!

**Me:** Maybe he changed.

**Bonnie:** Ha! Men like him never change. They get worse. That's what money and power do to people. The second he has you in his monster claws, you'll see his ugly face. What car does he drive? The more expensive the car, the douchier the guy.

I had no idea what car Ace was driving.

**Me:** *Shrugging no clue emoji.*

**Bonnie:** I'd bet my life and everything I own that he drives a sports car. You'll be much better off without him. Trust me. You should count your blessings if he *doesn't* hire you. Then, you'll find a better job. Chin up! Love you, girl! *Heart emoji.*

**Me:** Love you too.

**Me:** *Heart emoji.*

I locked my cell phone's screen and shoved it back in my pocket. "Oh, bonsai tree," I said to the little leafy plant sitting in front of me. "What am I going to do?" It didn't reply.

After a brief yoga routine, I decided it was time to shower. My apartment's selling point was its spectacular bathroom. The estate agent had called it its "crowning glory," and he hadn't exaggerated. It was what had convinced me to rent it in the first place.

The bathroom's back wall was occupied by a clawfoot bathtub that could comfortably seat an adult elephant. Its shower, which filled a third of the huge room, boasted two showerheads. My beautiful apartment was homey and humble in every department, except for that one room. I supposed that one of its previous owners must have had a "thing" for bathrooms. I liked to imagine it was a seventy-seven-year-old dethroned dowager duchess—I named her Elisabeth of Witherleicester—who poured all of her renovation capital into that room, just to be able to take a bubble bath in majestic surroundings, reminiscing of her time amongst the royals and her secret love for a handsome earl. I had no idea if duchesses took bubble baths, but in my fabulous fantasy, they did. I, for my part, didn't mind that all her funds had only covered the bathroom. If anything, I was grateful—and optimistic: The only reason the Dowager Duchess of Witherleicester hadn't renovated the rest of the rooms wasn't because she had run out of money or miscalculated the cost. It was because her blue-blooded hero had swept her away to his castle on his white steed before she had time to renovate the rest. Thanks to my duchess, I often sought solace in a piping-hot shower or a sudsy bubble bath, basking in the oh-*so*-very-romantic idea of her life.

The pretty ornate mirror above the bathroom sink was completely steamed up within minutes. Undressing quickly, I peeled off my layers of clothes and placed them on the counter next to the sink. My phone was resting on top of them. I had to keep it close in case Windsor Architects called.

Steam swirled around me like eddies of water around a smooth pebble. I drew a little heart in the steamed-up mirror and then got into the shower. The hot water battered my skin and gave me goosebumps. My head tilted backward, allowing the water to soak my hair and run over my face.

The day's worries washed off me like dust or dirt.

*I'll be okay even if I don't get the job. I've got everything I need to be happy: Me.*

*Ring. Riiiiing.*

My ringtone drowned out the sound of water running down the drain.

It was him.

Ace.

At least I hoped it was.

Immediately, I wiped shampoo out of my eyes and stumbled out of the shower, butt-naked and covered in soap bubbles. A small voice warned me not to get my hopes up, believing it was him or news about my interview at Windsor Architects. It was probably just Damon or Bonnie. The warning voice didn't decrease my speed. Unfettered, I slid across the bathroom floor like the world's most graceful figure skater and collided with the bathroom sink. *Ouch! Graceful as a figure skater my bruised ass.*

Scooping up my cell that had almost tumbled to the floor from the collision, I noticed that its screen read "Unknown Number." So, it wasn't Bonnie or Damon.

My heart fluttered as I answered the call.

"Hey there! You've reached Stella Copeland." I couldn't conceal the excitement in my voice.

"Hello, Stella." Ace's baritone crackled through my cell phone's speaker. "How are you?"

It *was* him.

"I-I-I am doing really well." It seemed like my tongue had been stretched and tied into a knot by someone with very clumsy fingers. The words I was formulating in my head simply didn't come out sounding the way they were supposed to.

"Do you have a minute to talk?" he asked in a deep timbre. "Or is this a bad time?"

I looked down at myself, standing—in a puddle of soapy water—in the nude. "Yeah, I mean, no, I wasn't busy with anything important," I said truthfully. "Your timing is actually perfect...at least comedy-wise."

"Comedy-wise?"

I tucked a wet strand of hair behind my ear and leaned against the bathroom wall. No way was I gonna tell him that I was standing here in my birthday suit, all wet and with pebbly nipples. Was it odd that I was glad I'd shaved? "Let's just say I was hoping you'd call sooner rather than later."

"Well," he hummed. It was a deep throaty sound that felt like it echoed through my chest (and other places). "You don't even know why I've called yet."

"Well...can't a girl be happy just because she's hoping for good news?"

"Not when she's waiting to hear back about her dream job."

I was surprised he was being so blunt, but then again, he'd never been one for unnecessary small talk. "Who said it would be my dream job?" I challenged him.

"I could see it in your eyes while I was interviewing you. I bet you've already imagined your own office up here."

Oh, my God. How did he know? "Well, it's called manifesting. However, 'dream job' is a really strong term. I would love to work at Windsor Architects, but life won't end if you're calling to tell me you've hired someone else. So, no need to beat around the bush. Just—"

"You got the job."

"That's great news." I wanted to jump up and down. I wanted to scream. Heck, I wanted to squeeze and hug someone until they told me to stop. *Gahhhh!* I totally held in my squeal of excitement.

"You start on Monday so you can catch up on as much work as possible. Mrs. Mills, she's our office manager, will be pleased if I stop piling paperwork on her desk."

I couldn't remember when last I had been as happy as I was in that moment, or as excited, but I didn't want Ace to know. It wasn't that I was feeling spiteful—not at all—it was just that I wanted to appear professional. From what I had experienced so far, he kept his staff rather "toned down," and I wanted to be at least as laid back as he was. All cool and professional, I said, "Monday? Yes, of course. What time should I be there?"

"By 7 a.m.," he said. "That will give us enough time to get you settled in before the day kicks off."

"See you on Monday?"

"See you on Monday," he rumbled darkly and ended the call.

My body was tingling all over by the time I put the phone back down. My knees felt weak, and there was a warm, heavy sensation in the pit of my stomach that seemed to be spreading to all kinds of places. Wings on my back, I shuffled to the shower and turned it on again to rinse off. The steam in the air made the tingling sensation seem even more pressing and urgent. It was a primal feeling—one I wasn't sure how to contain. I took a towel off one of the hooks on the bathroom wall and wrapped it around myself. The sensation of its soft surface brushing against my skin was almost too much to bear. I patted myself dry and proceeded to mop up the floor with an extra cloth by sliding around on it. Once that was done, I stared at myself in the bathroom mirror. My reflection became clearer and clearer as the steam dissipated.

I examined the contours of my waist and breasts, the valleys and peaks, and wondered what it would be like to have Ace touch them. The thought of it made the tingling sensation worse, but I couldn't rein in my imagination. I visualized his lips touching my flushed skin, his kisses getting lost in the nape of my neck, and his fingers exploring the most sacred parts of me.

The squirming in the pit of my stomach was almost becoming too much to handle, and yet I allowed my mind to wander further. I imagined Ace inviting me into his office for a "meeting," only to wrap his strong arms around me and push his body against mine.

I imagined him growling, "How badly do you want me?" in my ear as he sat me down on his desk—it was exactly as high as the countertop I was sitting on now. Bossy grump that he was, he would insist on my answer.

"So, so badly," I said aloud.

I imagined him growling, "Such a good girl." He would then nudge my knees apart with his strong thighs, slide my skirt up and rip my thong right off. What a bosshole! Hello? Couldn't he just slide them off like a normal man? Anyway, I had no time to voice my complaint to him because suddenly his manly fingers started to rub my clit—yep, he went straight for the gold, impatient jerk that he was. Whoa...jackpot! Not gonna lie. The intensity he chose was phenomenally perfect. He seemed to know my body almost better than I knew myself. He rubbed and rubbed and rubbed, and if he continued this exact pace and rhythm, I would come within seconds. Hard. I felt my orgasm building and building and building—until I fell over the edge, moaning my boss's name. "Oh...Ace."

I quickly opened my eyes.

Trust me. I was equally shocked about the turn of events here.

My phone vibrated. I nearly jumped out of my skin.

It was him! Again.

It was Ace.

My new boss.

The man I'd just masturbated to.

He knew that I'd masturbated to him.

Instantly, I felt guilty for allowing myself to think less-than-professional things about my boss, and to moan his name while orgasming.

With shaky fingers, I picked my phone up.

A message from Bonnie flashed across the screen.

**Bonnie:** Wanna go out for some cocktails? *Clinking glasses emoji.* It might help you take your mind off the interview thing.

Phew.

Oh, thank goodness. I was good. It wasn't my boss.

**Me:** Actually, I got the job... Ace just called. I'm starting on Monday.

**Bonnie:** WHAAAAT?!? No. Gurl. If I didn't know you better, I'd think you were dreading telling me. Meet you at Davy Dave's for a daiquiri at 7 p.m.?

**Me:** Make it a mojito, and it's a deal.

I grinned at my phone screen. Its screensaver was a picture of Bonnie and me with goofy faces, sticking out our tongues. The photo always made me laugh. If I explained everything, Bonnie would understand. It was only a matter of one or two mojitos until she would be on my side.

Everything was falling into place. I had the best friend, the best brother, and now—the *best* job. The thought of my brother reminded me that I needed to let Damon know I'd got the job too.

After I retrieved my panties from the sink, my bathrobe from the hook on the bathroom door, slipped both on, and as soon as I was "decent" again, I dialed Damon's number.

"Hey, sis," Damon answered on the first ring. "What's up?"

"Hey, Batman. I'm doing better than ever! In fact, I'm on cloud nine. No, I take that back—I'm on cloud ten. Ace just called me..." I left him hanging with a dramatic pause.

"And?"

"Guess."

"Just tell me, and hurry up," he said.

"I got the job! I got it! Of course, I got it because you guys are friends, but I'm fine with that."

There was a pause. "I'm sure you got it on your merits alone."

Hopping from foot to foot, I waited for Damon to express his delight. But there was nothing. "You don't sound too happy?" No one could say my brother was a talkative person, but even for him, that was a bit thin. A strange feeling spread in my stomach.

"I'm happy for you. Well done. One of these days you'll be a world-renowned architect, and Ace will have to go to extraordinary lengths to thank me for helping get you into his employ."

"That's a really sweet thing to say, mwah!" I felt oddly relieved and sent Damon a kiss. "I can't describe how thankful I am that you recommended me to Ace."

"I didn't have to recommend you. Like I said, I'm sure he hired you on your own merit. I was just the middleman."

"You're being too modest." I twirled my robe's sash around like a majorette might twirl a baton on parade day. "You're the best big brother in the whole galaxy, and I love you."

There was more silence.

"Well…I don't know about that," Damon said. "But I'm glad I could help. Actually, speaking of help, there's something I need to ask you."

"Yeah?"

There was another long pause. Something was odd. Then I heard a sigh. Finally, he asked, "Are you doing anything to celebrate?"

"Are you sure that's what you wanted to ask me? I'm going out for a few drinks with Bonnie. Why? Do you want to come with us?"

"No, I've got to work. Have an extra shot for me," he said. "We'll speak again soon."

"Love you."

"Love you too." With that, he ended the call and left me alone with my thoughts of my new boss.

# 12

# ACE

"Gracie, he's serious this time," Miles said to our wide-eyed waitress as she handed me my drink. "He wants a fresh beer in front of him every two minutes. Don't keep him waiting like last time."

"Fuck off," I grumbled and couldn't help but chuckle.

"Wasn't that what you were about to say, man?" Miles asked, grabbing the beer Gracie set down in front of him. "I thought that's what you were about to say."

"Get out of my ass."

Miles and Oliver laughed. The three of us were seated at our usual table in a dimly lit corner of Talia's. Music roared from the speakers: a combination of '70s music with some new-age beats. It wasn't to my liking, so I tried to block it out.

Gracie handed Oliver his whiskey, then scurried back to the bar at the other side of the almost-empty dance floor. "Like I was saying before we were interrupted," Miles said once she was gone and we clinked glasses, "Damon couldn't make it. So, no talking shop. Tonight is about having fucking fun."

"All right." Oliver banged his tumbler on the table's surface.

"Where's Damon?" I asked, lifting my glass.

"Working late on some shit."

"So how did that interview go, Ace?" Oliver asked me. "Did you end up interviewing Damon's little sister?"

"I did. Cheers," I said, and we clinked glasses. "Jesus, the beer is getting warmer each time we visit."

Miles shook his head after taking a gulp. "Dude, the beer is fine. Maybe something's wrong with your tastebuds," he teased and wiped foam from his upper lip. "So, wait now—how did that interview go with Damon's little sister?"

"I hired her. She's starting on Monday."

"*Excellent.* Dude, seriously, that's fucking *excellent.*" Miles seemed surprisingly excited. He raised his beer again, and we knocked glasses for a second time. "Cheers! I bet she's thrilled about it. Thanks for giving her a chance, man."

I eyed him with a certain suspiciousness. "No problem."

"Make sure to get her involved in everything as soon as you can. Is she... Wait, what was her name again?" Miles asked.

My bullshit alarm went off. His enthusiastic reaction was strange in itself, but it turned out he couldn't even remember her name. It didn't add up.

"Stella," Oliver answered for me.

"Right." Miles nodded. "Is she still as goofy as she was when we were younger?" He crossed his eyes and made an even goofier face than he had done back in Damon's presence.

Okay, maybe I was overreacting. He was my buddy, and maybe I was just overworked. Miles was the same clown as ever.

"Bro. You can't ask him that," Oliver warned him. "There's no right way to answer that question. Also, I bet you wouldn't call Damon's sister goofy if he were here."

"Exactly. He'd 'goof' up your face with his fist," I said.

"Well, Damon ain't here, is he?" Miles grinned, crossing his eyes again, but preemptively ducked when Oliver jokingly raised his fist.

"She's actually turned into a beautiful woman," I said almost contemplatively, trying to not conjure up an image of her in my mind.

Miles looked up. "*Beautiful?*" he asked, as if I had just said something utterly ridiculous.

"I'm just saying she looked well," I told him. "Nothing more, nothing less. Though, to be honest, the minute I saw her, I understood why Damon's been hiding her from us. She's...quite something."

"Really?" Miles asked incredulously.

"Close your mouth, bro," Oliver said to his brother. "I saw a pic she uploaded of herself on Insta the other day." Oliver's eyes flickered mischievously in the bar's dim light. "She was wearing a little black dress. I've just got to say, Ace isn't wrong. She's quite something."

"Sounds like I need to check that out," Miles teased, then added, "Just kidding. Married man. Happily so."

"*Exactly*. Tell you what, Ace," Oliver turned to me, "just a word of warning. If you so much as touch her, Damon will knock out every last one of your pretty white teeth. Not that I would blame him."

"Woah. Hold on, bro—what are you talking about?" Miles asked. "He might be cool with it. He's with our sister and no stranger to, let's say, 'inopportune romantic circumstances.'"

"He *is* with Aria, true," Oliver argued, "but I'm telling you, once you get into such an 'inopportune romantic circumstance,' as a by-standing older brother, you see fucking red." He faced me. "If you ask me, Damon *will* blow your brains out. And I, for my part, will not object."

"Okay, okay. True, with Damon, you never know. She's his baby sister, and he's very protective of her. He'd probably argue that his case is completely different."

"Chill, for Christ's sake." I emptied my beer glass and pushed it to one side of the table. Gracie made eye contact with me from across the room and gave me a nod. "Do you really think I'd go after his sister? No offense intended."

"Dude, no," Miles said, emptying his beer glass as well. "If his sister is still the way I remember her, all fidgety, and talkative, and happy, you guys are basically polar opposites. She's a ray of sunshine, and you're"—he leaned back in his chair and grinned—"...*not*."

"Jeez, thanks. Asshat."

"Opposites don't really attract, you know. That's a myth. Unless you're a magnet."

"Jesus Christ." I gave him a hard stare. "How often do I have to tell you? I'm not looking to get involved with any woman right now. I just got my heart ripped out by one." Well, that was a bit of an exaggeration, but I was fed up with the Stella talk. Let the boys think I was heartbroken. "Now let's change the fucking subject."

"Yeah, bro, we know," Oliver said. "Now promise yourself that you'd rather cut off your own dick than stick it in Damon's sister, and we all can stay friends."

"Ow," Miles grumbled.

I looked around and noticed that Miles and Oliver had instinctively moved their hands over their junk.

"Well, the only person I would need to give a promise to is Damon. But he isn't here."

"Well, in case he brings it up, tell him that Windsor Architects is your wife," Miles grinned a wide grin, "and architecture is your mistress."

"I don't know why you pursued architecture. You should have been a poet."

Before tensions could continue to rise, Gracie came shuffling over with a tray full of beer and another tumbler full of whiskey for Oliver, then handed us our drinks. "Can I get you anything else? Another round in thirty?"

"Good idea," I said.

Gracie nodded, scooped up our empty glasses, and left without saying another word.

"You know," Oliver said, "I really think we have a point here. It wouldn't be appropriate for you to pursue something with Damon's little sister."

"Jesus Christ, are we still on that topic? Let's fucking drop it."

"Hear me out." He patted my shoulder. "Not because she's Damon's little sister, but because she would be just a rebound after what happened with your ex. In all seriousness though, it wouldn't be fair to her. Damon's little sister seems like a good girl."

"For fuck's sake, stop saying it like that. Are you not listening? I said I'm not interested in her. I don't know what more you want me to say." I lifted my beer and noticed Emmie approaching. *Well, shit. Here we go again.*

"Guys! So happy to see you," she said as she drew nearer.

Emmie was wearing the same bright-green shirt and had the same matching nail polish on her fingernails as the last time. If I *had* wanted a one-night stand with a girl, I could have had one, but I refused to with an employee of a place I frequented. But the girl didn't know how to take no for an answer. It was...bothersome, to say the least.

"Still the same old grump as last time." Emmie threw her arms around my neck and squeezed, causing me to spill my drink.

"Hey, Emmie." I grabbed a napkin from the center of the table to dab at the wet spot on my chest.

"Today's my last day here." Emmie blew a large bubblegum bubble. It popped with a loud *bang*. She sucked it back into her mouth and continued chewing, oblivious to the fact she'd made a mess of my shirt by spilling my drink. She leaned in and whispered, "Let me know if you want to reconsider your decision from last time, hunk." She giggled and winked at me.

"No hard feelings, but no," I said to her with as much patience and kindness as I had inside me. It was difficult. Even if she no longer worked here, I was *not* interested.

She leaned back, saying, "I'm here until midnight." She blew another bubble, then turned and sauntered away to another table.

Miles whistled. "What was all of that about?"

"Nothing," I said. "Mind your business."

"Oh, I'm minding my business all right." Miles chortled into his beer glass. "Looks like Ace has set his eyes on somebody."

I threw my crumpled-up napkin at him. It hit him on the side of the head.

"Ouch. Dick."

"You're the dick. And shut the fuck up. It was just a napkin."

We spent the rest of the night reminiscing about college frat parties, old motorbikes, and all the youthful shenanigans we once got up to together, before we all had responsibilities and careers.

~

I stumbled out of Talia's more drunk than ever that night. On our way out, we had tipped Gracie generously.

The sidewalk felt like rubber beneath my feet, swaying and threatening to give way with each step I took. My black Sián was parked just across the road. Allison had loved the car. The thought of it made my guts churn. The whole ridiculous thing. Fucking ridiculous. I stopped midway across the road and doubled over, spilling the contents of my stomach onto the black asphalt below.

Fuck. What was I doing to myself?

The scissor doors automatically opened as I got closer, the microchip in my car key now within a few yards of the car. I barely had enough strength left in my limbs to slither onto the seat, the beers that Gracie had so dutifully supplied had stolen all of it from me. Leaning my forehead against the steering wheel, I waited for the world to stop spinning. I fucking shouldn't be driving. My light-headedness passed, and I called my chauffeur to pick me up. As luck would have it, he didn't take too long to get to me.

"Good evening, Mr. Windsor." He hopped in and turned on the engine by pushing a small button on its dashboard.

He steered the Sián onto the road and pointed it in the direction of my apartment on the Upper East Side.

~

I don't remember being driven home that night, but I do remember standing in front of my door, not wanting to knock.

The challenge was finding the right key and actually managing to insert it in the lock. I should have let that interior decorator talk me into buying automatic doors. Also, I shouldn't have had that last drink.

"Success," I mumbled the moment I finally managed to unlock the heavy wooden door. Walking into the foyer, I whipped my coat off, and attempted to hang it on a coat rack in the corner.

"Good to be home," I whispered, kicking off my shoes and leaving them lying in the hallway. The maid would pick them up in the morning.

My living room was large but cozy. Thanks to Tilly and my interior designer, several new brightly colored modern art pieces hung at eye height, depicting complex geometric shapes surrounded by large expanses of blank canvas.

The marble floor felt cool under my feet as I made my way into my bedroom.

Thank God Tilly and Teddy were fast asleep. I staggered over to my walk-in closet and retrieved a box. The word "Photos" stood sprawled across its lid in blue permanent marker. After a moment's hesitation, I opened it.

One by one, I started digging through the old contents, searching for a small photo album dating back to my time in college. There it was. Glad to have found it, I sat down on the floor, carefully placing it on my lap.

The first page contained photos of the guys. Miles, Oliver, Damon, and me on a biking trip. I kept flipping until I found what I was looking for: a group photo of all of us, one which we'd allowed Stella to join us for. She was wearing a cute purplish dress with little white flowers. I hadn't looked at her twice back then, but now I found myself running my index finger over her pretty face and the curves of her flawless body, perfectly captured by a very low-resolution camera.

"Stella," I muttered.

Time to go to bed. I struggled to get up, my arms and legs feeling like they were made from lead. It took all of my remaining energy to pull my shirt over my head and haul myself over to my bed. Bare-chested and still in my jeans, I flopped down onto it, face-first. I remained a minute or two in that position until I couldn't breathe. After managing to roll over, I lay with spread arms on my soft cotton sheets and stared at the ceiling. The world was spinning again.

What was she doing now? I knew the answer immediately. She was sleeping in front of an open window, in the nude, tits out, her body only lit by the brightness of the moon. A hint of a spring breeze was wafting into her room, carrying the smell of blooming jasmine with it, caressing her form. I imagined myself tracing my fingers over her goosebumps and pebbled skin like a blind man reading Braille. Before I could stop myself, my hand had wandered into my briefs. Stella's body was twitching at my touch. She liked my touch. The thought of her moaning my name nearly drove me mad. It was enough to bring my fantasy to an end.

Despite my drunken state, I came fast—and hard.

That night, I slept like a baby for the first time since returning to New York. My dreams were filled with images of Stella in a purplish dress with little white flowers.

# 13

# DAMON

"'Sup, bro. Have you spoken to your sister yet?" Miles's voice sounded via phone.

"Already you've pissed me off."

"Well, have you?"

"I haven't."

"Well, I've heard that Ace hired her."

"I know."

"So, when are you going to give her the good news?"

"For fuck's sake, Miles. Give her at least a week to get acclimated."

"Man, I don't know. You're stalling." I heard him close a door, likely making sure nobody was listening. "Dad is getting impatient. Oliver is on my ass. We need to get that information."

I knew he was right. We were running out of time. Mr. Humphries, the CEO, was known to not toy around when in doubt or left waiting. Only a fool would get on his bad side.

"Bro, you still there?" he asked.

"I'm here," I growled.

"You better talk to her soon. Don't waste any more time. We're all counting on you. Don't fuck this up."

"Don't tell me how to do my job."

"Chill, bro. Just saying it's time to inform her."

"You know I have several trips planned. My round trip is coming up in one week. São Paulo, Sacramento, Toronto, Boston." I listed the cities to give him a better grasp of the situation.

"Well, you better tell her before the trip."

## 14

## STELLA

*Monday*

The storm hit on Monday morning, just like the weatherman had predicted it would. Under normal circumstances, I loved nothing more than rainy weather. More specifically, I loved nothing more than curling up with a good book on a rainy day. However, today was my first day at Windsor Architects. I'd bought a whole wardrobe full of formal dresses and hung it neatly in the closet inside my bedroom. Unfortunately, the storm meant that it was far too rainy to wear any of the new dresses without risking being asked, "Aren't you cold?" by every person I encountered.

Consequently, I ended up fishing out an older pair of neat black slacks and a white button-up blouse. I looked a lot like a librarian. The boring cliché kind, not the cute real kind. To make matters worse, the button-up blouse didn't fit quite as well as it had when I'd purchased it two years ago. But I had a good hair day going on, so that was something.

I scarfed down a bowl full of fruit and yogurt for breakfast while listening to relaxing music, something I believed I needed more of (especially around my new boss). Jesus was I jittery. I'd called Jay earlier, my cab-driving friend, and I still had time, so I allowed myself a second helping.

Just as I was putting the bowl and spoon in the sink, I heard the car's honk. Perfect timing.

It was raining only a little as I closed the front door behind me. With my red umbrella covering me, I ran down toward the street where my cab was waiting for me.

Jay was staring at me out of the waiting car's window.

"Jay," I exclaimed as I opened the cab's back seat door and slid in. I held the umbrella out and opened and closed it a few times to get rid of as much moisture as possible. "You have no idea how glad I am to see your friendly face," I said. "Guess where we're going today?"

"Not a clue, love... I can tell it's somewhere exciting though," he said. He winked at me in the rearview mirror, and I knew he was just playing dumb so as not to spoil my fun. He was such a nice guy!

"We're going to the same address as last time—the one on Third Avenue. I got the job!"

"Yeah, baby! Ah, that's bloody brilliant news. Nice one!" Jay turned the cab's fuzzy steering wheel and merged with the traffic already flowing in Manhattan's direction. "The offices in that part of town are pretty bloody fancy. You must be one hell of a professional."

"Me? No." I giggled. "Not yet, anyway. I hope I'll be a 'hell of a professional' someday. For now, I'll just be the CEO's assistant."

"The CEO's assistant, la-di-dah. Don't do yourself down," he said, smiling at me. "That's a proper fancy job. I'll count myself honored to have a pal who works on Third Avenue."

"And I count myself lucky to have a friend with a cab," I joked, "or else I wouldn't even be able to get to my fancy job on Third Avenue."

"Well, that's true." Jay smiled from cheek to cheek. "I guess we've all got our own role to play in life... Just hope we don't get stuck in traffic this time."

I dreaded seeing another accident or a line of traffic as we crossed Manhattan Bridge, but I'd been dealt a good hand that day, and there was no more traffic than there would be during any normal morning commute in New York City.

"Fuck's sake, mate, have you lost the plot?" Jay tapped his horn when a black Lamborghini raced past us doing around two hundred. What a douche! He blared his horn, and without thinking, I raised my hand, giving him the bird. Honestly, I didn't even know what got into me. I never flipped people off. Jay laughed when the guy shot past us. "That car, though...*instant* boner." We kept the joke rolling, making fun of douchey sports car drivers, and then Jay spent the drive talking about a game the New York Mets had recently played against the Mariners. He admitted to being a San Francisco Giants fan. I wouldn't hold it against him—and *not* because that was where Ace used to live before he moved back to NYC.

The cab cut through the now-near-torrential rain like a bright-yellow arrow through a thick mist. I was glad I had packed my silk scarf in my handbag, just in case my coat and umbrella didn't manage to keep me from getting wet. We passed by a lovely French bakery and a small boutique with a cute sunflower dress in the window. It wasn't long before we came to a stop.

"Wow." Jay's mouth was open as he stared through the window, the wipers now running at full speed. "That is not just a fancy building. That is what I call a sick AF big-shot tower. Someone's clearly compensating for something. I mean, what I can see of it through the rain, anyway."

Laughing, I scanned the base of the imposing building that would be my new workplace. Through the rain, it seemed even farther away from the curb than usual. "I guess this is it. Wish me luck," I said as I opened the cab's door, while releasing the umbrella that immediately flipped inside out due to the wind.

"Good luck! Rob them of their senses," he shouted as I jogged toward the building's entrance, not bothering with the umbrella, instead holding my handbag above my head.

. . .

With my heart nearly beating out of my chest, I pushed open the heavy double doors far more urgently than I had the first time around, causing them to swing wide open with a *bang*. I basically fled inside and immediately soaked the marble. Water dripped down my umbrella and handbag, creating puddles of rain on the floor.

The receptionist glared at me over her half-moon glasses, scanning me from head to toe and landing on my stilettos.

Glancing down at myself, I realized that my coat had done its duty. My white blouse had turned somewhat transparent, but luckily not to the extent of any concern. Still, I was grateful to have packed my silk scarf, and I quickly retrieved it from my overly full handbag, ensuring that nobody would notice the outline of my white bra peeking through my blouse. And by nobody, I meant specifically Ace. No way was I reliving any white wet garment memories.

"So, you're on time today?" the receptionist taunted, her voice chilly. I glanced at my watch. It was 6:45 a.m. Perfect. She adjusted her glasses before she addressed me again. "I heard you got the job, so I guess an introduction is in order. I'm Glenda. Glenda Meeks. I was the one who phoned to invite you to your interview." She rose to her feet and stuck out her hand, waiting for me to take it.

So she wasn't left standing awkwardly with an outstretched arm, I hurried to close the distance between us.

"Hey, Glenda." I politely took her hand and shook it. "I'm excited to be here—and to have made it in time, despite the storm. Perfect Monday weather, isn't it?" I said jokingly, trying to break the ice. Clearly, she didn't appreciate my humor by the way in which she just stared at me. *Ohh-kay.* Trying to not let her bring me down and keep the situation both friendly and professional, I added, "We're going to have a nice time working together."

"Talkative, aren't you?" Glenda asked and sat back down, adjusting her minty leather skirt. "You'll need to learn to dial that down if you're going to be working successfully under Mr. Windsor. He doesn't like small talk. In fact, he doesn't like blabbermouths. With him, it's 'speak when spoken to.' You know what I mean?"

"Not really," I said meekly. "He seemed nice during my interview, and I don't think he minds. Although I'm sure he'll tell me if he does."

"I'm sure he will. Anyway, I like a double-double with oat milk, just so you know in case you ever want to make a coffee run."

She'd get straight black, burnt coffee from me, with a shit-eating grin. *Biatch.*

"All right," she continued, "Mr. Windsor is already waiting for you in the big conference room, 7th floor, down the hallway to your left. He's kind enough to spend a few of his precious minutes personally orienting you on your first day." She briefly pointed to the elevator and then started typing away at the keyboard behind her computer screen. "Enjoy orientation." She didn't look up at me again.

"Thank you, I appreciate your help," I said, choosing to be friendly despite Glenda's bluntness, and let's be frank, snide and overbearing attitude.

Greeting the first few people along the way, I made my way up the elevator to the 7th floor. I dried my sweaty hands on my slacks as I rushed down the long hardwood-floor hallway. From there, I headed straight to the conference room, this time careful to avoid head-on collisions.

Fortunately, unlike last time, I didn't run head-first into my new boss. He was already seated around the large table in the center of the conference room when I entered, my heart trying to make a go of catapulting itself right out of my chest.

"Ah, Stella," Ace said in his deep voice. "Welcome."

I caught him glancing at my somewhat-wet hair, and immediately ran my fingers through it, trying to adjust the curls. *So much for a good hair day. Thanks, rain!* "Sorry if I look a bit frazzled. It's raining cats and dogs outside."

He ignored my attempt to make small talk—well, my attempt to find an excuse for my wild hair—just as the receptionist had warned me. "Please, sit down, and we'll get started." Like Damon, Ace was not a man of unnecessary words. If I could handle an overprotective broody brother like Damon, I could handle a super grump like Ace.

I took a deep breath. "All right." I gave him a friendly nod, and in return, he gestured to an empty chair, beckoning for me to sit.

Obeying, I sat down and crossed my legs at the ankles. It made me look more elegant and professional—I hoped.

"I'm afraid I don't have a very interesting schedule laid out for your first day. Usually, I prefer to have an easy, if not fun task for my new employees before they really get started, but there won't be time for that."

"That's okay. I know you're a busy man."

"Very well. As part of the upcoming merger, you'll be getting started by filing documents for me in our archive room. It's just as exciting as it sounds, but I trust that you'll get it done quickly and efficiently, nonetheless. Please, follow me." He rose from his seat and motioned for me to accompany him. Instead of using the elevator, Ace led me up the staircase to the 8th floor. As we marched up, he explained that he was still waiting for paperwork to arrive from the old archive room in San Francisco. It seemed like some boxes had gotten lost or were shipped incorrectly to who knew where, but his team was investigating it.

We walked by the receptionist, who was busy on the phone. When she noticed Ace, she offered him a smile.

"Mrs. Mills will answer any questions you may have." He tilted his head toward the older woman as we passed her. "Your office is through there," he said once we made it through the hallway, motioning toward a door adjacent to his office. "We're having issues with the A/C on several floors, including your office, but it's getting fixed today. Your office used to be a storage room, but we've renovated it, just like the other rooms. Your predecessor was incredibly involved with decorating it." My ears perked up. There was something in his tone that I didn't quite know how to interpret. Before I could think about it any further, Ace continued to speak: "You're welcome to make any changes that you'd like to. If you'd like any new furniture, ask Mrs. Mills to give you a requisition form for it."

"I'm sure it's lovely just the way it is," I replied, sauntering over to the door Ace had indicated. With an excited smile, I pushed it open and peeked inside. Its appearance nearly knocked me off my feet—and not in the best way. A large metal desk with a bright-orange art-deco office chair stood against one of its purple walls. Two large flat computer screens were mounted on it, hovering above a keyboard that was lit up by blue neon lights. Three bright-orange filing cabinets stood beside the desk, and a big metal statue of a rearing horse occupied one corner of the room. "Wow! This is…more than I expected." The room looked like some nutty artist had acted out his idea of female reproductive organs, plus disco lights, plus horse stables. Somebody *clearly* liked orange too.

"As I said, you're free to make any changes you'd like. All right, let's head down to the archive room." Ace quickly closed the door behind him, which I could understand. The rest of the building was—as far as I could tell—an atmospheric mixture of old and new.

Ace led me to the elevator past Mrs. Mills' now-empty desk, hit the button for the sub-ground floor (the basement or, as the button indicated, "minus 1" floor), and we zoomed downward before the elevator doors opened again with an ear-piercing *ping*.

"This way," he said, leading the way.

The dark-gray walls were covered in modern art that stood out in a bright contrast and looked brand spanking new. I spotted prints by modern New York artists all hanging next to each other. There were several cool charcoal portrait drawings that stood out to me, a series by up-and-coming artist Josephine Graham. "This place is interesting," I said. "I've never been in an office building quite like it."

"I enjoy modern art combined with traditional interior design and old materials," Ace said. "People often get nervous about incorporating modern pieces into traditional settings. But that's one of the things that drew me to architecture."

"Who designed this building?"

"Funny you should ask. I designed this building myself many years ago at the start of my career. By a fortunate event, I was recently able to purchase it from the client who originally commissioned it. Getting my hands on this place made it easier to decide to move back to New York."

"And what was your main reason for coming back?" I asked.

"This is it," he said, ignoring my question and pointing at a closed door next to us. The words "Archive Room" were written across it in small silver lettering. Ace firmly gripped its doorknob and opened it. He flipped a light switch and light flickered on, revealing a huge dark rectangular room lined with oak filing cabinets and bookshelves holding a variety of files. A heavy and beautiful oak desk stood almost at the center of it. There was nothing on it except for a modern white lamp, a plastic pen holder filled with a handful of pens, and two big boxes. A cluster of bright light fixtures dotted the ceiling, filling the room with a strange artificial white light. "The files that you need to work through are in the boxes on the desk. You need to slot their contents into the correct folders. You'll find all the applicable folders in the filing cabinets over there." He pointed toward them and stared at me. "Do you think you could do that?"

"Yes, *sir*," I replied jokingly, but he didn't find my joke funny.

"I need you to start getting familiar with our biggest client projects over the last decade. The list is in the top box. You'll also get access to the new server. If you can't find a folder, go talk to Winifred or Mrs. Mills." He continued explaining my task, giving me a quicker orientation to help me find my way around the cabinets and color-coded folders inside of them. "I'll come around to check up on you later today," Ace said once I had no further questions. "Ask Glenda to call me if you need help with anything. Good luck."

With that, he left, and the door closed behind him.

When I stepped farther into the archive room, I noticed the A/C was definitely working down here. It was colder than I'd expected it to be, notably colder than the rest of the building, and I adjusted my scarf. Luckily, my clothes and shoes were dry by now. I sat down in the wooden chair behind the big desk and opened the box of files.

I had a to-do list. I loved to-do lists, and I started working through the papers it contained, reading pages and pages of construction contracts and progress reports.

The minutes slipped away and soon a few hours had passed. I decided that I'd try to find a restroom, believing that a short stroll would help me to regain my focus.

## 15

# STELLA

Sneaking through the archive room's heavy oak door, I crept into the subfloor's lobby. Looking around, I hoped to find a sign or something that would help me find the ladies' room. No such luck. But, I decided that setting off in any direction would eventually deduce the restroom's location. I headed down a hallway that ribboned out to my right.

*Thud!*

I found myself sitting on the hallway's hardwood floor. Again.

"Are you going to make a habit of running into me?"

Ace. My heart skipped a beat.

"Well, I told you it's sort of my thing," I joked and patted down three of my curls that had positioned themselves in a wild tangle during the fall.

Ace reached out to help me to my feet. He grabbed onto my forearm and pulled me up, and my feet stumbled toward him. More specifically, it was my body that was being pulled toward him, drawn to him as irresistibly as iron filings were to a magnet.

I gasped as my breasts brushed against his chest. Immediately, almost before the actual moment of impact, my nipples stiffened into little peaks. The fiery tingling sensation I'd felt during my interview had returned. The other parts of me that touched him started burning.

"You okay there?" he asked in his deep rumbly voice, still holding me. His icy-blue eyes scanned my face as the smell of his cologne washed over me. It was a musky scent reminiscent of ancient pine forests and petrichor. The burning tingle in my chest had turned into a raging wildfire, a wildfire that was burning between my thighs too.

"Uh-huh, perfect. Just a little clumsy," I blurted, trying desperately to ignore his hard muscles I felt under my hands and the crazy butterflies fluttering around in my belly. I needed to pull myself together before he noticed.

"Hmm. You sure?" he asked, his voice stern. "You look a little…dazed, if I may say so. Were you looking for something before you bumped into me, or were you just taking a stroll?" Letting go of me, Ace stepped back and tugged at his suit jacket sleeves. He straightened his tie, waiting for my answer.

"I wasn't snooping around. I promise," I said, feeling like I had been caught searching for Christmas presents in my parents' closet before Christmas. "I'm just looking for the ladies' room. I didn't want to bother anyone with it and thought I'd probably find one on this floor if I looked hard enough. I didn't think that—"

"No need to explain yourself," he said, cutting me off. "You work here now. You have free reign of the office, and you're welcome to walk around wherever you like. Restrooms are this way—let me show you. How is the filing going?"

"It's going well," I said, walking beside him. "I should be finished in a few hours. I can't wait to see what you have in store for me next."

We reached this floor's restrooms. "You'll have to wait until tomorrow to find out. You're welcome to clock out whenever you finish the filing I've given you. The electricians are working in your office now, and I've been called away to a meeting."

He gave me a nod and bid me farewell.

I rushed inside the restroom and headed straight to the closest sink. The taps used motion-sensor technology, and I had to wave my hand below one of them to get it to work. With my heart still racing from my encounter with Ace, I splashed cold water on my face and stared at my reflection in the mirror.

I couldn't let him affect me like this.

It was *not* professional. It was the *opposite* of professional.

A few minutes later, I sauntered back to the archive room, without straying from the route or stopping to look around. I didn't want to get caught on an "unauthorized tour" of the premises again, even though my boss had said I was allowed to take a look around. But somehow it didn't feel right to do so on my first day. I knew that "snoop" wasn't an attractive look, and I sure didn't want to be labeled as one.

The archive room was still unreasonably cold when I returned, and I made a mental note to bring a reserve sweater. I finished the rest of my filing as quickly as possible and prepared to leave. As I leaned over to grab my handbag's handle, three huge plastic bags resting against one of the desk's legs caught my eye. They were overflowing with ribbons of shredded paper. Strange. Where had all of this come from? And why would anyone at Windsor Architects need to shred a veritable mountain of papers from the archive room?

Sure, there were confidential parts to the projects, but it wasn't like the archive contained any confidential details such as billing or other classified monetary information or contracts. I decided not to give it too much thought. After all, I didn't have enough context to draw any conclusion.

I gathered up my things and headed back toward the elevator. Several minutes passed before its shiny double doors finally slid open. Once inside, I pressed the "Ground Floor" button. The doors closed again, and a speaker mounted in one of the elevator's mirrored corners started playing an instrumental version of Sting's "Fields of Gold." Was that a good omen? Yes, I decided. When the doors momentarily opened again, I was confronted with a foyer that was still filled with life. I saw two men and a woman waiting to get into the elevator, a handful of sales reps sitting in the waiting area, and of course Glenda behind the lobby floor's reception desk, looking just as "cheery" as ever.

She looked up angrily as I stepped onto the foyer's marble floors. My stilettos clicked as I approached her. "Done working already?" she asked in a snippy tone, that shouldn't have surprised me but did anyway. "Most of us work eight- or nine-hour days, but I suppose you can do anything you like when you have connections to the boss."

I wondered if she meant that I was Damon's sister, or if she was referring to my new position as Ace's assistant. I didn't want to jump to any conclusions as to what she might possibly be implying, but sure hoped she didn't suggest that my connection to my boss was unprofessional. Either way, something inside me thought it would be wise to avoid any rumors from spreading, so I replied, "Mr. Windsor said I could go home when I finished my filing." I forced myself to sound calm and unaffected. "I finished early, so I'm going home early. It has nothing to do with him and my brother being acquainted." I wanted to be mindful and make things clear right away.

"I don't see the rest of us getting that offer," Glenda said as she typed away on her keyboard. "But if I were you, I wouldn't get too comfortable. It's probably just some first-day clemency."

I smiled. "Whatever it was, it was a kind gesture that made me feel welcome."

"Well, anything you need from me? I'm sure you haven't just come over to chat or to ask permission to leave."

"That's correct," I said cheerfully, not letting her rudeness spoil my day. "I didn't come to ask permission, but to inform you of my leaving. I don't know if Mr. Windsor has returned from his meeting yet, and I don't want to disturb him in case he is busy with something important."

"He is *always* busy with something important." Glenda rolled her eyes while typing and looking at her screen.

"I'm sure he is," I said. Glenda didn't look up at me again, and I could tell she wasn't interested in continuing the conversation. Frankly, neither was I. "See you tomorrow morning." I tightened my grip on my handbag and started making my way toward the building's exit.

"Here's an idea," Glenda said loudly as I pushed open the double doors that led outside, "perhaps you could wear *quiet* shoes tomorrow? News flash: there are other people working here."

Jesus. What a beast.

# 16

# STELLA

The next morning was finally warm enough to wear one of my new formal dresses. Carefully, I pried the elegant creamy-white one I had set my heart on from a coat hanger in my wardrobe and stripped off my pajamas, leaving them in a heap next to my feet. I wriggled into the lacy white bra and panties I'd chosen as my first layer and pulled on a pair of stockings that were labeled, "Grecian blonde." I had no idea what "Grecian blonde" meant or why it was different from "beige," but it sounded glamorous and enchanting—two qualities I could only dream of embodying.

The creamy-white dress was formfitting, but modest. It had a knee-length skirt, and its cute neckline was just low enough to show off my décolletage without revealing too much. In the full-length mirror next to my wardrobe, I stared at my reflection and admired the way the dress looked on me. I completed my "look" with a pair of cute high heels and flower earrings with little faux diamonds. Satisfied that I looked like the esteemed architect I hoped to become, I sashayed out of my bedroom and strode down the hallway leading to the kitchen. There, I grabbed a granola bar out of one of the cupboards and strolled out of my apartment's front door.

Jay was already waiting for me.

Unlimited cab rides (preferably with Jay) had been Damon's gift to me after I'd got robbed on a train in New Jersey. At first, I'd said no, but Damon had insisted. It wasn't that I was afraid to take the subway or the bus, it was just that Damon had argued that he only had one sister and he wanted to keep her around. He had offered to buy me a car, but that was where I had drawn the line. If I got a car, I wanted to pay for it myself.

"Day two," I reported as I slid onto Jay's back seat.

"How's the new boss treating you, love?" Jay steered onto the main road and merged with the early-morning traffic.

"He's fine. But I'm not sure where I stand with him. I can't tell if he likes my jokes."

"Bit of a grumpy one, is he?"

"A hundred percent."

"Well, he better be nice to you, or else good old Jay here will have to have a little *chat* with him...*mano a mano*."

The thought made me beam. I tried to picture Jay wrestling Ace to the ground and winning. "I'll be sure to let you know if I ever need you to intervene. Somehow, I'm more nervous than I was yesterday." I fiddled with a loose piece of string protruding from one of my handbag's seams.

"Nervous? Or...maybe a bit excited?" he asked. I could see him grinning in the cab's rearview mirror. "Bit hard to tell the difference sometimes."

"It's definitely both, and I like neither of them. I prefer books and to-do lists. In fact, I've been known to actively avoid 'exciting' situations, especially the ones that make me nervous. When do you think I'll stop feeling like a fish out of water?"

"Heh, good question. Good-looking bloke is he...your boss?"

"Ehhh...well..."

Jay's eyes grew huge in the rearview mirror. "Oooooh, she's blushing. I'll take that as a yes then?"

I shrugged and sighed. "He's the most handsome man I've ever met."

"Seriously? Bastard," Jay said, his inner Brit leaping out, slightly competitive on the looks front, and I chuckled. "Well, in that case... maybe tomorrow. Maybe never. Kind of depends how things evolve. But what I do know is that you'll be perfectly fine, and you'll do a brilliant job. That's all that matters, innit? New jobs are always a bit uncomfortable. All new things pushing us out of our comfort zone are, aren't they, 'til we get used to them. That's just normal."

The cab pulled up in front of the Windsor Architects building, and my breath caught in my throat. "See you again late this afternoon?" I asked as I tried to hand Jay a tip, which he refused.

"A pack of wild donkeys couldn't stop me. Just drop me a line when you need me."

"Do you mean 'a herd of wild horses'?" I asked as I shoved my purse back into my overly full handbag and got to my feet.

"Eh?" Jay lifted one of his eyebrows and watched me through the cab's open window.

"People usually say 'a herd of wild horses couldn't stop me,' but you said 'donkeys.'"

"Donkeys are stronger than horses...and *much* more ferocious when they're traveling in packs," Jay said with a straight face, although I finally realized that he was joking.

I couldn't contain my grin. "Bye, Jay. I'll see you later."

As I approached the building's double doors, I took a deep breath, counted to five, and exhaled. The doors were heavy as usual when I pushed them open, ready to greet Glenda at the reception desk.

"Good morning, Gle—wait, you're not Glenda." I blinked. "Whoops! Now I feel silly."

A cheery-looking redhead with cute freckles mapping out her face like constellations, stood where the former receptionist usually sat. She smiled at me as I walked toward her. "Hey there! No need to feel silly. Glenda fell off her chair when she was trying to escape a bee and had to go for an emergency medical procedure. It's nothing serious, but she won't be in today. Anyway, I'm Terry. I'm an intern in our customer support department. You must be Ms. Copeland, the CEO's new assistant."

"It's nice to meet you, Terry," I replied. "Please, call me Stella. Will you be standing in for Glenda today?"

"Normally, I would. We called a staff replacement agency early this morning, but they said they'd only be able to send someone at about noon."

"Oh, I see. Well, better late than never."

Her Cheshire cat grin took on a more urgent appearance. "Yeah, it really is. I was supposed to man the reception desk until then, but I just got a call from my kid's daycare. My daughter's got a fever, so I need to go."

"Oh, no! I hope she's okay."

"Anyway, I asked my manager if I could leave, and he informed Mr. Windsor..." Terry paused, bobbing her head up and down. "To make a long story short, Mr. Windsor should be in any second now, and—"

"Good morning, ladies." Ace came strolling into the empty foyer. In his dark suit and well-polished dress shoes, he radiated an almost golden aura of confidence and power. His silver-gray coat hung across his arm.

"Oh! Hi there, Mr. Windsor," Terry quickly greeted. She got up from her seat behind the reception desk and stepped out from behind it. She seemed relieved to see him. "I was just about to ask Stella if she'd mind managing the reception desk while we wait for Glenda's replacement to arrive."

"Ah, I see." He shifted to face me. "Yes, unfortunately the agency's replacement won't be in until noon. Mrs. Mills is out too. It seems that receptionists are in short supply around here." At six-foot-four, he towered over us, casting a long shadow that encapsulated me. "I hope you won't mind helping out, Stella? If I remember correctly, you mentioned having some experience at the front desk."

"I'd be *happy* to help. Working reception will help me to familiarize myself with Windsor Architects' clients. I'm sure I'll learn a lot." I was kinda excited by the challenge, and frankly, the thought of spending the morning in the bright foyer instead of the lonely archive room energized me. Plus, I didn't want to make anybody feel bad about assigning the role to me."

"*Really?*" Terry asked, utter disbelief in her voice. Her eyes lit up like the sky on the Fourth of July. "Gosh. I've heard people saying you're nice, but that's an understatement."

Who said I was nice? I highly doubted that Glenda would ever say something like that about me. Other than that, I'd only had short interactions.

Terry must have noticed the surprise on my face because she clarified, "Glenda mentioned how friendly you are."

My face fell. Glenda did? Was her inside softer than her outside suggested?

"We're very thankful," Ace agreed and ended our small talk. "I don't think there's a single Princeton graduate in the country that has ever been asked to work reception, but it is an emergency."

"Except during my internship, and I love being the exception. It's nothing, really," I said with a dismissive wave. I supposed he hadn't expected my response because his reaction almost felt like Terry's, only on a much, *much* smaller scale. Even if I didn't have the experience—did he really think I would say no? "I'd never say no to doing something that could potentially benefit the company. You need me to run reception until a replacement gets here, and I'll be happy to. Besides, I love working with people, and this gives me the opportunity to do just that."

"I'll leave you two to it then," he said, and it was the first time he'd given me an appreciative nod. With that, he turned to the elevator and left Terry and me standing alone in the foyer once more.

"He never forgets a favor. He's a strict but fair boss." Terry and I simultaneously tore our eyes away from the closed elevator doors. "Now, let me show you how the telephone system works before I go." She waved her arm, gesturing for me to join her.

"That's a good idea." I wedged myself between a filing cabinet and her office chair. "I'm a fast learner."

After a few minutes of explaining the phone system, she concluded, "Once customers start bursting in, get their details and direct them to the foyer's waiting area. Oh, and usually, all calls for Mr. Windsor go through Mrs. Mills, as well as direct calls, but since she isn't here, try to filter them as best you can. I just know you'll rock this telephone system and everything else the day throws at you."

"Thank you. I'll do my best."

Terry's nose wrinkled up until it almost resembled a snout. "You're really like a little ray of sunshine, you know that?"

Before I could answer, Terry got up from the office chair, grabbed her purse, and practically bowed in front of me. "The kingdom is all yours." She gestured to the scarlet chair. "Good luck! You're going to do great."

"Good luck to you too." I pushed wayward strands of hair out of my face and smiled at her. "Tell your daughter I say hi."

"Thanks. Byeee!"

As soon as she was out of earshot and I'd made myself comfortable in the red office chair behind the reception desk, I sighed.

Something clattered to the floor. Leaning forward, I thought I saw one of my earrings between my shoes. *Darn*, I thought, reaching up to my ears to find the left one missing.

I knelt to retrieve my piece of fake jewelry. Just as I wrapped my fingers around the earring's shiny circumference, a loud *snap* made me gasp. My breasts bounced (and not in a good way), and I instantly knew what had gone wrong: my bra's clasp had broken. I could feel its well-padded cups brushing against my tender skin as I stood up. *Shitshitshit.* What was I going to do? I hooked my earring back into my earlobe, all fidgety. Were all of my work outfits going to be this disastrous?

Still kinda slouched down and hiding behind the desk, I committed to taking my bra off through one of my dress sleeves. In the middle of just that, the elevator pinged. *Are you kidding me? Now? I wish I could hide under this desk...* I had to hurry. In my mind, not wearing a bra was better than wearing a bra that was tunneling around in my dress like a lost mole. At the speed of light, I wriggled both arms out of the bra's straps and stuck one of my hands down my dress's neckline in order to remove the malfunctioning undergarment. Whipping it out, I momentarily brandished it in front of me like a victorious gladiator holding his opponent's severed head aloft.

"Stella?" A stern male voice sounded from above me.

All the blood in my veins went ice cold, but I quickly got up (being the professional that I was), the lacy bra clasped in my fist. *I'd like to die now, but I don't have time.*

"Hello again," Ace said, his baritone like warm honey, deep and thick.

Omg, had he seen me doing what I did?

"Oh! Hello! I didn't think I'd see you again so soon," I joked. Immediately, I stashed my bra behind my back and tucked a stray curl behind my ear. His gaze hovered over what I held in my hand, but he didn't acknowledge or mention the strange stance he found me in. I could hear my pulse. I gulped. "Uhm... Fortunate, isn't it? This time, no collision. Ha-ha. What are the odds?" I laughed awkwardly and tried to avoid making eye contact with him, my sweaty hand holding my bra. I wanted to sit down instead of just standing there, but then he would notice that I was hiding something in my hand, so I remained standing.

For a few seconds he stood tall and handsome, staring at me, assessing me. I could feel heat radiating off of him. "I had to grab something from my car." He tilted his chin toward a large folder under his arm. "Have you made plans for lunch yet? I had a meeting at 12:30, but it got postponed." His voice boomed, drawing me back to reality. "If you have no other plans, you can join me in my office, and we can have lunch together."

I gulped. He was asking me to a private meeting, just like he'd done in my fantasy—in the masturbating fantasy.

*No. Sorry. Can't.*

"I'd like that," I said, still trying not to make eye contact to minimize my embarrassment over the "bra incident" and the sudden memory of climaxing to him earlier. "How do you take your coffee? I'll bring you a cup," I offered, completely out of context.

"Black. No sugar. But I'm good. I'll let you know when I want coffee."

My knees wobbled under my weight as I lost myself in his Arctic-blue gaze. "Oh, okay."

"I'm on my way to the 7th floor to meet with our executive team. I would like all of my calls sent to voicemail."

"Got it," I said, wringing my hands together. "Easy."

Before the doors closed again, I looked back at Ace, who had stepped inside the elevator. He nodded at me just before they did, but there wasn't enough time to return the gesture. Shuffling my bra from one hand to the other, I stared at the thing and shook my head. There were no words to describe how relieved I was that he hadn't insisted on showing him what I was holding.

Sitting back down, I took the opportunity to compose myself. My first mission was to discard my broken bra in my handbag. I had a moment of silence for my fallen comrade before grabbing my small round folding vintage mirror from one of the side pockets. After opening it, I examined myself, readjusted the bobby pins in my hair, and used my thumb to wipe away a line of smudged mascara under my eye.

Satisfied that my makeup looked almost as good as it had when I'd left the house, I looked down at my outfit.

My dress was immaculate, but I worried a sharp-eyed onlooker might be able to see my nipples through its satin-like material. Making sure that nobody was in the foyer (especially *him*), I hopped up and down on my chair for good measure to gauge how much "chest movement"—to put it euphemistically—my dress would facilitate. I realized that the answer was "more than I'd like" and frowned. Did I have my scarf with me? No. Damn it. But it wasn't like I would be hopping around on my chair. "You're going to forget all about Ace Windsor. You'll let him know you won't be able to meet him for lunch, and you'll avoid him entirely until you've grabbed a bra from the boutique one block down *and* this silly feeling subsides," I sternly whispered, wagging my index finger at myself in the mirror. "He's your boss, and you're not going to allow yourself to fantasize about him."

Having given myself the antithesis of a pep talk, I breathed out. It wasn't long before clients started calling and coming through the door.

*Ring-ring.*

"Hello, good morning, thank you for calling Windsor Architects. This is Stella speaking. Who do I have the pleasure of speaking to and what can I do for you today?"

"Ecclestone Construction for Mr. Windsor," a deep male voice stated.

"Mr. Windsor is unavailable. May I put you through to his voicemail?"

"Thank you."

The name "Ecclestone Construction" sounded vaguely familiar, and not necessarily in a good way, but in my bustle, I couldn't place it. The hours passed in a blur of strange faces and voices. When I wasn't drowning in a perpetual ocean of walk-in customers waiting to meet one of our reps, I was busy tending to the barrage of phone calls that were streaming in through Windsor Architects' telephone system.

I connected calls, sent them to voicemail when required, and even answered a number of questions without any help. I was feeling confident that I was, indeed, doing a great job. Actually, I was having fun!

---

By the time that I wiggled the computer mouse on the reception desk again, its screen read 12:35 p.m.

Oh, no.

I was late meeting Ace for lunch. Yes, the same lunch I had decided *not* to go to earlier. Also, Glenda's replacement wasn't here yet! I didn't have a bra. Did the boutique have a delivery service? Unlikely. *Don't panic.* I just needed to call Ace and inform him I'd be late.

In the middle of my panic, my cell chimed with a message from Damon.

**Damon:** How about lunch today?

**Me:** Sorry, can't. Already have plans.

**Damon:** Okay. Call you later this week. Let's meet up soon.

# 17

# STELLA

*I* was still busy catastrophizing when the front desk's phone rang. Quickly, I scooped it up from its switch hook and pressed it against my ear. "Windsor Architects, this is Stella speaking. How can I help you?" As I said it, I realized the number flashing across the telephone's small gray LED screen was Ace's extension. I broke out in a cold sweat and my knees grew weak. *What a noob!*

"It's Ace." His voice rumbled through the speaker like an avalanche down a mountain pass. "How are you doing down there? Are you still joining me for lunch?" His tone made it clear he didn't like to be kept waiting.

"I'm so, so sorry." I sat bolt upright, and with my free hand tried to tame an unruly curl that was swooping into my view. "I didn't realize it was so late already. I've been so busy that I lost track of time. I promise, I'm normally very punctual. My mom always used to say, 'Fifteen minutes early is on time, on time is late,' and I've always kind of agreed with her that—"

"Stella. You can apologize to me in person," he rumbled, an almost growl-like quality to his voice. It was an animalistic sound that queued the return of the strange tingling sensations I was starting to become all too familiar with.

"All right," I said breathily.

"You've got five minutes to get here."

*Oh, no.*

He didn't say what would happen if I didn't arrive on time, but I was sure I didn't want to find out. Despite my affinity for Ace, as a boss I found him rather intimidating—and perhaps even a little scary.

"I'll be there as soon as I can. I'm just waiting for the replacement to get here." It was right then that a gray-haired woman in an elegant blue dress suit came rushing through the door. She gave me an apologetic smile that made me realize she was the woman sent by the agency. "Oh, here she is. As soon as she is settled, I'll be right up," I assured him.

"Good." With that, he ended the call.

The elderly staffing agency's replacement receptionist made her way over to me. "Sorry I'm late. Traffic. I'm Willette Washington. Systematic Staff Solutions Inc. sent me."

"Hey, I'm Stella Copeland." I leaped out of the red office chair. "Thanks so much for coming. Let me show you how the telephone system works and—"

"Honey, I've been working reception since you were in diapers. Trust me, you don't need to show me anything."

"Excellent."

"Honey, I was just kidding. I'm not *that* old. Although my grandkids would differ." Willette smiled mischievously, slipped past me (with an awkward but hilarious hip and belly touch), and sat down in the red office chair. "I was sent to man the reception desk over here last week, so I know how everything works."

"Oh, you're funny," I said, smiling. "Well, I'm Mr. Windsor's new assistant." Before I excused myself, I informed her that Mr. Windsor's receptionist was out, and his calls were to be sent to his voicemail. "Let me know if you need help with anything else. I've gotta run to meet him."

She nodded. "We'll work it out somehow. Don't let him wait. He hates to wait, so I've heard."

I grabbed hold of my handbag and dashed across the foyer toward the elevator. My breasts seemed to bounce with every step I took. *Damn bra!*

Five minutes, he'd said. *Well, he can wait,* I thought in a moment of silent rebellion, praying that the elevator wouldn't take an age and a half to arrive.

The elevator doors opened as soon as I pressed the button. Yes! I hit the button for the 8th floor. An instrumental version of Guns and Roses' "November Rain" was playing. Examining my reflection in my little hand mirror, I reapplied my lip gloss and wiped at a clump of mascara on one of my lower lashes. The doors slid open again just as the part played where Axl Rose would normally sing about how love was always coming—and always going.

I slipped through the doors and turned left, and this time, I didn't pause to read the silver name plaques on the doors that lined the hallway, nor did I stop to admire the artwork on display. All I did was fly down the hallway, at what could only be described as "warp speed."

If anything, at least I would be in great shape after all this.

One of the office doors that lined the hallway swung open, and an elderly man with a fun mustache stuck his head through it. "No running in the hallways," he shouted at me, triggering an array of middle and high school flashbacks.

"*Sorry,*" I squeaked as I passed him. I heard him chuckle softly—oh, he had been joking—but I didn't let his humor slow me down. Ah, wait. "A good run is like a cup of coffee." I tried a late comeback. "I'm much nicer after I've had one."

The man with the mustache laughed aloud. "Well, in that case I better have one too. Coffee, that is."

"Yeah, you better," I said, smiling (it was almost impossible to laugh when out of breath) and run-walking.

I reached Ace's office in a new record time. Tiny beads of sweat were forming along my brow and threatened to run down my temples. Jesus, why was I so tense and on edge? This was Ace, not the devil himself. I dabbed my temples with a handkerchief from my handbag and loudly exhaled.

He wouldn't eat me. I hoped.

"You better get in." I heard the warning voice of the man with the funny mustache again and turned my head in his direction. "He hates when people hover around doorways. So they say." He disappeared into his office, only to peek out a second later, saying, "What's with ya? Go on, go in. He doesn't bite." He paused. "On good days." His loud chuckle filled the hallway before he closed his door for good.

I put my handkerchief back into my handbag. Confident that I looked as good as I possibly could under the circumstances, I raised my hand to knock. Wait. My breathing was getting back to normal (kinda), as I stared at the door's glistening ornate doorknob with my hand still up to knock, and tried to calm my nerves.

"Stella? Is that you panting out there?" Ace's voice thundered from inside his office. "Come in."

Sweet Lord. *Nothing goes unnoticed by him.* I gulped, took a deep (silent) breath, and carefully opened his office door.

Ace was standing behind his desk, his lips curved at the edges in an almost-smile.

Wait.

Was this a fun game for him?

His gorgeous eyes sparkled.

My heart fluttered, and I could almost swear I felt it tugging itself toward my new boss. Its erratic beating filled my ears with the sound of my own blood rushing. My blood itself felt like it had been set alight. It was blazing through my veins like a wildfire.

"There you are," he said in a deep undertone. "I was starting to think you were going to disobey my instructions to meet here."

I pushed my shoulders back and straightened, although I hadn't the faintest idea how to interpret his words. "I'm so sorry I kept you waiting," I said professionally.

"Don't mention it. Thank you for helping at reception. Let's go." Before he stepped out from behind his desk, he made a point to lock its drawers and then grabbed his suit jacket. His muscles strained and bulged under his formal white button-up shirt as he slid it on. "This way please," he said, motioning toward a door on the left. He opened it, gesturing for me to step through and follow him upstairs.

The stairs led to his helicopter pad, where the pilot was already waiting.

Wait, what?

Heart pounding like mad—and utterly speechless—I sat beside Ace in the back. He handed me headphones and adjusted the settings, so he and I would be able to talk in private. I watched him signal the pilot to take off.

Oh, my poor heart. It began to race again when things got wobbly, and the ground moved farther away. "Whoa," I blurted, trying to take in the scenery that unfolded below me.

"You all right?" he asked, leaning in. His hand brushed my cheek and hair. "Stella? You all right?"

Because I was so ticklish, I giggled a bit. I didn't want to because his tender touch had been completely unexpected and caused a million butterflies to take off in my belly. He likely thought I was losing my mind—which I kinda was.

"Do you want me to distract you?" he asked.

"No. Yeah. I'll be fine."

"It's a short flight. We'll be there in a minute. Try to enjoy it."

He took a curly strand of my hair in his hand, tugging it down and stroking it. For a second, I gasped, thinking his fingers would brush my breasts, but they didn't.

～

After only a few minutes, we found ourselves sitting outside in a huge round balcony area, overlooking the astonishing New York skyline.

The air outside was pleasantly mild. It was a warm day, as we'd long passed the cooler months. But I could see a few rain clouds forming in the distance.

A white tablecloth had been set up with a single white rose serving as its centerpiece. There were two place settings, each with its own wine glass and cutlery. I tried to count the number of knives and forks beside each plate, but soon gave up. All of it was outlandishly lavish.

"Monsieur Windsor! We were *delighted* when your visit was announced," a man in a chef's hat said in a heavy French accent. "We're always excited when we get to welcome such influential clientele."

Two waiters pulled out the ornate wooden chairs positioned at either side of the table.

"Thank you for being willing to accommodate my request," Ace replied. He turned his head to face me and continued, "Stella, this is Mr. Perrault—"

My first thought was, *Ace knows my passion for Agatha Christie's mysteries*, that was why he brought me here. In the two seconds it took to understand that I had misheard, and that the chef's name was Perrault and not Poirot (as in Hercule Poirot, one of her most famous characters), I felt naked—and it wasn't a bad feeling at all. How wonderful it would be if a man like Ace—gorgeous, influential, and charismatic to the max—knew my little nerd secret and *still* took me out to dinner. *Sigh*. I was only disappointed until I remembered that this was a working lunch and not a dinner date. At the same time, I wondered what my mishearing—*let's call it misunderstanding*—said about myself and my fascination with my grumpy boss.

As I carefully sat down and tucked my dress skirt beneath me, I pushed all thoughts of "Ace, the Stunning Man" aside and focused on Ace Windsor, THE BOSS (clearly in all caps).

"...he owns Le Legendary Coq, one of New York's finest restaurants."

"Le Legendary Coq? I've heard of it." I tried to keep a straight face. Me and Bonnie had laughed our asses off when we'd learned a place like that existed in the city. What kind of man would call his restaurant the "Legendary Rooster"? Only one who was one himself! At first, we'd thought the name was a joke, but no, it was legit. Maybe it had been part of the branding strategy since it was rather...memorable. Who knew? It had all likely started out as a joke, but then it had taken off. Mr. Perrault seemed just the type for it. I imagined him lying in bed late at night, thinking, "Only in America." Bonnie would *die* if I told her I had been to the Legendary Coq.

I glanced up at Mr. Perrault, who now stood at the edge of the table, and before I could stop myself, I asked, "So, what is so legendary about it?"

Ace gave a chuckle at my question.

"*I* sure hope *everything*, Mademoiselle." Mr. Perrault smiled smugly. "We have three Michelin stars."

"Oh, that's wonderful. Three stars? Congratulations, well done!"

Mr. Perrault gave a proud nod and served the wine—a favorite of Ace, a French Cheval Blanc from the Bordeaux wine region of France—then waved his arms, and servers swarmed our table, placing a plate in front of each of us. "Today's menu consists of the following: venison tartare with wild berries, Umber escabeche with earth fruits for the main course, and chocolate tartlets with vanilla ice cream for dessert."

"Oh, how..." I trailed off, searching for appropriate words. Tartare with wild berries? How did that fit together? And what were Umber escabeche and earth fruits? "...promising," I concluded.

They lifted the silver cloches on our plates and revealed an array of delicacies. The scent that filled my nostrils made my mouth water.

"Thank you, Perrault," Ace said. "You've outdone yourself. I promise the next time you see me, I'll have made a proper reservation."

"Monsieur Windsor, we're always happy to make an exception for you." Mr. Perrault bowed. "Enjoy your meals. I hope they'll be satisfactory." He stepped through the sliding-glass door and motioned for his assistants to follow him.

Ace waited until the trio were entirely out of earshot before saying, "You can tell me if you don't like it. I can get you something else."

"No, it looks lovely," I assured him.

"In that case, cheers." He lifted his wineglass and beckoned me to do the same. We clinked our glasses together. "To your first day."

"To my first day," I echoed nervously, raising the glass to my glossy lips. Technically it was my second day, but my first had been chaotic for Ace. It was nice of him to treat me to lunch. The wine was intense and complex, and completely unlike the boxed wine I was used to drinking. It tasted of red fruits, dark chocolate, and cassis. "Do you have lunch like this every day?"

"No. This is a special occasion."

"If I were the boss, I'd have lunch like this every day," I joked (but not), picking up one of the numerous forks to my left to sample the dish. I stabbed a bit of the fish, along with the ground fruit a.k.a. potatoes and popped it into my mouth. It was like landing in culinary heaven with just one bite. The taste exploded on my tongue, a mixture of sweet, earthy, and sour-salty, while the tender fish and crispy potatoes melted together. "It's more than lovely—it's delicious, legendary delicious," I confirmed. "Monsieur Perrault is an artist."

"I'm glad you like it," he said, allowing his eyes to scan my face. It wouldn't be the last time I'd feel the intense touch of his gaze. Chewing away at the world-class meal in front of me, I tried not to react to his piercing stare. I wondered if my dress's material was a tiny bit more see-through in direct sunlight than anticipated, but instead of being embarrassed, I felt glamorous. In fact, I couldn't help but feel a little goddess-like while caught in his sights. It was like being adored by Apollo himself. I knew that his glances were likely just a typical male reaction, but a large part of me hoped they were more than that.

We spent the rest of our shared meal making small talk about the economy (a subject I found boring, but one that he clearly found fascinating) as well as my tasks for the upcoming merger, which basically consisted of me assisting him and Mrs. Mills with, in his words, "the initial attestation and documentation of company history and financials, in order to allow both entities better assessment of the deal's benefit." Or specifically, compile a presentation with the most profitable clients' projects from all the years in order, with samples, numbers, plans, and charts. Even though the important boxes were still lost, my task this week was to continue organizing the archive room, help with the material that the company had available, and assist with the daily tasks until the boxes arrived.

Over dessert we discussed current and upcoming architectural projects we would be working on, and their timetable. Maybe it was the delicious melt-in-the-mouth chocolate crust of the tart, or the best vanilla ice cream that had ever touched my tongue, but the time just flew by. Ace told me about one of his new projects, a children's hospital, and we quickly came up with some ideas that would round out the project.

No work lunch had ever felt as good as this one. Or so luxurious.

The sky was growing darker, and small droplets of rain were beginning to fall.

When it started raining even more, it was time to go. "I'm going to drop you off at the office," Ace said, "before I head to another meeting."

M idway from the rooftop door to the helicopter, it started pouring so heavily, I feared I'd get wet on the way to my seat, even with my trusty big handbag covering my head. It was worse. The gusty wind picked up. To my shock, within only five seconds I was drenched to the bone.

By the time I sat in my helicopter seat, my creamy-white dress had turned almost see-through. And I wasn't wearing a bra. My nipples were poking right through the material. *This see-through business is becoming an unwanted theme. Can I have one day? Just one day...*

I couldn't believe I was reliving my worst nightmare. Quickly, I tried to cover myself with my hand, fully expecting to hear Ace laugh.

He didn't.

He quickly reached for his silver-gray coat that he had left in the helicopter earlier and placed it around my shoulders, making sure to fully cover me.

"You all right?" he rumbled.

"Uh-huh." Sitting in the helicopter with his coat all around me and the beautiful manly scent enveloping my mind and body, you'd think I was going to do just fine and relax. You'd be wrong.

Even though the pilot waited for the rain to pass before initiating the start, it still felt windier, and the start was way wobblier than the first time around. By the time we took off, Ace had removed his wet suit jacket and relaxed into his seat. I watched him run a hand through the wet hair that hung into his face. His perfect hair that looked perfectly sexy, no matter what. He put his headset back on and made sure that mine was sitting properly. It was still set to private.

When he realized that I hadn't loosened up even after we reached altitude, he smiled and scooted closer. I thought it was sweet of him to try and comfort me, but somehow, the sudden closeness made it worse.

"Hey, hey, relax." He leaned in and pulled me closer.

*Thump. Thump. Thump.*

"It's just that my heart is pounding really fast," I admitted.

"Yeah? You'll be fine. I promise." He leaned even closer. "I'm right here."

*Thump-thump-thump.*

My poor heart. At this point, I was unable to think, let alone calm down. "It might be getting worse."

He chuckled. Judging by his facial expression, he didn't believe me.

In a moment of rebellion, I took his hand and placed it under the coat, right on my breastbone so he could feel my heart. "See? Feel it?"

His eyes darted to my chest, pausing for several seconds, trying to feel my heartbeat with his strong manly hand.

Those were the sexiest seconds of my life, and they made my pulse speed up even more—so much so that I heard my heartbeat in my ears.

*Thumpthumpthump!*

He gazed up at me and nodded. "It really is beating fast."

There was a cute smirk tipping the corner of his lips, and he didn't remove his hand. His smile stopped my breathing, it made me melt, it made the world around us stop. He scanned me with his icy blue eyes, causing the tingling feeling in my chest to migrate downward. Seconds seemed like minutes. His manly scent of cider and sandalwood invaded my senses. Suddenly, his hand moved. It slid tenderly across my breast, and my heart nearly stopped. His hand remained on my breast while his thumb brushed my nipple softly (that made it way too obvious that I wasn't wearing a bra), causing me to gasp. A million electric currents rushed through my body at once. My nipples grew so hard that the one left untouched rubbed painfully against the cloth of my dress, and the other against his thumb.

"You have gorgeous breasts. I've always thought that," he murmured softly.

Did he really say that? No. There was absolutely *no* way I would be able to hear that through all the noise.

His hand slid back up my chest to my neck, and from beneath the coat, then across my cheek. There, he softly caressed my jaw, looking at me like I was the most precious thing in the world. He released my face and rumbled, "We're almost there."

Ace made sure the coat was closed and then cast his eyes toward the window, indicating that I watch the landing. Everything had happened so quickly that I wasn't even sure if it had *really* happened or if I had just imagined it.

I hoped I hadn't.

But I thought I probably had.

Shifting my gaze, I stared out the window and started breathing again. The rain had completely stopped, and the sun was shining. Nothing made sense. All I could concentrate on were the crazy butterflies in my belly that were still flying around in circles unwilling to land, and the dampness between my legs.

## 18

## STELLA

After Ace dropped me off, I watched him fly away to his next appointment. Back in the office, I took the elevator down, rushed past Willette who was busy on the phone, and headed to the small boutique I'd noticed from Jay's cab only one block away. They still had the cute sunflower dress. They also had cute bras. As soon as the friendly sales lady handed me my size for each, I swiped my card. Less than fifteen minutes later, I was back on the 8th floor, wearing dry clothes and feeling happy.

I returned Ace's coat to his hanger and updated his schedule to what we'd discussed sitting in Le Legendary Coq.

Seriously, I had never seen a schedule like his. Compared to his tight timeline, the timeline of my former boss during my internship had been a vacation on a tropical island where everyone was rottenly lazy, never worried about a damn thing, chillaxing at the pool, guzzling caipirinha all day like it was nobody's business. Ace never did any of that. He was the type who got up at 4 a.m. and went home after midnight to an empty apartment only to catch a few hours of sleep, just to get back up at 4 a.m.

Once I was finished, I took the elevator down to the reception desk again, this time to ask Willette if she needed any help. I was still slightly wobbly (not from the wine), but I tried to play it cool. As I helped

Willette open a new ream of printer paper, I realized that I liked working at Windsor Architects more than I'd thought I would, but I couldn't help but wonder whether I liked it because it represented an incredible career opportunity, or just because I found it madly exciting to be around my new boss. We could never be together, I reminded myself, but that didn't have to mean I wasn't allowed to enjoy being around him.

"Excuse me," a raspy voice said from the other side of the reception desk. Willette and I jumped—neither of us had seen or heard them come in. I spun around, the ream of paper still clasped in my hands.

"Apologies, we didn't hear you—" I started.

The person on the other side of the desk was the delivery man who had gotten me to my interview on his scooter on time.

My mouth hung open. "It's *you*."

"Hey! You got the job."

"I got the job."

"I knew you would," the delivery guy said. One corner of his mouth pulled up into an almost menacing smile. "A smart girl like you probably gets everything she wants."

"Well, not quite." I tried a friendly laugh.

"Do you two know each other?" Willette interjected, arching one of her grayish eyebrows at me.

"Yeah, we do," the delivery man replied before I could.

"This man helped me out of a pickle once, and didn't even ask for payment," I clarified.

The delivery man nodded proudly but didn't say anything.

"So," I said, trying to break the tense silence, "are you here to deliver something?"

"Nope," the delivery man answered.

"Then why are you here, sir?" Willette demanded. I loved her.

"To see my damsel in distress, *of course*." He grinned. "I think she owes me a date after all that effort I went through for her."

"Oh." I gulped. "No, I think you got the wrong impression."

"Awww. Come on," the delivery man insisted. He pushed away from the reception desk and started walking toward me. "Don't be such a tease! I felt how you held onto me when you were on the back of my scooter."

"What? No, really," I replied, growing even more uncomfortable. "I'm so sorry if I gave you the wrong impression, I didn't mean to. I must kindly ask you to leave."

"You heard the lady," Willette said without hesitation. "Sir, please leave the premises immediately," she addressed him, pointing at the door. "Before I call security."

"Hmm," the delivery man hummed, drawing ever nearer. "I don't think I will. Not before I get a little sugar." He chuckled and moved closer, his hand reaching out to me. Somehow, I was frozen, clutching the ream of paper.

"Excuse me." A voice boomed from behind him just before he touched me. The voice didn't sound apologetic in the slightest, and it was so deep that it almost caused the pen holders on the reception desk to rattle. "You've got one chance to tell me what's going on." Ace positioned himself between me and the scooter man. His shoulders appeared broader than ever, and he seemed to have grown since I last saw him—which of course was impossible unless you were Bruce Banner a.k.a. the Hulk.

"And who the fuck are you? Some wannabe hot shot? Yeah, I don't think so." He raised his fist and propelled it forward.

Ace evaded the punch, so instead, it hit me.

It wasn't hard. It was more my own reflex that caused me to stumble back, trip over a plant, let go of the paper, fall to the floor, and land directly on my butt. "Ow!" I yelped. Loose papers were flying all around me.

"Willette, call security." Ace spoke calmly as he bent down to me, asking, "Are you okay?"

I said, "Yeah," and at the same moment, the delivery guy made a move.

That was his mistake.

Ace was quick. He grabbed the guy and pressed him against the wall, holding him there by his neck. "Touch her again, and you will die," he growled, baring his teeth.

"Yo, I wasn't touching her, I swear, dude, and I didn't mean to touch her, it was an accident! I was just leaving," the delivery man spluttered, but Ace didn't seem convinced, so he continued in a pleading voice. "Me and the girl just had ourselves a little misunderstanding, but I'm leaving now. I swear!"

Ace looked at me, and I gave him a nod. He let go, and the guy stumbled.

"I'm sorry," the delivery guy muttered again, before turning on his heel and sprinting past me out of the door. He looked back as he stepped over the threshold, likely checking to see whether Ace was following him, but he wasn't. Instead, two huge security guards blocked his way.

Ace directed his attention to me, his eyes still dark. He held his strong hand out toward me and helped me to my feet. "Are you sure you're okay?"

"That man wanted to *molest* her," Willette exclaimed as she picked up the papers. Her hand was still clasped over her chest when she placed the stack on her desk. "Excuse me, I will need to use the bathroom. Sensitive bladder. Excitement like this always gets to me. I'll be back in a minute." With that, she entered a few keys into the phone system (turning on the voicemail, she explained), got up and left.

"Is that really what happened? Do you want me to call the cops?" Ace asked, wrapping one of his arms around my shoulders to keep me steady. My legs threatened to give out beneath me as a rush of adrenaline coursed through my veins.

"No, no. I don't know the guy. He helped me out of a traffic jam when I needed a ride on his scooter."

Ace leaned back and gave me a dark look. "A ride on his scooter?"

"Yeah, funny story, actually. I was in a cab on my way to my interview here, and there was an accident...anyway, I guess he thought I owed him something." I shrugged.

"Why didn't you use the train?"

"One time I got robbed on the train. I just froze when that happened too—like a deer caught in the headlights. Damon insists on me using the cab company."

"You don't need to be scared of anything," Ace said, pulling me against him. "I won't let anything bad happen to you," he added, "and we'll talk about getting you a car allowance as part of your benefits soon, so you don't need to worry about transport either."

"Damon is paying for the cab, and also Jay, my cab driver, is a sweet friend. You don't have to—" I started.

Ace held up his hand, cutting me off. "You don't need to say anything. I know I don't have to. I *want* to."

I smiled, not just because he had been my savior, but because...because...his concern for me sounded so surprisingly genuine. "Thank you." He'd do the same for any other employee in distress, wouldn't he?

Ace pulled away from me and took a step back as one of the security guys approached him. They exchanged a few words.

"Stop this guy or anyone from the same delivery company from entering the building without an escort," he ordered. "Make sure no one walks in here without you knowing about it."

"Roger that," the security guy said. "We monitor the camera above the building's entrance twenty-four-seven. Boss, we have it handled."

With that, Ace straightened his tie and glanced at me one last time. "Stella, when you're done helping Willette, come up to my office and I'll give you the private cell number of the head of our security team. Just in case you ever need it."

"Oh. Thank you," I said. "For everything."

Ace nodded once, and with Willette's reappearance, he pivoted on his heel and left.

"Wow. Mr. Windsor can be pretty intimidating," Willette whispered to me. "But I don't blame him for getting touchy-feely with the guy. Rumor has it that there was an incident with his former assistant and a delivery guy. Apparently, Mr. Windsor caught them in the act in his office, if you know what I mean. I doubt that it's true though. Are you guys close? He seems very protective of you."

"He would have done that for anyone," I said, not wanting to start any rumors. "He's just a good guy."

# 19

## ACE

Anger and blind rage were the only emotions thrumming through my body—they'd seized my mind. I wanted to kill him. Just for a split second, but nonetheless, it had taken all my self-control not to squeeze the guy's throat until he gasped for his last breath.

I'd never been so possessive in my life.

As I stomped into the elevator, the texture of his grubby, oily skin still marred my hands. The elevator doors slid closed behind me. My reflection in one of the mirrored walls stared back at me. My face appeared deceptively normal.

*Calm down*, I told myself as I tried to exit beast mode. She was safe.

I pressed my forehead against the wall. It felt pleasingly cool to my heated skin.

*Ping.*

The elevator doors slid open, revealing an empty foyer. Mrs. Mills had taken the day off. She'd said something about her daughter having an out-of-town wedding, or something like that. I made a mental note to ask her about it in the morning.

After a quick visit to the bathroom where I washed my hands, I headed down the hallway to my left, and marched toward my office.

The inside of my office was bright, even though the blinds were drawn and not a single sliver of sunlight wormed its way through. I took off my suit jacket and hung it from a hanger on my office door next to my silver-gray coat—that had looked perfect around her shoulders hours earlier—before strolling over to my large leather office chair and sinking into it.

My head tilted backward and I closed my eyes, forcing calm back into my body, and most importantly, into my mind. I shook my head. It wasn't working today. After a moment of quiet contemplation, I unlocked my desk and took a small pack of bond paper from one of my drawers. I began to sketch a house. A small, modest, beautiful house with a large garden in Camana Bay. Nothing like I'd usually design. But I made a point to add a pool.

Sometime later that day, Stella came up to my office, and I gave her our security manager's number, and then watched her working through her office's open door. She took all of her tasks very seriously. I watched as she frowned at a pack of papers on her desk, thumbing through them like they were eviction notices. There was something endearing about the way she went about doing the most ordinary things while putting her whole heart into it.

When 5 p.m. rolled around, I was in the middle of prepping for an upcoming presentation. As the CEO, I was free to come and go as I pleased, but my day was far from being over. As soon as I saw Stella close her laptop, I packed up my briefcase and walked her to the cab that was waiting outside for her. Next, I made my way to my Sián in the building's underground parking garage, switched on its ignition, and revved the engine. It was loud, sure, but not what I wanted it to be. Probably time for a new car. *I'll call the dealership first thing in the morning,* I decided as I pulled out into the street, heading toward the Upper East Side—*I'm going to buy an Aventador.*

Tilly and Teddy were in the kitchen, busy cooking up a storm by the time I set foot in my apartment.

"That smells good," I announced, hanging my suit jacket on the coat rack next to me. I loosened my tie, rolled up my sleeves, and strolled over to my sister. My nephew was cradled in one of her arms while she stirred a large pot of boiling soup with her other.

"It's nothing fancy," she said, smiling at me over her shoulder. "Just onion soup like Mom used to make."

"Why don't you go sit down with little Teddy, and I'll finish this off?" I reached for the wooden spoon in her hand.

"That's sweet of you, but I think *not*." She pulled the spoon away from me and playfully scowled at when I didn't let go at first. "I'm a new mom, not a baby, Ace. I can still make soup. Also, you suck in the kitchen."

"Have it your way." I released the spoon and ignored the jab. Instead, I dug through my fridge and withdrew a container full of strawberries. One after the other, I popped them into my mouth. They were sweetly sour, or sourly sweet, I couldn't tell.

"How was your day? Did anything exciting happen?" She started adding pinches of thyme, rosemary, and dried parsley to the steaming pot in front of her. The entire apartment was filled with the smell of cooking herbs.

"A little too exciting."

"What do you mean?" she asked. "You didn't get in trouble for something, did you?"

"Why would I get in trouble?"

"Why wouldn't you?" She grinned.

"Hmph. Well, it wasn't anything like that. It happened to Stella. My new assistant. I just intervened. A delivery guy she met once showed up at reception and basically tried to force himself on her."

"What? Another delivery guy?" Her eyes widened until they were as big as saucers, and her forehead wrinkled. "And Glenda didn't beat him to death?"

"She would have, if she had been there. She took the day off, so it was just Stella and Willette, the staffing agency's replacement. By the time I walked in, the guy was almost all over her."

"What did you do?"

"I wanted to break his neck."

"Please tell me you didn't."

"I didn't," I said, leaning against the far wall of the kitchen. "Just scared him off. That was probably a mistake. Security grabbed him."

"You'd be spending the night in jail if you had done more, so, no, no mistake." She shook her head and continued stirring the soup. "Is your new assistant okay?"

"She's a little rattled, but she's fine. When I saw that man reaching for her—" I stopped myself, and the next moment, I wondered why. It wasn't like I had done anything wrong. Like telling my best friend's little sister that I'd always thought she had the most beautiful breasts.

"You're not usually that concerned about your assistant's feelings."

"Are you calling me an asshat again?" I asked in a deliberately light tone.

"No...I'm just saying that sometimes, you don't exactly show that you're the compassionate human being I know you are, now, do you?" She smiled and shrugged, pulling her bony shoulders up to her ears. "Am I right or am I right?"

"You're wrong."

"But you even remembered that replacement's name, I'm impressed! You've been in a slightly better mood lately too. Perhaps that new assistant of yours is changing you."

"Don't be silly," I growled.

"Silly? Me? I'm just saying that you've been working way too much ever since your breakup—today not included—and have had your mind on your projects instead of on your employees. When was the last time you made small talk with one of your staff? There's more to life than barking out orders."

"Hey, I make plenty of small talk."

"Yeah, is that before or after you put someone's nose out of joint?"

"I don't like beating around the bush. I'm an honest person, and I like honesty in others."

"I know, but that's not how society works. People don't have a clue that you're a fun-loving guy inside, and not the grouchy jerk you make everyone believe you are. A smile goes a long way."

Teddy woke up and started crying, ending the conversation.

## 20

## STELLA

*Saturday*

I sat in front of my laptop while an episode of *MasterChef* was playing in the background. My third attempt at making éclairs was baking in the oven. The key to success was fairly simple: Don't give up. The sweet smell of vanilla and sugar filled my apartment.

Still, I wished I was elsewhere.

Before I'd started working at Windsor Architects, Saturday was my favorite day of the week. Monday was—surprise surprise—my least favorite. Now, I found myself counting the hours 'til Monday morning. My boss was the "forbidden fruit," but I found myself longing for his company regardless. It wasn't just that he turned my body into a living flame, I truly enjoyed conversing with him too. He was inarguably the most intelligent man I'd ever met, and I could listen to him discussing just about anything for hours on end. It wasn't just a slight infatuation, no, I was in awe of him. His recent "rescue" of me at the reception desk hadn't helped put a damper on my feelings for him either.

"Ooh. That looks a little burned," one of the *MasterChef* presenters said. I looked up just in time to see the camera pan across a blackened piece of cookie. My stomach rumbled, prompting me to reach for a half-empty packet of Oreo minis on the small coffee table in front of me. I scooped a few of them into my mouth and chuckled.

My kitchen timer's loud beeping filled the room just as I had settled on watching another episode, and I jumped up off the couch and made my way down the hallway. When I opened the door, I smelled smoke before I could see it. *Nonono.* A thin cloud of it appeared just under the ceiling as I got closer to the kitchen.

"What the heck!" I rushed toward the oven.

Grabbing my tattered pair of oven mitts from the kitchen counter, I heroically went in after my éclairs. I whipped them out of the oven—but I was too late. They were nothing but unshapely coaly versions of what I'd hoped they'd be. "Oh, *crap*," I exclaimed, slamming the tray onto the stovetop.

At least the alarm didn't go off, so there was progress.

Was the oven broken? It *had* to be.

I turned all the oven's dials to zero and stomped toward the kitchen window to open it. Smoke rolled out of it like water escaping through a sluice. I guessed I would try again next weekend. My first batch of *unburned* éclairs had better be absolutely heavenly to make up for all of this trouble.

My Miss Marple ringtone interrupted my train of thought.

Ace!

It was him—I could feel it.

Quickly, I withdrew my cell from my jeans' pocket and unlocked it. My heart sped up. The word "Brother" flashed across my phone's screen. Okay, not *him*.

I swiped left and held it up to my ear. "Hey, big bro."

"Hey, lil sis," he answered. There was music playing in the background, and I could hear people loudly conversing around him. I wondered where he was.

"Where ya at?" I asked.

"What you up to?" he asked at the same time.

I looked at the black baked goods I'd left on the stovetop and said, "Not much."

"I'm glad to hear that," he said, "because I'm calling to find out if you'd like to join me for a drink at Swayze's."

"Is Ace there?" A flutter of hope stirred in my stomach.

"No, he isn't. He might show up later. But, I'd like to talk to you about him."

"Oh. Why? Is he in some kind of trouble?" I asked jokingly.

"No. Or at least, I *hope* he isn't."

"Wait, you're serious? I was just kidding."

"I'm very serious."

That was odd. "What could Ace possibly be up to that would get him in trouble?" I asked. "He's the poster boy for success."

"I'd prefer to talk about it in person."

"Fine, I'll be right there."

"See you," Damon said, ending the call.

*I'll tidy this up later*, I thought, standing in the center of my war-torn kitchen. I was far too overcome with curiosity to delay the meeting even a second.

After dialing the cab company's number, I asked the woman on the other end of the line to send a cab to my location. "If Jay is free, I'd appreciate it if you could send him."

"Jay the Brit, or Jay the Hunk?"

"Jay the Brit," I said without thinking. *Jay the Hunk? Who was Jay the Hunk?* I had to ask Jay about him.

"I'll see what I can do," the woman replied. "One of our drivers will be at your location in the next fifteen minutes."

"Perfect." I stowed my cell phone back in my pocket.

Looking down at my red shirt and blue jeans, I realized they were covered in flour and sugar. It was not exactly a flattering look, and I needed to change. While standing in front of my antique wardrobe, I decided to don a cute floral crimson summer dress I'd purchased two seasons ago. It wasn't quite "little summer dress" weather, but I wanted to look as pretty as possible in case Ace showed up, and I was willing to bear the chilly spring breeze to do so.

I wriggled out of my clothes and pulled the dress over my head. The dress's waist was tight around my middle, and its skirt stopped mid-knee. I twirled in front of my mirror, admiring the way it looked on me and wondering where Ace's gaze would pause if he saw me in it. The mere memory of how he had stared at and touched my body in the helicopter (I still wasn't sure if it had actually happened) was enough to make my heart pound harder against my ribcage. I wondered what his soft, warm hands would feel like on other places.

"Ugh! Stop that," I chastised myself. "He's your boss, for heaven's sake." I shook my head in an attempt to loosen the fiery thoughts of Ace that were forming in my mind.

The old wooden cat-shaped clock that hung above my front door read 1 p.m. by the time I was ready to leave. Once outside, I locked the door behind me. The breeze playfully tugged at my dress, threatening to lift it. I held it down with one hand and jogged on my beige heels toward the yellow cab waiting for me.

"Hey there," the cab driver exclaimed, waving at me through his open window. He was a slight man with a shock of bright-white longish hair trying to cover a bald head. Not Jay.

"I'm Jay…the Hunk," he added when he noticed my perplexed expression. "Where are you headed today, ma'am?"

"Hello, it's nice to meet another Jay," I replied as I slid into the back seat, wondering why they called him "the Hunk." He wasn't tall, strong, or really that attractive—even though attractiveness was subjective, of course. I contemplated asking why they called him "the Hunk," but I stopped myself. It would be rude, and I didn't want to hurt his feelings. "I'd like to go to Swayze's, please."

"Of course. I'll have you there in a jiffy." He turned the cab onto the road and turned up his stereo system's volume.

"Where's Jay today? The Brit?" I asked as I made myself comfortable. "He's usually the one that's on my route."

"He's writing an essay or something today. He took the day off. Are you two close?"

"I know him from yoga class," I replied, "and yes, we're friends. What kind of essay is he writing? And why is he doing it on a Saturday?"

"Full of questions, aren't you, ma'am? He's writing a fancy-shmancy college essay, but I have no idea why he's writing it on a Saturday. All I know is that he said he's trying to 'better himself.'"

"He didn't tell me he's taking college classes. What is he studying?" I pried, suddenly realizing that I didn't know nearly as much about my friendly gym buddy and neighborhood cab driver as I thought I did.

"Psychology, if I remember correctly," he said. "He wants to be a head doctor."

Oh! Nice. That was why his advice always seemed so meaningful. "I think he'd be a great one."

Jay the Hunk stopped the cab in front of Swayze's and rotated in his seat to look at me, telling me the price. He knew it was to be deducted from my account.

"One moment, please." I dug through my handbag and withdrew my wallet. I leafed through it and handed Jay a sizable tip. Nothing made me happier than being able to leave someone a tip that was big enough to make them smile, although the Copeland financial planner called it an "irresponsible expenditure." It did make him smile, and I knew that no financial planner's approval would be a better feeling than that. "See you around," I said as I slid out of the cab's back seat. "Say hi to the Brit."

"Have a nice day, ma'am. I'll tell Jay you send your regards when I see him again."

"Thank you. I really appreciate that."

Swayze's was buzzing with activity. Peeping through the thick glass door that served as its entrance, I saw rows of glass tables with ornate metal chairs around them. Most of them were filled with rambunctious occupants drinking liquor and enjoying each other's company. There was something infectious about the atmosphere of a busy bar that even I couldn't resist.

A youthful hostess with a face full of dark makeup and shoulder-length black hair came jogging up to me as I entered the establishment.

"Welcome, welcome," she greeted me in a Southern drawl, and led me to the table where Damon was already seated, his favorite drink—a bourbon—in front of him. Ace wasn't there.

"Hi, Pancake." He gave me a hug.

"Hey, Muffin."

"Can I ask the waitress to bring you anything?" the hostess asked as I sat down across from my brother.

"An extra-creamy strawberry milkshake would be nice, please," I said, smiling across the table at Damon.

He shook his head at me. "An extra-creamy strawberry milkshake?"

"Don't judge."

"An extra-creamy strawberry milkshake it is," the hostess said in a friendly tone and nodded. "Coming right up! Anything else for you, handsome?"

"I'm good, thanks."

"An extra-creamy strawberry milkshake?" Damon asked again as she left. "Weird."

"Says the weirdest guy in the room." I rolled my eyes and stuck my tongue out at him.

"Don't be silly. How am I weird?"

"You called me weird first, so you have to explain yourself first," I insisted. "How am *I* weird?"

"Hmm, let me think, I don't know, Miss *Extra-Creamy Strawberry Milkshake*."

"You've got me there," I said, giggling, "but you're the worst kind of weird: the kind that looks normal."

He chuckled softly.

I put my elbows on the table and rested my chin on my hands. "So, what do you want to talk about? How is Ace in trouble?"

"We're diving right in, then? I thought we'd make small talk first. Perhaps talk about your first week at your new job? Anything exciting happening?"

"Nope, you first. I want to know why you asked me to come. I'm dying of curiosity. I won't be able to talk about anything else until I know." I chose not to tell Damon what had happened with the creepy delivery guy for fear it might cause him to worry about me, or worse, make him doubt that I was safe at work. I knew he'd worry, and I didn't want that.

"Okay, fine." Damon furrowed his brow and pinched the bridge of his nose. "I invited you here because I'd like to ask you a favor."

"Of course! Anything. You know I'd do anything for you. But I thought you said it was about Ace?" I asked, biting my thumbnail.

"It is." He nodded and took a sip of bourbon. "You know Humphries Properties is in the process of merging with Windsor Architects."

"Yes?"

Our waitress, Sadie, appeared with my milkshake in hand. It looked deliciously thick and creamy. She put it down in front of me and stuck a thick (environmentally friendly) metal straw in it. "Bon Appétit! Enjoy!" she said in her Southern drawl.

"Thanks, Sadie," I said. "Can you bring me some curly fries too, please?"

Damon gave me the "weirdo" look.

"Of course, hon." Sadie smiled. "I'll get those for you right away." She flipped her black hair behind her ear and shifted her attention to my brother. "Can I get you anything else, handsome?"

"No, I'm fine. Thank you." Damon only looked up briefly at her, despite her obvious attempts to get his attention. "Actually, on second thought, please bring me another bourbon." He held up his almost-empty glass. The remaining amber liquid in it swirled around like a stormy whirlpool.

"Sure thing," Sadie replied and smiled at him. "Let me know if you'd like absolutely anything else." She winked at Damon as she turned to leave. He didn't lift his head to watch her sashay across the room, although I noticed most of the other men in the bar turning their heads to ogle her.

"What's all of this about?" I asked, accidentally slurping loudly at my beverage, trying to suck the thickness up the straw, earning an annoyed glance from my brother. The shake was cold and decadent, and it reminded me of the summers I'd spent at the rocky beaches in Maine as a kid with him.

"I'll get right to the point: The guys and I are worried that Windsor is caught up with Ecclestone Construction, or worse yet, that Ace has buddied up with Edmund Ecclestone himself. If that's the case, we can't let this merger happen."

"Did you say Ecclestone Construction?"

"Yes."

"Yesterday, someone from Ecclestone Construction called, and I forwarded them to Ace's voicemail."

He lowered his glass. "Are you sure?"

"Yeah, I was helping out at the front desk when they called."

"*Fuck*," he grumbled.

"What?"

"Was it Ecclestone himself?"

"No idea. It was a man, but he didn't give me his name."

Damon looked upset.

"Why? What's wrong?"

"Edmund Ecclestone is one of our biggest competitors. They call him the desperado—the miscreant, the cutthroat—of the building industry."

That rang a bell. "Wait! Oh! I've read about him in the papers. Is he the construction shark with the skeletons in his closet, yet he remains untouchable? That the one?"

"Yeah."

That was why the name sounded familiar. Yesterday, in the hustle and bustle, I hadn't given it any further thought. Looking into my brother's concerned eyes, I started to understand. Any association with Ecclestone would be catastrophic for Humphries.

"But maybe it was just a cold call, you know?" I tried. "I'm pretty sure that's what it was. A sales rep. Trying to get a bite of the cake by getting in business with the rival. There were tons of rep calls, it doesn't mean anything."

Damon wasn't happy. "I'm not liking this."

"I'm sure Ace isn't doing any of that shady stuff," I said firmly. "He wouldn't team up with Ecclestone. He's not like that."

"The problem is that we can't be sure of that. We know for a fact that he was drawing up blueprints for properties in Short Hills, the exact same location where Ecclestone is currently building a bunch of new developments."

"That's probably just a coincidence though." I tried to suck up more of my strawberry goodness. "I mean, it doesn't prove anything."

"You're right, it doesn't. That's where you come in."

"How?"

"I need you to keep an eye on Ace for us. You have access to Windsor Architects' files and his meeting schedule. All you need to do is ascertain whether he has met or is still meeting with Edmund Ecclestone or one of his partners."

I looked at him, shocked. "I can't do that! *No*," I blurted, nearly knocking over my milkshake. "You're asking me to snoop on *Ace*. Hello? He's my boss. Even worse, you're asking me to snoop on your friend. That's a terrible favor to ask. Wait, is that why you helped me get a job there? That's horrible! *You're* a horrible person."

"I know. But it's important." Damon took off his glasses and placed them on the table, pinching the bridge of his nose again.

"I thought you were helping me out of the goodness of your heart, not to *use* me!"

"Calm down. Nobody's using anybody. It might be an unpleasant task, but it's crucial to the well-being and future of Humphries Properties. To *our* well-being." He met my gaze. "Stella, there's no other way. You *have* to do it."

"Are you threatening me, Damon?" I asked, arching a rather irritated brow. "You know how much I appreciate that you're helping me pay my bills and offer certain luxuries while I get settled in. I'm also well aware that you've always been willing to help when I needed it, no matter the cost, but that doesn't mean I'm obligated to do your dirty work for you."

"I'm not threatening you. I'm asking you to do me a favor. Not because you owe me, but because I'm your brother, and I need your help. You know I wouldn't be asking you if I had any other choice. I know it's fucked up, and I tried to think of other ways, but there are none."

"Why don't you just ask him yourself?" I asked. "I'm sure he'll understand why you're wondering, and I'm even more sure he'll be honest with you."

Damon rubbed at his temples, ruffling the edges of his dark hair. He sighed and put his glasses back on. His almost-black eyes bore into me as he kept me locked in his gaze. "I *did* ask him, but he weaseled his way out of giving me a straight answer. He's hiding something. That's all I know."

I didn't like where this conversation was heading, not a single bit. My brother was excellent at knowing people. He was smart. He was intuitive. He was the best at what he did, and his sixth sense hardly ever let him down. I couldn't just dismiss his thoughts because they didn't align with what I wanted to hear.

In a weak attempt, I said, "I'm sure you just misunderstood him."

"I didn't. My gut is telling me there's something we don't know. My hypothesis is that Windsor Architects got into financial trouble somehow because Ace teamed up with Ecclestone—likely by getting involved on the Short Hills Development with him or maybe even some earlier project—and that's why he's looking to sell Windsor Architects."

"Are you really sure, Damon?" I fiddled with a piece of paper I'd found on the table and folded it into intricate shapes. "Ace is a good person. I don't believe that he'd be dishonest with you."

"Ace might be a good person, but Ecclestone is an absolute fucking bastard. You know that. Everybody knows that."

"Yes." I dropped the piece of paper I'd been playing with and stared at it mournfully on the glass top of the table, remembering one article I'd read in the comic section of a construction magazine. "If the two worst people had a baby, and that baby was raised by the worst people, it would probably be almost as evil and sadistic as Edmund is." Nobody wanted to be tied to him, unless you were either ruthless or uninterested in a successful Whitehat career.

"So, you understand I don't have a choice? I need to find out if Ace is connected to him, no matter the cost." Damon looked at me, his eyes illuminated by the bar's unnatural lighting.

"I understand. I don't want to do it, but I understand. If I were in your shoes, I'd want to know if Ace was working with Ecclestone too." I sighed and leaned back. "I trust you, Damon. Now I really want to know. Maybe Ace stumbled into it by accident?"

"Maybe. But I doubt it. If all of it had been some kind of mishap, he would have confided in us. He's covering something up, and you need to catch him."

"I can't see myself working for him if Ecclestone is part of the package." Solemnly, I did my best to suck more of my thick milkshake through the straw, but nothing came out. I shook my head, unhappy. "So, what exactly do you need me to do? Catch him how?"

"You need to find out if Windsor Architects is in any kind of financial trouble, and more importantly, if they're doing or have done business with Ecclestone. All this could be the case, but it could also be neither. Either way, I need to know."

"Okay, but I don't like it one bit," I finally said.

"Honestly, neither do I." Damon lifted his bourbon glass to his lips and emptied it. "He's one of my best buddies."

"And my boss," I reminded him just as my curly fries arrived.

I looked at my watch. It was 2:05 p.m. Only forty-two hours until I got to clock in on Monday morning.

I wasn't looking forward to it.

Not one tiny bit.

# 21

## STELLA

*Monday*

*Knock. Knock. Knock-knock.*

My fingers grazed shakily against Ace's office door. It almost seemed to shudder at my touch. After the meeting with Damon, I had hardly closed an eye. Was Ace really a ruthless, dangerous businessman, an evil monster who would stop at nothing to get his way?

"Come in." His deep voice boomed darkly, menacingly from somewhere behind it.

The door's ornate handle felt like ice in my palm as I twisted it. Inching open the door, I could hear Vivaldi's *Gloria in D Major* playing softly in the background. A waft of air hit me as I opened it further. It smelled of whiskey, coffee, and Ace's cologne: invigorating, fresh, and powerful.

"I've been waiting for you," he rumbled sternly.

There was something merciless about the way he looked at me from across the table. It reminded me of the way a raptor looked at their desperately fleeing prey just before they pounced.

"I'm sorry if I'm late," I squeaked as I stepped inside. His office was dark. The only source of light was a handful of candles on his desk. And white roses. That was so odd! I looked up and saw him lock his drawer, get up from his office chair, and approach me rapidly.

"You know I hate being kept waiting," he practically growled, getting closer and closer to me. He paused when he was about a foot away from me and reached out, bracketing his hands on either side of my head, pressing me against the wall. "But you're worth waiting for. Now—on your knees."

"Wh-at?" I stuttered.

My nervous system called a "code red," and my body started going haywire. My knees trembled, my heart raced, and beads of sweat formed along my brow and between my heated breasts. My tight nipples pressed against the fabric of my new sunflower dress, rubbing against it teasingly. To make matters worse, I suddenly realized I wasn't wearing a bra or panties. A chilly breeze waltzed in through Ace's open balcony door. It swirled up my dress and caressed the area where my underwear should have been.

How could I possibly have forgotten to put on underwear? I mean, wearing no bra during office hours, yep, been there done that, but no panties? That was a whole new level of taboo. There was no excuse for that.

I gulped and put my hand on my quivering chest, trying to calm my frantic pulse. "I think there's been a mistake of some kind—"

"Now, I'm only going to say this one more time. On your knees."

*Holy shit*. I dropped to my knees.

"Atta girl." His upper body leaned down toward me and he cupped my chin, his face moving closer and closer to mine as I prepared for our lips to meet. His mouth almost grazed across mine, almost touched but did not, and my heart almost stopped when his deep gaze penetrated mine.

"Such a good assistant," Ace growled against my lips.

He leaned back up to a standing position without kissing me (you tease, you...you...*bossy grump!*), and his free hand reached for his belt, unbuckling it.

Oh, my goodness.

With a tug, he suddenly held my head and messy hair in his palm. "Open wide."

I began to wonder whether I would be needing a bra and panties after all.

*Beep! Beep! Beep!*

Sitting bolt upright in bed, I slammed my fist down on the red collector's item alarm clock on my bedside table.

It had all just been a dream. *Whaaat?* How? *Noooo.* How anticlimactic. *Seriously?* Now I was mad! I wiped my eyes with the back of my hand. For a moment, I allowed myself to hope it might have been possible. I considered lying down again and doing *that*, but glancing over at my pretty alarm clock, I realized I didn't have time to slip back into my saucy slumber for even a minute or two unless I wanted to risk running late—which I didn't. Begrudgingly, I kicked on my fluffy white slippers and stretched my arms above my head.

Over the next several minutes, I tried to forget the specter of Ace that had visited me in my sleep, and prepared for work. Definitely a bad hair day, just like in my dream. My hair was all over the place, and I was barely able to get the frizz under control.

Gulping down a bowl of fruit salad and yogurt for breakfast, I tried to erase my highly inappropriate dream from my memory. "Hey, Bossy Grump," I muttered to myself, "stop living rent free in my mind. I am a good assistant, but nowhere did I sign up for *that*. Not happening, nuh-uh. I'm a professional, not a teenager with a crush."

After making sure that I was, in fact, wearing a bra *and* panties, I skipped through my front door. Northern Cardinals were singing their early-morning songs in a loud string of clear down-slurred or two-parted whistles, heralding in the blossoming spring, and the sun's optimistic rays painted the city a soft golden color. It was a beautiful morning by anyone's definition. I paused to breathe in the smell of jasmine that was wafting from my old neighbor's garden before crossing the lawn that lay between me and the bright-yellow cab that awaited me.

"How'd your essay go?" I asked Jay as I slid onto the cab's back seat.

"My essay? How'd you know about that?" he asked happily, tapping his fingers against his fluffy steering wheel. He waited for a gap in the traffic and merged onto the road.

"I got a cab on Saturday and Jay the Hunk told me you were writing a psychology essay. Why didn't you tell me you were studying to be a psychologist?"

"S'pose I didn't think it was important."

"Well, it is," I insisted. "And I'm proud of you."

"Aw, thank you," he said. I could see him smiling in the rearview mirror.

"How'd it go?"

"Eh...so-so. Pretty mediocre, to be honest."

"Keep me updated. Also, why is Jay the Hunk called 'the Hunk'?"

He grinned. "Nothing hunky about him, eh?" He chuckled, as I couldn't wait for his answer. "Except for one thing..." he teased. I was dying of curiosity. "His last name. Jay's last name is Hunkell. Jay Hunkell. That's why they call him the Hunk."

"Ohhh. That's so funny."

"Bit of a laugh, eh? So, where did *you* go on Saturday?"

"Nowhere special. I just met with my brother at a bar."

"Oh, Damon! How's he doing? My hubby's brother's name is Damon too." He chortled as he overtook a slow Prius. "But honestly, that guy is a supreme donkey. That's why he wasn't invited to our wedding."

"My brother is a good guy. But he can be one, too...sometimes." I grinned, but at the same time, I was glad Damon hadn't been here to witness me calling him a "supreme donkey," or rather a "supreme dumbass." I would never call him that to his face. We liked calling each other names, but they were always of the funny, playful nature. "But he usually means well. He asked me to do something that I really don't want to do though."

"Err...nothing illegal I hope?"

"Is espionage illegal?" I laughed, but I was only half-joking.

Jay turned serious. "Your brother asked you to spy for him?"

"Well, he didn't put it that way. He needs my help to catch someone who might not have told him the truth."

"Ooh, right." Jay relaxed. "You're like Miss Marple, you are, love."

My mouth fell open at that. "What? No. Sorry, Jay, that doesn't make sense." It was funny he would compare me to my beloved Miss Marple, of all people, but the comparison *so* lacked accuracy and validity. "Miss Marple isn't a spy, and apart from that, she is everything I'm not." I tried to explain, counting down my fingers. "She isn't scared of anything, unlike me, she doesn't trust people, unlike me, and last but not least, she's extremely intuitive, unlike me. If anything, I'm the fidgety, easily agitated person, the pedestrian who stops and waits at the red light with no cars in sight."

"Nope, sorry, you're just like her," Jay protested. "You're witty, just like she is. And just as headstrong! *And* you're a good sport. I assume your brother gave you a secret task, and now you want to get to the bottom of it. Okay, so maybe you're not an agent…you're…an investigator. Anyway, it's for the greater good. I know Damon, and he's a top bloke. So, he's a vigilante—and thanks to the both of you, the baddie will get what he deserves."

"I guess…" Being a detective sounded better than prying or snooping or spying.

"Just be careful, eh? Real-life detectives—sometimes they get shot."

Gah. "Darn. That kind of spoils my new identity," I replied and pulled a pair of thick-rimmed tortoiseshell sunglasses out of my handbag, put them on, lowered them onto my nose, and then peered over them at Jay. "Call me Miss Stella Marple," I said dramatically.

He chuckled as he brought the cab to a stop in front of Windsor Architects' offices. "You'd make the *perfect* detective—just make sure *you* catch *them*, not the other way around."

"Don't you worry. That'll never happen. I'll be extremely careful, trust me." I chuckled as I opened the rear passenger-seat door. "See you this afternoon?"

"Wouldn't miss it. Just give me a bell when you're ready."

I closed the door behind me and made it up the steps that led to the imposing building's entrance.

## 22

# STELLA

The foyer was entirely empty, except for its usual occupant, Glenda. She was paging through her folder and didn't see me approaching.

"Good morning," I greeted. "Glad you're back. How are you feeling?"

"Don't even ask. I'm in terrible pain," Glenda gestured to her leg, then looked back in her folder, "but this place would crumble without me, so it's not like I could take more time off."

"I'm sorry to hear that. I hope you feel better soon."

"Do you know who handled the desk down here yesterday?"

"Yes. Me. I manned the reception desk in the morning until your replacement arrived. Terry had a family emergency."

"Well, that explains a *lot*," she deadpanned, without pausing to look up from her folder.

I knew she was in pain, but more than that, Terry's compliment yesterday had given me the patience to oversee the direct jab. Also, I needed something from her, so I needed to tread carefully.

"I thought it went rather well," I said. "For the most part, anyway. That's not why I'm here though. I have an unusual question to ask you." Leaning forward, I rested my hands on the reception desk and stared intently at her while the first workers started pouring in.

"Yes?" Glenda impatiently turned a page.

"Who knows the most about Windsor Architects' business dealings? You know, other than Mr. Windsor, or Mrs. Mills?" I did my best to *not* lean further over the reception desk's counter and speak in a low whisper like someone who feared being overheard.

I needed to be cool.

I needed to be as inconspicuous as possible.

I couldn't reveal that I had other motives.

"Mr. Windsor, naturally, and Mrs. Mills." She repeated the names of the two people I had mentioned back to me. "Why don't you talk to Mrs. Mills?"

"I don't want to bother her. I know how busy she is." That wasn't entirely true. If I asked her certain questions, she might tell him. I was not getting caught.

"That she is. Wait, I would assume that Winifred knows almost as much. She is our typist, so she creates transcriptions of audio recordings, fills out forms, types all the higher-ups' letters, memos and documents, that sort of thing."

"Then I need to see her. I need some help with...something." The last word accidentally came out as an almost-whisper. "I mean," I raised my voice to a normal low-key level, and said confidently, "I need help with some research." I watched Glenda shut her folder, punctuating its closure with a loud sigh.

"Her office is on the 2nd floor. It's the first door down the hallway on your left. Maybe I should call her to find out if she's busy—"

"No, that won't be necessary. It'll only take a few minutes. I won't bother her if she's occupied with something else," I insisted. "I won't make a nuisance of myself."

She waved her hand. "That's what they all say, and yet, most of them are nuisances. I suppose I can't stop you though, so—"

The phone rang.

Glenda picked it up, her voice suddenly a warm, welcoming tone. "Good morning, Mr. Windsor." A pause sent chills down my spine. For one crazy moment, I was convinced Ace knew what I was up to. "Yes, she just arrived, I'll tell her, Mr. Windsor." She hung up and looked at me, her voice back to normal. "Mr. Windsor needs you to report to Mr. Hardy's office. Immediately."

"Thanks," I said, flashing the brightest and most innocent smile I could muster. "Feel better soon."

Mr. Hardy was Harvey Hardy, the funny mustache man, one of the higher-ups I'd met last week, and his office was on the 8th floor, just like Ace's and mine.

I headed to the elevator. Despite my boss's order, I decided to make a quick stop on the 2nd floor at Winifred's before reporting to Mr. Hardy. It would only take two or three minutes, tops, and doing it now would save me a trip. Also, I wanted to get this over with as quickly as possible. With a bit of luck, I could report to my brother sooner rather than later that Ace wasn't in league with Ecclestone.

I squeezed into the elevator, positioning myself between five people who looked like accountants. "Good morning," I said cheerfully to the small crowd around me.

"Good morning," one of them greeted back.

The trip up to the 2nd floor was a short one. The elevator doors opened, and three of us spilled out of it, scattering off toward our respective destinations. I hesitated for a second, trying to take in the 2nd floor's lavish design. Sparkling modern lamps hung from the ceiling, casting bright specks of light on the floor beneath it.

I drank in my surroundings as I headed toward the hallway on my left. Glenda's directions had been accurate. The first door I arrived at had a sleek silver plaque on it that read "Mrs. Winifred Thomas: Senior Copy Clerk." Copy Clerk seemed to be the official title for typist. I took a deep breath and knocked.

"Come in," a warm, full voice said from the other side.

"Hey there, Mrs. Thomas. I'm Stella, Mr. Windsor's new assistant."

A large office with huge shelves awaited me.

"Oh, I know who you are, dearie. Gossip spreads like wildfire around here. Please, call me Winifred," said the pretty African American woman seated behind a glass desk at the center of the room. She wore an elegant green dress with a matching green ribbon in her curly hair.

She got up from her office chair slowly, and shook my hand, then sat back down, equally slowly. "Nice to meet you."

"It's nice to meet you, Winifred," I said. "I think we'll likely be working together a lot in the future."

"I'm looking forward to it." She smiled warmly. There was something about her that reminded me of my mother—perhaps it was her kind smile and keen eyes. "May I have a seat?" I gestured to a chair at one side of her desk.

"Oh, of course! Mint?" she asked, holding out a bowl full of wrapped candy.

"No, thank you," I said, "but I appreciate the offer. I'm actually here to pick your brain a little."

"About what, dearie?"

"About Windsor Architects in general."

"I don't know if I'm the best person to ask about the *entire* workings of Windsor Architects. But I get it, our CEO is too busy answering questions, am I right?" She laughed a friendly laugh. "I've only been here for a few months. Mr. Windsor's previous copy clerk didn't want to move to New York when he decided to move Windsor Architects' offices here." She took a mint from the glass bowl and started nibbling on it.

"Oh, I'm sorry, I just assumed you'd been here for a while."

"I suppose that's an easy enough assumption to make. I wish I'd worked here longer. This is the most fulfilling job I've ever had. I'm sorry if I'm disappointing you with my lack of seniority, but I'm sure—sooner or later—Mr. Windsor *will* be happy to answer any questions you may have that I might be too new to answer properly." She finished off the piece of candy with a toothy grin.

"The reason I'm asking you is that I'd like to impress him with my knowledge of the company." It was a little white lie, and immediately, I felt terribly guilty about it. A bead of sweat ran down my spine. Was I doing the right thing? I hid my hands under the table so Winifred's sharp gaze wouldn't see them trembling.

"I see, I see," she said. "In that case, I'd be happy to answer any questions you may have to the best of my ability, but I still can't guarantee that

I'll know the answers to all of them. I'm rather busy, especially now after the move, there's all that work to be done, but I know that you're assisting Mr. Windsor with the merger documents, so I'll help you in any way I can."

"You have no idea how happy I am to hear that," I said, trying to hide my guilt and my profuse happiness at how she had played the merger card into my hands. I hadn't even thought of that. It wasn't even a lie. Ha, perfect! "So I guess my first question is this: Do you know how Windsor Architects is doing? Financially, I mean?"

"Dearie, I like you! We're really getting right to the serious stuff." She laughed. "I can honestly and confidently tell you that Windsor Architects is doing *very* well financially. Of course, Martha and Mary in the finance department know more about that, but last year was our most profitable year ever, and at our current trajectory, we'll do even better this year. You can also read about it in the annual reports that we prepare every year."

"*Phew*. That's good news." I feigned relief and wiped my brow. "That means Mr. Windsor can afford to pay our salaries."

"*Exactly*." Winifred snorted as she took another mint out of the bowl. "You're a cheeky one, but I appreciate your attitude. Are you planning to make Windsor Architects a part of your long-term career plans?"

"I am. This really is the best place for me I believe."

"It sure is," she agreed. "Mr. Windsor is an inspiring CEO, so that's an added bonus. He's very good at what he does."

I was growing confident. Talking to Winifred felt as if I had known her for years, as if I could ask her anything. "Next question. Does Short Hills ring a bell?"

"Of course. Has Mr. Windsor shown you his marvelous blueprints for the properties he's working on there? If he hasn't, ask him about it. Well, when he has a minute. They'll blow your mind."

"Aren't there a ton of construction and architecture companies busy with projects and developments there?" I tapped my chin and pretended to think for a moment. I couldn't just outright mention Ecclestone Construction—it would be too suspicious. "I read something like that in *Architecture Weekly* a few days ago."

"I'm afraid I don't know the answer to that one." Her chirpy smile slowly faded, and I didn't know what to make of her reaction.

Despite her facial expression, I decided to go for it.

"*Wait...*" I started. "I remember the names of the top companies that are busy building real estate around there: Bulsara Renovations, Thorne Architects...and Ecclestone Construction." My armpits were getting sweatier and sweatier, the guilt continuing to gnaw at my insides. "Is Windsor Architects contracted with any of them? I would like to...familiarize myself with our subcontractors."

Did that sound plausible? Probably only half, because she stared at me intently. "Hmm... Thorne Architects sounds somewhat familiar, but I don't think they're involved in the Short Hills project. I honestly don't know about the rest. Is there a particular reason that you're asking about these three specifically?" She raised one of her thin dark eyebrows at me.

My blood turned to ice. I should have thought this through better. The thought of getting caught in a lie was enough to make me want to crawl and hide under her desk.

In a desperate attempt to make my worries dissipate, I shook my head. A ball of guilt the size of an elephant was forming in the pit of my stomach regardless, but I needed to ignore it. When I noticed Winifred concernedly staring at me from across the table, I finally said, "No, no. There's no specific reason. I just get anxious if I make a mistake. Mr. Windsor can be pretty intimidating." I repeated Willette's words, only in a different context. It was too late to back out anyway, so I grabbed the bull by the horns and tried the other way around. "Is there any way I could find out if Windsor Architects has worked with one of those construction companies in the past? Just hypothetically speaking."

"Doesn't sound very hypothetical to me," Winifred noted. "But I think you're a smart girl, and I trust that you know what you're doing. If you wanted to read through the company's previous contracts, you'd need to visit the archive room—"

Oh, Jesus. Why hadn't I thought of that? Of course. *Duh. Duh. Duh.* I wanted to kick myself. Agatha Christie would not only be ashamed of me, she'd also kick my butt out onto the street.

"Fantastic idea. I know exactly where that is," I said, quickly getting up.

"Wait, wait. Hold on a moment." She gestured for me to remain seated, and my breath hitched. "The old archive room is still in San Francisco. It didn't move when the new offices did. The new archive room downstairs only has our current contracts."

I slumped into my seat, discouraged. Ecclestone had his fingers everywhere, not just in New York. I still didn't believe Ace was involved in any shady dealings with him, but to fully satisfy my brother, I had to dig into Windsor Architects' past as well. "So, there's no way to find out about those companies?"

"Nope. Not unless you want to drive or fly almost three thousand miles to do it."

"Are those files eventually going to be shipped over?" I asked hopefully, biting at my lower lip.

"I can ask them to be couriered to me, but I can't guarantee we'll have files on those three companies. If we haven't worked with them before, we won't have any information on them of course. I'll send a few emails. I hope we don't run into shipment issues this time. We, well," she paused, seemingly thinking of the right words, "ran into some issues recently, to put it mildly. Dearie, I'm sure you have already heard all about it, so let me be frank—it's a huge mess. Twenty boxes are still missing. Unfortunately, during the move, the server broke, and we lost access to the digital files as well. And as if that wasn't enough, some folders in our new archive room downstairs got shredded because they were labeled incorrectly. The former assistant, who had been in charge, well, her system was...let's say, *flawed*. I've never seen Mr. Windsor so enraged."

Oh! That explained the three huge bags of shredded paper I'd found. As far as the rest went, Ace had already mentioned the issue to me last week, but he had seemed confident that his team would solve the issue.

"Anyway, if you ask me, the boxes that got lost, I doubt we'll ever see them again. And those were important boxes with paperwork we need for the acquisition."

"Wait. How did they get lost?"

She shook her head, seemingly exasperated by the mishandling of company property. "They never arrived."

"I mean, aren't there usually tracking numbers?" My friend Bonnie, who was an operations agent at a transport firm, always mentioned tracking numbers when she talked about the crazy stories that happened at her job.

"I'm sure there are, but as far as I know, Mr. Windsor's former assistant arranged the shipment with MKY Shipping using her private account, instead of creating one for the company. That's why MKY can't help us, even though she used the company's billing information. Now she's gone, and we don't have access to her login. That's all I know. I'm sorry I can't be of more assistance."

I could imagine that Windsor Architects wasn't the only company that had lost shipment through such an unfortunate series of events. As soon as I possibly could, I had to ask Bonnie if she knew of a solution, or at least a shortcut, on how we could get the missing boxes back—pronto! "No, no need to apologize, you've been very helpful, thank you. I appreciate it." Composing myself, I smiled at the kind woman. "I'm just grateful you took the time to talk to me."

I made a mental note to check the archives. Maybe there was a more recent project that involved Ecclestone that Winifred didn't know about. Highly unlikely, but not completely out of the question. My curiosity was killing me, and I itched to go to the archive room right away, but I couldn't. First, I needed to report to Mr. Hardy. The conversation with Winifred had already taken up more time than I thought it would.

"It's a pleasure, dear," she said. "I'm going to let you know once something arrives. Now I've got a little favor I'd like to ask you, if that's okay."

"Of course."

"This might seem like a silly request," Winifred said, "but would you mind fetching me a few new black pens from the supply closet? It's on the 3rd floor, next to Mrs. Hoffman's office. I've got arthritis in my knees, and it makes the walk down the long hallways a horribly unpleasant experience. I'm having a terrible flare-up today, and I'd be in your debt forever if you could spare me the trip."

Darn. I would be even later for the meeting with Mr. Hardy, but he'd understand. "Sure. I love exploring this place. A walk to the supply closet would be a treat," I assured her, rising from my seat and straightening my pencil skirt.

"Thanks, dear," Winifred said.

"I'll be back before you know it." With that, I grabbed my bag, slipped out of her office, and made it back to the elevator. Acquiring those pens for Winifred couldn't possibly take more than three minutes, and that would tick another, less important item off my to-do list. Right after that, I would go up to Mr. Harvey and help him—without a thousand other things floating through my mind.

## 23

## STELLA

The elevator was empty this time around. I rushed inside and pressed the button. When the doors opened on the 3rd floor, I found myself standing face to face with Terry.

"Oh! Hi there," she squeaked as I stepped out of the elevator and onto the foyer's elegant ceramic tiles. "I didn't think I'd see you again so soon." She hopped into the elevator.

"Neither did I," I replied, nodding. "I'm on my way to the supply closet to get some new pens."

"Well, you better hurry up then. Mr. Windsor hates when employees loiter around…that's what his former assistant told me. I heard he caught one of the previous interns reading a comic book in there once and ended their internship right there and then." She hit one of the silver buttons on the elevator's panel. "Thanks again for yesterday!"

"I don't think he'd do tha—" I was unable to complete my sentence before the elevator doors closed. Firing someone over a comic book? *No way.* But who knew? People had been fired for crazier things than reading. It wasn't like I knew Ace all that well. For a second, I'd forgotten he could possibly be involved with Edmund Ecclestone and maybe shadier than we all thought.

Trying my best to not look like I was dawdling, I quickly marched along the wood flooring to the supply closet.

The supply closet's door looked different to the others that lined the hallway. It was matte and cherry-red, and it had a silver plaque on it that simply read "Supplies." It was situated about ten feet away from Mrs. Hoffman's office door, which appeared exhaustingly ordinary in comparison.

Out of habit, I knocked timidly, but there was no reply. After opening it, I stepped inside and flipped a light switch on the wall to my right. No windows. The darkness that had lain over the expansive room like a thick blanket blipped out of existence, and the bright white lights that dotted the ceiling started humming.

The room was filled with four rows of gray steel shelves. I could see the tops of rulers and the handles of scissors sticking out of boxes stacked on the shelf to my left, and headed directly toward them. Everything from staplers to highlighters were inside the boxes, but I didn't see any pens. I started weaving between the rows of shelves, opening random boxes and peering into them. A sense of dread started setting in when I reached the fourth shelf and still hadn't found any evidence of pens in the supply room. On my knees, I started digging through a few boxes on the floor.

I heard the supply room's doorknob twist and quickly hid behind one of the large boxes lining the third shelf I'd been going through. Don't ask me why I was hiding. It was a reflex—likely from reading too many thrillers. I regretted it immediately. There was nothing more suspicious than a person hiding behind some boxes, sweating profusely. If anyone saw me here! I peeked over the large box and watched as the glossy red door slowly opened.

Damn it. Too late to come out from my hiding spot without being seen.

*Thump. Thump. Thump.* My heartbeat was audible. I clutched my handbag.

I just hoped whoever was approaching wouldn't be able to see or hear me. Any one of them would totally give me away. Sure, I hadn't done anything inherently wrong by being in the supply room, but

Terry's words of warning were still ringing in my ears, causing the voice inside of my head to pipe up, "You are so fired!"

"Who's in here?" A gruff baritone echoed through the shelves, causing some of them to rattle.

Gulp.

I knew it would seem even more suspicious if I *kept* hiding after being asked to identify myself. My legs wobbled as I stood upright. Lifting my head, I realized that the person standing in the center of the supply room was none other than *him*. My boss. Of course. Just my luck. Who else would it be? Of all the people, of all the employees working in this huge building, why, oh, why, did I keep running into *him*?

"I-I was just looking for some pens," I admitted. "Winifred sent me. Am I in trouble?"

"Hmm. Do *you* think you're in trouble?" Ace practically growled.

"I don't know. Maybe?" My blood rushed to my cheeks, causing my ears to burn. "I thought perhaps I'd been gone too long, and you came here to chastise me."

"To chastise you?" Ace stared at me intently, watching me, assessing me, while I stared back at him, and into his cool blue eyes that sparkled like icebergs caught in the bright Arctic sun.

"Yeah, well, I can't find the pens anywhere, so I've been here longer than I suppose most people normally are. At this point, I'm starting to think there are no pens in here whatsoever." The tingling feeling was returning. It had started spreading from my navel to between my thighs and to *there*.

Without saying a word, he brushed past me. The smell of his cologne wafted over me. It smelled like the air did after the first rain that ended a dry spell. He nonchalantly strode toward a box right next to me, stuck his hand inside, and withdrew a fistful of pens. "Are these what you were looking for?" he asked, holding them out toward me.

"Oh. Yes." Hand outstretched, I went to retrieve the elusive stationery. "I can't believe I didn't see them there—" My breath caught in my throat when our skin touched.

"No, sorry," Ace said, closing his fist around the pens and withdrawing it. "I can't give these to you quite yet. First, there's the matter of your punishment to discuss." He stowed the handful of pens in his slacks' pocket and glared at me.

"Why, for...loitering?"

"You clearly disregarded my wish to report to Mr. Hardy. You were late for your interview. You were late for lunch. Now this. So, tell me—what do you think your punishment should be?"

"My punishment?" I squeaked. "But I told you, I've only been up here for so long because I couldn't find the pens. I'm just a *little* late. It wasn't on purpose. Normally I'm Miss Punctuality." I didn't tell him that I'd known of his request before I'd decided to visit Winifred's office, and indeed had disregarded his order. "Besides, I can always make up the time." The tingling feeling turned into an urgent type of burning sensation. Every inch of my skin screamed to be touched.

"Oh, can you?" He took a step closer to me. His icy-blue eyes bore into me. He put one of his arms around my waist and tugged me toward him, nearly lifting me clean off my feet. My handbag slid down my shoulder, landing on the floor with a thud.

"Wait, wha—" I started, not really protesting *that* much.

He leaned into me, his lips nearly brushing against mine. This was no dream, no imagination. This was really happening. I was pushed against his chest, my breasts delectably flush to his front, and I could feel his heart racing through his thin cotton shirt. The pens in his slacks' pocket poked into my stomach, or at least that was what I thought it might be. I closed my eyes and prepared to surrender to him, to feel his fiery kiss on my lips. The burning feeling inside my chest—and between my legs—was now an unstoppable magnetic tug. I needed his touch as much as I needed air.

"Turn around," he ordered, sitting down on one of the boxes. "Lap. Now."

"Hmm, what?" I asked while I was turning around.

His eyes gestured to his lap. "Bend over."

"Hmm?"

"I'm not going to repeat myself."

I bent over his knee, sticking my ass out as my skirt rode up.

"I feel a spanking is in order." His hand was grazing the curve of my ass. If I hadn't already been a little wet before, I totally was now.

Omg, this was so embarrassing. And *so* hot.

I couldn't help but wiggle my ass and giggle a little at his touch. I was so ticklish! His hand stroking my butt tickled!

He pulled my skirt up to my waist, exposing my ass. Heavens. This wasn't actually happening, was it? He was teaching me a lesson for being late? What happened to good old write-ups?

The sound of the supply room's doorknob twisting open sent me flying up. Ace's expression seemed to say, "Saved by the bell."

I grabbed my handbag and hastily hid behind one of the large boxes lining the third shelf. Please do not ask me why I was hiding again. (Obviously, I was an utterly hopeless case.)

From my hiding spot, I watched Ace calmly stand up.

The door opened. I was still trying to straighten out my skirt. It had gotten a bit roughed up during my...erm...almost punishment.

"Mr. Windsor! Apologies, I didn't know you were in here," a portly bald man said loudly, sticking his head in through the doorway. "Can I come in? I just want to fetch some paper clips."

"Of course. Go right ahead," Ace said, motioning for the man to enter.

Still frozen behind the large box, I was trying to process what had just happened. My heart was still racing, and my body was still yearning for Ace's. I felt a drop of sweat running between my breasts as I tried to slow my breathing.

"Thank you, sir," the bald man said, shuffling into the room and catching sight of me. "Looks like I've come during rush hour, hello."

"Oh, hello." I pretended to be searching for something. Not sure what. I was just doing a lot of mindless looking around.

"Flint, this is Stella Copeland. Stella, Flint Walter is one of our account executives. He also helped to organize this room."

"I did," he said proudly. "So, what are you looking for, young lady? I know where everything is in here. Let me help," he offered.

"Oh, Mr. Windsor already helped me," I said. It totally didn't make any sense since I had just pretended to be looking for something.

Just before I could get myself into more trouble, Ace held out the fistful of pens he'd brandished at me before "the incident." I took them without making eye contact with him.

Instead, I held them up for Flint to see. "There they are," I said brightly.

"Alrighty then." Flint smiled. "Well, is there something I can help *you* with, Mr. Windsor?"

"I just came up here to fetch a file I left in here this morning," Ace said, strolling away from us toward the back of the room. As he walked by me, I could have sworn he winked at me.

Did that really just happen? No. I was still trying to process the fact that a) Ace had almost kissed me, b) he'd almost spanked me, and c) we'd almost been caught doing just that—and now he was mischievously winking at me as my mind kept replaying how his hand had felt on my ass. My mind liked it—a lot.

In fact, my mind was so preoccupied that I nearly didn't see Ace reaching down to pick up a file that lay on one of the boxes stacked against the back wall. The file's cover read "E.C." and the word "Classified" was sprawled across it in large bold red lettering.

E.C.?

As in Ecclestone Construction?

Another bead of sweat rolled down my skin.

Ace tucked the file under his arm and headed toward the door. "Stella, after you've taken those pens to Winifred, report to Mr. Hardy's office, *immediately*." As he said that word, I thought I noticed a small tug at one corner of his mouth—but I couldn't be sure. "He owes me a set of blueprints before noon, and I just know he won't get them to me unless he has help. See how you can assist him. Once you're done there, please come to my office. I have some paperwork that needs to be tended to." Ace turned to the bald man who had nearly walked in on us. "Have a good day, Flint." He nodded at the man and strode through the supply room's cherry-red door.

"Thank you, Mr. Windsor. You too! You too," the bald man said eagerly, and then faced me. "Are you feeling okay?" he asked, likely because I was still standing behind the box, staring at the pens in my hand, and *still* trying to imagine what Ace's lips and his punishment (there was that too) would have felt like. "You look a little pale. Maybe you should sit down or something?"

"No, I'm okay," I assured him. "It's just a little...*hot* in here. I've got to run. Have a nice day." I made a beeline for the door.

"Have a nice day too," he yelled after me.

I found myself racing toward the elevator, stowing the fistful of pens I'd gotten for Winifred in my handbag. I wasn't sure where I was headed, but I knew I needed to find somewhere to clear my mind before I went on with the rest of the day. Ladies' room. Yes! As soon as the elevator arrived, I dove in and hit the 3rd-floor button. The elevator's speaker played an instrumental version of "Bad Romance." How appropriate.

The elevator doors opened, and I flew out, heading straight toward the ladies' room. I burst inside like a marathon runner powering over the finish line, startling an older blonde lady who was washing her hands at one of the sinks.

"*Sorry,*" I immediately apologized.

"No one that's sprinting toward the bathroom *that* fast ever needs to apologize to me," the lady said. "Been there, done that. One word: prunes. I'll leave you to it. Good luck!"

"Oh, trust me, I'm going to need it."

She dried her hands on a paper towel and smirked at me before slipping through the bathroom door.

From the bathroom's mirror, my reflection stared back at me. Someone had drawn a bright-red heart in lipstick in one of its corners, with the letters "AW" inside.

AW?

Ace Windsor. Naturally. Who else? Well, the lipstick drawing hadn't been me (but totally could have been in my teen years). I wet my hands and tried to rub it off. I smudged it but didn't remove it.

Now if someone came in right then, they would think for sure it had been me. And by the way ridiculous gossip spread around in this company, no doubt my boss would hear about it too.

*CEO's Assistant Madly in Love*

### with Her Boss Who Almost Spanked Her for Loitering Later Caught Drawing Hearts in Company Toilet

I entered one of the stalls and peed. Phew. Better, much better.

My phone started ringing as I stepped away from the toilet and flushed. I quickly pulled it out of my handbag, digging past Winifred's pens to get to it. "Bonnie" flashed across its screen. I swiped to the right to answer and held it up to my ear.

"Stella." Bonnie sounded excited on the other end of the line before I could even say hi. "I hope I'm not bothering you. I'm just calling to ask how your day is going. Are you at work?"

"Yeah, I am. I'm in the bathroom now." The invisible connection between my best friend and me was reliable. "I'm glad you called, and as always, at the right moment! I need your help. You're an operations agent. How does a company find lost packages without a tracking number?"

"Depends on who the company used."

"MKY Shipping. The boxes were shipped from San Francisco to New York City, and they never arrived. But we don't have tracking numbers or login info to the account it was ordered from. Apparently, the former assistant signed up with her private account. Now she's gone."

"Gone...as in got fired, am I right? Well, are you sure she labeled them correctly? Maybe somebody else is really happy about those boxes."

"I don't know. All I know is that twenty boxes are missing. Thing is, we need them, and urgently."

"Tell you what. You're in luck. I happen to have a former colleague who is now a branch manager at MKY. I can ask him what to do."

"Oh my goodness. That would be great!"

"Just send me the info, and I'll see what I can do. But first, tell me how your new job is working out. What exactly happened after Ace hired you?"

"To be honest, it's a long story. I'm having a bit of a weird day. I've actually had a few weird days lately." I leaned against the bathroom's tiled wall. "Is it okay if I call you at lunch?" Although I'd already spent too much time in my Miss Marple role, I was hoping to squeeze in another half hour once I'd finished the blueprints with Mr. Hardy.

Bonnie laughed. "It sounds like your lunch break is barely enough. Call me when you have time to tell me all the juicy details. Until then!"

We hung up at the same time.

Glancing at my watch, I noted it was getting late.

I needed to take the pens to Winifred, inform her that I was going to help her look into the whole MKY issue, and then report to Mr. Hardy.

When I opened the door to the hallway, I almost expected *him* to be standing in front of it, tapping his foot, expecting me, ready to go through with his punishment this time. He wasn't. With a sigh of relief, which contained just a tiny bit of disappointment, I went about my tasks.

## 24

## ACE

*A* knock at my office door jolted me.

"Come in," I barked, irritated.

"It's meee, sir. Good old Mrs. Mills," she said enthusiastically. "Sorry to disturb, well, you're used to that by now, are you not? But I thought this would be less intrusive than calling you."

"Why would you think that?" I asked, pinching the bridge of my nose in an attempt to keep a gradually building headache at bay.

"Truth is, I just had to get up and walk a little, you know, to avoid neck stiffness and muscle cramps in my legs. I'm not the beautiful young woman I once was anymore. Folks might disagree." She laughed. "Sorry, sir, I'm getting off topic," she added, without sounding sorry at all. "I've got a Mr. Ecclestone on the line for you. He says it's urgent. Can I put him through?"

*Ecclestone?*

"No," I growled. "I don't have time."

"Yes, sir. But it seems urgent. He keeps calling. Glenda says it is the fourth time he's asked to speak to you this week—"

"Send him to voicemail," I said gruffly. "I'm heading out to meet with a few investors. I doubt I'll be back before the end of the day. You can tell him that too, if you think it'll stop him from calling."

"All right, sir. I'll do that. When will you be back?"

"Probably not until tomorrow."

"Very well, sir. Is there anything I can do for you before you leave?" she asked, holding her hands behind her back like a sergeant on patrol.

"When my assistant returns with Mr. Hardy's files, inform her that I'm leaving a note for her on my desk. Ah, and Mrs. Mills? How was your daughter's wedding?"

She looked at me over the rim of her glasses. "Thank you for asking, sir. It was entertaining, I can say that much. But telling you everything would take up too much of your schedule."

I nodded. "Thank you, Mrs. Mills."

"It's a pleasure, sir. Enjoy your meetings. Cheriooo." She backed out of my office. I could hear her shuffling footsteps slowly fading to her reception desk.

I did have two more meetings lined up, which was a good thing. I didn't trust myself to stay in the same building as Stella Copeland for the rest of the day without trying to recreate our encounter. No. I had to get out of here before I did something I would regret. No matter what, I couldn't have her.

My thoughts were interrupted by one blink of my voicemail's pickup. I played it back. "Mr. Windsor, this is Edmund Ecclestone speaking." There was a unique quality to his calm, rusty voice, which vibrated with a French accent. "I'd like to talk to you. Please call me back at your earliest convenience."

Getting up from my chair, I walked over to a filing cabinet next to the balcony's door, retrieved a stack of forms and information requests, and strolled back to my desk. I placed the pile of papers on my desk, forming a wobbling tower, and scribbled a quick note to Stella.

How could I have let myself lose control like that? No woman had ever had that effect on me.

I left the office building. My facial expression must have reflected my mood, because not a soul spoke to me.

The interior of my brand-new blue Aventador was a welcome reprieve. The Lamborghini dealership had dropped it off at the office that very morning. I was glad to be rid of the Sián. It had been nothing but a reminder of Allison. I melted into the Aventador's smooth leather driver's seat. Its engine came to life, roaring just as loudly as a sports car of that caliber should, but indefinably warmer, livelier than the Sián.

## 25

# STELLA

*I* spent the rest of the morning helping Mr. Hardy draw up the blueprints that Ace expected from him. Working with him was a pleasant experience, and we were done in no time.

Having finished the job earlier than expected, I had time for a quick side tour to the archive room to check if I could find anything related to Ecclestone Construction. My search resulted in zero finds, and secretly I was relieved. Immediately afterward, as promised, I called Bonnie and filled her in—with all the embarrassing details that I'd found myself in.

I started with my meeting with my brother Damon and what he'd asked me to do. My tale of woe was wrapped up with a recounting of us having lunch at the Coq—Bonnie thought it was beyond hilarious and asked me if I'd had the "Coq Special" (almost!). I continued with what had happened on the helicopter, with the creepy delivery man the previous Friday, and my "encounter" with Ace in the supply room earlier in the day.

"Girl, I can't believe he almost spanked you, but okay, carry on."

"I'm caught between a rock and a hard place. My brother wants me to snoop on Ace...and after I saw that classified 'E.C.' file with him, I'm starting to worry that he might be right about Ace being up to no good.

Especially after hearing about all the crazy mishaps during the move: missing files, shredded papers, lost boxes..."

"Oh, my. He's hiding something," she said.

"Huh? Ace, you mean?"

"Yeah! Who knows what's inside those boxes? I bet he's the one who got rid of them, and then he fired the poor assistant just to keep the act up, you know making it seem that she was the one who lost them? You better keep your guard up. Or, oh my God, what if her body is in them?"

"What? *Noooo*, I doubt that. Stop it. I mean, as far as I know, Ace wants us to find the boxes. But honestly, I'm confused about many things. What's worse..."

"Yeah...?"

"What's worse is that at the same time, it feels like there's something happening between him and me, but I don't know what to do about it. I know we can't be together. I mean, he's my boss and my brother's best friend, but I can't get him out of my head. I can't stop wondering what would have happened if we hadn't been interrupted by that Flint guy."

"Oof," Bonnie grunted. I could hear her fidgeting on the other end of the line. "I'd hate to be in your shoes, but family is family. Damon has a point. I'd pry on my boss if my sexy superhero-like brother asked me to, too. I guess that doesn't make it any easier for you, does it?"

"You think Damon is a sexy superhero-like brother?"

"Heck yeah. He wears that cape perfectly, plus, let's face it, he's panty-melting hot. I'd drop my panties for a stud like him any day. Besides, if Ace has defected to the dark side, it's in your best interest to know. You don't want to be with someone that hangs out with pricks, or worse, someone who is a prick."

"Also," I sulked, "it's not like we can be together anyway."

"Right. You cannot."

My lower lip started trembling, but I didn't want to surrender to the flood of emotions that was threatening to draw me under. "I just wish we'd really kissed, you know?"

"Oh, honey, I know," Bonnie cooed. "But I think it would be best if you were careful around Ace. My alarm bells are ringing. Loudly. You should guard your heart, at least until you know whether he's involved with that Ecclestone guy or not. You've got to try to forget about what happened in the helicopter and in the supply room, for your own sake. Maybe you should try to avoid him for a while? Just to make it easier to resist him."

"Avoiding him will be difficult, but I guess you're right. I'll do what I can."

"I'm always right."

"Well, mostly, but not always."

"What car does he drive?"

Damn. Proving her point, I said, "A Lamborghini. A 3.6 million-dollar Sián." I had Googled the price, and frankly, I still wasn't sure how anybody could drive such an exorbitant car without maneuvering it right into the first post from the nerves of driving it. Funnily enough, it was the very same car brand I'd given the bird to when I was in the cab with Jay. Something in me suspected it had been *him*. Luckily, my boss had sped past us too fast to recognize me. Fast cars also had their advantages.

"*Three-flipping-point-six* million…for a car? Uh. Sorry. Small Barry energy. Tiny Barry energy." I could hear the dismissive shake of her head right through the phone. "Remember the guy I dated about a year ago and I thought something was wrong?" Bonnie had no luck with men, that was for sure. She was the kindest, loveliest, most beautiful woman I knew, and she always fell for the same type of man: handsome jerks who left her with either an empty wallet or an empty heart, or both.

"Of course I remember. You mean the guy who said you were the other half of his torn-apart soul? His name was Barry, wasn't it?" Secretly, I found the idea of two lovers finding each other across time and space incredibly romantic. It had to be wonderful to find someone who would accept you for who you were. In my case, a hopeless endeavor—too nerdy, too curious, and far too convinced that every human being had a good core. In Bonnie's case, it never ceased to amaze me how stupid men were to have let her go.

"Exactly him," Bonnie confirmed. "It turns out he was just pretending to be unemployed. The truth is he had a super-rich dad—

something to do with oil or IT tech or both—and he had not one, but three Lambos. And his you-know-what was—"

"Stop," I interjected. "Now if you tell me details about his...about little Barry and how certain compensating methods could also apply to Ace, I'll have nightmares tonight and I won't be able to sleep."

Bonnie laughed. It was a wonderful sound that, despite all thoughts of Ace, warmed my heart. "You can always call me if you need someone to talk to, day or night."

"Thank you, Bonnie," I said. "I've got to go before I get in trouble for dawdling. I love you."

"I love you too, girlie. Stay away from that man, and his car, and his evil manly seduction powers. You can do it. I believe in you. I promise I'll get back to you on those lost boxes as soon as I speak to my colleague. Something's fishy! I'd get your two weeks' notice ready if I were you." With that, Bonnie ended the call, and I was left alone with my thoughts.

Bonnie was right, without a doubt. Along with Jay, she was now the second person thinking that Damon had a point. I couldn't let Ace get into my head. Not until I knew what he was up to. I couldn't let myself give in to my desires, let alone fall for him.

~

After lunch, I headed straight to Ace's office. I wondered how much paperwork awaited me.

Ace's office manager and fill-in secretary, Mrs. Mills, an elderly woman with a friendly face and frizzy gray mane, was busy in his office, digging through one of his files.

"Oh, good morning, dear," she chirped, whipping her head around, her hands on the files in the cabinet. "I don't think we've formally met yet. I'm sure Mr. Windsor has been meaning to introduce us, but I was gone most of last week and well, you know how busy he is! I'm Mary Louise Mills, and you can just call me Mrs. Mills. Everyone else does."

"Hi." I waved at her from a few feet away. "I'm Stella Copeland, but just call me Stella."

"Stella? Did you know that the Latin word for 'star' is 'stella?'" Mrs. Mills asked, finally withdrawing the paper she'd been searching for from between the file's covers.

"My mom told me." I smiled as we shook hands. "I have her name. My mom was a Stella too."

"How lovely. Not many people know what their names mean." She shrugged, putting her hand on her hip. "Oh, Mr. Windsor left a note for you before he left. On his desk." She rushed to the desk and handed me a piece of paper. It was so romantic he'd left me a note—sorry, I mean, it was so surprising my boss had left me a note. I loved getting notes.

"Oh, wonderful, thank you," I replied, more excitedly than I should have, taking it from her and unfolding it quickly.

It read:

*Stella,*
*The paperwork I need you to take a look at is on my desk. Put it back where you found it when you're done. I'll likely be gone for the rest of the day.*
*I'd like you to attend the Garfield client meeting with me tomorrow evening. It's an important meeting. Get up to speed about profitable developments in the area.*
*Stay out of trouble while I'm away.*
*Ace*

Stay out of trouble? No problem, as long as he wasn't near me.

"Is there anything I can help you with before I go, dear?" Mrs. Mills asked.

"I think I've got everything I need." Yes, anything but definitive evidence for or against Ace's association with Ecclestone. For a second, I considered asking Mrs. Mills outright, contrary to my earlier decision, but then it was past the moment when I could have done so.

"See you around! Cheriooo." With that, she slipped out of Ace's office and left me standing in there alone.

A part of me was relieved I wouldn't have to see Ace for the rest of the day (and consequently that I wouldn't have to try to resist him, or worse, resist falling for him), but an even bigger part of me was a teensy bit disappointed. Spending time with him was my favorite part of the day, even though I knew I shouldn't allow myself to enjoy his company as much as I did.

*He's your boss and your brother's best friend*, I reminded myself as I picked up the stack of paper from his office desk. *And for all you know, he could be buddied up with the evilest man in the construction biz.* I made a quick scan around, but the E.C. folder was nowhere to be seen.

My own lecture didn't dissuade my heart though, and I soon found myself daydreaming about our almost-kiss again.

∼

The next day

As I slowly worked through the paperwork Ace had given me the previous day, I felt like I was edging ever closer to madness. Some of the forms were overdue by weeks. On any ordinary day, this fact would have sent me into a panic, but I was still expending most of my mental energy on imagining what would have happened if that portly bald man, Flint, hadn't interrupted Ace and me while we were in the supply room. I thought about how his hand had slid down from the hollow of my back and onto my bottom, how he'd lifted my skirt, and I imagined how he would have smacked my butt and gotten closer to the origin of the tingling feeling he gave me. After the spanking, our lips would have collided in the best kiss of my life.

My bright-orange office chair started to get uncomfortable underneath me. It was harder than any other chair in the whole building, and my tailbone was starting to ache. I got up, but continued paging through the stack of paper.

*Ring. Riiiing.*

"Girlie! Hey," Bonnie said from the other end of the line.

"You'll be happy to hear that I spoke to my friend at MKY Shipping. Let's just say, he is willing—and able—to help. According to him, there are exactly twenty boxes sitting in their storage room that fit the description. They were all labeled incorrectly and have been sitting there waiting to be picked up. I'm going to send you a form to fill out. If you send it over to me in the next half-hour, we'll get things processed right away. And girl, make sure to put the correct address on it."

I laughed. "Bonnie?"

"Ya?"

"I really love you."

"I know you do."

With the help of Winifred, I filled out the form and shot it back over to Bonnie. I was curious to know what was hidden in those boxes.

*Knock, knock!*

"Come in," I exclaimed.

"It's just me, dear! Mrs. Mills," she chimed, sticking her head into the room. Her big bun bobbed around like an angry hedgehog, emphasizing every single word. "Sorry to bother. I just wanted to ask how you're feeling about the meeting this evening?" She shook her head and the hedgehog wiggled. "I remember how nervous I was before the first big client meeting I attended with Mr. Windsor. Sweet Lord. A nervous wreck, that's what I was. What time is it starting this evening? Half past six?"

"Half past six," I confirmed, and looked up from the stack of paper I was examining. "Have you got any advice for me?"

"Sure! Drink *lots* of coffee, but not too much either, if you know what I mean. Trust me. You'll need it to stay sharp. Mr. Garfield is a difficult client, and it won't be easy to win him over, even though Mr. Windsor is an excellent strategist. I'm sorry I have to throw you into one solo so soon, but my granddaughter is performing in her dance theater's rendition of *Sleeping Beauty* this evening, and I promised her I wouldn't miss it. Family means everything to me."

"That's okay, Mrs. Mills. I understand, and I'm sure I'll be fine, even though I'm pretty nervous," I clarified, "but I'm prepared."

"Of course you are." She smiled encouragingly. "The meeting is on the 7th floor at the end of the hallway in the executive boardroom. Be up there ten minutes before everybody else to prepare the coffee. Mr. Windsor likes his coffee black. But I'm sure you know that by now."

"I do, thank you, Mrs. Mills."

"You're a superstar, and you're going to do an amazing job. Don't let the vultures intimidate you. Good luck! If you need anything, I'm here until six. Tudelidooo!" With that, she closed the door behind her and popped out of view.

~

Despite my trepidation, I was excited to attend an important meeting at Ace's side. Gah. I knew I needed to stop myself from getting riled up at the thought of spending time with him, but I couldn't muster up enough self-control to do it.

After I quickly returned a couple of folders to the filing cabinets next to my desk, I grabbed an empty notepad and two pens from my desk. I slung my handbag over my shoulder, mentally preparing myself for the trip down to the 7th floor where the Garfield meeting would be taking place.

The walk to the conference room was somewhat nerve-racking. I knew what I needed to do during the meeting and what was expected of me, but I couldn't help but start feeling a little out of my depth. My heart beat faster and faster as I drew nearer. While power walking, I pulled out my little folding mirror to examine my appearance. I reapplied my red lipstick and took a bobby pin from my handbag to tame a curl that had escaped from my neat ponytail. My winged eyeliner was miraculously just as symmetrical and un-smudged as it had been when I'd applied it this morning. I took the staircase instead of the elevator and met a short mousy man in a brown suit strolling down.

"G'day," he greeted me.

"Good evening," I replied, before quickly proceeding.

The 7th floor's foyer was just as immaculately decorated as all the other floors I'd seen so far. This one was especially impressive. A large copper globe the size of a child stood in the center, refracting light in every direction. Pulling myself away from the room's furnishings, I headed down the hallway on my right. I'd never seen the executive boardroom before, and I was curious what would set it apart from the conference room Ace and I had sat in during my first day.

The hallway in front of me was empty, so I increased my pace to a brisk walk. I lifted my left arm and read the time on my wristwatch: 6:25 p.m.

"Executive Boardroom," a silver plaque on the door at the end of the hallway read.

Stepping inside, I found it empty except for its furnishings. Neither Ace nor the clients were there yet. Good. A large wooden table stood in the center of the room. Twenty-six chairs were tucked neatly around it: eight on each side, and five at each end. The walls were painted a pretty shade of creamy white. Architectural photographs and awards lined them. One end of the room was dedicated to a projector and a projection screen, while the other was occupied by a coffee table. I hurried over to it and hastily prepared piping-hot coffee. The cups were placed on the table in no time, ready for Ace and the clients to arrive.

I decided to make myself comfortable, and chose one of the middle chairs on one side of the large table to sit down on. I put down my notepad and pens in front of me, prodding at them until I was completely satisfied that they were entirely straight and parallel to each other. An ornate clock with a black rim hung above the projection screen. Its loud ticking was the only sound that reverberated through the room.

There were voices. Someone twisted the doorknob. I whipped my head around, pulling my gaze from the clock's glistening face.

"This way, please." Ace's voice echoed from the other side. He opened the door completely and confidently strolled in. He was followed by a group of four men, each wearing a fitted suit in a different hue of navy. Ace was in all black: black suit, black shirt, black tie. "This is the executive boardroom. It's still a work in progress. As I'm sure you know, our offices recently relocated back to New York." He strode toward me, grinning boyishly. "And this is Ms. Copeland. She'll be assisting me."

I smiled at the four businessmen. "Hello, gentlemen." I extended my arm toward each of them to shake their hands. My legs felt wobbly beneath me.

With that, they walked around and sat on the other side of the table, removed their laptops and notepads from their briefcases, and set them out in front of them. Ace sat down next to me.

As soon as the businessmen settled down, it was as if a switch flipped in Ace, and he went into "meeting mode." He was always assertive, a born leader, but now he became almost inhumanly charismatic. He continued to sell Mr. Garfield—and the others seated in front of us—a whole host of services, answering their questions with the kind of self-assuredness I could only dream of having.

"Look, I like you, Mr. Windsor," Mr. Garfield, the evident leader of the pack of men said. "You seem like a good man. I like your no-bullshit approach." He paused and leaned back, swiveling his gaze between the men sitting on either side of him. They exchanged brief nods, and Mr. Garfield looked back at Ace. "Let me make this quick. We're looking forward to a bright future with Windsor Architects."

"I agree," one of the other men said as we all shook hands and sat back down. "It's an honor and a pleasure to work with a businessman as acclaimed and successful as you are."

"You won't be sorry," Ace replied, leaning over the table as if he were preparing to share a secret. "Look, I don't usually do this, but I have a development in Hudson Yards in the wings. I haven't offered anyone a buy-in on it yet, but if you're interested, I'd be happy to involve you. We're expecting to make upward of $12 million on it." He turned to face me. "Stella, anything else interesting out there?"

"What about the development in Noho?" I chirped, confident of my skills. "Buying in on Hudson Yards and Noho together makes sense. It's the same market that's driving demand for housing in both areas."

"My assistant makes a good point," Ace said, nodding at me. "You don't want to miss out on Noho either."

"It's *impossible* to say no to you," one of the men said.

Mr. Garfield gave a curt nod, saying, "Send over a proposal to my secretary for the kind of buy-ins you have in mind for both developments, and I'll look it over."

"We will send it over first thing in the morning," Ace replied and looked at me.

I nodded in agreement and scribbled "Draw up a proposal" on my notepad. That was more for show for Mr. Garfield and his colleagues, because I certainly wouldn't forget it.

The four businessmen started packing up their things. Ace rose from his seat and extended his arm toward each man, and I watched them enthusiastically shaking his hand. One of them grimaced at his vise grip.

"I hope I'll see you gentlemen again soon," Ace said as the meeting ended.

"Definitely. You will."

One by one, the businessmen filed out of the room until only Ace and I were left. He strolled back to his chair and slumped down on it.

"That went well," I chortled.

He ran his hand through his dark-blond hair. "It sure did."

## 26

## STELLA

"You did good in there," Ace praised me.

Pride swelled my heart. I had been so nervous, but I was glad everything had gone well. "Are you ever worried that you'll mess up one of these meetings?"

"Sure."

"Really?" I smiled—more from my relaxing nerves than his answer—turning on my chair to look at him. "I didn't know 'The Great Mr. Windsor' got nervous."

"Ha. 'The Great Mr. Windsor,'" he repeated. "What a title—maybe not nervous, I've been doing this for too long, but of course I get tense. I'm human, just like you."

"I'm intrigued to hear more about your apparent humanity," I said, closing my notepad in front of me. "Tell me more about the kind of things that make you nervous."

"Nothing out of the ordinary," he replied. "Sharks, venomous snakes, that kind of thing."

"No, no, no. Give me something better."

"Hmm. There are a few other things too, I suppose...sometimes I get"—he made quote fingers—"'nervous' when I get a call from your brother."

"Damon? Oh, me too! Especially lately."

"Why? What's been happening lately?"

*Oh, darn. What do I say? What do I say?* I couldn't tell him the truth about, you know, my new side hustle as a spy—set on him, but I didn't want to lie. "Damon's just being Damon: overly protective, you know him," I said, keeping things vague, hoping he wouldn't press the subject.

"Yeah." His lips curved upward. "Oh, you might be surprised to hear, but public speaking used to make me nervous. Any kind of public speaking, really."

"I stutter sometimes when I'm anxious, as you might have heard. But I've never heard *you* sound nervous when you speak."

"I guess I hide it well. Today, I'm more nervous about being late. I dislike being late. Punctuality is a form of respect. In school, I was the kid who always forgot something. The time, a book, or homework. Most of the time, though, I was late or forgot things on purpose, just being a lazy kid, you know. I preferred hanging with my friends than having my nose in a book." He winked. "Mom and Dad knew. I can't even count how many times I got grounded. In fact, I got my ass beat so hard I couldn't walk the first time they caught me in a lie. My mother insisted that honesty, punctuality, and being prepared are the keys to life. So, I try to be whenever I can. I guess I should be grateful: it would be harder leading client meetings like this without certain standards. Not impossible, just harder. People have a sixth sense for BS."

"Oh, they absolutely do," I said, somehow taken aback by the little glimpse into his childhood. It seemed like his parents had been quite strict. "I'm sorry your parents gave you a hard time as a kid. But you're a pretty impressive speaker. The best, really."

"Thanks, Stella."

"You're very welcome, boss. Anytime."

"Hmm," he said, arching a brow. "You're not trying to butter me up, are you?"

My cheeks burned. "No, of course not. I would never."

"Well, I think you owe me an embarrassing childhood story of your own now that you know mine."

"I'm willing to bet I have *way* more of those than you do. Give me a moment to think."

"Give me a good one."

Pensively, I tapped my index finger against my chin and stared upward. Then it hit me. "Ah, I think I've decided on a suitable embarrassment." I looked back at him as he watched me intently. "It all happened on Valentine's Day, just before my tenth birthday. I had my first ever crush."

"Who was it?"

"It was a cute boy named Mikey. Mikey was always caked in mud, but I thought he was just *everything*. I knew he didn't like me back because I was this chubby nerd with thick glasses. Anyway, on this particular Valentine's Day, I decided to slip a Valentine's card into his locker. And I did, I committed the deed, with all my courage! I swear I almost *died*. I waited until recess to do it."

"How gutsy. I'm impressed."

"*Well*...I realized I'd forgotten to sign the card, but it was too late. It was already in his locked locker. I thought, 'Maybe this is for the best.' Like I said, I wasn't exactly the girl of his dreams—in fact, he thought I had cooties, so I told myself it was better that the card remained anonymous."

His eyes widened. "Did he find out it was you?"

"Nope. But he loved the card. He laughed and said it was hilarious. Which was a pity."

"A pity? So what happened? Why didn't you just tell him it was your card?"

"Because when he was going on and on about how it was the best Valentine's card he'd ever received, a pretty girl named Becky took credit for it, and Mikey gave her a peck on the cheek and asked her on a date. She said yes. At that point, it was too late to claim copyright without looking like I was desperate for Mikey's attention. So, I just let him believe she had made it for him."

"That's heartbreaking." He grimaced. "Ultimately, his loss."

"Yeah, oh, well. Don't be so sure about that. Imagine if I'd left the card in *your* locker. Ha-ha." An awkward laugh escaped my throat.

Ace didn't laugh. "You know, if you had left a Valentine's Day card in my locker, I would've been happy about it. Surprised, but happy."

"Really?" I knew he was just messing with me, but my heart was pounding against my rib cage like a trapped animal trying to make an escape. My eyes dropped to his lips—his beautiful, manly, kissable lips.

"Really," Ace grumbled firmly, nudging my chair in his direction. He started leaning toward me, his lips coming closer and closer to mine.

All I could think was: *finally*.

Goo. I was gonna be goo... I wanted nothing more than to be kissed by those lips.

*Now.*

"I've got so much tidying up to do," I squeaked, chickening out at the last moment. I jumped out of my chair and made my way around the table, collecting all the cups and saucers the clients had made use of, dropping a few and collecting them back up again as I went. I could feel Ace's gaze following me.

"You all right there?" he asked. "Did I do something to offend you?"

"No, not at all. I just thought I'd better get this boardroom back in tip-top shape before it gets too late. Tomorrow's another busy day."

Was there amusement on his face?

I bent over to pick up a plastic spoon I had dropped on the floor. When I was getting back up, two hands firmly gripped my waist and spun me around so I was facing him. The impact almost made my contacts pop out.

"Oh," I exclaimed, feeling his muscular frame against my body.

"We have some unfinished business," Ace growled. His eyes radiated a bright light of their own. Despite the intensity of his gaze, there was something icy about it.

"Bu-ut," I stuttered, unsure what to make of what was happening.

He looked down at the table. "You don't need to do that." He swiped away the stack of saucers and cups and spoons, and sent them flying across the room.

"But I—"

He moved his hands around my waist and picked me up like a rag doll. "I want you, baby," he rumbled as he set me on the table. My legs were dangling off its side as I was still processing the fact that Ace Windsor had called me "baby." It was hotter than hot. He nudged my legs open and wedged himself between them. With a firm grip, he pulled my waist against his hips, secure and confident as if he'd done it a million times, letting me feel his erection press against my center.

"Oh," I practically moaned, "but what about—"

My train of thought was forgotten when he put his hand at the back of my head, nestling it between my curls, and pulling me toward him. He stopped one inch from my lips.

"You want me to kiss you?" he growled. "Say yes."

"Yes." It came out as a hoarse whisper.

His lips brushed mine, teasing at first, and a jolt of energy raced up and down my spine. The butterflies in my stomach flapped their wings. They were just as shocked as I was at the unexpected softness of his touch.

But then they took off all at once.

The world spun around me.

My lips met his with an almost feverish urgency. The impact of it parted them just enough for his tongue to slip through. My heart raced, threatening to leap from my chest, and the throbbing sensation between my thighs turned into a scorching ache that I knew only his touch would cure. Our tongues intertwined like sparring fighters, each trying to take in more of the other. His hand grabbed one of mine and placed it on his chest. I could feel his pulse growing faster.

"You feel this? You feel what you do to me?" he murmured, only disconnecting his lips from mine for a mere second.

*I do*, I nodded, unable to speak, his tongue back in my mouth. I kissed him like my life depended on it.

The strong heartbeat under my palm made me melt further into him. I had always imagined that my first kiss with Ace would be magical, but I had no idea how intense it would be. Why did he, of all people, have to be the world's best kisser? His lips tasted of black coffee, but his familiar piney scent urged me to kiss him more, and I bit his lower lip. In response, his hands ran down my hips and he playfully squeezed my butt. An involuntary squeal escaped my lips.

He released my mouth, growled his appreciation, and tightened his grip around me, pulling me even closer, then ran his hands up my shoulders.

For a moment, he just rested his forehead against mine and stared into my eyes, saying nothing—just looking at me with his intense feverish gaze. We stayed like that for long breathtaking moments. His blue eyes reminded me of the cold bite of winter mornings, the kind before the first snow falls, and the icicles that hang from tree branches when the snow starts melting again.

"Ace—" I started.

"No. Hush." He pressed his lips against mine before I could finish my sentence, making me forget any protests I might have possibly had. He brushed the tip of his tongue against mine, over and over, and I could feel another smile forming on his face.

Why was he smiling?

He released my mouth, pulling away just enough to speak. "Tell me what you wrote in Mikey's card," he mischievously said.

"Ehhh...I don't remember." I tried to kiss him again, but he playfully jerked his head away.

"No, you *do*," he replied. "Tell me. I'm curious."

"It's really dumb and embarrassing."

"Even better. Tell me."

"Only if you promise not to laugh."

"Just tell me."

"Ugh," I groaned, trying one last time to kiss him against his will before yielding. "It said, 'Roses are red, violets are blue. You are my Squirtle, and I'm your Pikachu.'"

He snorted, turning his face away from me, placing a hand over his mouth. He did it so I wouldn't see how hard he was laughing. "That's... beautiful," he replied, chuckling, turning back to me. I gave him a death stare. He was still laughing.

"I liked Pokémon a lot back then."

He gently brushed his lips against mine. "You're cute. Kinda nerdy, but cute. Seriously." He kissed me. His lips felt like fire against my own. "Can I be your Squirtle instead?"

"You're too hot to be a Squirtle. You're more like a Charmander," I said before crashing my lips into his.

I slowly pulled his shirt from his pants and slid my hand under it. His washboard abs were rock-hard under my fingers, almost inhumanly hard. I wondered what he looked like with his shirt off. I'd seen photos of his college swim team, but I strongly suspected he was even more attractive now. Maybe he had even more tattoos? I ran my hand from his navel up to his back and down again before cheekily pulling at the waistband of his pants, feeling his erection press against me. That was no little Barry. If anything, it was the opposite of little Barry.

He paused, drew away from me, and looked into my eyes. "You're playing with fire. Look what you're doing to me," he groaned.

"To you? Look what you're doing to *me*." I ran my free hand through my messy hair.

"Do you like it when I touch you?" he rumbled. He put one of his hands on my naked knee, not breaking eye contact for a second.

"I'm not supposed to, right? But I do."

Painfully slowly, he started running his hand up my leg and slipped it under my skirt. His fingers left what felt like a trail of flames behind it, and then continued pulling my skirt up and up. My skin burned at his touch, and yet I wanted him to explore every inch of me.

His fingers reached my panties, and he pulled them to one side.

He paused again. "Tell me to touch you," he demanded. "Ask me to."

"Touch me, Ace," I whimpered. "Please, touch me."

A mischievous smile spread across his face as his fingers finally made contact with the fire between my legs. "Good girl."

I moaned when his fingers brushed my clit, but he silenced me by pressing his lips against mine. His thumb ran teasingly over my clit, playing with it, causing me to jerk and moan. My groans were muffled by his writhing tongue in my mouth. He slipped his hand out of my panties and started unbuckling his belt.

"Ace," I gasped.

"You open it," he growled, casting his eyes toward his zipper, and sliding his hand back into my panties.

Without hesitation, I reached forward, unsure of what to expect, and felt something in his pocket. It was vibrating. What was that? Oh. Duh. "Oh, gosh," I said, jerking my hand away. "I think your cell phone is ringing."

"Fuck," Ace grumbled, annoyed, removed his hand from me, and reached into his pocket. He stared at his cell screen and muted his ringtone. "Bad timing."

"Aren't you going to take that?"

"I'm not." He tried to shove his cell back into his slacks' pocket, but swiped right instead, accidentally answering the call. "Fuck," he muttered under his breath.

"Hello? Hello? Ace, are you there?" Damon's voice crackled from its speaker.

I froze.

Ace held it up to his ear and frowned. "Yeah, I'm here."

"Hey, bro. Good to hear your voice. Do you want to come out for drinks? Miles, Oliver, and I are headed to Talia's."

My hands fumbled desperately at my skirt to pull it down.

"Umm," Ace hummed, looking at me. I was still seated on the boardroom table with my legs spread wide enough to allow him to stand between them, with wet panties and a drenched clit, and his belt unbuckled. "I can't right now, bro. Bad timing. Another time."

"You sure? Just a quick drink," Damon insisted. "You don't have to stay out all night." I could hear his voice booming from the other end of the line, despite Ace pressing his cell tightly against his ear.

"Another time," Ace groused. "Tell the guys I said hi." With that, he ended the call.

"What are we doing, Ace?" I asked as soon as he slid his cell back into his pocket.

I pushed him away, and he looked down at me. "What do you mean?"

"I don't know," I said. "You initiated it."

He shook his head. "No, baby, *we* initiated it. And you know it. Don't just put it on me."

"Well, I'm not doing it on purpose," I said, crossing my legs. I crossed my arms too, and frowned at him. "I thought you were enjoying my presence…"

"I was," he said bluntly. "I *am*. And that's the problem. I shouldn't be."

"I know it's wrong." I shrugged. "But it doesn't feel wrong. It feels so right."

"It's unprofessional of me to even have put you in this position." He buckled his belt, then locked eyes with me, his features deadly serious. "Listen, I apologize, Stella. As your boss, I shouldn't be making advances on you. It's unethical, on top of everything else."

"It's okay. Really," I assured him. I got off the table and straightened my skirt and blouse. "We can pretend this never happened."

He straightened his shirt and tie, then made his way toward the opposite end of the table and collected the broken saucer shards on the floor from the crockery he'd so urgently shoved aside. For a second, I was taken aback. Why would he worry about the saucers? Cleaning staff would be in during the late night. It was odd to see the CEO of a soon-to-be billion-dollar company cleaning up. I rushed to him, helping to collect the last dirty cups on the boardroom table.

He stood and looked at me. "If you were anyone else but Damon's sister, things could have been different. Hypothetically. But we can't let this happen. We can't get involved. I know how betrayed he'd feel if he knew what just happened between us."

I gulped, feeling terrible. "Agreed," I said, cups in my hands. "We won't let this happen again. No problem. No hard feelings. We'll keep things professional and write this one off as a weak moment. One of many, but it was the last one."

We locked eyes. "Thank you for not making this harder than it needs to be, Stella," he said calmly, taking the dirty cups from me. "You can come in later tomorrow to make up for having to stay later today."

"Thank you," I replied. "I'll take you up on that offer."

"Good night."

"I'll see you tomorrow." I wanted to hug him, but instead, I gave him an awkward wave and turned to rush out of the room.

"Oh, before you leave."

I turned back around to face him. "Yes?"

"I've been meaning to tell you, Winifred called me this afternoon and said that she got a call from MKY Shipping. The lost shipment was found. The twenty boxes are being sent overnight to us. I understand you had your helping hands in all that? This means we can finish the papers by the end of next week and send them off to Humphries. Good job, Stella. Very good job."

I smiled at his honest praise. I could tell that a huge stone had been lifted from his shoulders. "Oh, that's wonderful news. Glad to be of help, anytime."

"I appreciate it. It was smart to bring you on."

Feeling a rush of weird mixed emotions—happy about his words, bad for not really deserving praise due to the stupid circumstances, I quickly turned to leave. It was a good sign that he was glad we'd found the boxes. He would have reacted differently if he was hiding something like Bonnie had suggested. "Good night." I waved, no less awkwardly than before.

"Hold on. Winifred also informed me that she got some files for you from our offices in San Francisco."

*Shoot.* I felt my body tense back up.

## 27

## ACE

Stella drew to a halt, stiffening. "Oh?" Her eyes were huge. "She asked me to tell you there weren't any files on the three companies you'd specifically asked about, but she'd gotten you the last years' annual reports. What's that about? What companies did you ask about?"

"Ehhh...well..." She stalled.

I narrowed my eyes on her. "Yeah?"

"Oh. Let me think..." She stared back at me, fidgeting. "It was all related to...the upcoming merger."

I had asked for a basic list of Windsor Architects' most profitable clients' projects from the beginning of time to be prepared and listed in order, with samples, photos, and numbers. "You're talking about the basic list?"

"Uh...yes. Exactly," she said curtly and turned to leave.

"Thank you for your help with that." Hiring her had been a good decision. She was on top of things. I owed Damon.

"Perfect. Yeah. Good night."

I watched Stella basically flee the meeting room. The way her hips swayed from side to side when she stormed out was enough to drive a man insane. The smell of her perfume lingered long after I lost sight of her. It smelled of mandarin and jasmine. I inhaled and tried to remember how strong the smell of it had been on the nape of her neck. Shaking my head, I put the dirty cups I'd taken from her back on the boardroom table.

I couldn't believe I had just let that happen again. What fucking spell did she have on me? I'd never been unable to resist temptation.

The stars in the night sky twinkled through the boardroom's large windows. I looked at them and tried to spot some of the constellations I was familiar with, all in an attempt to distract my ravenous mind. It didn't work for long. My reflection in the windowpane looked like I felt: a hungry animal. I put my hand against it and felt the evening air's cool touch behind it.

"This has to stop," I said aloud.

That texture of her skin and that wetness between her legs. Sweet Lord. How soft and warm her skin had felt against my fingers. My cock jerked at the mere thought of exploring more of her than I'd been able to.

In vivid pictures, I imagined what might have happened if my phone hadn't rung. I would have made her beg for more, plead for me to do unspeakable things to her on the tabletop. Being the gentleman that I was, I'd have obliged, of course. But not before I'd put her on my lap and spanked her until her bare ass cheeks turned blushing red—I hadn't forgotten the spanking I'd promised her. Then, I'd spank her pussy. Thoroughly. Once I was done with that—and only if she promised to behave—I'd offer to kiss the places all better. I'd allow my lips to tickle her thighs and everything between them.

*Stop.* I caught myself getting feverishly embroiled in my thoughts. I wouldn't allow my mind to run away with itself.

I took a deep breath and tried to calm my pounding heart. *She's off-limits*, I reminded myself, *and you need to put all this—whatever it is—aside.*

*Now.*

## 28

## STELLA

When I finally got home, I headed straight to my bedroom and flung myself onto my bed. Damn. Damn. Damn. I ran my hand from my chest down to the hem of my panties and sighed. How was I ever going to pretend that it never happened? Realizing what I was doing, I jerked my hand away and stared up at the ceiling.

After a moment of contemplation, I pulled my cell phone out of my jacket pocket and dialed Bonnie's number. She answered before my phone had the opportunity to ring a third time.

"Girl! How was your day? Have you been managing to avoid that apparently sexy boss of yours?"

"Ehh...Not quite," I ashamedly conceded. "It happened again, but *worse* this time."

"Worse this time? What do you mean?" I could practically hear Bonnie raising her eyebrows as she always did when she heard something surprising.

"He and I had to work late today because we had a client meeting at half past six."

"Oh, no. If I've learned anything in life, it's that nothing PG-13 ever happens when two adults end up working late."

"I guess I'm a cliché then," I said. "Because that's exactly what happened. It wasn't rated R, but it was pretty steamy. After the clients left, I started tidying up the boardroom, and before I knew it, we were making out on the conference room table. One minute I was just collecting dirty cups, and the next we had our tongues in each other's mouths. And then he touched my—" I paused, searching for a tasteful term.

"What? Your Hoo-hoo? Bajingo? Minky? Your Underwater Treasure Grotto?"

I laughed a little. Bonnie always knew how to crack me up. "Yeah."

"Oh, shit. I think I can deduce what happened next. Did you end up going all the way?"

"No, nothing like *that*. Not even close." I sighed as she didn't say a word. "But I kind of wish we had."

"Girl. Stella. This is bad," Bonnie chastised me. "That's the opposite of what I *advised* you to do. I told you to *avoid* him, not suck his face. What would your brother say?"

"Ugh, don't remind me about Damon," I said. "I feel guilty enough."

"Why? Please tell me you didn't suck his you-know-what."

"Confetti Dispenser? One-eyed Wonder Weasel? His *weapon*? His *loaded* gun?" Uhh, I liked that one.

"Exactly. His little Barry. Whatever you wanna call it. *Did you*?"

"I didn't. He only unbuckled his belt...and that was *so* hot. But that was it."

Bonnie's relief was audible through the phone. "Thank goodness. So it's not going to happen again? It can't happen again!"

"I know. We both agreed that we shouldn't allow it to happen again," I replied. "Am I silly for being sad about the fact we can't be together? I know he and I haven't been close for very long, but I feel so many things when I look at him or even think about him. Don't they always say, 'Follow your heart?'"

"You can follow your heart, as long as it doesn't lead to your boss," Bonnie said matter-of-factly. "Look, lots of people have chemistry and don't act on it. You two will just need to learn how to do that. You're not the first person in the world to have a crush on their apparently madly sexy boss."

"This feels like more than a crush though."

"You still shouldn't act on it. There's too much at stake: your relationship with your brother, your job, and your future as an architect. It's not worth it."

"You're right," I said. "I know you're right."

"Look. There are lots of cucumbers in the sea. You'll find someone that makes you even weaker in the knees and whose whistle is even slurpier, and then you'll forget all about Ace Windsor."

"I hope you're right. Or else, I'm totally screwed."

"You've got this, girlie," she said. "I believe in you. You can resist his sexy wiles! If anybody can resist falling for him, it's you."

"Thanks. I needed that. You always know what I need to hear."

"What are best friends for? Anyway, have a good night. I'll talk to you again in the morning. I've got to get up early for tennis class." She ended the call before I could thank her again for her help with MKY, and before I could invite her—again—to yoga class. I really thought Bonnie would enjoy yoga, but she always had some "believable" excuse. She had to groom her neighbor's cat, she accidentally washed all her pants at once, she downed a rum and Coke, thinking it was just Coke.

Feeling tiredness take hold of me, I put my cell on my bedside table and lay down on my back. The sensations that Ace evoked in me hadn't gone away yet, I still felt it stirring in my chest—and between my thighs.

After half an hour of just staring at the ceiling, I gently ran my hand over the parts of me that felt like they were burning. An involuntary moan escaped my lips. I closed my eyes and pictured Ace on top of me. I tried to imagine what his weight would feel like, crushing against my body as he kissed my lips and thrust himself inside me. I pushed my panties aside just like he had done, and tried to relive what it had felt like when he'd done it.

My own touch didn't scorch my skin like his had. I fell asleep splayed out on my bed, trying to imagine him kissing every inch of me, starting on my lips, then the nape of my neck, and ending where the erotic sensation was most prominent.

## 29

## STELLA

*Three days later (Or: Bad Hair Days Are a Thing)*

"So, how have things been?" Bonnie asked, her voice crackling through my cell phone's less-than-admirable network connection. I found myself sitting on my bed, talking to Bonnie, and secretly wishing I didn't have to try to control my feelings for Ace. Sadly, I'd never been good at keeping secrets—or controlling my feelings.

"Apart from me having had a bad hair day for three days straight, better than I thought they would be," I said, pressing my cell tightly against my left ear. "The last few days have been pretty...ordinary. No invites to lunch dates, no working late, no 'flirting' in the supply room— just normal work stuff." I stared at the outfit I'd laid out beside me. Not dressing in a way that would distract my new boss was top of my list, so I'd chosen a plain pair of dark-blue slacks, a loose-fitting white blouse, and a matching navy blazer. "Ace winked at me the other day," I continued, "in the breakroom. At first, I thought, 'Here we go again,' but then he just nodded once from across the room and left. There was no follow-up, or quick chat, or even the tiniest hint of flirtation. It was just a normal wink between friends." Gah. My insides churned. I really didn't want to be "friends" with Ace. That was the last thing I wanted to be.

"Ah, I see. Perfect! A purely platonic wink," Bonnie said happily. "To be honest, I was worried things might be a bit awkward between the two of you when you told me what happened after the client meeting. At least the fact that they aren't proves that Ace is a more mature guy than I thought he would be."

"I guess," I agreed, running my hand over the dark-blue slacks next to me. It was the first time I'd heard Bonnie say something nice about Ace. "To be honest, the rational part of me is relieved that things have gone back to normal, but at the same time, I can't stop thinking about what happened."

"Well, you're only human. The important thing is that you're both trying to put it behind you, and you're maintaining a sense of professionalism in the process. It'll get easier as time passes. You'll forget all about kissing him eventually, trust me."

Hmm. I wondered whether I'd ever be able to forget the feeling of Ace's body pressed against mine. "At least there are no hard feelings, and we get to be friendly."

"And you still get to be the CEO's assistant," Bonnie chimed in. "And work at Windsor Architects, arguably *the* fanciest architecture firm in the whole of New York. At least according to the *New York Times*."

"*And* I get to play detective," I added sarcastically. "Damon is still on my case about digging up more information about Ecclestone, and it's freaking me the heck out. I have been keeping my eyes open—without any real results thus far—and I don't know what more to do to get him the answers he wants. It's not like I can hack into Ace's emails or anything."

"I bet he hides the incriminating papers in his desk. That's where *I'd* keep my dark and dirty secrets if I were a CEO. In my top drawer. That's where nobody suspects anything, because it's too obvious, right?"

"Hmm. I did notice that he keeps it locked at all times."

"See? He's hiding something."

"Right. But I would never go through his drawers. That's out of the question."

"I'm sure you'll think of something," Bonnie said hopefully, trying her best to encourage me. "You always do." There was a commotion on the other end of the line, although I couldn't quite hear what was happening. "Anyway," she said, "I've got to go. UPS is here and the delivery guy is hot. Talk to you soon! Love you, girlie! You've got this!"

"Love you too," I said, just before we ended the call.

A reel of memories of my last "meeting" with Ace ran through my head as I slipped into my chosen outfit, discarding the old white T-shirt I'd slept in. I slid on the modest pair of flat leather pumps I'd taken out of my wardrobe and walked over to my full-length mirror to examine my appearance. Neither the slacks I was wearing, nor the blouse I'd donned were particularly flattering. More the opposite, really. But that was okay. I wanted to respect our agreement. I could never provoke Ace with a sexy outfit, it wouldn't be fair. Not after what had happened.

The bright-yellow cab was waiting for me at the curb in front of my apartment building by the time I walked through my front door. The morning sun beat down on me like a fiery downpour as I made my way over. I immediately regretted including a blazer with my outfit. I'd likely end up taking it off during the first hour of the day. A pair of larks loudly sang at me from a large tree growing in my landlord's garden, spurred on by the surprising early-morning heat.

Jay waved at me through his window as I drew nearer. Excitement to see him flooded me, more so than usual. I needed his advice.

"Good morning, Jay," I greeted after I slid onto the back seat. "Can I ask your advice about something…weird?"

"Oh? Well, you know you can *always* ask for my advice, love," he replied, turning the cab's steering wheel to join the line of traffic. "The weirder the better." He grinned at me through the rearview mirror.

"What does it mean when a man winks at a girl?" I asked. "Do men wink at girls they just want to be friends with, I mean?"

"Yep, you're right—that *is* a weird question." He chuckled and shook his head. "Can't speak for every bloke, of course—but I do know I've never winked at a guy who I only thought of as a friend. Does that help?"

"Yeah. Kind of," I replied solemnly. "And kind of not. But thank you nonetheless."

"My pleasure—and if it helps, I'm sure he likes you back."

"It does, Jay. It does." I gave him a sad smile, not really believing him.

Once we arrived, I slid out of the cab's back passenger seat, smiled at him one last time, and slung my handbag's strap over my shoulder. Taking two steps at a time without breaking a sweat, I quickly made my way up and pushed open the double doors leading into the foyer.

"Don't do that," Glenda chastised me from behind the reception desk as soon as I stepped in.

"What did I do?"

"You don't need to open both doors to come in. Just open one, like a *normal* person."

"I guess I'm not a normal person," I said as cheerfully as my mood would allow, and walked toward her. "Any messages for me today?"

"Mr. Windsor won't be in until later this afternoon. He's meeting with investors at the country club. Mrs. Mills told me to tell you that she left paperwork for you to complete and file. She already had it brought down for you to the archive room. Satisfied?"

"Yes, thanks," I said. "Have a nice day, Glenda."

"Hmm," she grunted.

The archive room was unpleasantly cold—cold enough that I felt increasingly thankful for my blazer, despite my earlier regrets. A tall stack of paper was waiting in the middle of the desk, exactly where Glenda had said it would be. For the last few days, I'd been helping to get the contents of the twenty boxes unpacked and sorted. They really were just boxes of client paperwork (no body parts). None of the papers were about Ecclestone. Winifred hadn't been kidding when she'd said that the former assistant's archiving method had been *flawed*. It almost seemed as if someone had made it a point to dishevel the papers. It had taken Mrs. Mills, Winifred, and me, plus four interns, three full days to get an initial order into things, but now we were finally seeing a light at the end of the tunnel. One of the interns had started to digitalize the now-sorted papers.

I sat down on the new, much-more comfortable office chair behind the archive room's desk (Mr. Windsor's interior decorator had surprised everyone with new chairs) and started working through the almost unimaginably large pile of documents. I'd gotten so good at filing that I almost instinctively knew which filing cabinet I'd find the right folders in.

Every now and then while I was slotting a document into a hanging file in a filing cabinet's drawer, I'd catch myself daydreaming about Ace. I knew it was wrong, but I couldn't help myself. I imagined him barging through the door, pinning me against the wall behind me, and having his way with me. *Or perhaps*, I thought, *he'll call me up to his office and "punish" me for not doing this paperwork fast enough*. Maybe I should slow down. Maybe I should work at a punishingly slow speed. The thought had me giggling and giddy and caused the familiar tingle to return.

Naturally, all my recent fantasies ended with him declaring his eternal love for me. But that was just a pipe dream. Sigh.

Finally, I reached the last pages of the stack that was clipped together. I turned it around. It was a contract of sale for some property in the Cayman Islands. I'd never heard of it before. There was a note in Mrs. Mills' handwriting stuck to it.

It read:

*Hey, Stella, dear.*
*Please make three color copies of these for me (my scattered brain forgot). You'd save me and my old legs a trip.*
*Thank you! M.*

The copy room with a color copy machine was located on the 4th floor. With the papers that needed copying clasped in my hand, I got up from behind the desk and ventured out into the hallway. It was quiet as usual down here. There were no interns running around looking for offices they'd never been to or businessmen making hushed phone calls.

The elevator arrived quickly. It stopped on the ground floor, and Terry stepped in. "Oh, hey there," she greeted. "Long time no see!"

"Hey, Terry." I smiled at her. I hoped she wouldn't notice my less-than-cheerful composure. She was exactly the kind of person who'd ask me about it, and I wasn't in the position to provide any acceptable or believable answers. "How's your daughter doing?" I quickly asked before she had a chance to catch on. "Has she made a full recovery?"

"Yeah, she's back to her old self. It wasn't anything a round of antibiotics couldn't fix. I'm just sorry it deprived me of the opportunity to prove to Glenda that her job isn't as hard as she thinks it is. But then again, I doubt anyone could prove that to Glenda."

"She's a trip, that's for sure."

Terry pressed the button for the 5th floor. "As far as she's concerned, not even Mr. Windsor works as hard as she does. 'This place would crumble without me!'" She mimicked Glenda's strict tone of voice.

I smiled, amused by how well Terry hit the tone. "And maybe it would. Who knows? I hope we'll never have to find out."

She looked at me, smiled, and finally said, "You're the exact opposite of Mr. Windsor's last assistant, you know that?"

The elevator doors opened on the 4th floor with a loud *ping*.

"I'll take that as a compliment? This is me," I said. "See you around, Terry."

"Have a good one," she exclaimed as the doors started closing. With one last wave, I headed down the hallway to my left.

Without too much effort, I found the door labeled "Copy Room." Anxiously, I opened the door that led inside. A part of me almost expected—let's face it, *hoped*—to collide with hard pecs, but I didn't. The room was entirely empty except for two high-tech copy machines—one black and white, the other color—and a small stationary cabinet containing reams of paper and ink cartridges. I walked straight toward the color machine and stuck the papers I'd brought with me in the top of it.

The copy machine's user interface was an overengineered touch

*Assistant to the Billionaire CEO*

screen. For a second, I struggled to input the correct commands, but eventually got it to work. Loudly, it whirred to life and sucked the contract of sale with floor plans into it like a hungry beast devouring its struggling prey. Its inkjets hissed as it started creating the copies. I leaned against it and felt its pleasantly warm surface vibrating against my skin. My eyes fell closed. The back of my eyelids almost instantly turned into some kind of movie screen onto which my tormented mind projected every memory I had of Ace's touch.

Distracted by my thoughts, I almost didn't hear the copy room's doorknob turn. The door creaked open, and I heard the steps of men's dress shoes crossing the floor. Probably one of the interns sent to make copies for one of the top dogs.

I turned and looked up.

"Ace," I practically exclaimed. I had not expected him. For a moment I struggled to find words, but then an innocuous question popped into my mind. "How was the country club?" I felt light-headed as he drew nearer. He looked at me, not breaking his gaze for even a moment.

"Fine," he replied. "Actually, pretty good. The investors I met with play a mean round of golf."

Mr. Hardy sauntered in through the door and headed toward the unoccupied copy machine. "Don't listen to Ace. He's just being modest," the engineer said in passing. "I played golf with him once and swore never to do it again. There's no way those investors even came close to winning."

"No, we should play again, Harvey," Ace said seriously.

"Nope. Not gonna happen." Mr. Hardy was probably the only man who could get away with a no. The engineer made his copy and exited the room while my machine was spitting out the last pages.

Ace stepped closer until he was practically towering over me. "Do you mind if I use the copy machine you're using? I need to color print something off a flash drive."

"Of course," I said, grabbing the copies I'd made. "I'm done, I just need to check everything. It's all yours. Do you want me to do it and bring it into your office?"

"No thanks," he replied. "I'll manage." He stuck his hand into one of his slacks' pockets and retrieved a small black flash drive. Inserting it into the copy machine caused the layout of its user interface to change. Ace was *not* a seasoned professional at the copy machine. But eventually, he navigated through it and started printing the document.

It came to me then that it was odd he hadn't sent Mrs. Mills or me to do it for him. But then again, we were all busy, and maybe he just thought it would be quicker this way. Also, I had no idea flash drives were still a thing. That was, unless you wanted to ensure that a specific document had minimal connection to the internet, because you wanted to keep this specific document extremely secure...

"Are you having a good day?" Ace asked as he waited for his prints to finish. Too bad I couldn't see what he was printing.

"Great! I'm having an awesome day," I said, smiling at him as I *diligently* counted through my copies and *religiously* organized them, making sure I had perfect sets, hoping to stick around long enough to get a glimpse at his printouts.

"How's the paperwork going?" he asked.

"Well, not to try to get in your good books or anything, but I'm almost done with the paperwork you left me."

"Good," he replied. "You're a fast worker." His documents finished printing, so he retrieved the papers from the tray and removed his flash drive. He turned over the pieces of paper and briefly scanned them. Whatever one of them contained made him scowl. He crumpled it up into a little ball and tossed it into a silver knee-high trashcan in the corner behind him. "Come up to my office when you're done with whatever you're busy with, and I'll give you something else to do."

"Sure thing," I replied, nodding enthusiastically. "I love being kept busy." My eyes darted to the trashcan in the corner. What was that all about? Ecclestone, maybe? A spark of curiosity ignited in the pit of my stomach, erupting into a roaring flame that demanded action. But I couldn't act, not yet.

"All right," Ace said, turning to leave.

With clammy hands, I waved at him as he strolled out of the room like a man certain of his next destination.

"See you," I answered, although I knew he was already too far away to hear me. As soon as I could no longer hear his shiny leather shoes stepping down the hallway, I darted into the corner like a startled shrew and hovered over the trash can. *What secrets do you contain? Tell me, tell me, tell me.* My heart sped up. I was so nervous when I reached down to retrieve the ball of paper. It felt prickly in the palm of my shaky hand. My heart was beating at least a hundred beats per minute. Seriously, I was surprised I didn't hyperventilate and sweat bullets—I was more than scared of being caught.

Carefully, I unfolded the paper, cautious not to tear it.

The page was titled "Short Hills Development." My heart sank into my shoes. I reached out to my copy machine and leaned against it to steady myself. Oh, no. This was it. This was the document that would incriminate Ace and spoil any chance I might ever have had of being with him.

Just when I was about to fully open the document and read all of its contents, the copy room's doorknob turned again. I found myself standing with the now-somewhat uncrumpled paper in hand as Ace came strolling back into the room.

Shit.

*Oh, shit.*

"Uhm. What are you doing?" He stopped mid-stride.

Quickly, I tried to shuffle his paper amongst my own, as inconspicuously as possible. It was too late.

"Are you *spying* on me?" He gestured at the pieces of paper in my hands.

Blood rushed to my cheeks and my heartbeat hummed in my ears. My physical reflexes might have been a bit slow, but my mental ones certainly weren't. They never let me down.

But now—nothing.

Nothing, zero, zilch came to mind to get me out of this terrifying mess.

More sweat ran down my skin.

I had to confess. I had to tell him everything, tell him the whole truth. About Damon and me and this awful, *awful* plan to spy on him—no, wait, I mean, be a detective for the greater good.

But then I had an idea.

"Yes, yes, I am," I said in a teasing tone. "I'm Miss Jane Marple, and you've caught me—*red-handed*." I held my breath and hoped I'd be able to hide the truth under a thick layer of humor. I was basically betting on a double-bluff working, something I'd only ever seen successfully pulled off in cartoons.

"Hmm," he hummed. For a few seconds, he just stood staring at me, and I wondered if he even knew who Miss Marple was, but then his lip curved up. "Stella, I was just kidding."

Oh, my gosh.

It had worked.

My tactic had worked.

Excellent! I realized he hadn't seen me going through the trash can and he had no actual reason to believe I was holding *his* crumpled paper in my hands. He probably thought it was one of my own. Thank goodness I hadn't confessed. I shuffled more paper around, to let his disappear deeper among the stack of mine (just in case) and smiled innocently, ready to leave the room. Victory!

I was such a perfect detective. Agatha Christie would have been so proud of me. That was some true Miss Marple magic.

"But still, you know what this means, don't you?" he rumbled darkly, mischief in his eyes slowly spreading across his entire face.

"That you feel honored to know the world's most amazing detective?" I laughed, hoping the truth of my words wouldn't ring clear and he'd continue to take it as a joke.

"Even the world's most amazing detective can't be allowed to get away with a crime like this." He waggled his eyebrow once. "Lock the door."

Oh, my God.

*Lock the door?* Was that what he just said? Was he still playing, or was this real?

Something squirmed in the pit of my stomach, and the familiar tingle returned, quickly spreading to my chest and the space between my thighs. I walked over to the copy room door, closed it, and locked us inside.

After I returned to where I had been standing, I gulped playfully (well, not really *that* playfully). "What are you going to do, boss?"

Ace started walking toward me, and I took a step backward. One of his hands was in his pants' pocket. It made his chest look even broader than it usually did.

"I sentence you to one kiss," Ace growled.

"One kiss?" I asked, my eyes wide. One kiss? That didn't sound like a punishment and— "I thought you said we shouldn't—"

Someone rattled the door handle. It startled me.

*Knock. Knock. Knock.*

The door handle rattled—again. It startled me—again.

Ace remained all cool.

*Knock. Knock.*

"I need to make a copy!" a voice drawled from the other side of the door.

"Coming," Ace replied loudly, like he was calmness personified. He tore himself away from me, winked at me, and went to unlock it.

"The lock must have slipped." He stepped out as the intern who had been waiting to come in entered.

"Oh, hello, Mr. Windsor," the intern said apologetically, getting out of Ace's way. "Sorry, Mr. Windsor. Have a nice day, Mr. Windsor."

I waited until I could no longer hear Ace's footsteps and followed suit, all papers clutched firmly in hand, making my way back down to the archive room where I'd left my paperwork. The chair at the center of it rolled backward in my rushed attempt to sit down.

I pulled the crumpled piece of paper I'd recklessly stolen—*borrowed*—from the copy room's trash can from my stack of copies, the very same piece of paper I worried would be the evidence I needed to incriminate Ace (who had just about kissed me) in all kinds of nefarious dealings with Edmund Ecclestone. With shaky hands, I finished straightening out the page for all the text to become readable.

*Here goes nothing.* Hastily, my eyes scanned through the rest of the information on the paper. It was a letter from a company called DC Developments. They wanted Ace to help them design high-end lofts in the Short Hills area, and they were definitely *not* Ecclestone Construction. Oh, thank goodness! I exhaled. Okay. Good. This was good. Not great, but good. Of course, this didn't conclusively prove that Ace wasn't working with Ecclestone Construction. It was enough to make me twirl on my office chair in happiness.

I let my mind dwell on our encounter for a moment and then shook my head, hoping to gain more clarity of thought. "Focus," I muttered under my breath, stopping the chair. "Don't let yourself fall in love. You've got a job to do."

A sense of regret, and worse, shameful guilt welled up in my chest. I'd lied to my boss and then crossed a line with him (again), all in the hope of keeping a useless piece of paper in my possession.

I wasn't the greatest detective, but I told myself that Miss Marple had setbacks too.

## 30

## ACE

The previous day's happenings were still fresh in my mind when I left my car and glanced at my watch. I had an early meeting with investors on the 7th floor, and I resented the fact that I felt unable to completely focus on it. I'd always been a man of numbers, a lover of graphs and statistics, and it had taken me longer than usual to prepare for this presentation. Instead of creating a slideshow in my usual efficient manner, I'd spent half the night trying to remember the taste and feeling of Stella's body. Now, I was almost late.

The fact I couldn't control myself around her both thrilled me and left me feeling frustrated at my own indiscretions. I knew it was a losing battle. No amount of moral agonizing was going to erase what I felt for Stella Copeland.

*Ring-ring.*

"I'm almost there," I informed Mrs. Mills, who had called to inform me that all the gentlemen were waiting for me.

"You better hurry! They don't look happy."

I ended the call. They would be after I was done with them.

The hallway leading up to the elevator was bustling with life as my employees streamed in for the morning. "Good morning, Mr. Windsor," sounded from all around me as everyone weaved through the crowd to make it to their offices. There was enjoyment for me in seeing the office at its busiest and I pushed through the throng of people, nodding, greeting, my laptop bag firmly tucked under my arm.

Finally, the elevator arrived, and a number of people and I stepped inside of it in unison. We crammed into it like sardines. I made it a point to chat with everybody. We discussed the weather and a recent football match. I realized it was out of character for me, but a little small talk, as Tilly had mentioned, wouldn't hurt me. To be honest, I hoped it would take my mind off the one person invading my thoughts and distracting me to no end.

When the elevator doors slid open on the 4th floor, it revealed a single waiting figure.

"Good morning, Mr. Windsor, good morning, everyone," Stella half-sang as she stepped into the elevator, several folders in hand. Her hourglass figure, wearing her sunflower dress, brought in a sweet smell of mandarin and sugar that enveloped the elevator.

Stella wasn't part of my meeting. Now that the missing boxes had arrived, I found her time best spent helping everybody involved to get the merger papers prepared.

"Good morning," I formally replied as the others said their friendly and warm hellos. It seemed like she had made many friends in the short time she'd been here.

The elevator doors slid closed again with a loud hiss.

"Why can't every morning start with a smile from Miss Copeland in an elevator?" one of the young men joked, and I gave him a hard look. *So much for small talk...*

"What floor, Miss Copeland?" one of the account executives asked her eagerly.

"The 8th, thank you," she said, and he beamed at her as he pressed the button for the 8th floor.

"Excuse me," she said in a friendly tone, "so sorry, excuse me," she continued, squeezing past the elevator's occupants, and positioned herself so that she was standing directly behind me.

"It's a lovely day, isn't it?" she asked into the crowd and received enthusiastic comments.

The elevator jolted as it started moving upward again, causing Stella to stagger behind me. Tits. No doubt. Her tits pressed against my back as she tried to regain her balance. An involuntary chuckle escaped my lips, one that clearly made no sense. I hid it behind a small cough. I felt her tits again. Hmm. Oh, I see. She was doing it on purpose. My dick twitched.

"You better not," I muttered quietly to my back.

She didn't listen. In fact, the little minx spent the rest of the next agonizing moments we were gliding upward toward the 7th floor—with stops and goes on every damn floor—pressing her tits against my back or "discreetly" rubbing her undoubtedly puckered nipples against my arm.

My cock appreciated the gesture. I didn't.

"You wait," I hissed under my breath.

"Did you say something, Mr. Windsor?" she asked loudly, all innocently.

Ping.

The doors slid open on the 7th, and I stepped out of the elevator, ready to head to the executive boardroom where the investors were awaiting me. But instead of proceeding to where I was expected, I turned around to look back at the crowd of people inside. "Stella, please join me."

"Oh…yes, sir, of course," she said. Her eyes twinkled like diamonds caught in sunlight, and I knew that her little stunt hadn't just heated me, it had heated her too. She wrung her hands together and cautiously slipped through the now-smaller group of people in the elevator, making her way toward me. "Bye, everyone."

As soon as the doors closed, I glanced over my shoulder to make sure we were alone. We were. The only two souls currently in the hallway were my assistant and me.

Stella was avoiding eye contact.

When I didn't say anything, she asked, "What do you need me to help with, boss?" She was staring down at her stilettos.

"I didn't say I needed your help with anything," I grumbled, sticking my free hand in my pocket to avoid giving in to the urge to touch her. "What were you doing? And look at me."

"I don't know what you mean," she replied, meeting my gaze. Her lips quirked.

"You know exactly what I mean," I said. "You were brushing up against me like a cat." I lowered my voice to a deep register. "You were trying to seduce me."

"No. I would never. Ever. If I brushed against you, it was accidental. I'd never try to seduce *my boss*."

She blinked at me, twice.

That little minx.

I stepped closer, almost brushing against her, but made it a point *not* to touch her, unlike she had done in the elevator. It wasn't what I wanted to do. Not in the least. What I really wanted to do was push her against the wall, press myself between her legs, deeply, and take her right there for her insolence.

"Don't lie to me," I rumbled. "How wet are you right now?"

"You *wish*," she said cheekily. "I am not. I don't get wet that easily, and definitely not by bossy grumps like you." Her eyes widened. Her hand flew up to clasp her mouth. Obviously, that had slipped out, her mouth faster than her brain. "Shoot. Forget I said that. I mean, I don't get wet by bosses like you...wait, no, eh..." Her eyes grew larger as she realized that hadn't really made things better. She lowered her hand. "I mean, I don't get wet by *any* bosses, not just y—"

"Stella," I hummed, catching her gaze. "Bossy grumps like me? That's how you see me? Hm? As some surly, bad-tempered *grouch*?" I needed to teach her a lesson for that too.

Her eyes were round as saucers—round *dancing* saucers—and her brown curls bounced around on her shoulders. She clearly thought it was hilarious. "Uh...like I said, forget I said that." She didn't even try to correct her assessment of me. She didn't have to. *That's exactly what I think*—that was what her expression and the tug at her lips were saying.

Even so, I liked that she didn't try to convince me otherwise.

"Luckily for you, in *this* case and moment, I don't believe corporal punishment is the best way to get someone's cooperation." Also, I didn't have the time. I was in no mood to be interrupted a third time, which, if tendencies held, would likely happen. "Thus, in lieu of current circumstances, I'm going to have to insist that you hand me your panties."

Her mouth fell open. The impudent smile was gone from her face. "You want my panties?" she squeaked in outrage. "For what?"

"So I can investigate whether you're lying," I said in as flat a tone as I could manage. "If they're dry, I'll know you were telling the truth."

"Eh." She stalled. "I was."

"Good. If you were truthful and they're dry, you get to keep them. If they're not, your punishment will be spending the rest of the day without underwear."

# 31

## STELLA

*A*ll right. Maybe I *had* taken things a bit too far in the elevator. "Ace?"

"I'm only going to say this one more time. Underwear. Now," he rumbled darkly.

I knew "the bossy grump" had won the minute he'd stated his terms. There was *no* way my panties would be dry when I handed them to him, but what chance did I really have? He would never let it go. I wiggled out of my panties, slightly lifting my skirt to do so. Luckily, I'd put on a nice pair this morning. His eyes were on me the whole time.

Scrunching up my lacy black G-string in my hand, I held it out to him. "Here you go, Mr. Windsor."

He wrapped his fingers around the bundle of cloth. "So I was right," he replied, his voice dropping in pitch by at least two octaves. "You little tease."

"I am *not*," I replied.

"Oh, yes you are," he growled, triumph in his eyes. He shoved my wet panties into his pocket. I tried not to allow myself to think about what he'd do with them when he was alone.

"When can I have them back?" I asked. "They're my favorite pair," I added, not even sure why I would say that—as if it would convince him to return them to me any quicker.

"When I'm done with them," he said in a deep baritone.

"That means?"

"As you should be aware, I have an investor meeting right now, which I'm late for, and after that, I have a number of off-site meetings to attend. I'll likely only be back at the office late this evening. You may have them then if I'm back before you've left for the day—or else I'll return them to you tomorrow. Until then, you are not to put any other panties on. Understood?"

There went my idea of storming to the boutique one block down to get an extra pair. At this point, the friendly saleslady would probably be expecting me. First a dress and a bra, now panties—what was next? A "daily underwear delivery subscription" right onto my office desk?

"Just as long as you know you're the cruelest boss ever."

"I know," he growled in his deep timbre. "And I'm going to make you put them back on in front of me when I give them back to you too." He winked at me and then turned to leave, heading toward the executive boardroom down the hallway to our left.

He was such a bossy grump. How was I to concentrate on work? Honestly now. I loudly exhaled, trying to release some of the tension from my body. It didn't work. Not gonna lie, it was kinda hot, but it was so bosshole-y! The tingling sensation between my legs still felt urgent and pleading, like I needed Ace's touch on my little clit to ever feel normal again.

He said I deserved punishment. I didn't deserve punishment. At least not like that. Having no panties and him enjoying knowing that I wasn't wearing any the whole day, stood in *no* way in proportion to the little teasing in the elevator.

Wait.

Ace had said he wouldn't be here for the rest of the day. That meant his office would be empty, and consequently, that I could go and take a *teeny* tiny look around. Take that, Grumphole!

Here was the plan: I would take one quick look at what was in there, and if I didn't find anything, I would be able to tell Damon to screw off once and for all. I was tired of living with the undeniably awful stress of being Miss Marple.

With my perfect plan fully hatched, I summoned the elevator and rode it up to the 8th floor. I spent the rest of the day in my office, glued to my chair. There was *no* way I would be parading around without panties. Ace's office, adjacent to mine, remained empty all day, only guarded by Mrs. Mills' watchful eyes.

But eventually, Mrs. Mills popped into my office to say goodbye for the day. She was typically the last person to go home (excluding Ace, of course), so I knew that her departure meant the rest of the office building was empty too.

My feet heavy as lead, I snuck out of my office and trotted down the empty hallway to make sure there was no one lurking about. The floor was truly empty. Good. With a horrible feeling and a heartbeat that was dangerously close to race speed, I opened Ace's office door and slid inside, just one step. The scent of coffee and Ace's cologne hit me like a truck. It smelled like I imagined a forest would when it rained. The scent was enough to cause the longing sensation to return. It was as if my body had learned to react to the mere suggestion of Ace's presence.

*Why am I doing this again?* I wondered as the guilt of being in here hit me. How had I even gotten into this mess in the first place? I was barebottomed, with a racing heart, about to snoop around in my boss's office for material to incriminate him, while having a tingly clit. How had I ended up here like this? I kept playing with fire, that was how.

I already saw myself in all of New York City's gossip papers.

*Billionaire CEO Ace Windsor Catches*
*New Assistant Stella Copeland (a Princeton Graduate)*
*Rummaging Through His Office*
*Bare-Bottomed in the Middle of the Night*

Nobody would hire me again. Ever.

This had to be the last time I snuck into my boss's office. Anybody's really. I couldn't make a career out of it. I couldn't afford more near heart attacks by nearly getting caught like I had been in the copy room.

Carefully, and with shaky hands, I closed the door behind me. The room was dark, but I didn't turn on the light. Ace's large desk stood almost menacingly near the back of the room. The city's evening lights that slipped through the cracks of his closed blinds cast bright white stripes on it. An open file lay on top of his desk, nestled between two crumpled-up pieces of paper, a pen holder, and his keyboard.

A clock mounted on the wall above the door ticked loudly, counting down the seconds menacingly (had it always been that loud?), as I made my way toward the desk with slow and silent steps. For the first time, I was incredibly thankful that Glenda had advised me to be more aware of my loud footwear. I felt like a thief. My knees were shaking, and my heart was still racing, and it was starting to cause my ears to ring. I could feel a trail of sweat running down nearly *every single* part of my body. This was *seriously* becoming a daily issue—a highly uncomfortable one. Oh, my goodness. I felt like a lamb being led to slaughter, and I was almost certain I'd get caught. No way this would go over well. Not in a hundred years.

I would end up in jail. I wouldn't last half a *second* in jail. Oh, this could end so badly… I wasn't just a terrible detective, I realized—I was the worst ever. You'd think I would have gotten used to "the excitement" of it by now, but no. I sucked at this in the worst possible way, and if I got caught again, Ace would never ever give me the benefit of the doubt.

The file on top of Ace's desk was the E.C. file I'd seen him with in the supply room.

*Thump-thump-thump-thump-thump.*

My pulse was audible to me. A bead of sweat rolled down my butt—not stopped by panties—and right into my butt crack. *Just…eww. I can't think about that right now. I'm showering as soon as I get the hell out of here. Curse you, Damon.*

I took my cell phone out of my jacket pocket (almost dropping it, twice, with my freaking sweaty hands) and used the light from its screen to illuminate the file's contents. A list of ongoing construction and architectural projects was roughly scribbled down under the page's heading. The page was titled "East Cleveland."

Oh. So, that's what E.C. stood for.

It wasn't Ecclestone Construction after all.

Thank goodness. I put the file back down, making sure to leave it as I had found it.

The crumpled papers contained uninteresting scribbles. I crumpled them up again.

My eyes were drawn to the ornate golden handles attached to the desk drawers. There were tiny wild animals intricately carved into the beautiful wood of the drawer, and none of them resembled each other. It was clear they'd been hand carved. The top one stood slightly open. Wait, what? No way! He must have forgotten to lock it. Bonnie's theory about him keeping his dark and dirty secrets in there came to mind.

My boss must have been in a real rush before he'd left for his off-site meeting. It was the chance of a lifetime.

No. I would not go through his drawer.

That was out of the question. Damon would probably want me to open it. I could almost hear him say, "Just take a quick peek."

But I couldn't bring myself to do it. I could not and would not violate Ace's trust or privacy like that. A folder lying on top of his desk for the world to see was one thing, but looking inside drawers that he usually kept locked was a different story. Those were my exact thoughts while still staring at the glistening handles.

Enough. I couldn't do this anymore. I had to leave. The feelings I had for Ace... It wasn't right for me to snoop on him.

Yes, I was more certain than ever that I had developed feelings for my grumpy boss—and what was worse, they *almost* felt like love. Consequently, I didn't want a hand in betraying his faith in me. I bent down to close the open drawer. My index finger ran over one of the handles. What a nice antique. Ace liked beautiful things. Did he think I was beautiful too?

I would never even glance at something of his again unless he asked me to. I needed to trust him as much as he trusted me.

# 32

# ACE

There were three fucking things I hated more than anything else in this world: piss-warm beer, dishonesty, and meetings being canceled at the last minute. Especially if I had to drive halfway across town before finding out through a fucking automated message that the meeting was "delayed until further notice." I was in a foul mood as I drove back to the office, and I decided the next meeting would take place at Windsor's—or nowhere—as I pulled into my designated parking spot.

The parking area revealed empty spots nearly everywhere. Everyone had gone home already.

It was just a short walk from my blue Aventador to one of the elevators that would whisk me up to the top floor—and at this time of day, luckily without interruptions. I gnashed my teeth the whole ride up, still infuriated.

Animated entirely by my frustration, I promptly stormed down the hallway toward my office. I couldn't wait to throw myself down onto my office chair and make the phone call I'd been itching to all day.

My office door's ornate knob felt familiar in the palm of my hand, and yet something was amiss. Something didn't feel right. I wouldn't go as far as saying I had a sixth sense, but I'd always had a talent for sensing trouble.

I pushed open my office door, more carefully than usual.

Stella was bent down at my desk. Her sunflower dress stood out like a sore thumb and gave her away immediately. The skirt was lifted up, exposing her pale bare ass. The first thing that went through my mind was, "She's here to surprise me." My cock twitched.

"Stella?" I asked loudly, announcing my presence while turning on the lights with a *click*.

She whipped her hand away from my desk drawers and shot upright. Beads of sweat were running down her forehead, and I could see her gasping for breath. She looked terrified, perplexed, and out of place.

"What are you doing here?!" she squeaked, her eyes widening.

"Well, this is my office," I said, trying to grasp the situation, flashes of déjà vu rushing through my head. "What are *you* doing here?"

"I-I-I..."

"I saw you pull your hand away from my drawer. Were you going through my things?"

"I...just held onto your desk for balance," she said, biting her lip. "I mean...well, funny story...I lost my contacts, and I was looking for them on the floor. I swear!"

"You're a shitty liar," I replied, still reeling to understand what was going on here. "You couldn't lie if your life depended on it. For the last time. Were you going through my things? What the fuck are you looking for? Are you selling information to one of my competitors?"

"I'd *never* do that." Tears were now flowing freely from her eyes, leaving dark trails on her cheeks and chin.

"Just admit it," I barked. "You don't need to try to fool anyone. Tell me the fucking truth!"

"I didn't look inside. I just tried to *close* your drawer."

"In the fucking dark? Are you a rat?"

"What?" She clasped her hands together and held them against her chest. "No! You know me, Ace. You know I wouldn't do something like that."

Past events rushed into my mind. The copy room incident. The crumpled-up paper in her hands. Her request to Winifred. Now this? It all made sense now. "Apparently, I don't know you as well as I thought I did. I thought I could trust you, and clearly that's not the case."

"No, pleas—"

"I suppose you really *did* dig out that piece of paper I threw away in the copy room?" I stated coldly. "Get out of my office. *Now*."

"Wait, wait," she pleaded. I could see her trembling. "Yes, I did, but I can explain." She gulped, her face pale like paper, squirming painfully.

I was silent. Not because I had nothing to say—I did, and a lot—but because I wanted to give her a chance to come out with the truth.

After an eternity, she straightened her shoulders, put her hands on the table, and looked into my eyes. "It was Damon's idea," she said quietly. "He asked me to find out if you were working with Edmund Ecclestone. He meant no harm."

What?

*Damon?*

"*He* put you up to this?" I stared at Stella intently, waiting for a reply. I couldn't fucking believe it, although it was clear to me why that bastard had sent his own sister after me.

"Yes, he did," she finally whispered. "I'm sorry. I'm so, so sorry," she cried. "He meant well, I promise," she repeated. "After I saw that the E.C. file on your desk stood for 'East Cleveland' and not for 'Ecclestone Construction,' I was planning on telling him to go stuff it, but then you—"

"But then I caught you digging around in my office," I finished the sentence for her. I still couldn't fucking believe Damon would do this. Worst of all, I couldn't believe that *she* would do this.

"Ace, I am so sorry," she sobbed uncontrollably. "I'd never do anything to hurt you, and I swear I was going to tell Damon I wouldn't keep tabs on you anymore. I was going to call him when I got home. It's the truth!"

Rage was burning like fire in my chest. It took every ounce of self-restraint not to scream.

"Get out of my office right now, Stella. I'm serious. Get out before I ask security to escort you out."

"Does this mean I'm fired?" she asked, her lower lip trembling forcefully. Her eyes were already red and puffy from crying. "Because I'm so sorry, and I promise that nothing like this will happen ever again. *Never.*"

"Just go home," I grumbled. "Go. Go home before I lose my temper."

She sobbed as she stormed out of my office, pushing past me. Only her mandarin scent lingered. I walked over to my office chair and slumped down onto it like a defeated, dying man.

After a minute or two, I propped my elbows onto my desk and rested my head in my hands. Without the crying, rueful Stella in the room, I found it a lot easier to calm down. I read the first page of the open file between my arms. There was nothing exciting about it. I couldn't believe she'd really thought I'd work with Ecclestone. What type of person did she fucking think I was?

I glanced at my drawer. I was certain she hadn't peeked inside. Had she discovered what I was concealing in there, her reaction would have been quite different.

I did not regret returning to the office. If I'd just gone home, I could have been blissfully unaware of all of this, and Stella and I could have still enjoyed each other's company. But at what price?

Now that all the cards were face-up on the table, there was hope for us.

I got to my feet and started pacing the length of my office with my hands behind my back. The smell of Stella's perfume was starting to fade.

Damon.

"You asshole," I muttered.

I wasn't sure why I was really that surprised. A few days back, he'd asked me about Ecclestone on the phone. Apparently, my answer hadn't satisfied him. And so he'd sent his sister to find out whether or not I had been lying to him.

What a bastard.

I pulled my cell phone out of my pocket and dialed his number. It rang twice before an idea suddenly dawned on me. I ended the call before he could answer and shoved my phone back into my pocket.

The only reason I couldn't pursue a relationship with Stella was—apart from my being her boss, but *fuck* that—because it would piss Damon off. Now that he had clearly proven he was no friend of mine, I could have her without any consequences for our "supposed" friendship. She might have tried to get information on me behind my back, but she had done it in his name, because her "dear brother" had told her to. He'd probably left her no choice, the fucker. Everyone knew how persuasive Damon could be.

Well, served him right!

If he decided to call back, I wouldn't tell him what I knew. I would never throw her under the bus.

I had an advantage—one I didn't intend to waste. I was sure Miles and Oliver were in on the whole spying shit as well. Part of me understood why they were being careful. I would be too. The other part hated the distrust. The question wasn't whether I still wanted the merger. The answer was yes, because it would give me what I needed: time.

Why play my cards to lose? Only a fool would.

I couldn't bring myself to be "grateful" to Damon for his shoddy tactics, but he had gifted me something I intended to exploit mercilessly, now that I didn't have to feel guilty anymore.

Something good could still come out of this.

First, she deserved a verbal spanking. Then, the other kind.

This time, she wouldn't get out of it.

## 33

## STELLA

*A*ll was lost.

For as long as I could remember, I'd loved learning new things. I'd devoured books throughout middle school and high school, and I'd taken every possible extra credit course during college. There were very few lessons I hadn't enjoyed learning, likely only a handful in total, but two of them were learned when Ace had caught me in his office.

First, I'd learned that love wasn't always enough to stop someone from hating you, and second, I'd learned that there were some things that you should never do for your family.

The sound of Ace yelling at me was still ringing in my ears and playing and replaying on a loop in my mind as I stood at the curb in front of Windsor Architects' office building, flapping my arms, trying to hail a cab. Tears were streaming down my face and staining my sunflower dress with mascara-tainted droplets. I looked back over my shoulder at the building's entrance and wondered whether I'd ever walk through it again, which only sent a new surge of sobs through my body.

A yellow cab pulled up next to me just before I could completely dissolve. "Good evening," the cab driver greeted. He wasn't Jay, but he appeared friendly enough. "Are you okay, Miss?"

"I'm fine," I lied. I used the back of my hand to wipe the tears from my eyes and tried to compose myself. "I'm just headed home." I gave him the address to my apartment building and sighed, leaning against the back seat's headrest. New York sped by outside the window as we drove past. The sight of it normally had me in awe, but it seemed bleaker than ever before.

Once we arrived, I handed him his fare, plus a sizable tip, and slid out of the cab. I inhaled a deep breath of spring air, but it didn't smell as pleasant as it normally did. Everything felt blander. The larks in my landlord's tree were not singing. (They were sleeping.)

When I got to my apartment, I headed straight to my bathroom. There was no better place to cry than the shower. It had always been a place of respite for me, a place of reflection. I hoped that standing under a stream of water would wash away the trauma of the day's events.

He hadn't said I was fired. He'd just said to go home. Was that what he'd done to his former assistant, only to officially fire her the next day? I had never seen him that angry. The expression on his face. His eyes. The disappointment in them was so hard to bear, and thinking about it gave me chills. His utterly crestfallen face—I would never forget it. I'd lost him.

"You blew it," I mumbled as more tears rolled down my face. My heart ached so badly. How I wished I could go back in time. I should have known. I should never have listened to Damon.

I undressed and realized I was still without my panties. Ace had never gotten an opportunity to give them back to me.

The water that came out of the showerhead was cold as ice. I whipped my arm out from under it and shivered, a wave of goosebumps skating across my skin. Stepping backward, I decided to wait a few moments for the water to warm up before getting in.

There was a towel on the countertop next to my bathroom sink where my cell was lying, and I wrapped it around me. My phone's glowing screen caught my eye. I needed to call Damon and tell him what had happened. Right? I dialed his number and pressed my phone tightly against my left ear.

It rang, but there was no answer.

*Darn. I'll try again later*, I thought. I just hoped he wouldn't be mad that I'd let myself get caught.

Maybe the best thing to do was wait it out.

It'd give me more time to think up a strategy on how best to tell him. Damon had mentioned something about a long business trip, so I had time. I remembered him saying something about flying to Sacramento and Toronto and other cities upstate for some kind of business deal, so that was probably where he was. A thought came to mind. Maybe I wouldn't tell him at all. Wouldn't it be best to just tell him that I hadn't found anything to avoid opening that can of worms?

No, that wasn't right either. It would only work if Ace didn't tell him either. Damn. I was stuck between a rock and a hard place.

Setting both my cell and towel on the countertop, I stepped into the steamy shower. The water spraying from the showerhead was now pleasantly warm, kissing my skin like tropical rain. Tilting my head upward, I let it wash over my face, erasing any trace of the tears I'd cried. When the boiler finally ran empty and the water came out cold again, I stepped out and wrapped a towel around myself.

After I wiped my foggy mirror, my reflection stared back at me. I smiled at myself weakly, but no matter how much I contorted my face, I still looked sad. It was hard to put your big-girl panties on when someone had stolen them.

*Ding-dong.*

My doorbell's shrill sound reverberated through my apartment. It had to be Damon. Maybe his business trip had been canceled? He must have noticed that I'd tried to call. He was the only person who showed up unannounced whenever he was in the area on his motorcycle. Quickly, I exchanged my towel for a robe.

*Knock! Knock! Knock!*

Jesus Christ. "Coming!"

## 34

## ACE

*Knock! Knock! Knock!*

I rapped my knuckles against the light-brown surface of the apartment door and scanned my surroundings. There were two flowering potted plants placed neatly at the top corners of the welcome mat. The mat itself read, "Visitors welcome. Pet lovers extra welcome." A small cactus on the windowsill sat next to the front door beside a tiny white porcelain bird. I knocked again.

The door swung open.

"Jesus, Damo—" Stella started, then froze as her eyes met mine. "You're not my brother." She gulped.

"Thank God for that," I growled. "Otherwise this would be more of a sin than it already is."

I put my hands on her curvy hips and pulled her against me. She parted her lips like she meant to say something, but I didn't give her the opportunity. Instead, I pressed my lips against hers and parted them further with my tongue. She responded by getting weak in the knees. I tightened my hold around her. She wasn't going anywhere. Her moan filled my mouth like the sweetest honey, and my tongue slipped deeper inside. Pressing myself closer, my body was flush against hers.

I would devour her. She was mine, and mine alone.

Stella moaned into my mouth and pushed her hips against mine. My angry cock pressed into her.

"Eww! Yuck! PDA, much?" a blonde-haired girl in a red dress said, making gagging sounds as she walked down the hallway just past the door, with a tiny Chihuahua in tow.

Stella pulled away, obviously startled by the youth's sudden appearance. "Oh, gosh," she muttered, catching her breath, "That was little Jilly from Apartment 601. Her mom and I are in the same yoga class. Little Goliath has a weak bladder."

"Let's get inside now," I growled, tugging Stella into her apartment and closing the door behind us. Without wasting any time, I put my arm around her and pushed her against the wall, caging her in. The feeling of her curves pressing against my chest made me want to rip off her robe. Without thinking, I grabbed her wrists and placed her arms above her head. I leaned in to devour her mouth, my other hand already on the satin belt of her robe.

"Wait," she said, interrupting me. She drew away and made eye contact. "What changed? You told me to go home... I'm not fired like your last assistant?"

"No, you're not."

"Oh, my God, really?"

"I didn't fire my last assistant because she fucked up," I stated calmly. "I fired her because she lied to me. You told me the truth."

Her shoulders visibly relaxed. "And I thought you never wanted to see me again."

"I had to return the souvenir you gave me, otherwise I'd be a thief," I grumbled darkly. I stuck my hand into my pocket and withdrew her black G-string. Dangling it in front of her, I leaned in again, stopping just a breath from her mouth. "Plus," I rumbled, pausing just long enough to throw her underwear somewhere behind my shoulder—she wouldn't be needing them—and leaning in, my lips brushing hers, "you've been a bad girl. You need a spanking." I stood straight.

"Haven't I been punished enough?" she almost purred. Her hands started fiddling with my belt buckle, and I knew she'd have it undone within seconds if I didn't intervene.

"Perhaps you'd be punished less often if you weren't such a bad girl. But you were naughty, and once I'm done with you, you won't be disobeying me again," I growled, grabbing her hand and removing it from my belt.

"Wait... What are you doing?" she asked, wriggling around to free herself from my grasp.

"Commencing your punishment. Finally." I let go of her and took up position on the chair next to me. "Now, I'm only going to say this once. On my knee."

I'd never seen a woman crawl on my lap so quickly *and* eagerly. It almost caused me to chuckle. She was ready to accept her spanking, and I would enjoy every second.

Taking my time, I unbuttoned my right sleeve and rolled it up to my elbow. I did the same with my left. "When I'm done with you, you won't be sneaking into my office ever again." I slid my hand over her curves and moved the robe up, revealing her bare ass. Her round bottom jiggled at my touch.

I smacked it, and she let out a sound that resembled a laughing gasp.

"It tickles!"

"Oh, yeah?"

"This doesn't feel like punishment." I heard her gasp again and she shook her head, as if she wondered why she'd just admitted that.

"How about now?" I growled and smacked her again, this time sharper.

"Ouch," she hissed.

"Better?" I smirked and smacked her harder. "Does it still tickle?"

She ground her hips against me, writhing, and trying to gain a bit of friction. "Ouch! Definitely better." She bit her lower lip in eager anticipation.

Damn. She was naughty and flawless.

I knew she was already wet for me, and I'd just gotten started. Stella was the perfect girl for me. This time, I really smacked her ass.

"Ouch, that was almost *too* hard," she protested.

"Hush. Count down from ten."

"Okay...one. I mean ten."

I smacked her ass.

"*Ouch*! Nine. Seriously, Ace...*ouch*."

"Atta girl." Chuckling, I smacked her ass again and again, taking pleasure in her heavenly gasps and moans.

"Eight...seven...sex...I mean six..."

We continued until she counted down and her ass was somewhat red from my hand. She promised to behave after I'd softly rubbed comforting circles on her ass cheeks, and I rewarded her with a few slight strokes of her clit. It was wet and swollen and ready for me. "A little pleasure mixed with a little pain? It all melds together."

"Oh, Ace..." She turned her head, and her eyelids fluttered.

With that, I flipped her on her back, circled my arms around her lower body, and picked her up. "Hold on tight, baby." She immediately wrapped her legs around me. We fit together perfectly. Our lips met as I carried her to the kitchen counter. With my free arm, I swiped a wooden bowl full of apples off the table and set her down. The apples rolled off the edges and scattered all over her floor. Not that I gave two fucks.

I drew away from her to untie her robe before I pulled it open, revealing her gorgeous round breasts. I inhaled sharply as I took in the sight of her.

"You're fucking perfection," I murmured, my fingers teasing her pebbly nipples while I started kissing the nape of her neck. Stella groaned as I gently bit the sensitive skin there, and she threw her head back in pleasure.

She started squirming, and I kissed and nibbled my way down between her tits, until my head was nestled between her thighs, my stubble grazing her perfect little clit.

Stella continued to squirm beneath me, laughing. "Stop *tickling* me." She put her hand on the top of my head and grabbed hold of my hair.

My tongue brushed over her swollen clit, softly, teasingly, with just the slightest bit of friction to bring her *close* to ecstasy.

"Oh, gosh," she gasped, her laugh replaced by delicious moans. Her legs opened wider. "Ohh...Ace...you're killing me."

That was the idea—sort of. Torturing her—in the best possible way.

My tongue glided across her slick heat, brushing it in teasing circles, over and over, keeping the intensity light, not allowing her to gain enough pleasure, depriving her of what she needed the most.

"From now on, I'm the only source of your orgasms," the beast inside me rumbled. "Understood?"

"Okay," she whisper-moaned, and I let out a contented growl.

My hands tightened on her hips, and my tongue intensified the movement on her clit, sucking on it, playing with it, teasing it, forcing her legs to open farther as her breathing continued to speed up.

I didn't stop—I devoured her until she was flailing around on the countertop, crying out my name, the inner walls of her pussy spasming around my tongue.

She tasted like honey—and *mine*.

Just. Fucking. Perfect.

"I think it's best if you tell me where your bedroom is," I grumbled, scooping her up in my arms again. Her legs dangled from one of my arms, and her upper back rested against the other. She was still gasping for breath, but she pointed to a door to my right. I didn't need much more than that. Forcefully, I shoved it open, and a lamp noisily clattered off her bedside table.

I laid her down on the bed. "No escaping now," I growled as I undid my belt buckle.

She sat up and shuffled to the edge, but I yanked her back to me and slipped her robe off her shoulders. More blood rushed from my brain, southward to my iron-hard cock.

After I got rid of my jeans and other clothes, I pushed her back down onto the bed, and leaned in further. Her eyes landed on my tattooed chest. They moved from my pecs to my shoulders and back down to my stomach. It was evident she liked what she saw. I pinned her underneath me.

"Wait... Do you have protection?" she asked.

Fuck. *Where's my head?*

"Yeah. Hang on a second," I rumbled and reached down to my jeans to retrieve a condom from my wallet. I gave myself a few strokes while she opened the foil, her eyes sparkling.

Her hands were trembling when she slid it on.

She was tense.

"I've got you, baby. Try to relax."

"Okay...I'll try," she breathed.

I took her hands and kissed them. Next, I cupped her face, and cradled her sweet flushed cheeks to kiss her lips. She wrapped her arms around my waist, begging me to bear down on her.

She didn't have to do much begging.

I crawled over her body, positioning myself on top of her, my elbows on either side of her shoulders, caging her in. "Yeah, keep looking into my eyes, just like that."

Slowly, I began to push inside of her. Her eyes widened, and she released a "Hhhh."

*Ah, fuck.*

She felt warm, slick, tight. Too tight. "Relax. Open up for me...let me in, baby."

I made tender progress, pushing deeper, pulsing in.

"That's it, baby, you're doing so well for me." When I was all the way inside her, she gasped, digging her nails into my back, breathing out. "Ohhh..."

Jesus Christ, she was made for me. "Look away for even a moment, and I will stop."

"I...won't," she breathed.

I stared into her tender eyes. Time paused as we melted into each other. Then, I slowly pulled out and pushed inside her again.

*Fuck.*

"Baby. You're so perfect," I groaned sharply, and thrust myself deeper, grabbing a fistful of her dark-brown hair in my hand. "Look how well you're taking my cock," I praised. Her mouth was parted, and her eyes were sparkling as more delicious moans escaped her lips.

"This is too fucking good," I growled as I fucked her slowly, taking what belonged to me.

My forehead was now resting against hers, and our lips met. Our tongues connected in a dance, circling, and tangled with each other as my cock drove inside her.

Stella's moans played in harmony to the rhythm of my thrusts like a metronome keeping time with the most primal form of music.

The sinful expression on her face was enough to almost push me over the edge—but I had to force myself not to come too soon. I pulled out.

"Ace?" she whispered.

"Don't move," I warned, resting on top of her, wet and warm, letting the agonizing seconds pass, trying to avoid the jump off the edge my body urged me to take. "Don't move," I breathed.

"Okay," she whispered, her body lying still below mine, her breathing near my ear. "But you're tickling me."

Then she wiggled.

Within seconds, I slammed back into her—couldn't help it. I fucked her hard, and we were moving in rushed unison like a well-oiled machine. I sped up even more when she started begging and screaming my name, giving her what she asked for.

Seconds later, we jumped off the cliff together.

Our bodies collapsed.

I flipped her over onto her stomach and playfully bit her round bottom. "Grrr."

"Ah!" She giggled and squealed. I slapped her bare ass with a loud *smack*, before I pulled her back into my arms.

Stella and I spent the rest of the night repeating that routine. After all, I had promised her several things that night, and I was a man of my word.

# 35

## STELLA

"I didn't think I'd ever wake up next to you," I whispered. The bright morning sunlight streamed in through a crack in my curtains, casting a golden trail from the edge of my bed to my window. The larks in my landlord's tree were singing so loudly that I could hear them from my spot next to Ace.

A part of me waited for him to tell me what we had done was a mistake, but he didn't.

"You're mine now," he murmured instead, wrapping his strong arms around me and pulling me closer. "We'll wake up next to each other often."

"I like the sound of that," I said, humming as I pressed my ear against his tattooed chest, listening to the beating of his heart. The huge tattoo of a dark eagle was eye-level with me, watching me. With my finger, I traced its shadowy wings. Was there a growl as I did so? "So, you're really not mad at me for what happened?" The eagle's claws appeared ready to grab me at any moment, so Ace—no, the eagle—could devour me.

"No, I'm not. You were acting on your brother's instructions, and there's no point in directing my anger toward you. I can understand that you wanted to help your brother."

I looked into his eyes, which had turned winter blue. "I could and should have said no. Even when I...when we didn't...you know." I gestured between us. "Even then I knew you were anything but dishonest. I just wanted to prove Damon wrong."

"That's what I thought," Ace said. "However, baby, if you ever think about snooping on me again, you'd better up your game. You need to." He kissed the top of my head and grinned. "I'm surprised I didn't catch you sooner."

"I don't know. I think I was an *excellent* detective under the circumstances," I teased. "*Ex-ce-llent*," I repeated.

"Yep. Excellent detective work there. Way to go," he teased right back.

"Hey! I said, under the circumstances."

"What circumstances?" With one hand, he tilted my chin upward. Our eyes met, but it was different this time. It wasn't a joking or teasing gaze, but a loving one.

"Well, it's pretty hard to snoop on someone when you have feelings for them. So, those circumstances."

He arched an eyebrow. "Feelings for them?"

"Yep. You heard me." I smiled, turned my face, and kissed his chest. Maybe I was being too bold here. Maybe it was too early to tell him, but I just had to. I would burst if I didn't. His breastbone was hard under my lips, and I could feel his calm pulse.

"You've had a crush on me since the beginning then?" he asked.

I looked up at him and nervously bit my bottom lip. "Wanna know a secret?"

"Shoot."

"I've had a crush on you since the first time I saw you," I admitted.

"The collision in the hall? Phew. In that case, I'm glad you collided with me." My head bounced around on his chest as he chuckled.

"Well, actually, it was earlier than that..."

First, he just looked at me, but then realization dawned. "That long, huh." He gave me the cutest smirk. After leaning forward to kiss my lips, he tenderly placed my head back onto his chest and caressed my curls.

"I'm glad to hear that. I applaud your exquisite taste in men—even as a teenager."

Smiling, I enjoyed the feeling of his arms tightening around me.

"Does all this mean that we're...you know, a thing now?" The moment the question was out of my mouth, I wanted to take it back. It was way too early to express boundaries and expectations. Yes, I did like him, obviously, but maybe he didn't like me back, at least not like *that*.

"A thing?" he asked, staring at me as if I had asked him to have a baby with me or something crazy like that. Which I hadn't. Maybe for him it was just a one-night "wham bam, thank you, ma'am" kind of thing.

"Yeah, like in a relationship." Jesus. I was making things worse. What the hell was wrong with me? How pathetic to ask your childhood crush *and* boss *and* brother's best friend if they wanted to be in a relationship just after hooking up. Sure, I was pretty awesome, but *way to scare off a man, Stella.*

"A relationship?" he asked.

"Yeah, because let's face it. I'm a catch," I said. No way was I going to take the question back. It was now or never. Also, it was fun to be sassy with him, and so far, he had responded well to it. Men liked brave women. "You don't want to miss *all this*." I pointed from my head down to my toes, making circular motions.

He released a cute laugh. To my utter surprise, he said, "You *are* a catch, and it does mean we're in a relationship." He pressed his lips against the top of my head as his hands caressed my back.

Omg. I didn't expect that.

*Okay, act cool. Act confident.* It worked.

"Do we tell Damon, you know, about the whole 'snooping on you' thing?"

He answered without a moment's hesitation. "No."

"All right. Good. Let's wait with that until the furor dies down."

"But," he said, "I think it's best if we keep our relationship quiet as well, at least for now. There are a lot of people who need to be told about us before we make it public."

*Ouch.* I tried my very best to hide my disappointment.

But he was right. It was probably for the best.

"Okay." I looked up at him and kissed the underside of his stubbly chin. "I kind of hoped I'd never have to keep another secret ever again, but I guess I can keep our relationship secret for a little while. Just as long as I never have to investigate you or anyone ever again. I'm done being a detective."

That was the one thing no amount of love would *ever* get me to do.

"I'm all for that," he said. "And yes, I agree, you can rule out that side career of yours for sure. Despite being so *excellent* at it."

I laughed. "And I gladly will." I sat up and lifted my cell off the bedside table.

Speak of the devil. Unlocking its screen revealed that Damon had tried to call back twice. *Oops.* I hadn't noticed his calls. He'd be worried by now, and I needed to call him back ASAP.

"How do mustard pancakes sound for breakfast?" I chirped, glancing over my shoulder at Ace, whose head was snuggling into the pillows.

"Mustard pancakes?" he asked, eyes still closed.

"Yep. With a side salad and chocolate sauce." I giggled. "They'll be *almost* as delicious as you are."

"Ah. I see we're already in the food-pun stage of our relationship."

"Food puns are my lifeblood. I'll go get them started. Salad with chocolate sauce and mustard pancakes coming right up, I'm starving."

"Can't wait."

"Where are my slippers?" Not seeing them, I moved quietly out of my bedroom and tiptoed barefoot over my cold floor, making my way toward the kitchen. Most of my baking supplies were in a modest pantry next to my oven. I dug through it and retrieved the necessary ingredients before unlocking my cell phone again. I stared pensively at its screen.

No time like the present.

I dialed Damon's number and listened as it went straight to his voicemail. His cell was turned off.

Damon was still on his business trip, likely on a flight now. I guessed he wasn't that worried about me after all. I measured out a cup of flour.

With my floury fingers, I shot Damon a "Hey, D, what's up?" message, you know, so he wouldn't worry. I didn't mention Ace. I didn't feel great for hiding our relationship. In fact, it did nag at me a little—seriously, living a secret life was exhausting—but it was for the best. It was what Ace and I had agreed on, at least for now. I consoled myself with the thought that one day very soon we would reveal everything and laugh about it together.

"How are those mustard pancakes coming along?" Ace waltzed into the kitchen groggily, handing me my slippers. "They were under my jeans." He ran his hand over his disheveled hair, trying to smooth it down. He then rubbed his arm and moved his fingers. "I woke up with a numb arm this morning."

"Oh, no. Because I was lying on it for too long?"

"Not complaining. You're welcome to do so any time."

I smiled at his cute sex hair, slipping my cold feet into my comfy house shoes. "You're just in time."

"Wow." He smirked. "That was pretty quick."

"Oh, no, they're not done yet. You're just in time to help me make them."

He smiled his breathtaking smile. "That so?"

I walked over to him, stood on my tiptoes, and kissed him. "I hope that's not a problem." I smiled too, and turned back to my mixing bowl.

"Of course not." He stood behind me as I measured out a tablespoon of butter and wrapped his arms around my waist. "I'll help you make pancakes any day. Hell, I'd even fight the fiercest of dragons, get you the moon and all the stars, go through hell and back...or search for these adorably furry slippers for you." He winked at me. "Although I have to admit that, at first, I thought there was a rabbit hiding under my pants."

"I would never keep a live animal in my small city apartment. Not even a canary, although I love birds more than anything." I thought of the dark eagle on his chest. Was it getting warm in here? Hot, to be exact?

"And you don't quite need to go through hell and back." I laughed. "But I would appreciate it if you could get the almond milk from the fridge for me."

He shuffled over to the fridge. Observing him, I realized I was the happiest I'd ever been. I ignored the tiny voice urging me to not get too excited.

He placed the milk onto the counter next to me. "Just a heads-up. We have one hour, then I'm meeting a client."

"You should do something about that crazy schedule of yours. Both my mom *and* dad died way too young. It is crucially important to take time for yourself."

"I'm working on it," he muttered.

I used to believe he was grumpy because of his breakup, but it seemed more like his impossible schedule was the main cause of his grouchiness. Did he ever slow down, even for a day or two?

## 36

# STELLA

*J*ay appeared more somber than usual when he picked me up in front of my apartment building the next day. I noticed that he didn't smile at me like he usually did when I slid onto the back seat of his cab.

"What's up, Jay?" I asked, leaning forward to put my hand on his shoulder. "Are you okay? You look a little upset."

"I handed in my notice today," he replied with a sad expression. "So this is my last month as a cab driver. And that means it's my last month driving you around, love. I just wanted to give you a heads-up." I caught his eye in the rearview mirror to see if the reason for his resignation was good or sad. "Thinking about it makes me feel a bit sad, to be honest. Don't worry, I've got a lot of trusty colleagues ready to take over—Jay the Hunk, maybe? Don't ride with Hans, he'd have his 'hans' all over you. Susie's a sweetheart too, if you'd prefer a female driver. I hope you're not upset?"

"Upset? No, of course not. Okay. Maybe a little bit. That's…that's big news. It feels like everything's changing, hmm?"

"Sure does." He sighed. He turned the cab onto the main road and followed the flow of traffic toward Manhattan Bridge.

"So, why did you quit? It has something to do with the essay you wrote a few days ago, doesn't it?"

He shook his head at a red pickup truck that tailgated us near an exit. Normally, he'd swear at the other driver in his fun way, but instead, he just focused on me. "All in the bag, love. Just finished my degree. The last essay I needed to wrap up my bachelor's in psychology."

"Wow, Jay. I had no idea. I'm so happy for you." I wrapped my arms around him—and the driver seat—from behind. "I can't believe I know a psychologist, a real psychological expert. That's *so* cool."

"Thanks," he humbly replied, solemnly smiling at me in the rearview mirror. "I mean, I'm not a psychologist yet. I need to get a PhD before I can join the American Psychological Association—and before that, I've got to get my master's."

"What are you going to do then?" I arched an eyebrow and placed both hands on the backrest of his seat.

"I applied for a gig as an assistant at a psychologist's office in Hoboken." The cab came to a stop in front of Windsor Architects' office building, but I didn't get out, gesturing for Jay to continue. "It's a foot in the door, y'know? I'm kind of hoping the guys who work there take a liking to me and give me a hand with my postgrad studies," he admitted.

"I'm incredibly proud of you, Jay," I said. "Even though you won't be my cab driver for much longer, you'll always be my friend. My mate. My lad."

"And you'll be mine too," he said. "Hang on a minute. Sit tight." He got out of the cab, walked around, and opened my door for me. "And thank you for being you, mi'lady. You've always made my day."

I slid out of the back seat and stood facing him. "That's because you're freakin' awesome."

"Too right, love."

I put my hand on his shoulder. "And you're going to be an even more awesome psychologist someday." While standing next to the cab, I wrapped my arms around him and gave him the best bear hug I could muster. "Now, I think it's time that you promise to stay in touch and still come to yoga class, especially after you start your new job."

"Errrr...it hasn't been me skipping yoga classes these past two weeks." He smiled. "Don't worry, though—I will definitely drop you a line when you become a bigwig here to find out whether you need counseling."

"Oh, trust me. I'm sure I *will* need it." I chuckled.

After we exchanged another hug, he turned to make his way back to the driver's side door.

"Jay? Can I ask you something before you go?"

He stopped mid-step. "Sure, what's up?"

"I need advice about something. Psychological advice."

"Of course."

"It's just hypothetical. And odd."

"Sounds bloody perfect. That's what I'm here for. Fire away." He rested one of his arms on the roof of the cab and the other on the half-open door. "I'm all ears."

"All right then. Well, I was just wondering what happens if a boss sleeps with his new employee, and that new employee kind of admits that she has always liked him? Like *always* liked him. Do you think a boss would do something like that if they didn't like the new employee back?"

"That's an excellent question," Jay said, rubbing at a patch of dark hair on his chin. "Has he told you he likes you back?"

"*Jay.* Was I that obvious?"

"Oh, *one* hundred percent." He chuckled. "I'm a psychological expert, remember? So, your boss hasn't told you he likes you back yet?"

"He's said a lot of things," I replied. "It's not the things he's *not* saying that I'm worried about... He asked me to keep our relationship on the down-low. He doesn't want other people to know about it."

"Uh-oh. That's not good. Major red flag, love. Have you ever been to his house?"

"No, I've not been to his house, but I'm not worried about that. Thing is, it kind of feels like he's hiding something."

"You reckon he's married?"

"No, that's not it."

"Sure?"

"Well...yeah...I think—"

"Okay. Well...here's my advice. Ask him how he feels," Jay suggested. "Maybe he really is sincere, and maybe you're worried about nothing."

I bit my lower lip. "Or I could have a reason to worry."

"Pfff, well...you'll never find out by standing around stressing about it."

"Yeah, you're right. Thank you."

"No probs, love. Am I seeing you after work? You're still stuck with me for another month, remember?"

"Yes, and gladly so."

"See you later, alligator," he said before getting back into his cab. It sounded funny in his "Brit tries American" slang. "Good luck!" He waved at me through the window.

"Thanks. I'm totally gonna need it." I waved back at him as I made my way up the stairs toward Windsor Architects' entrance.

Due to all the storms and wind, the tree growing beside it had lost most of the little white flowers it had sported, but there were still a few lost bees buzzing around. I pushed open the double doors in front of me.

"Close the door before those damn bees come in," Glenda huffed from the reception desk. "I'm allergic."

I quickly closed the door behind me and spun around to ensure I hadn't been followed inside by any of the little yellow and black buggers. The coast was clear. "Don't worry. I think you're safe."

"For now," she sulked. "One of them is bound to get in eventually." She swiveled her office chair around and held up an envelope. "Mrs. Mills asked me to give this note to you from Mr. Windsor before she left to run errands."

"Oh, okay, coming." I walked over to her and took the letter just as she spun around to answer a call.

"The phone has been ringing all morning," she mumbled before answering it.

I stared at the letter in my hand. It was a closed envelope. I wondered why Ace would possibly close the letter, unless it was just meant for my eyes.

"Thank you, Glenda," I mouthed to her, quiet enough so as to not disturb the conversation she was having with whoever had called. I waited for her to put down the phone again before I said, "And if one of those bees gets in here, just call me and I'll escort it back outside for you."

"You'd do that?"

"Of course. I'm always willing to help my friends." I heard her "Pfft" as I turned and headed toward the elevator.

Once I was alone, I ripped the flap of the envelope open. The flapping envelope looked like a disembodied mouth, chattering away inside my hand. When I was sure no one would be able to read it over my shoulder, I unfolded it and skimmed its contents, all giddy and excited.

It read:

*Stella,*
*I have an unexpected presentation at 9 a.m.*
*Please fetch me the file I left on the executive boardroom table and get the room ready. Meet me in my office directly thereafter.*
*Hurry.*
*P.S. Your panties aren't invited.*

## 37

# STELLA

I reread the P.S. and gasped. Quickly, I folded the letter back up again. As luck would have it, no one else was waiting by the elevator, so I took a moment to compose myself.

He wanted me to come into his office without my panties? *No way.*

I unfolded and reread the P.S. again, just to make sure. Nope, that was, in fact, what the note said. I examined my reflection in my hand mirror.

*How naughty.*

As I waited, I coated my lips in my bright cherry lipstick and made sure not a single hair was out of place in the intricate French braid I'd spent an hour crafting that morning. Good hair day. Perfect.

*Ding.*

The doors slid open, and I stepped inside the *empty* elevator. Luck was on my side. An instrumental version of Meatloaf's "I'd Do Anything for Love" was streaming out of a speaker, mounted in its corner. *Of course,* the soundtracks of my life would follow me as elevator music. The irony wasn't lost on me, I was a little amused by it.

I hit the button for the 7th floor and waited for the doors to close. They slid shut with a loud *whoosh* just as the song reached its chorus.

*I shouldn't do it.*

*But no time like the present, right?* With my heart thumping loudly, I reached up my pencil skirt and took hold of my underwear at the hips. I wriggled out of them, slipped them over my ankles, and stuffed them in my handbag.

*Just another day at the office.*

Suddenly, on the 3rd floor it got crowded. Thank goodness I had already taken off my underwear and didn't have to worry about it now. I nodded politely at all the friendly faces and pretended to be busy on my phone (not even saying hi as usual because: no underwear). With an innocent expression, I spent my ride up watching people come in and leave the elevator, floor by floor, wondering what exactly Ace was planning to do with me.

On the 7th floor, I got out.

The file that Ace had sent me to fetch was labeled "Hudson Yard Development." It belonged to the project we'd sold the clients on during our first client meeting together. After I prepped the room, I scooped the file up off of the table and headed directly back to the elevator, but took the stairs up instead.

A sense of pride filled me knowing I'd played a role in closing the deal that had led to the creation of the file in my hand. On a normal day, I might have spent some time imagining what the next steps of the Hudson Yard project would be. However, I already knew that this moment was no ordinary moment. Many of my moments had been extraordinary lately.

By the time I got to the 8th floor, my legs were trembling and my heart rate was steadily climbing (and not because I'd climbed the stairs). I knew Ace would have something risqué in store for me, and the thought of it was enough to cause my pulse to race like a rocket. But I tried my best to contain myself and maintain my demure appearance.

I dashed into the hallway that led to Ace's office.

One of the office doors that lined the hallway swung open, and Mr. Hardy, with his fun mustache, stuck his head out. "No running in the hallways!" He teased me as he'd done before, only this time, I knew he was joking.

"But I have to. It's a life-or-death situation!"

"In that case, better hurry up. No corpses in the hallways!"

We both laughed, and he returned to his office.

Ace's office door was closed. I took a deep breath, straightened out my pencil skirt, and knocked.

"Come in and close the door behind you," he growled from the other side.

I obeyed and slipped inside.

His office's familiar smell engulfed me, pulling me in deeper, akin to a wild animal following the scent of its mate's pheromones. When I inhaled, my light-blue button-up blouse pulled tight across my chest.

"I got the file you asked for," I said after closing the door.

Ace was seated behind his desk. His elbows were propped up on it and his fingers were laced together. He stared at me over his folded hands, his icy-blue eyes sparkling menacingly in his office's dim lighting. "What took you so long? Bring me the file," he demanded sternly, still holding me in his gaze.

Oh, my goodness.

"Yes, *boss*," I said, having decided to play along. I walked toward him, making a conscious effort to do so as seductively as possible. I swayed my hips from side to side with each stride and pushed out my chest in hope that it would look perkier. I was totally *not* having a déjà vu white bikini walk, which had started just as promisingly and ended in a total fiasco.

"Put it on my desk."

He was talking about the files, not my thong, right?

Ace unfolded his hands and motioned toward the pile of paper on his left. "And then come sit here so I can run through my presentation with you. I'd like your input on it before my meeting."

He pushed his office chair away from his desk and patted his thighs.

Oh. He wanted me to sit on his lap.

"Yes, boss," I squeaked as I placed the file on his desk and shoved my handbag onto the chair across from him. I sashayed toward him until I was standing directly in front of him.

"On your lap? That's what you mean?" (Like I hadn't gotten the message.)

"On my lap," he growled. "Now."

All right. I nodded, unable to speak. He was the boss. I turned around and lowered myself onto his lap.

Heavens. I could feel him harden under me instantly.

One hand now circling my waist, he slipped his other one beneath my pencil skirt. He squeezed my thigh, and my heart nearly leaped out of my chest. The familiar tingling sensation returned, and it was stronger than ever. I wanted to beg him to touch me more, to touch me *there*, but I knew I couldn't. It wouldn't be professional. It would be *so* unprofessional.

"Open the file for me. My notes for the presentation are on the first page. Then we can begin." I felt him repositioning himself underneath me. His thick erection was right at my center.

"Very bossy today, aren't you?" I reached out to pull the file closer and opened it. A note circled in red at the top of the page read, "Start with ROI conversion."

"That's because I *am* your boss," he grumbled. "Pay attention." I could have sworn his voice sounded even deeper and "growlier" than it usually did.

He started running his hand up my thigh while reciting his speech. Oh, I was paying attention all right. I could tell he'd put a lot of thought into it (into the speech that was), which I concluded meant that the investors he was meeting with intended to invest a considerable amount of money.

By the time he reached the delicate portion on construction costs, he'd reached the delicate area of my skin where my underwear would have been if I hadn't stashed them inside my handbag. In between sentences, his fingers stroked over *that* spot as his mouth brushed the nape of my neck until I was squirming around on top of him. He kept exploring the secrets my skirt hid while he used his other hand to undo a few of my blouse buttons, exposing just my collarbones—mindful not to reveal too much in case someone knocked, *and* I happened to have a heart attack.

But who would be knocking? Mrs. Mills was gone, and it was too early for the other execs to come bursting in. Still, just the thought of getting caught made everything that much more exciting. It was sort of good that I wasn't wearing my thong, or it would have been drenched. Actually, flooded. Not that I cared. I felt perfectly content where I was with his thumb doing its magic. Did he just call me a good assistant? I could barely hear, let alone think.

He reached his presentation's conclusion just as I was reaching a conclusion of my own.

At this point, things sounded promising, thrilling, *peaking*.

My breaths were fast, and I was physically incapable of stopping my gasps and moans. I was also unable to rhythmically move my hips, grinding over his very, *very* impressive erection.

"Nope, I'm not letting you finish just yet," he rumbled darkly, glancing at his watch, and withdrawing his hand from beneath my skirt just before I could orgasm.

What?

No.

"No... That's cruel," I panted, resting my head on his shoulder and leaning back into his embrace. "No, that's criminal."

"Do you want to press charges?"

"Yes," I panted, frustrated. "Don't change the subject. Please let me come. Ace, seriously."

"You've been a good girl, and I'm going to let you finish, I promise. Just hold on a little longer. Until after my meeting."

"Until after your meeting?" Was that what he just said? I must have misheard. "No, I don't want to hold on so long. I *can't* hold on that long. I don't want to. Please let me come now. Please, *please*." I sounded desperate, and I was totally fine with that.

"Are you begging me, Miss Copeland?" he asked, amusement coloring his expression. "Are you begging your boss to make you come?" He kissed my shoulder and chuckled when he saw my you-better-believe-it eyes. It was a throaty sound that felt like it reverberated through my chest.

"No, of course not." I shook my head and closed my legs, coming to my senses. I stood from his lap—all wobbly—and straightened my skirt, just like I had before I'd entered his office. Just like I had done on many other occasions in this building. "That would be improper. You are my boss, after all, Mr. Windsor."

With my shirt all buttoned back up, I was ready to turn and make a beeline out of the office, when he said, "The reason for having to *delay* is because Mr. Hardy will be here any second now. He's going to present with me, and he's always punctual."

*Knock-Knock. Knock-Knock.*

Oh.

"Come in," Ace said, giving me a subtle wink, just as Mr. Hardy entered and greeted us, his fun mustache twirled up to perfection. "Sit down for a minute, Harvey." Mr. Hardy lowered himself onto one of the chairs in front of Ace's desk.

I straightened, returned the greeting, then shifted back to Ace, collecting myself. "Would you like me to sit in on you...sorry...sit in on the meeting with you? I know Mrs. Mills is out this morning."

"No. That won't be necessary," he said, already busy scribbling something onto his notepad. "But I'm going to need you once it's done."

"I'll be waiting with a fresh cup of coffee." I slung my handbag over my shoulder and turned to leave in a way that I *hoped* looked innocent, or at the very least, not like I almost got caught begging my boss for an orgasm on his lap. "Good luck, gentlemen."

"I've got one last favor to ask before you go," I heard Ace say, and I spun around to face him. He held a note out to me. "Please take care of this later."

I took the note and left his office.

Once I was at my desk, I unfolded the paper.

It read:

*Stella,*
*When I get back, I want you to be waiting here for me—on your knees.*
*I'll give you a special treat.*
*P.S. Although I wouldn't mind a fresh cup of coffee too.*

. . .

It wasn't hard to guess what his special treat would be.

∼

It went without saying that what was to come after his presentation wouldn't be like anything that had come before–and I was ready for his "special treat." Ace returned in a good mood, having landed another million-dollar deal.

"Thanks, baby," he said, taking the black coffee I'd brought him before I knelt on the floor as he'd demanded. *I mean, why not, right? Just your regular office procedure.*

He caressed my cheeks and leaned down to give me a kiss, grinning. "Hang on for a second. Well, I mean you can get up," he said, taking my hand and helping me to my feet.

For a moment, I was confused.

"Remember when I caught you in my office the other day?" he asked.

My heart sank. Where was he going with this? "Yeah...?"

"I'm glad you didn't go through my drawer, or you might have spoiled a surprise for yourself."

Perplexed, I followed him with my gaze as he walked behind his desk and opened his drawer (his "dirty secret drawer"). He removed a piece of paper, and something else.

Wait, what? "Didn't you want to give me a 'special treat?'" I made quote fingers.

"I do."

"I guess I totally misunderstood your note?" I laughed.

"Okay, I don't want you to freak out," he said, ignoring my question. "Close your eyes."

"Close my eyes?"

"Yeah."

I did as he asked.

"I *do* have a special treat for you. Hands out, with your palms face-up."

As requested, I put my palms face-up and felt him putting the paper on one of my hands and something heavy dropped in the other. "Can I open my eyes?"

"Open your eyes."

I did. Slowly, I glanced down, feeling his smiling eyes on my face. In the middle of my hand was a brand-new car key. The paper was the title. An Audi, *no way*! That was what he was hiding in his drawer? Car keys... for me?

My mouth formed into a wobbly downward curve, and I looked up at him. *No freakin' way*. Tears started filling my eyes. It was perfect timing too, since Jay's announcement had made me so sad.

I was not going to cry.

"You have a driver's license, don't you?" he asked.

"I don't."

"No? No worries, I'll teach you."

I jumped into his arms.

"Thank you so much! Really? But...but...I can't accept this. I can't." I let go of him, staring at the key.

"You can and you will," Ace said firmly, closing his hand around mine. He kissed me so tenderly as if I were the most precious thing in the world.

"Ace." I looked up at him. "I'm such a bad person. I thought your special treat had something to do with *your*, you know...'most prized possession.'" I made quote fingers and directed my head downward.

He chuckled, and whisper-rumbled, "Well, that's because you're a naughty assistant with a dirty, dirty mind."

"Ace! I am *not*," I protested as I fumbled with his belt and pulled his zipper down.

He paused, his eyes on my hands. "Oh, yes, *yes*, you are," he rasped.

"So, you didn't set up the note like that to fool me?"

## 38

## ACE

"Of course I did," I growled.

A mischievous grin spread across her face. "Just to prove how grateful I am," she began in a sexy whisper, "I won't even ask for a promotion for what I'm about to do."

I knew a lopsided smile meant trouble when the person wearing it was Stella Copeland.

She dropped to her knees, her hands back on my belt.

"That's what I call a good assistant," I praised, knowing exactly where this was going, but my smile was stolen from my lips by a groan. No woman had ever made me feel the kinds of things that Stella could invoke in me.

Within seconds, she did something fantastic with her tongue, and my knees almost buckled.

"Fuck," I moaned, cupping both her cheeks and caressing them tenderly while pushing in and out of her. "Holy fuck."

She held onto my thighs and dug her nails into my skin and did the tongue thing again.

Holy fuck.

*Holy fuck.*

"Baby," I groaned, my thumbs stroking her cheeks, "I'm going to—"

I pulled away from her right at the moment that I most desperately did not want to.

"Open your mouth. Wider. Stick your tongue out."

And sweet paradise, if she didn't obey right away.

A second later, I orgasmed harder than I ever had. I moaned as more of my come jetted out of my cock, all over her sweet small tongue, and into her mouth.

"Swallow…atta fucking girl." Fuck… Once I was done, I stared down at the most beautiful face. My Stella.

Picking her up, I set her on my desk and spread her legs wide. My lips crashed against her sweet pussy. It was a good thing she wasn't wearing any underwear, because I would have torn them off to get to her if she had been.

"The only man's name you're going to scream from now on is mine."

A few moments later, that's exactly what she did.

## 39

## STELLA

It had been two days since I'd helped Ace "prepare" for his presentation and "unwind" thereafter. We'd spent the days that followed making out—and possibly hooking up—in his office (on his desk), the copy room (on the color copy machine), the archive room (behind the third shelf), the executive boardroom (yep, there's that too), and at my apartment (bed, clawfoot bathtub, on top of my *running* washing machine) every chance we got.

Bonnie took note of the fact I'd become something of a recluse and promptly invited me out for cocktails.

The restaurant she'd chosen was a small Italian-looking place with a charismatic waiter named Giovanni and a bunch of white tables nestled in a green and red garden. The sound of bees and other animals buzzing around the tiny flowers surrounding us was almost deafening, but it was a pleasant type of white noise that was comforting to me.

"He has a new car."

"Really?" she asked, disbelief coloring her words. "He got rid of his Lambo?"

"Yeah."

"What'd he get?"

"Well, so...he got another Lambo. But it's a *smaller* one. A much smaller one. At 393K, an almost ten times less costly reprieve." That was the wording the website had used.

"Sorry. Lambo is Lambo. Like banana is banana. Like douche is douche."

"I guess," I agreed, albeit begrudgingly.

Over the next few minutes, I brought Bonnie up to speed about all that had happened after having been caught snooping, and all the sex—the mind-blowing incredibly, fiery-*hot* sex—that had followed, all around the company and my apartment.

Bonnie just frowned. "So, you're dating him now?" she asked, clearly unimpressed, sucking her bright-red strawberry daiquiri through a bamboo straw. Bonnie and I bonded over all things strawberry.

"I think so," I replied. I'd ordered a "Frullato alla fragola," a true strawberry heaven of a milkshake. It was sweet and creamy, and it had a real strawberry on top. "I asked him whether we were in a relationship, and—"

"Let me guess, he said no?"

"—and he said yes. He just wants to keep it quiet for a while. I guess he doesn't want to face the drama that will ensue when people find out just yet. I mean, people at the office would gossip. Let's not even start with Damon. It's such an important time for Windsor Architects. Ace just needs to invest all his energy in the company right now."

"Nope. That's a major red flag if you ask me," she said, taking another sip, confirming Jay's words. "Keeping things quiet means *no*." A lazy bee buzzed between us, drunk on the late-spring sun. She sighed when she saw my wide eyes. "But, I'm happy for you...as long as you're happy."

"I am happy." I slurped at my heavenly milkshake and then promptly tore up the white paper straw sleeve into a bunch of small pieces. They fell onto the table like snowflakes. "And I'm worried." The words just burst out of my mouth. "I'm starting to think all I am to him is a 'dirty little secret.' I mean, he's never even invited me over to his place. What if I'm just a plaything, a fling, a little distraction at work—"

"Hold on. First: You're wifey material, and if Ace is as smart as you say he is, he should know that, right? If not, *screw* him." Bonnie clicked her tongue at me. "But yeah, I'm worried too. What if you're his side chick?"

"No. Bonnie. Stop. I'm sure he's single."

"Okay, if you say so..." she said. "In that case, don't listen to me. Ignore the past. Ignore the facts. Ignore the red flags. Just enjoy it."

"But I want more than just a fling," I sniffed, averting my gaze to avoid having to make eye contact with her. "I want him to love me."

## 40

# DAMON

*Thursday*

I had two things to do: talk to Stella, talk to Ace—in that exact order.

"What's with your face?" I asked my sister after I sat down.

"Nothing. What do you mean?"

"You look guilty."

"I do *not*." Stella was trotting between her apartment's modest kitchen and the living room, ferrying around a variety of snacks and a pot of tea she'd prepared for us.

"Try this," she said, pouring a crisp-looking brown liquid from the teapot's spout. It swirled around in my teacup like a whirlpool stirred up by a tempest as she handed it to me. "It's vanilla chai. Did you know chai means tea?"

She was trying to change the subject.

"Everybody knows that," I replied, taking a sip. It was sickly sweet. "How much sugar did you put in this?"

"Not enough." Stella sat down on the couch next to me and crossed her legs at the ankle. She looked out of the window and adjusted her glasses. "But I suppose you didn't just come for the tea."

"Can't a brother visit his sister without having an ulterior motive?" I teased her. I knew she knew that I was onto her.

"Not when that brother is you," she replied. "I love you, D, but I think you've been in my apartment only a handful of times since I moved here."

"I'll make a point of visiting more often." I took another sip of my sickly-sweet tea. Stella's apartment always smelled like baked goods, vanilla, citrus, and lavender. I wondered if it was a scent she cultivated purposely, or whether it was merely the result of her baking attempts. "However, you're right. I didn't just come to have tea with you."

"See? I *knew* it." She attempted a grin, but I wasn't wrong, there definitely was a guilty look on her face, now more than before. She was fully aware that I knew she was hiding something. Just like when we were kids and she had stolen an apple from the neighbor's tree—which she'd felt awful about, and had taken the apple back the next day. "I've come to find out whether you've learned anything about Ace and Ecclestone."

"Would you like a chocolate chip cookie?" she asked, reaching forward to scoop one up off the silver tray full of snacks she'd put down on her coffee table.

"No, thank you." I raised one of my palms to emphasize the sentiment.

"How about a shortbread cookie then?"

"I'm not hungry," I said. "In fact, I've got to run soon. So, if you could tell me what you've learned, I'll get out of your way."

"Well, you've got to try a caramel swirl, whether you're hungry or not." She wrapped her fingers around a frosted pastry and pointed it at me. "I made these yesterday evening, and I think they're my best batch yet."

"Stella. Just tell me whether you've learned anything useful. I'm sure your baking is delicious, but I'm here to hear how your 'intel-gathering mission' is going."

"Why do you always have to be so impatient?" she asked, frowning at me. "I'm trying to be nice to you. I worked really hard on these cookies."

I could see that I'd pissed her off. "First, you show up uninvited, complain about the sweetness of my tea, and then you question me like I'm a suspect and you're a cop. How is that fair?"

"I don't appreciate that you're avoiding the question," I said, careful to keep my temper under control. "With all the effort you're putting into it, the question is no longer *whether*, but *what* you're hiding from me."

"You want an answer? Fine. Here's what I think: you're a terrible friend. An absolutely horrible friend! A supreme donkey."

"A supreme donkey?"

"Yeah. What kind of person asks their sister to snoop on their best friend?"

"Stella, we've been over this. You were onboard with helping the guys and me keep an eye on him." I paused, watching her. She could barely look at me. "Did something happen between you and Ace?"

She stiffened. "What do you mean?"

"What's up with the sudden rage? That's what I mean. Are you sleeping with him?"

"I'll tell you what's up," she said, whipping the snack tray from the table and carrying it back to the kitchen. She returned and took the cup of sickly-sweet tea from my hands. "I've learned nothing about Ace other than that he's a good person—a better person than I am...and you are, you bet! I, at least, feel horrible about even agreeing to help you. And now, you've overstayed your welcome."

I got up off the couch and shook my head. "You're throwing me out?"

"You're dang right I am." She put my teacup down on the coffee table, stomped over to her front door, and swung it open. "Goodbye, Damon."

I sighed. "I mean well, Chicken Little. Ace isn't looking for a relationship, trust me, he's made that point clear to me and the guys many times. I can't blame him. No man would jump from one serious relationship to the next. I mean, think about it." Her demeanor didn't change. Damn, she was stubborn. "Just...just be careful. I don't want you to get hurt."

"Goodbye, Damon," she repeated.

"Bye, sis," I grumbled as I strode through the front door. "I'll see you at Frosty's this weekend?" Frosty Sugar Rush at Prospect Park West in

Brooklyn was our favorite ice cream place. According to Stella, they had the best strawberry ice cream on the planet, and so we'd made it something of a tradition to meet there once or twice per month.

She slammed the door closed behind me. Jesus Christ. A blonde woman wearing an olive-green yoga outfit shuffled past me in the hallway, grinning at me like I was some cheating high school kid kicked out by his mad girlfriend. My rage level multiplied, and all the feelings of unrest I'd kept reined in while talking to Stella came rearing up, but I knew when to stop.

Pushing her would only lead to her pulling even farther away. Instead, I decided to follow my plan. Time to direct my irritation toward the person who was really the cause of it: Ace.

∼

I kicked down. I knew where he lived from having dropped him off several times after a night out, but I'd never been inside his apartment before. It was a fact that I'd never found strange before, knowing he had just moved his sister in with her child. There was just enough time to think about what I'd say to him when I got there. I knew the Upper East Side like the back of my hand and found his place without any problems. The street running past his apartment building was buzzing with life: Pedestrians marched up and down along the sidewalk, and the cars flowed over the asphalt like water. I parallel parked across from the building's entrance, got off my motorcycle, and waited for the street to quiet down. As soon as there was a lull in the number of cars rushing past, I crossed the street and strode through the apartment building's stately wooden door.

I didn't know if he was at home, still, I wasn't planning on announcing my presence. The security guy remembered my face (thanks to a memorable evening where I'd been dragging Ace to the elevator under his eyes) and let me up without double-checking with Ace. Good. It also meant he was home.

Ace lived in the penthouse. There was only one door leading off to the 12th floor's round hallway: Ace's front door. I took another deep breath, trying to calm the frustration that was still unfurling in my stomach like a pissed-off snake, and strode over to it.

I knocked and waited.

Someone shuffled toward the door from the other side and peered through the peephole. I recognized Ace's light-blue eye staring out at me.

"Damon?" His door beeped electronically as he unlocked its electromagnetic lock. He opened it and peeked out. "It's really not a good time."

"I really need to talk to you," I said.

I heard Ace muttering something under his breath.

"Let me in," I insisted. "It won't take long."

He slipped through the door and closed it behind him, preventing me from catching even the slightest glimpse of the inside of his apartment. What the hell?

"We can talk out here."

"Sure." I didn't really care what Ace was hiding in his apartment—unless it was a chick.

"Speak your piece."

"I'll get right to the point: Are you fucking my sister? I just saw her, and she's not... Well, she doesn't seem like her usual self."

"That's a weird assumption to make," he rumbled. "Maybe she's just having a bad day."

"She was fine until I mentioned you. So, be honest with me. It's the least you can do." The irony of it all didn't escape me: I hadn't been completely honest with Ace myself and was now urging him to tell me the truth. But here and now, it was more important than the merger. It was about family, about my little sister. "Are you and Stella fooling around?"

He stared at me. His face was entirely expressionless, but I knew he was thinking about how to respond to my line of questioning. We'd been friends long enough that nothing either of us could do would be unpredictable to the other.

He leaned against the hallway's blindingly white wall and crossed his arms. "Why did you mention me?" he asked.

For the first time in years, my heart stopped beating—out of distrust, not out of shock. "That's not the point." I stepped closer to him and put my hand on his shoulder. "Tell me."

He shook my hand from his shoulder and grimaced. "Does Stella know you're here?"

"No, she doesn't," I said seriously and narrowed my eyes as if that would allow me to see inside his stubborn head. "For the last time. Are you fucking my sister? Are you stringing her along? Don't lie to me."

There was a long pause. "Damon," he finally said, nodding solemnly. A sound came from inside his apartment. "I gotta go."

"Why? Are you hiding a chick in there?"

"What the fuck?" He shook his head. "Are you high? My sister is staying with me, and her baby is sleeping. Enough of the interrogation, Damon. I have a workload to manage, tasks to complete, and a deadline to meet. Go home."

"Wait. How are the acquisition papers coming along?"

"Good. We got the last shipment from the San Francisco archive and are soon going to wrap things up. You'll have the information on your desk as planned: in two weeks, Monday first thing."

"Fine," I said. "I'll see you around then. Mr. Humphries is waiting for it. Don't be late or the deal is off."

"Sure," he said.

With that, he slipped back into his apartment and closed the door behind him.

There was nothing I could do about the fact he hadn't given me a real answer to either question. Damn slick *bastard*.

I walked back toward the elevator and whipped my cell out of my pants' pocket mid-stride. I started dialing Miles's number just as the empty elevator arrived.

"Damon, is everything okay?" Miles's crisp voice echoed through my phone's speaker as I stepped inside and pressed the button.

"No," I said as the elevator started descending. "I think Ace is screwing my sister."

"*Hell* no. Ace wouldn't do that," he said. I could tell he was trying to sound as reassuring as possible.

"Dude. I don't care if he does, we're all fucking adults. If they like each other, I can't and won't stop them. What I dislike is the shadiness."

"Look who's talking. You tried to hide your feelings for Aria from us too."

"What the hell are you talking about? I wasn't trying to hide shit. Also, my situation was completely different."

"Yeah? What was so different about it?"

"For one, I hadn't just come out of a serious relationship, plus, I had *three* people on my ass. Do I need to remind you that you, Oliver, and your father weren't exactly fans of me being involved with Aria? You all wanted to chew me up for breakfast. I'm one guy here. It pisses me off that he just doesn't come straight out with it. Makes me think I'm spot on with my hypothesis on him and Ecclestone too."

"Okay, fair. But keep in mind that you, Oliver, and I learned our lesson the hard way when you started dating *our* baby sister. At that time, Ace was still in San Francisco, about to tie the knot."

"So?"

"He has no idea how all that went down. He has no clue how to act. It's his first rodeo, so give him a fucking break. I mean, even if there was something between the two—I'm sure there isn't—you still can't blame him for thinking you'd go berserk on him. It's only human. So chill. And again, you're just seeing things. If I remember correctly, Stella doesn't even like him."

"Then explain to me why she suddenly decided that it goes against her moral compass to keep an eye on him when I went to see her just now?"

"Maybe she's just a better person than we are, bro." He laughed loudly. "She's always been fucking nicer than we are, anyway."

"No, this is more than that," I replied. "I know her."

"Perhaps not as well as Ace knows her—if you know what I mean," he teased and chuckled mischievously. "Just kidding. Relax, I didn't mean to offend you. You make it way too easy, bro, ha-ha. Anyway, do you think we should involve Harris? I know we talked about this, but I don't see how else we're going to get the information we need if Stella isn't willing to help us anymore."

"No, it's too risky. Your dad will find out if we do. You know that. We can't take that chance. Also, Ace is sending us his paperwork in two weeks."

"So, what are we going to do until then?"

"I don't know. Not yet, anyway," I rumbled.

"I've got a great idea. How about a beer? As in, right now."

"Sure. See you in twenty."

We ended the call just as I stepped out of the elevator. There was only one place I wanted to be: Talia's. The best plans were always hatched over a cold lager, or better, a bourbon, and I needed a good one.

## 41

## ACE

*Fuck.* As soon as I closed the door, I pulled a black jacket over my shoulders and turned to face my sister, Tilly.

"I'm heading out," I announced.

She was stirring sizzling onions around a pan. Baby Teddy was sound asleep in his room. Luckily, we hadn't woken him. His T-rex-themed baby mobile was quietly playing its happy tune. A feeling of warmth filled the apartment. It was the feeling of home.

"Where are you going so late?" she asked, not looking up. "Work? All you do is work, work, work." She scooped up a piece of onion with the wooden spoon in her hand, blew on it, and popped it into her mouth. With a "yum" face, she turned and looked at me. "And who was just at the door? You look like you've seen a ghost."

It hadn't been more than two minutes since Damon had had the audacity to come up to my apartment to accuse me of sleeping with his sister—just like that. He wasn't wrong, of course, because I *was* sleeping with his sister (and quite happily so)—but in no way was I going to pick a fight with him, even though I was still fucking mad at the shit he'd pulled. What the hell was wrong with him, sending her to dig through my stuff? But *damn*, that guy had a hell of a Spidey-sense.

This was my plan: Rush out and inform Stella that Damon was fucking onto us. She needed to know as quickly as possible. Fuck knew what the guy would do when he found out how I felt about her.

Somehow, it was all fucked up.

But I had to tread twice as carefully. I would not put her on the line.

"*Ace?*" My sister snapped her fingers at me, and the sound pulled me right back from my thoughts. The onions were still sizzling, the mobile was still playing its song, and I was more certain than ever before that I was willing to cross oceans for Stella Copeland.

"Sorry," I said. "Lost my train of thought there. I got things I need to get to."

"Oh, *really*?"

I wasn't ready to tell her about my relationship with Stella just yet. Not before I had figured all this shit out. Tilly had enough on her plate now that little Teddy was here.

"What things?" she pressed. "Work?"

"I'll tell you later. But I won't be gone long."

"You better," she said excitedly as I hurried to the front door. "Don't forget. You know I have my doc appointment later this evening, and you need to watch Teddy." She'd made the evening appointment so as to not interfere with my work schedule.

"I'll be here. Be safe while I'm away."

"I promise I won't open the door for strangers. Unless they're hot. Or tattooed. Or drive a motorcycle. You can bet your ass I'm opening the door to them." She laughed and rolled her eyes.

The elevator doors slid open and I stepped inside. It jolted and then started descending. There was something unnerving about making the journey to Stella's apartment, especially not knowing what her reaction would be when she heard that her brother had shown up at my front door to question me about us. Sure, I could have called, but I wanted—*needed*—to see her face to face.

The elevator doors *whooshed* open, and I headed straight to my black motorcycle. In no time, I put on my helmet and kicked down.

. . .

An eternity passed between hauling ass through the streets and parking in front of Stella's apartment building. I rushed to her front door and knocked on it like someone trying to outrun a zombie attack, or something equally dramatic.

She opened it with the same sense of urgency, wearing a beautiful crimson dress. Her hair was all over the place. Her face lit up as she realized it was me. Then her eyes grew wide, and she attempted to straighten some of her messy hair strands, only to realize she was wearing glasses. She quickly removed them, hiding them behind her back.

"Ace!" Her eyes were red and puffy. I could tell she had been crying. This had to be Damon's doing, I had no doubt.

"Hey, hey. You all right?"

"Yeah...fine. Bad hair day. Don't look," she sniffed. "What are you doing here?"

"I missed you." I smiled, hoping to hide my internal turmoil and to cheer her up at the same time.

"That's so sweet. Well, come in. It's not like I can turn you away now."

I stepped past her. "Would you want to?"

"No," she replied, closing the door behind me and putting the glasses she had just hidden from me on the side table. I wrapped my arms around her waist and pulled her against me. She stared up at me.

"Good." I softly kissed her lips. "I have something to tell you though."

"Uh-oh, that doesn't sound good." She grimaced and led me over to her couch. We sat down next to each other, and she stared into my eyes, rubbing at her forearm and biting her lower lip.

"Go ahead, tell me," she whispered.

"Okay, but you have to promise me that you won't freak out."

"I can't promise that, and now you're just making me nervous."

"All right," I said. "Your brother was just at my apartment. He showed up to ask me if we're seeing each other."

"Oh." She gulped. The color drained from her face. "What did you tell him?"

"Basically nothing," I said. "You and I said we were going to keep this thing quiet for a while."

"We did," she whispered, bobbing her head up and down. "But we can't keep it a secret forever."

"I know. It's not my plan to keep it a secret forever." I picked up her hand from her lap and kissed it. "But I do need to ask you to keep it a secret just a little while longer."

"I don't understand," she said, her lower lip trembling. "Who are we even hiding this whole thing from? I'm pretty sure that Damon already knows, considering he has asked both of us about it already."

"It's not just about Damon though," I replied. "There are other factors. But we've thrown your brother off our trail. Hopefully he'll leave it be, at least for a while."

"I doubt it. My brother isn't the kind of person who just lets things go, you know?"

"I do, trust me. I know him better than most."

"You didn't tell him that you know he sent me to snoop on you, did you? Because that would be opening a whole different can of worms."

"I didn't," I murmured softly, caressing her long hair. "Of course I didn't." I leaned in and kissed her furrowed brow, hoping to chase her fears away.

"He wouldn't be happy to find out," she said sadly. "I know we need to tell him eventually. He'll be so angry at me." She shook her head, got up off the couch, and sauntered into her small kitchen. "Would you like some chai? Maybe some matcha tea? I think I need some."

"Do you have whiskey?" I craned my neck to watch her as she made her way over to her stainless-steel kettle. She lifted it up and walked over to the tap to fill it. I couldn't help but be mesmerized by the swaying of her hips. It was like all the light in the room bent around corners and crevices to wrap itself around her beautiful body. Each curve of it was like the most breathtaking landscape you could possibly imagine, an enchanting scenery upon which the sun always rose, but never set.

"I have wine?" she offered, her words sounding more like a question than a statement. I watched her smiling over her shoulder at me. Her face was almost enough to stop my heart in its tracks. I didn't believe in magic, but I knew she had cast some kind of spell on me.

"What kind of wine?" I asked, trying not to reveal how taken aback I was by her beauty.

"They're in a box in the closet. Mooncake Vineyards...I think," she said. "Sorry, let me go find it, I don't remember."

I shook my head. "Wait. No, thank you. I'll have some tea."

"Coming right up," she said as the scent of tea filled the apartment, swirling into the living room like eddies of water. She returned carrying two cups and handed the larger one to me. "I hope I put enough sugar in it." As she leaned forward to give it to me, her enticing breasts threatened to pop out of the neckline of her dress. I didn't avert my gaze, because why would I? I was already imagining tearing her crimson dress right off.

"Thanks, babe."

"Did you know that chai means tea?"

"I didn't. Not much of a tea drinker."

She sat down again and smiled at me. She knew perfectly well I was thinking less about the tea and more about her beautiful breasts and how they felt under my hands. "Try it."

"All right." I took a sip of my tea, surprised at the pleasant nutty taste. It was sweet, but not overly sweet. "This is pretty damn good."

"Right? Damon gave it to me as a gift for my last birthday. He imported about four pounds of the matcha from Japan after I told him how much I loved it."

"Hmm," I hummed. "He's not always an asshole."

"No, he's not," she agreed. "I know he loves me very much." She took a drink of her matcha and stared contemplatively at a painting of colorful birds sitting on a tree branch, hanging on the wall across from us. After a moment of silence, she shifted her weight around nervously. "Can I ask you something? It's something I've been meaning to ask for a while, but the opportunity just never presented itself." Her chest heaved as nervous breath after nervous breath passed through her lungs.

I took another sip of my matcha.

## 42

## ACE

"Ask away," I said, curious as to what she wanted to know.

"Okay, but don't freak out when I do." She took a deep breath and put her hands on her lap. "What happened between you and Allison? Why didn't you two work out?"

Not what I expected. I was slightly taken aback.

Although, I supposed she had the right to know. "She left me." I knew, of course, that Stella would follow up, but that was all I could say about Allison.

"Oh." She gulped and looked away. "Why?"

I put my cup down on the small table in front of us. "She fell in love with somebody else."

Stella inhaled sharply and went pale. "Oh, my gosh. I assumed—"

"It's okay." I waved my hand dismissively. "You didn't know, and I should have told you earlier. I found out after she accidentally sent me a text meant for him. It was...explicit, to say the least."

She emptied her teacup, lowered her head, and put her hand over her mouth. "Oh, heavens. I'm so *sorry*. That's so bad, it must have been really hard for you."

"I thought she was the one. The media made our breakup into a public spectacle, the asshats. I'm glad the reason for it never got out—it would've humiliated both of us. Some private matters are best left private." I paused and let out a breath. "Worst thing, I didn't see it coming. I'm not sure who to be more pissed at, her or myself. I trusted her with my whole heart. I should have fucking seen it coming."

"It's not a character flaw to see the best in people," she said softly after a moment of consideration. "Ace, I feel bad about admitting this, but I read an article online about your breakup. The article didn't mention the reason, but it had a photo of the two of you standing on a beach together in it."

"Oh, yeah? Sounds like one of our engagement photos. We had them taken on a beach in Zanzibar during a vacation."

"She is beautiful though. Much prettier, *and* blonder, *and* skinnier than I—"

"Don't compare yourself to her," I said, shaking my head, somewhat amused. Women. Grown real-ass men didn't care about any of that shit.

She just looked at me.

"What?" I asked. "You've never caught me staring?" I winked at her.

"Well..." She shrugged softly.

Maybe I hadn't told her, but she was absolutely spectacular. Even as she sat next to me on the couch, I couldn't stop myself from stealing glimpses of her. Her beautiful face. Her stunning eyes. Her gorgeous curves. Her thighs. They were full and round, and I wanted to wrap them around my head. She was real.

"You're the most beautiful woman in the world," I said, meaning every word. "I also like your glasses—they look cute on you. No need to hide them."

"You don't have to say that." She blushed and wrung her hands together. "I know I'm not *that* beautiful, but I have other qualities—"

"Stella, shut up." I interrupted her. I put my arm around her and pulled her closer to me until we were tangled together on the couch. "You're nothing short of a goddess. It's insane that you don't see that. My ex-fiancée doesn't have anything on you. No other woman does."

With sparkly eyes, she looked up at me and kissed my stubbly chin —the spot she liked to kiss. I hadn't shaved that morning like I usually did, and my beard was longer than usual.

"You make me blush," she whispered.

"I love to make you blush," I rumbled.

Hooking a finger under her chin, I tilted her face and kissed her. Her lips tasted like matcha and vanilla, and I lost myself in the tenderness of her skin. I could feel the urge to do *very* naughty things to her rising inside me, but I didn't want to interrupt the moment's sweetness. My lips brushed along hers, over her cheeks, making her giggle a little because she was ticklish, and I muttered in a low voice, "It's not just your breathtaking exterior that's captured me. You're everything that's right with the world. Because you don't consider yourself as something better. You're unbelievably kind to everyone around you, and the most empathetic person I've ever met. You're funny and witty, and smart. You see the world with your heart, and you go the extra mile for what you believe in and for the people that mean the most to you. You always give your best. Every inch of you is perfection personified, and best of all—" I paused for dramatic effect. "You know what's best of all?"

"No, what?" It was barely a whisper. Her eyes were filled with tears.

"Best of all—" I locked eyes with her. "You're all *mine*," I practically growled, kissing her again, harder this time.

Stella laughed, and she kissed me back feverishly, leaning into me, letting me feel her longing. Her breasts bore into my chest, and her hips wiggled against mine. She was so innocent and sweet. Me? I was the carnivorous animal about to devour its prey. I put my hands around her waist and encouraged her with slow pushing and pulling motions to writhe against me. It was hot. I was getting into it. My dick was getting into it. The thought of pushing myself into her depths was all I could think of. My hands ran over her thighs, pushing her dress up with them.

"Let's go to my room," Stella practically purred, suddenly pushing herself away from me and getting up. She extended her dainty hand toward me. I took it and allowed her to lead me to her bed. She flung herself down onto it back first and gestured with a funny head motion for me to join her.

All right.

Wait.

*Fuck.*

"I don't have protection with me," I said, cursing myself. "My wallet is at home. Forgot my phone and everything in my rush to come here."

"What makes you think you'll need any? I'm just inviting you to lie down next to me."

"Oh, really? That's all you wanna do?" I winked, pulling my shirt from the back over my head, throwing it somewhere across the room. Bare-chested and on all fours, I crawled across the bed toward her and up over her body until I was towering over her. I pinned her arms under mine and kissed her. "You have nothing else in mind?"

"I...didn't...not until you got on top of me." She laughed, trying to wriggle free from my grasp in a weak-ass attempt, which I eventually allowed, only to undress her, of course.

Pulling her toward me, I slid her crimson dress over her head. She was wearing a lacy white bra under it. I circled my hands around her to unlatch the clasp.

"Oh," she gasped as I threw it across the room to the pile of clothes I had created. "How am I supposed to resist you?"

"You're not. Stop trying." When I pushed her back down and ran my fingers to her panties, she started squirming under me like I was tickling her.

"Stop wiggling around," I playfully scolded her. When she didn't comply, I started kissing her nipples. That didn't make her lie still either.

"I'm ticklish." She giggled.

"I know," I rumbled.

Before I could stop her from squirming, or before I could take her panties off, she'd reached down and loosened my belt. Her hands were all over me. Obviously, she was in a hurry to have me inside of her, and I could work with that. Stella ran her hands down my back, let them slide past my hips, and started fiddling with my belt buckle.

"You're so eager for my cock, aren't you?"

She smiled, busy undoing my button and—*clearly*—I wasn't going to stop her. Her dainty hand slid into my underwear and took hold of my shaft.

*Fuuuuck.*

"I sense a shift of power," Stella proclaimed in a sagely accent. Masterfully, she maneuvered her hand around, leaving me stuck in an erotic paralysis. I wouldn't—or rather, couldn't—move for fear that she'd stop. "I think *I'll* be the one making demands from now on," she announced.

All right.

"Fucking fine by me." I gnashed my teeth and nodded in agreement.

"Hmm. Does Mr. CEO like it when I'm in charge? Does Mr. Grumpilicious enjoy giving up control?" she teased, then wrapped one of her arms around my shoulders, and I allowed her to roll over so she was on top of me. Proving herself a true master multi-tasker, her other hand never left its post.

"Yeah, baby," I rumbled deeply.

Her sweet mandarin scent hung over me like a cloud.

"Call me 'boss.'" She giggled, increasing the intensity of her touch.

I frowned at her and groaned. My dick was hard as fuck. She released her grip and started sliding her hand back up toward my stomach.

"No. Wait," I grumbled. "I'll call you anything you like. You don't stop."

She grinned and then slid down until she was face-to-face with the seam of my pants. She yanked them down and gasped, giving my shaft the softest lick. "Is all this for me?"

More blood rushed downward. "It's definitely not for anyone else," I replied, not even trying to control myself. Her breath felt hot and sticky against my skin.

"Good. That's what I want to hear. Now, I'm only going to say this one more time," she said as she threatened to place her soft lips exactly where I wanted her to put them. "Call me 'boss.'"

I didn't even hesitate for a second. "Yes, boss," I groaned, and laughed.

"Good boy."

I laughed again. Her mouth felt hot and heavenly as she closed it around me. At this point, I'd fucking call her anything. I'd fucking let her do or say anything. A groan escaped my lips and my eyes fell closed.

She sucked me like a lollipop until I knew I couldn't last another five seconds.

Four. Three.

Two.

Just when I couldn't stand it anymore, she pulled away from me, denying me my release.

"You're playing with fire," I grumbled.

Her eyes sparkled mischievously, and she raised herself again until she was staring right into my eyes.

"Who's your boss?" she asked, pushing it, smiling impudently.

I closed my eyes, letting my head fall back.

There, I took a deep breath, and then effortlessly flipped her onto her back so I was on top again.

She let out a loud squeak. Her eyes widened, and her mouth gaped open in surprise. In one fluid motion, I pulled her panties down. She wasn't expecting that. "If anyone's the boss here, it's me," I growled.

"Ace," she whimpered, biting at her lower lip.

"You know what I'm about to do to you." I nodded before lowering myself onto her, and sliding my tip in. "You want this, baby? You want my cock inside of you?"

She gasped. "Oh, so, *so* badly."

"Yeah?" My hips pushed against hers as I bore down into her, giving her what we both wanted.

Her eyes widened further as I slid into her, deep.

I pulled out slowly, and thrust back in.

Delicious moans escaped Stella's lips.

I truly believed a good boss should be able to take direction as well as give it—at least to a certain degree—like in this very instance, and let's just say, I embodied that belief fully. My fingers rubbed her wet little clit while our hips met each other over and over again until I could feel that we both were about to edge off the cliff. I tried to withdraw from her by pulling away, but she wrapped her arms around my waist and pulled me closer.

"We don't have protection," I growled, trying to pull away again. "I can't hold on much longer—"

"We should be fine," she moaned into my ear. She didn't release her grip on me for a second.

"We don't want a kid."

"Right. I mean, I do want one eventually," she clarified breathlessly, "but not now, of course. It's my infertile days," she explained.

There was no going back now.

I pushed back in.

"Ohhhh...."

Three, two, *one*.

*Fuuuck.*

She came in my arms. The orgasm exploded around her. Her warm heat squeezed and pumped me, while I released all my manly possessions into her. This was heaven. This was paradise.

This was all I wanted.

We flopped down next to each other, both groaning and twitching as the waves of pleasure started subsiding. "Come closer," I muttered and patted my chest with my right hand.

She rolled over, rested her head on my chest, and smiled up at me. "That was amazing." Stella was still breathless.

"You're amazing," I replied, kissing the top of her head and wrapping my arms around her.

"So, who's the boss?" she asked.

"Me." *Obviously.*

"Not in this bedroom you're not." She laughed.

"Sorry, baby girl. I'm the boss anywhere, and everywhere, and this bedroom is no exception. It's my rules, or nobody's. That clear? Or you want me to show you again?"

"Well..." She giggled.

The clock on her bedside table caught my eye.

Shit.

*Shit. Shit. Shit.*

I'd been here for two and a half hours, I realized. God damnit. I'd promised Tilly I'd watch Teddy while she was at her checkup.

I pulled out from under Stella's arm and sat upright. "Sorry, but I have to leave."

"But...but...you just said...I thought it was amazing."

"It *was* amazing. You're amazing. I promise if I hadn't made prior plans, I would stay."

Stella sat upright too, and glared at me. I could see an amalgamation of anger and disappointment swirling around in her eyes.

"Really?" she asked. "Because that sounds like a flimsy excuse for running."

"It's not, I promise." I stood up and started gathering our clothes from the floor. Damn, why did I forget my cell? My sister had gotten a new number after moving back from California, and I didn't have it memorized. I got dressed and walked over to kiss Stella. She was still sitting on the bed, but turned her head away from me when I leaned toward her. "Stella, I promise. I'm not looking for an excuse to leave, I just promised my si—"

"It's okay." She interrupted me. I could see from the expression on her face that it wasn't, but I didn't know how to make her believe me. She didn't want to hear my explanation.

"If you don't want to hear my reason, you just have to learn to trust me. Like I've had to learn to trust you."

"*Right*. I'll let you out." She slipped off the bed, pulled a robe on, and led me out of her bedroom.

"I'll see you tomorrow," she said. She tried to smile, but I could tell it wasn't heartfelt.

She closed the door, and I found myself standing in the hallway in front of her apartment alone.

# 43

## STELLA

*A* minute or two passed before I finally heard Ace walk down the hallway, heading away from my front door. Once I was sure he was gone, I leaned my back against it, sank to the floor, and dissolved into tears.

I had been right all along.

I was nothing but his dirty little secret. Bonnie had been right. Damon had warned me too. As had Jay. Why had I ever thought a man like Ace would commit to a girl like me?

I tried not to let my imagination run wild, but it wasn't long before I found myself wondering where Ace was now. *Probably in the company of whoever he really wanted to keep our relationship from*, I sulked. Maybe it was another woman. A beautiful, gorgeous, fit, and trim bombshell of a woman with blonde hair and soft blue eyes.

I shook myself out of my grim doubts and those awful little voices trying to bring me down. No, Ace wasn't a cheater. I knew that for a fact. More than likely, he was with the guys.

He just wasn't ready for a relationship with me. That thought stung. A lot. What it boiled down to was: He didn't have enough feelings for me.

Could I settle for what Ace was willing to give me? Over time, would he learn to really love me with all his heart if I just learned to wait? Patience had never been my forte, but I could learn if I had to. It was the idea of getting half of Ace's attention, half of his love, which tipped me over the edge. It would be synonymous with a slow, painful death. I saw myself hungering for his touch, and him shutting my apartment door behind him over and over again because something or someone else was more important than me.

Sobbing like my life was ending, I lifted my hands to my face and emptied my tears into them. I cried until I thought I'd tapped every ounce of moisture from my body. When I finally had no more tears left, I quietly got up and shuffled over to the corner of my living room where I'd set up my dedicated home office. My laptop's fan whirred as it came to life. I sat down behind it and wiggled the mouse until my bright screensaver lit up the room.

The Internet connection wasn't great today, and it took Instagram forever to load. Once it did, I typed Ace's name into the search bar and navigated to his profile. There hadn't been any recent activity on it. I knew he didn't think much of social media, or those who overindulged in it. Nevertheless, I started scrolling through his gallery. I stopped when I got to a photo of Oliver, Miles, Damon, and Ace standing huddled together around a campfire. They couldn't have been more than eighteen or nineteen years old. Ace sported a patchy beard, a testament to how long they'd been camping, but none of his friends had managed to achieve the same level of facial hair (except for Damon, but he didn't count).

Originally, my plan had simply been to longingly stare at a few pictures of the man who'd stolen my heart (because: masochist), but I soon found myself staring at a montage of photos that could only be described as a homage to Ace and Damon's friendship. They'd always been inseparable, despite Ace's "stopover" in San Francisco. Then there were more "homage" pics of Ace, Damon, Oliver, and Miles. All on their motorcycles, the four of them. They were practically brothers. They all were.

A realization hit me like a ton of bricks. The feelings I had for Ace—which, let's be honest here, he didn't really want—were doomed to break *my* heart (stupid fool that my heart was, I was practically shopping for wedding rings, while he was only in it for a friend-with-benefits situation). Not only would our relationship poison Ace and Damon's friendship, it would damage the bond between all of them.

If that weren't enough, all that combined would ruin the merger.

The merger, the one thing he, the workaholic with the impossible schedule, wanted and needed the most.

Even if Ace decided—for whatever crazy reason—that he did want a relationship with me, it still wouldn't be possible.

I couldn't be the reason why the life he'd worked so hard for fell through.

I might have been able to make peace with the fact that I'd never be more than a little fun to Ace, even if it hurt, but I couldn't reconcile myself with the thought of prying him and my brother and the guys apart. Especially not while I sat there, confronted with photographic evidence of their bond. In no way did I want to be the woman who was pressuring him into a relationship that he didn't really want or wasn't ready for, nor did I want to be the woman he had to give up his hopes, and dreams, and friendships for.

What it boiled down to—we weren't meant to be. It was a dead-end situation that would lead to heartbreak, for him and me both. I wouldn't stand in his way.

I knew exactly what I needed to do.

I knew what I *had* to do.

∼

The next morning, I woke up feeling the way I imagined I would if I were a soldier being sent off to war. A horrible sense of doom, fear, and trepidation filled my bedroom like helium filled a balloon, entirely and invisibly. You wouldn't know it was there, except if you came into contact with it, and boy, was it suffocating. Worst hair day ever. I know I've said it before, but there was no salvation this time.

Jay and I were both quiet as he ferried me off to work. He tried to start up a conversation once or twice, but eventually gave up. "I can tell there's something bothering you, love." I felt bad for not chatting with him like I usually did, but I was too busy planning my next move. But Jay understood, and the silence between us was a comfortable one, like the silence that lingered between old friends.

He dropped me off in front of Windsor Architects' office building. "You know, I'm here for you if you do want to talk about it."

"Thank you, Jay." I opened the cab door. "You're a good friend. I'll tell you all about it once I've had some time to process." I closed the door and smiled at him through the window.

He waved as he drove off. I returned the gesture and then staggered with heavier legs than ever up the stairs leading toward the building's front door. It was cloudy and humid. The sun didn't peek through the thick gray clouds for more than a second at a time, and when it did, it only did so to stir up the sticky heat that hung in the air like a question mark. The birds that usually sat on the branches of the tree were silent. I couldn't blame them. I wouldn't sing on a day like today either.

Even Glenda seemed less on edge than usual as I stepped through the large double doors.

"Good morning, Stella," she politely greeted me, lifting her head momentarily to watch me make my way across the foyer, likely surprised by my quieter-than-usual demeanor. "Are you okay? You seem a little reserved today."

"Good morning, Glenda," I greeted. "Yeah, no, of course I'm okay. How about you?"

"I'm fine. It's this damn heat. It makes me groggy," she replied. A small desk fan next to her keyboard did its best to stir up a cool breeze, but failed.

It did feel warmer here than usual. "It'll cool down once it rains. The weather report said that should be sometime tonight."

"We're all essentially living in hell until then," she said, dramatically placing the fan directly in front of her face.

"No air-conditioning today?" I asked, walking past her toward the elevator.

"They're busy doing maintenance on it. They said they'll only be done at noon, so I have to suffer until then."

"Maybe they'll surprise you and finish up before then."

"I wouldn't bet on it," she replied disheartingly.

"I'm sorry. I wish I could help."

"There's no need to apologize. You're not in charge of the maintenance schedule."

"I'm not," I agreed.

"But maybe you could suggest to Mr. Windsor that the A/C maintenance schedule should be based on the weather prediction," she said almost hopefully. "He seems to take your input seriously, or so I've heard."

I stopped in my tracks. "Who'd you hear that from?"

"Just around the office."

"Well, it's not true. I don't think he listens to me more than he listens to anyone else," I replied somberly. Glenda frowned. I couldn't tell what she was thinking, but I suspected she assumed I was just being modest. "I'll see you around."

I traveled up to the 8th floor with a single-minded determination. *It's better to rip off the Band-Aid*, I thought, recalling the picture of Ace, Damon, and the guys on their bikes I'd stumbled across the previous day. I was doing the right thing.

An instrumental version of Rod Stewart's "Maggie May" started playing through the small speaker mounted in one corner of the elevator.

I tugged at my formal black dress's hem to straighten it out and then pulled out my little hand mirror. My lipstick was a pale pink that matched the color of my eyeshadow, and I'd meticulously applied multiple layers of—waterproof—mascara that morning to ensure my eyelashes were extra fluttery. I can't explain why I felt the need to look my best for the occasion, but I did. Probably so I would at least feel pretty on the outside while I felt like crap on the inside.

*Ping.*

The doors slid open. Taking a deep breath, I stepped out

8th floor. The hallway leading to Ace's office was quiet, but I knew it wouldn't be for long. I had to hurry.

Heart beating against my chest, I made the short trip down the hallway to Ace's office door.

I took one last breath and knocked.

*Knock. Knock. Knock.*

"Come in," Ace grumbled sternly from the other side of the door.

My hand trembled as I reached out and wrapped my fingers around the handle. With a twist, it slowly swung open. The smell of Ace's manly cologne hung in the air as I stepped inside. He was seated behind his large desk at one side of the room, flipping through a stack of papers.

"Good morning," I said, and he looked up at me.

"There you are," he said as a relieved smile spread across his handsome face. "I was hoping I'd see you first thing this morning."

He stood up and made his way over to me. As he tried to wrap his muscular arms around me, I stepped away from him.

"Ace," I quietly said. My voice was barely more than a raspy whisper. "We need to talk."

His smile slipped from his face and inverted itself into a frown. "Sure. What's going on?" He took my hands in his and supportively squeezed them. "Are you okay?"

I gently pulled my hands from his grasp and put them at my side. "How did we end up here?"

"End up where?" he asked, arching a brow. His beautiful icy-blue eyes bore into mine. I knew he was trying to figure out what I was thinking. "Is this still about yesterday and my leaving?"

"We were never supposed to get involved with each other. We said we wouldn't. We knew we shouldn't."

"So this *is* still about yesterday."

"Yes...and no." My eyes fell to the floor.

"I thought you were enjoying spending time with me."

"I was, but that doesn't make it right." I still stared at the top of my shoes, unable to make eye contact with him. I was scared that if I did, I'd burst into tears, and crying in front of him was the last thing I wanted to do. "We're two totally different people. I'm...just me, and you're the 'Infamous Billionaire Ace Windsor.' Besides, this whole thing could have an even more devastating consequence."

"I'm not worried about Damon," Ace grumbled, as if he knew which direction I was heading.

He stepped closer to me.

I took another step back to keep the distance between us.

"We're different," I said.

"We have more in common than you think."

"My brother is your best friend. He has been since college. Of course you care about your friendship with him and the other guys, even if you won't admit it," I insisted.

"The other guys?"

"Well, yeah, they all were involved in this snooping thing, not just Damon. You don't want to say goodbye to the merger, I know you don't. And even if despite everything, the companies do merge, how sensible is the whole idea if there will only be arguments and fights between the top dogs?"

He shook his head. "Stella—"

"And we *are* different. For example, I'm the kind of person who wants to scream that I'm in a relationship with you from New York's rooftops, I want *everyone* to know it, and you're the kind of person who wants to keep me a secret."

"I don't want to keep you a secret. Stella, listen."

"No, you do," I said resolutely. "I've spent a lot of time thinking about this. Trust me, I've made up my mind. You don't feel the same way about me. We shouldn't be together. That's that."

"You can't be serious," he said.

"I'm done."

"I'm not," he said. "I won't let you go."

## 44

## STELLA

I gulped. "What?"

"You heard me. There's something between us. There always has been." He took another step toward me, and I took another step back. "I know you feel something for me," he added. "Why do you want to give up so easily?"

Okay, that was surprising, even shocking. I hadn't seen that coming, especially after what Damon had told me about him not wanting a relationship, but I couldn't let it deter me. I shouldn't forget that Ace's first instinct had been to keep our relationship hidden.

Besides, the outcome would still be the same. The outcome would still be a total disaster, for both him and me.

I needed to crush the dangerous hope he had just instilled in my heart. I knew if I let him touch me, I'd melt in his arms, and that was the last thing I wanted. "Yes, I have feelings for you too, I've made that more than clear." I said it as matter-of-factly and coldly as I could. What I really wanted to tell him was that I didn't just have feelings for him, that I loved him, but luckily, my brain was able to stop me. Instead, I said, "But that isn't enough."

He paused. This time, he didn't come closer. "No. You can't be sure about that."

"I'm sure. Can you trust me that this is for the best?" I said it with a hard expression.

He stared at me, not saying anything.

"I'd like us to still be friends," I added, and my heart knew he would hate that. Band-Aid, remember? I needed to not waver.

"I want you and me, I want what's between us, for fuck's sake," he said, his eyes on me, nearly breaking my resolve. But I refused to waver. Not now.

"You have to accept that I don't. And consider this my two weeks' notice." I fumbled around in my bag to retrieve the note. I walked to his desk and placed it in front of him.

A pause.

He shook his head, in a kind of a way that said, "This is getting better and better." He sat down, staring at the note, but not taking it into his hands.

To put it simply: I couldn't continue working here, it would only mess with my heart. It was important to me that I helped finish up the paperwork for the merger, but then it would be time to move on.

I reached into my bag. "And here is the car key back. It wouldn't be right to keep it." I placed it and the title next to my two weeks' notice.

"At least keep the car. You'll need it."

"I can't. I'm sorry."

He ran his hand through his hair, leaving it in a sexy mess. After about ten seconds that seemed like hours, he looked up at me. "I can't pretend I'm not saddened by this, but I'd do anything for you, including accepting this. If that's what you want." He paused, narrowing his eyes at me. "Is that what you want?"

"It is," I said, although it wasn't. My decision was entirely altruistic. If I had made it based on what my heart wanted, I would have been on his lap already, feeling his arms around me. "It will give us enough time to finish up the papers for the merger."

"Very well," he said coolly. "We have a meeting with Mr. Hardy and our IT team at 2 p.m. sharp to discuss the new scheduling software they have in mind for us. I'll see you then."

"I'll see you then." I turned to leave but hesitated once I got to the door's threshold.

Glancing over my shoulder, I faced him. I wanted to say something, but I couldn't find the words to express how I felt. Instead, I just nodded and left. His office door closed behind me as I walked down the hallway toward the elevator. No way could I just sit down in my office and go about my day. If only for a few moments, I needed to get away to take my mind off him, even though I didn't quite know where to go.

I summoned the elevator, still pondering my next move. Its doors opened with a loud *whoosh*, and I wanted to slip inside, but was stopped. A beautiful woman with blonde hair and a baby in her arms was trying to get out, but a toy dropped to the floor.

"Hang on, let me help." With one foot against the door so it wouldn't close, I picked up the soft toy.

"Thank you so much," she said, smiling brightly, putting the toy into her bag.

"You're welcome," I said in return, trying to hide my dishevelment. The baby in her arms caught my eye. "What a cute little baby," I added, waving goofily at the sleeping infant. "What's their name?"

"Teddy," she replied proudly. "He's almost two months old."

"He's the most adorable thing ever," I quietly cooed, careful not to disturb him. "Just look at that chubby little face."

"I might be biased, but I think so too." She laughed, her soft blue eyes shining. "Do you have any of your own?"

"Nuh-uh, no," I said, shaking my head.

She must have noticed the sadness on my face and quickly replied, "I'm sure yours will be even cuter someday. Hopefully they'll poop less too. This tiny dude is a poop *monster*." She smiled and walked past me toward the left hall, waving at me like an old friend saying goodbye.

"We can only hope." I smiled, waving back and trying not to let my emotions overwhelm me. I got into the elevator and pressed the button for the 1st floor. For a moment I wondered who the pretty young mother was. Maybe Mr. Hardy's young wife?

. . .

At the reception desk, Glenda was busy helping a rep with a query. I waited for him to leave in the direction she indicated before asking, "How's your day been going?"

"Too hot and too busy." She laughed. I hadn't seen her laugh often, but there was something contagious about it. Her mood appeared to have improved since I'd arrived at the office that morning, even though it was still warm, if not warmer. Maybe the cool drink in front of her had lifted her spirits. She took a sip and asked, "Hey, you didn't get a chance to make that maintenance schedule suggestion to Mr. Windsor, did you?"

"I'm so sorry. I didn't." Shoot. I totally forgot. "If it makes you feel any better, I'm this close to getting heat stroke too." I held my index finger parallel to my thumb with basically no room to demonstrate just how close I was.

"We should go on strike until the A/C is fixed," she joked, piling some documents in front of her into an orderly tower. "Then we'll see how much time they really need to fix it."

"That's a good idea." I smiled. A part of me really did like the idea.

"You know, Stella, I think you're pretty awesome. I know we've had our ups and downs—"

Oh. That was…unexpected. "No need to apologize."

"No, I should say sorry," she insisted. "I judged you too early. Mr. Windsor's previous assistant thought she was better than everyone else around here, spread tons of lies and rumors about everyone, especially about the CEO, and let's face it, nobody liked her—and when I heard you graduated from Princeton, I thought you'd be even worse. I think most of us did. You're not, though. No one around here has ever had a single bad word to say about you. We're all so glad you're here."

Oh. "Really?" It was welcome news after the morning I'd had.

"Really," she said, smiling kindly. "Now, not to be rude, but I have some calls to make. But we can have lunch together today, if you'd like?"

"That'd be nice." It was nice to know that I'd won over Glenda. It felt a bit like defeating Goliath—a female Goliath—and it seemed, unknown to me, my only pebble had been persistence. It made me happy to know why so many people had been reserved or had seemed cold in the beginning. I had thought they were reserved because of Ace's grumpy leading skills, not because of me and thinking I would follow in his former assistant's footsteps. Funny how it turned out to be so different from what I'd initially thought.

Glenda and I did end up having lunch that day. She told me about her three cats (Monkey, Saruman, and Fuzzy) and described each of them and their habits in detail. And it seemed, *nomen* really *est omen*. It was a pleasant distraction from the sad mess I felt my life had become.

Glenda must have enjoyed spending time with me, because we had lunch together again the next day. And the day after that, more and more ladies accompanied us, Mrs. Mills included.

∽

The following days, most of my time was spent perfecting the paperwork with Mrs. Mills. We were finally on top of things.

I still caught myself staring longingly at him during meetings or presentations, and I often imagined that I noticed him doing the same. His appearance was somewhat changed. Apart from looking handsome and professional as always, he seemed distraught, weary, almost unhappy—and I never saw him smile.

The following Friday, I placed the cleanly prepared merger files on Ace's desk for the information exchange. They contained information such as financials, company history, and client roster with the projects, neatly ordered by size and value, with color photos. Everything was perfectly prepared, ready for Ace to go over one last time before sending the big folder off to Damon.

Ace informed me that he had to leave for a short, unexpected business trip tonight to meet one of our clients, but he was planning to take a last look and hand the folder to Damon once he returned on Monday morning, meeting the deadline.

From there, the acquisition could go into the valuation and offer stage.

My work was done.

Ace thanked me and jumped right back onto the Zoom call I had waltzed in on. Our goodbye was short and trivial.

Was I doing the right thing?

Had I made the correct decision?

His bright eyes seemed to have lost all their sparkle.

I imagined I didn't look much different, but I was still resolutely convinced that my choice had been the right one.

## 45

## STELLA

*The next day*

Can you remember a time when you were little and worried that there might be a monster living under your bed? I could. More specifically, I recalled worrying about the monster and simultaneously being too scared to look under my bed to find out whether it was there.

That was the same feeling I had as I stared at the white plastic wand resting on my sink's rim.

The pharmacist had said the results would be compromised if I didn't follow directions, and it would take about three minutes for the results to appear. I unlocked my phone screen to check the time and realized the three minutes were now over.

I stowed my phone in my pocket and gulped.

Taking a deep breath to steady myself, I took a small step forward. I wrapped my hand around the piece of plastic and held it face-up in my palm. Scared as I was, I couldn't bring myself to peer down at it. I felt queasy, but that was nothing new. Feeling nauseous was exactly the reason why the pharmacist had recommended I bring home this anxiety-fuel.

I was sure I'd be sick, so I sat down on the toilet and placed the white wand on my lap.

*Three. Two. One.*

My eyes caught the screen. It displayed a big fat plus.

Oh, no. *I'm pregnant.*

My first thought was, "not possible," but then I remembered... Ace hadn't had protection when he'd visited me the day Damon had confronted him about us. He had warned me he didn't have protection, and that "we" didn't want a kid, and I had told him that it wasn't my fertile days. So much for being reckless and trusting an app.

I wanted to throw the pregnancy test halfway across the room and run away, but I knew this wasn't something I could run away from.

What was I going to do?

My hand found my stomach, and I tried to imagine the little life forming in there. "Who will you be?" I asked aloud. "And why on earth did your timing have to be so bad, little one?"

Leaning against my cold bathroom wall, I tried to stop myself from hyperventilating. The beautiful woman and her baby I had met in the elevator at work came to mind. She'd looked so composed and so calm—unlike me. I wondered whether she had been terrified when she'd found out she was expecting—maybe it was just a normal thing—or whether I felt terrified because my life was the opposite of structured and promising.

And what was Ace going to say? What if he didn't want anything to do with me or the baby? He wanted to keep me a secret—would he want to keep the baby a secret too? I tried not to think about it, but I knew I'd have to tell him. My brother's reaction would be even worse. It would just confirm his suspicions. Oh, he'd be so furious, and my pregnancy would end up ruining both his friendship with Ace and his plans with the merger—despite me having broken up with Ace partly in an attempt to try to stop that from happening.

I wanted to cry, but the tears didn't come. Part of me was happy too, and I supposed that stopped the floodgates from opening. The woman's baby had reminded me how much I wanted one of my own someday, and now I would have it. Sure, the circumstances were crushing, but I knew it would all be worth it when I held my own infant in my arms.

My cell phone vibrated in my pocket. I lifted my hand from my stomach, retrieved it from my pocket, and unlocked its screen.

**Bonnie:** Guess who just bought a Gucci handbag on sale?

I smiled at her message. Typical Bonnie.

**Me:** Umm...No idea. LOL

**Bonnie:** LOL! This bitch! Come visit, and I'll show it to you. Pictures don't do it justice.

**Me:** I'll be over in a bit. I have something to tell you too.

**Bonnie:** Nothing bad, I hope? *Heart emoji*

**Me:** I hope so too. See you soon! *Heart emoji*

If I had to tell someone first, that person might as well be Bonnie. She was my most trusted confidant, after all. She might have advice on how to handle this mess.

My phone buzzed again. At first, I thought Bonnie had replied, but when I lifted it up, I realized it was a message from Damon.

**Damon:** Available for Frosty's, usual time?

I decided not to reply. Not once had I ever *not* replied to one of his messages. I loved my brother as only a sister could, but I was angry at him too. I couldn't help but blame him for the fact that I was in this whole mess, and also that I'd broken up with Ace, so I ignored the message.

Instead, and with sweaty fingers, I dialed Ace's number.

*Tuuut. Tuuut. Tuuut. Tuuut.*

Just when I was about to end the call, I heard a woman's voice on the other line.

"Hello?" she said warmly.

"Hello? Yes! I mean...can I please talk to Ace Windsor?"

"I'm sorry, he's on a business trip. He forgot to take his phone. He'll be back tomorrow. Sorry, but who is this?"

"I'm Stella Copeland, his...assistant. And who is this?" I asked.

A baby cried in the background.

"Oh, sorry about that. Teddy's been fussy all morning. Did you say you were his assistant? I think we met on the elevator the other day," she said brightly. "Ace told me all about you!"

"Oh…" It was her.

My heart dropped. The beautiful blonde with blue eyes.

So it was true. Ace wasn't single. He was living with her. That was why he'd never invited me home. My mind was spinning. "A-are you and Ace…I mean Mr. Windsor…" *married, together, a couple,* I didn't know what word to use, "…close?"

"Close? You're funny. Of course! Very close. I *love* him more than anything in this world," she said happily and laughed. "Well, most of the time. But honestly, I'm starting to feel like his secretary. He keeps leaving his things at home." The baby continued to cry. "I'm so sorry, I've got to run. I'll tell him that you called, Stella."

She ended the call.

I gulped.

Ace was in a relationship, probably married, with a kid.

For about one minute, I tried to hold back my tears. *No. You're not going to cry. You're not going to cry.*

## 46

## DAMON

*Sunday*

Stella hadn't returned my messages or calls in days. I knew she was physically okay because she was still sharing a relentless barrage of memes on her social media pages. Unfortunately, that meant I was also cognizant of the fact she was purposely ignoring me. However, my concern peaked when she missed our plan to meet up at Frosty's, and I'd been wondering how to approach her ever since.

I sent her another message.

**Me:** Hey, Chicken Little, call me.

I waited until 7 p.m. before leaving my house. I knew she'd likely be home from work by then. It was warm outside, but the sun was quickly setting, bringing a cool breeze rolling off the ocean with it. I stared at the bright-orange horizon as I jumped in my car and steered it up my unnecessarily long driveway. I listened to the news while I drove to Stella's apartment. Fuel prices were up, the NASDAQ was down—nothing new.

The sky turned black as I pulled up in front of her apartment building. I checked my cell to make sure she hadn't replied to me yet. She hadn't, so I made my way up to her front door. When I got to it, I could hear her television blaring, but nothing else.

"Sis," I called as I knocked. "It's me. Open up. I'm worried about you."

"Go away," she exclaimed from the other side of the door. I heard her pause the show she was watching.

"I'm not going to. I'm going to stand here and wait until you open up. Save us the time and open *up*."

I heard her stomping toward the door. She flung it open and angrily looked up at me. "You're a pest," she grumbled, "and I said go away." She started closing the door again, but I stuck my foot through the entrance before she could.

"Talk to me," I insisted.

"*No*."

"For fuck's sake." I pushed the door open and walked into her apartment. It was in disarray. She'd never been particularly neat, but she'd never been as disorganized as her apartment currently was. "What's with the mess?" I asked directly.

She folded her arms in front of her chest, making it a point to not talk to me.

I sighed, frustrated. "I know you're ignoring me, so tell me what I need to do for you to forgive me for whatever I've done wrong."

Silence. *Jesus Christ*. This would take all night.

I said, "Stop being stubborn. Are you still mad at me because I asked you to keep an eye on Ace for me?"

"So that's what you call it now? The fact that you don't know what you did wrong is laughable," she huffed. She stomped over to her couch, shoved an almost-empty packet of sour cream and onion chips aside, as well as one empty brownie box, and one empty tub of hazelnut ice cream. There was a half-empty tub of strawberry sorbet on the table, all melted. Finally, she sat down among some Hershey's kisses wrappers. She didn't gesture for me to do the same, but I joined her anyway.

"That's all you've eaten? You must be starving," I teased.

Nothing. Only an evil glare.

"Look, I don't have time for this. I'm not a mind reader," I said, trying to keep my impatience at bay. "How am I supposed to know what unforgivable sin I committed if you won't talk to me about it?"

"It's really convenient that you've forgotten how you showed up at my apartment and accused me of sleeping with your best friend. Ace told me you went to his apartment too."

"That's it? That's all? Okay, I'm sorry that I wrongly accused you. It was unfair of me. Please forgive me?" It sounded like it could be a joke, so I lowered my voice to a friendlier register. "Hey...you know I'm just protective of you. You're my baby sister. You're my little pancake. You're my little éclair." I looked at her as she dissolved into tears, and I immediately worried that I'd said something wrong again. The goal was to make her smile, not burst into tears.

She sobbed loudly and violently, holding her hands over her face to catch her tears. The couch jerked under me, and all the wrappers fell to the floor as her wailing rocked it. I knew this wasn't a "normal" Stella weeping session—something was seriously wrong.

"Hey, hey, stop, Baby Cakes, please. Tell me what I can do to make things right," I said with the warmest voice that I could muster. "I hate seeing you like this." I wrapped my arm around her shoulder and squeezed. In response, she rested her head against my chest.

Oh, good. *Now we're getting somewhere.*

I stroked her head and her cheek, feeling tears dripping down onto my skin.

"I-I'm pregnant," she finally blurted, her voice shaking as she said it.

I inhaled.

Finally, everything made sense.

I exhaled.

I wrapped my other arm around her too, and hugged her firmly. I didn't let go of her until she was pulling away from me.

"You're not mad?" she asked, looking up at me with red-rimmed eyes full of tears.

"Mad? No, of course not," I said. "How could I be? I can see that you love him."

"You know it's Ace's?" The color drained from her face, and I knew she was bracing herself for my reply.

"Who else's could it possibly be?" I smiled gently, trying to not give her "duh" eyes. But that was exactly what I was thinking. *Duh, sis.* I didn't want to upset her further. Of course, I was shocked, but Stella and her unborn baby were more important than my thoughts.

"How did you know?"

"I took an educated guess." Again, I tried my best to not "duh" eye her. I wanted to give her so much shit, but now wasn't the time.

"Did you know he saved me from a creepy guy who showed up at the firm?" she asked, biting her lower lip.

A creepy guy? My alarm bells went off. "I didn't, but I'm glad he did, or I would have done it," I growled. I wasn't *that* surprised that she was in love with Ace. I knew him, and he was a good guy—aside from the whole Ecclestone shit I still hadn't figured out. It didn't shock me to hear he'd done something heroic for her.

"It's true. A delivery guy who gave me a lift once when I was stuck in traffic came to the office and tried to force himself on me." She sniffled. "Ace showed him who's boss and had his whole security team on high alert for weeks afterward in case he—or his friends—showed up. The guy never came back. I wouldn't have either if I were him. I was almost certain Ace would kill him when he grabbed him. And then he gifted me a car."

"That sounds like something Ace would do," I said sympathetically. "Have you told him yet?"

"No," she replied quietly, her voice still trembling.

"You should, and soon," I said. I couldn't possibly imagine how scared she had to be. "He needs to know, and you'll feel better once he does."

Tears were still streaming down her face, but at least she was no longer violently sobbing in my arms. I suspected being able to reveal her secret to me was the cathartic release she'd needed.

"H-h-e has a woman. He has a b-b-baby, too."

"Stella? Stop."

"No, I'm not...crazy. I called him. This gorgeous woman picked up.

Thin. Silky blonde. With soft blue eyes. P-perfection." She sobbed. "In the background was a baby crying…Teddy."

"Stella, listen. It's his sister."

She blinked once, twice. Her eyes widened. "W-hat?"

"Tilly. Yeah. She just moved in with him recently. You have nothing to worry about."

"Oh."

I chuckled a little when she still blinked. I could practically see the gears rolling. Then I saw a rock the size of an elephant lift off her shoulders, and she completely stopped sobbing. Within two seconds flat, she'd gone from doom and gloom to hopeful—it was hilarious.

"I had no idea." Light entered her eyes. "I mean, I knew he had a sister, but I thought she lived in a different state."

"Well, she did. Until recently," I said. "Ace is not exactly a sharer."

"I know." She smiled a little—finally.

"But you, you are. You need to inform him that you're pregnant."

She stiffened again, panic back in her voice. "What if he isn't happy about it? You said he didn't want a relationship. And now this!"

"He will be happy."

Hope flared up in her. "Are you sure?"

I nodded once. "I'm sure."

"What if he isn't?"

"If he isn't, I'll be here for you. We're family." I didn't have to say more about it.

"You're right." She nodded and wiped at her tear-streaked cheeks with the back of her hand. "Thanks, Damon. That doesn't make it any easier to tell him. But okay, I will tell him. Tomorrow, I promise. Let me sleep on it. Even though I doubt I will close an eye. It won't be easy."

"I know," I said quietly, pulling her back into my arms.

## 47

## DAMON

The door fell closed. I left Stella's apartment with a heavy feeling bearing down on me. It was an unfamiliar feeling. It wasn't frustration or anger—the usual fucking suspects—no, it was something else. As I meandered back down to my car and opened its driver's side door, I realized what it was: fear. I was scared for my sister. Ace was a good guy, I wanted to believe that with my whole heart—but who knew how he'd react to an unplanned pregnancy?

God dammit.

My car's engine roared to life just as my cell phone started ringing. I grumbled and stuck my hand into my slacks' pocket to retrieve it.

The word "Harris" flashed across the screen.

Harris? What could our P.I. possibly want at this time of the evening? My cell felt heavier in the palm of my hand than it usually did. Calling this late in the day was never good.

I swiped left.

"Harris? What's going on?" I asked without greeting, pressing my phone against my ear.

"What? No hello?" he chortled in his usual raw tone. His voice was the result of years of chain smoking and screaming matches in interrogation rooms. He was a retired detective, and still one of the best, a fact he wouldn't allow anyone to forget.

"Get to the point."

"All right," he said unaffectedly. "I've got some news for you: I took a little initiative and did some digging on that guy whose company you're merging with."

"I didn't ask you to do that," I hissed as I lowered my handbrake and pulled away from the curb.

"I know you didn't, but I overheard Oliver mention something, and I thought you'd be pleased as punch that I did it for you anyway." He coughed violently and continued, "Besides, you'll definitely be interested in what I found."

"You know how I feel about anything being done without my express go-ahead," I said, trying to mask the frustration that was causing my voice to shake. I paused for a moment and tried to prepare myself for what was coming next. "What did you find?"

"A photo of your friend, Mr. Ace Windsor, having dinner with Mr. Edmund Ecclestone."

My jaw dropped.

No way. Fuck.

*Fuck.*

"Are you sure?" I sucked in a breath and turned onto the main road. "Where did you find it?"

"I found it in an extra insert of a magazine that's gone out of print. I'm the proud owner of the last existing copy they published. It wasn't easy to find, but I have...well, let's say connections."

"Is there any way it was tampered with?"

"Nope," he replied, and coughed again. "It's a bit older and Ecclestone's face is in partial shadow, but the beard is unmistakable. It's him. Edmond 'Edmund' Ecclestone, born and raised in Marseille France, his mother Céleste Lavogne, French, his father Emmet Ecclestone, American."

*God dammit.* An intersection forced me to stop, and I changed lanes. The initial plan was to head home, but instead, I turned toward the

Upper East Side where Ace's apartment was located. "Harris, send me a copy of the damn photo. And keep this to yourself for now, clear?"

"Clear, boss," he said.

I ended the call and pulled onto the street leading to Ace's apartment building. While parallel parking in front of it, my cell phone vibrated again. I unlocked it, revealing the picture Harris had sent me.

He was right. I gritted my teeth as I examined it. Ace and Ecclestone. Shit. This couldn't have come at a worse time. Stella's tear-stained face flashed before my eyes, and I felt a red-hot rage rising up in my chest.

That lying bastard.

Angrily, I flung my car door open and got out.

People stepped out of my way as they saw me enter the lobby. I got onto the waiting elevator without saying a word to any of its occupants, who left the elevator the higher we got up, until it rode empty all the way up to the top floor.

Ace's front door was the final frontier.

*Bang! Bang! Bang!*

Nothing. I raised my fist again and pounded against it furiously.

"Open up! We need to talk. *Now.*"

His sister's baby cried from the other side of the door.

Fuck. I forgot.

"Coming!" I heard him reply.

## 48

## ACE

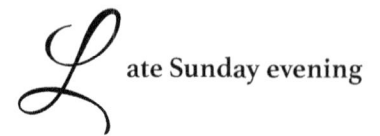

*Late Sunday evening*

Damon glared back at me when I opened the door. His gaze was fiery and intense. As I supposed, he hadn't popped around for a social call. Like I needed more shit to deal with.

It was late, and I was back from my trip, mood sour. I had just been going through the last page of the merger folder before stuffing it into a big envelope, ready for delivery, when I'd heard someone banging at my front door. What the hell?

I frowned at him. "Hey, Damon."

"You look fucking terrible," he said.

"I feel worse."

His expression softened, and the rage that had previously molded his expression appeared to wane. "Can I come in? We have a few things we need to talk about."

I opened the door further, stepped backward, and extended one of my arms to invite him inside.

"I forgot Tilly was here with the baby," he said, gesturing at the array of baby toys and spit rags scattered around my apartment. At least my sister had been quick to calm him. "Is there a good place where we can talk?"

"My sister and her baby are in the other room." I beckoned for Damon to follow me into my expansive kitchen. "Coffee, or something stronger?" I asked as I started up the coffeemaker.

"Coffee," he said. "Living with your sister and her baby, how's that been going?"

"Good. I thought it'd be better for her to have someone around to help her while she recovers and acclimates to motherhood. Being a single mom isn't easy."

"How do you get along with the baby?" he asked.

It was unusual for Damon to press about the baby. "The baby's pleasant, love him like my own. He doesn't fuss too much or too often, you know? Anyway, I doubt you came here to talk about my sister's newborn."

"Do you know why I'm here?"

I did. This wasn't about the merger files.

This was about *her*.

He knew. He knew I'd slept with his sister.

With a sigh, I retrieved two coffee cups from a cabinet to my left and filled them up with the midnight-black liquid that came gurgling out of the coffeemaker. The smell of ground coffee beans filled the room. It was one of my favorite smells, and on a better day, I might have paused to appreciate it.

I handed one cup to Damon. "Stella."

"Bull's-eye."

"You could have saved yourself a trip. We're no longer seeing each other."

"But you *were* seeing her?" He took a drink of his steaming black coffee and stared at me over the rim of his mug.

I needed to be honest. "Yeah, I was. I didn't mean for it to happen. What can I say, she hit me like a ton of bricks. I tried to stop it. Both of us did."

"Clearly you didn't try hard enough. She's pregnant."

I stared at him.

"Slppp." He took a loud sip of his coffee as if to punctuate the silence that followed.

It was like the world fell apart and came together all at the same time. A million thoughts ran through my head, followed by even more questions. My pulse raced, and my vision narrowed. When the sensation passed, I steadied myself and shook my head. "I gotta see her. How is she?"

He stopped me from turning to leave. "She looks even worse than you do. I was just at her apartment. She's a nervous wreck, to say the least. Did you knock her up just to get back at me, you asshat? Because if that's the case, I'm going to absolu—"

"What do you mean? Get back at you for what?"

He slammed his cup down. The sound of ceramic striking marble rang through the room like a bell. "Don't play dumb with me, Ace. You know *exactly* what I'm fucking talking about. I had her spy on you, do detective work in your firm, whatever the fuck you wanna call it. I know that you know."

"How do you know? From her?" It was highly unlikely she'd told him.

"No. Because I know her. My sister is an honest soul who wouldn't keep it from a man she fucking *loves*."

My shoulders dropped.

There was a pause as I tried to collect my thoughts.

We locked eyes. "You're a real piece of work, do you know that, Damon?" I asked. "First, you send your sister to fucking spy on me because you don't trust me, and now you're accusing me of using her to spite you? You're a fucking idiot, man. I'm not a fucking traitor or a liar, and I got nothing to hide from you. But I'm fucking mad because you, Miles, and Oliver apparently don't trust me. What, you think so little of me you go behind my back? It might disappoint you, but there are no secrets, or dark machinations, or any other shit you were trying to conjure up. She'll tell you the same."

"Oh, yeah? What's *this* then?" Damon growled, whipping out his cell and brandishing a picture he'd saved. It depicted Ecclestone and me sitting almost next to each other around a restaurant table. "Is this or is this not fucking Edmund Ecclestone?" he demanded. "The one person I specifically asked you about and you specifically denied working with!"

I could hear Teddy wailing again.

"Keep your voice down, for fuck's sake," I hissed, lowering my own. "You're upsetting the baby. How the hell did you get this fucking photo?"

"Harris found it, our PI."

I set down my coffee cup and rubbed at my temples. "Wait. Let me get this straight. You didn't just set Stella on me, but a fucking private investigator, as well?" I huffed. "Jesus. This is getting better and better."

"Well, I didn't want to, but I guess I did. Long story. So, confess."

"*This* fucking photo," I started, taking his phone out of his hand, and waving it at him, "was taken at a business dinner that I was invited to by a colleague several years ago. I completely forgot about it. I fucking didn't know Ecclestone would be there, let alone be sitting at the same table. I didn't speak a single word to him all night."

"Why didn't you tell me that when I asked you?"

"I didn't tell you that I'd *briefly* met him before, because I didn't even know who he was back then. To me he was some nameless construction guy. This is before his 'rise to fame.'" I made quote fingers around the term.

"You said you've never met him," he pressed. "You clearly met him."

"Jesus. I've never met him in a sense of meeting, and shaking hands, and talking, and doing fucking business together."

"Why is he calling your office?"

Jesus fucking Christ. "Because he's a pushy son of a bitch."

"You gotta give me more than this, Ace."

I paused, then sighed. I did have more, but I wasn't sure if I should even mention it. I never intended to. But he gave me no choice. "Full disclosure? I've got a theory on that."

"Shoot." He made an impatient hand motion, urging me to go on.

"My theory is that my former assistant was a spy sent through Ecclestone, channeled in to provoke agitation."

I'd never thought I'd see Damon drop his poker face. Tonight was the night. Surprised disbelief was written all over his face. He shook his head, mumbling, "Ace."

I continued, undeterred. "A real spy, a trained fucking rat. Goal: cause disarray, rumors, and scandal inside and outside my firm. She has disappeared from the face of the earth. Ecclestone hired her, I'm sure. The timing. The onslaught of errors. The lies. When I fired her, I saw a caller ID on her phone displaying 'E.E.' I believe he set his eyes on my firm. A merger wasn't in his interest, for obvious reasons: He didn't need another king on the chess board. As far as I was concerned, I had other motives, but the only way to save my company was to push the acquisition through with the giant he knew he'd never get his hands on: Humphries Properties. It's in his best interest to do anything to make sure the acquisition goes south. I can't prove anything, of course. The only way to get out of his line of fire was by letting him lose interest and being clear that no matter what shady attempts he tried to dish out, he wasn't going to crowbar himself into our business—in short: letting him know that he can go fuck himself."

Damon's brows were still furrowed, but his expression had lost some of the earlier disbelief. "Why didn't you tell us that?"

"Because it's a *theory*, man."

"How am I supposed to believe a word you say?" he huffed, shaking his head and stepping closer to me. "You've been dishonest as a business partner when I asked you about Ecclestone, and dishonest as a friend when I asked you if you were sleeping with my sister—and now you've changed the course of my sister's life forever. Do you fucking know what she's going through?"

I stared at him. The beast inside me narrowed his piercing eyes, mutated into a black predator, puffed his large wings, opened his beak, and unleashed a loud screeching noise.

A single angry tear ran down my cheek.

All the frustration I'd bundled up inside of me evaporated like mist.

"For fuck's sake, Damon. Do you know what *I'm* going through?" I demanded. "I love her, you fucking *asshole*. I love her more than life itself. I didn't fucking want anybody in my life, and she hit me like a freight train—but turns out, she doesn't want me. She left me because I fucked up, lost her trust, and because of this fucking merger. Fuck this merger. And fuck all of you who doubted me and thought I was in cahoots with that Ecclestone bastard."

I ran a hand through my hair, and slid my sleeves up my arms, enraged. "You know what? I don't want this merger, I couldn't care less anymore. I want *her*." I moved away from him.

Damon followed me. "So that's it? The merger is done?"

"Yeah. Done, over. *Fuck it*."

I went and grabbed the thick envelope that included the merger files Damon, and Humphries, and the board were waiting for, switched on the fireplace, waited a few agonizing moments, and threw it into the burning heat.

Satisfied, I turned, but stopped in my tracks when I noticed Damon's expression.

Was that a fucking smile creeping up his face?

He put his hand on my shoulder and sympathetically nodded. "Buddy. I'm sorry I riled you up, but that's what I wanted to hear. I didn't think I'd get the truth out of you unless I pissed you off."

*What?*

He rushed to grab the file out of the glowing coals. The envelope and its contents were already on fire, but Damon managed to put it out.

I sank to the floor and rested my back against the wall. "You played me?"

He placed the burned papers next to the fireplace and retrieved a handkerchief to wipe his fingers. "Kind of, but I know you have the emotional capacity of an eggplant. So, I had to. I needed to know that you love my sister. You should have told me right away."

"I thought you'd be *mad*. Miles and Oliver were all over my ass because of the whole thing."

"Well, next time talk to me instead of them. We're both fucking adults, not immature dickheads with hormones up our asses. Sure, I'm mad that you didn't tell me the truth, but I'm not proud of what I did myself. I guess we're even."

He offered me a bro-fist, and I bumped it, still trying to wrap my head around what had just happened.

"*What?*" he asked. "You seem disappointed. You wanted me to beat you up? Jesus, I'm not twenty—but I *can*. If that'll make you feel better."

I chuckled. "You're good."

"You should see her," he said. "She's terrified and fragile. She's going to need you. No more of that 'I'm not ready for a relationship' bullshit. You fucking be ready."

"I am."

He sat down next to me and slapped my shoulder. "You're going to be a good dad. I trust you. I do, man."

"Oh, you do?"

"All right, got me there. Well. If Harris couldn't find more than this on you, then there isn't anything else to find. Besides, I trust Stella's judgment, and she trusts you."

"Did *she* tell you that?"

"No, but like I said, I know her. I think she just needs you to reassure her that you love her *and* the baby."

"I will." I nodded, coming to grips with the news Damon had shared. "Actually, I'm excited. You know I always wanted to have my own family. I'm a family man, you know that. Can you imagine a tiny Ace-Stella hybrid running around?"

"I'm trying my best not to." Damon shook his head. "You should mention it to Stella though. Women eat that shit up. It'll mean a lot to her to hear that you're excited she's expecting. Like I said, she *needs* to hear it."

"I'll go to her right away." I started scrambling up, but he grabbed my arm.

"Don't fuck it up," he said kindly. "Maybe give her tonight to gather her thoughts. You can go see her in the morning. Everything's always clearer in the morning."

"I can't. I need to see her now."

"In that case, don't let me stop you." He inclined his head toward the burned envelope. "Also, we can't send this to Mr. Humphries and the board like this. You have to send me a clean set of prints. And pronto. In case you need a helping hand, I know somebody, who a few days ago, resigned from her assistant's job."

I chuckled, getting to my feet.

Tilly stuck her head out of her half-open bedroom door just as I reached for my helmet. "Is everything okay out here?" she quietly asked. I could barely hear her voice from across the apartment. She slipped over the threshold, closed the door behind her, and sauntered toward Damon and me. "Teddy's finally sleeping."

"Everything's all right." Damon winked at me and added, "But your brother here has some pretty big news."

"Spill the beans then," she demanded cheerfully. "Now I'm curious." She smiled past Damon at me.

I took a deep breath and said, "Teddy's getting a cousin."

Her mouth dropped. "Whaaaat? Holy cannoli!"

## 49

## STELLA

There was a fresh batch of éclairs in the oven. It was in the middle of the night, but I couldn't sleep. This time around, I was certain I'd absolutely shine making them. Why? Because I was staring at them through my oven's tiny window. The most important rule—so I'd Googled—was to never leave your éclairs unsupervised. Okay, maybe that wasn't the most important rule for everyone...but for me it was.

My hand fell onto my stomach. Of course I wasn't showing yet, but I knew I would be soon. My mom always said she'd looked pregnant the moment she'd conceived, and if genetics were anything to go by, I'd have a huge belly by tomorrow morning. Perfect time to tell Ace all about it.

Éclairs were a fantastic distraction. Not taking my eyes off them, they slowly turned golden brown, and the kitchen began to fill with the most delicious scent there was. I kept staring at them and found myself completely distracted from my current predicament. On top of that, I was consumed by a state of "momentary baker's bliss." *(I'm sure that's the official term.)*

The doorbell rang, and I jumped. Who was that? I accidentally caught a glimpse of my reflection in the oven's window: My hair was messy, and I had a streak of flour across my forehead. But I didn't consider running to my room to fix my appearance, because it was just Damon to check up on me, and consequently, such "drastic steps" weren't necessary.

Knock. Knock.

"I'm coming!" I gave my éclairs a last mournful glance and whispered, "Please don't burn."

As I wrapped my fingers around the doorknob, I hoped Damon wasn't planning on staying too long, and not just because of the éclairs. The reason was, I still had to come up with a reasonably good strategy for tomorrow on how to tell Ace I was pregnant, while dealing with my anxiety, excitement, and fear. It was a pretty weird time for me, but I was certain I would get through it if I was left alone to process all of it.

I flung the door open. "He—" I stopped short.

It wasn't Damon.

I blinked.

Beautiful, deep, soul-piercing bright-blue eyes. Intense. Powerful. Larger than life.

Ace.

Was it really him? Was I dreaming?

I exhaled.

"Stella," Ace gasped. He stared at me from the dark hall.

It was him. I came to my senses. "Ace!" I wanted to sound calm and composed, but my voice came out as a squeak. "What are you doing here? I thought I told you—"

"I know what you told me." He rubbed his forearm and bit his lower lip. He looked so breathtakingly handsome.

The tingling sensation I'd started feeling when I'd first laid eyes on him returned in full force.

"Can I come in?" he asked. "I have some things I need to get off my chest. Please."

No.

*I'm not ready yet.*

*My reasonably good strategy for tomorrow is nowhere finished.*

This would be so bad.

"Okay." I gulped and stepped to one side. "I'm just busy making éclairs."

"They smell great." He stepped into my apartment. As soon as I closed the door, he shifted to face me. "I'm sorry I hurt you."

Oh, I hadn't expected that. "Well," I said, "it's in the past now anyway, and it's not like we can't still be professional—"

"I don't want to be professional. Or friends or colleagues or anything shitty like that. Ever since you told me you didn't want to be with me anymore, I've been dying on the inside. Slowly. Torturously. Stella, I love you."

His declaration caught me by surprise. Speechlessly, I stared at him.

He stepped closer and took my hands into his. "No matter how hard I try, I can't stop thinking about you. I miss falling asleep with your hair in my face. I miss waking up with a numb arm because you've been curled up in it for too long. Fuck, I miss being able to hold you, touch you, and talk to you, fucking tickle you, damn it, laugh with you, and spend time with you. You have no idea what you've done to me."

Everything about his appearance suggested he was sincere. His demeanor was confident and strong—with that sexy grumpy touch—as it had always been, but I'd never known his eyes to sparkle with so much warmth.

My chest was burning with the affection I felt for him, but I suspected it was too early to completely break down the walls I'd built around my heart.

"Then why did you want to keep me a secret?" I asked, letting go of his hands. "And please tell me the truth," I added when he opened his mouth.

He gave me a "When have I ever lied to you?" look, and said, "I wanted to give us both time. I wanted to protect what I knew was still so new and fragile. With us having to face all the odds, I didn't want to risk losing you. I wanted to shield you, keep you safe. It was never about keeping *you* a secret. You know that."

"Of course I understand your last relationship made you careful. But what about all the 'I don't want to be in a relationship' talk to Damon and the boys?"

"Who told you that?"

"Damon."

"Jesus Christ. Your brother has set out to ruin my life, hasn't he?"

"Of course he hasn't. He just means well. Don't change the subject. Haven't you claimed a million times you're not ready for a relationship after your failed engagement? And that's not an accusation. I totally get it now. I've had time to think as well, you know. I get it, I really do. You just went through a bad breakup. I shouldn't have been so clingy and—"

"No. Wait. Please be clingy, baby, seriously. This thing between us is different. You've always been on my radar. Ever since the pool party."

I blinked. "What, wait? The pool party?"

"The white bikini. Remember?"

"Oh, I remember. Ace!"

He chuckled. "It's been living rent free in my head for a very long time."

His laughter made me laugh. "I thought you didn't see anything."

"I saw *everything*."

"Oh, my God." I paused, thinking. "Back then I thought you had negative feelings towards me, that you hated me, but the reason you avoided me wasn't because of that..."

"Not at all, Stella."

"Are you telling me I can't be mad at Damon anymore for splashing me with all that water?"

"I guess you have to be thankful to him." His lip tipped up into a half-smile. "By the way, Damon knows about us. I just talked to him."

"You did? So, I'm really *not* your little dirty secret?"

"Woman. You were *never* my dirty secret. Maybe my dirty girl," he brushed some of the flour off my cheeks, "but never a dirty secret. You know, I'll scale the highest building for you and declare my love for you from its peak if that's what you need me to do to prove that I'm serious about you."

I leaned my shoulder against the wall and stared into his eyes. "If you're so serious about me, why didn't you ever invite me to your apartment? I've never even seen the inside of it." I crossed my arms.

"Because that's where my sister, her baby, and I live. That's why I never invite anyone to my place. Baby Teddy sleeps most of the day, and I simply didn't want to disturb him or my sister."

"You know what's funny?"

"What?"

"I met them in the elevator. I thought she was your girl, and the baby was yours."

He laughed. "I guess Damon told you they weren't?"

"Yeah." I grinned.

He stepped closer to me and cupped my face in his hands, his expression serious again. "It was never, ever my intention to keep our relationship secret forever. I want to spend my life with you. I want to laugh at all your jokes until we're wrinkly and old. Please, baby. Are you finally believing me?"

"And what about Damon?"

"He showed up at my apartment, and we made peace."

"Really? How? How did you convince him?"

"I threw the acquisition papers into the fire. He fished them back out."

That made me speechless for a moment. "Really? You were ready to give up the merger, for me?" Tears started streaming down my cheeks. "But that was the most important thing to you!"

"I know, right? You must be pretty special," he teased. "I love you more than any man has ever loved a woman. You are the most important thing to me. You're everything to me. And you always will be." He kissed my forehead, and then wrapped his arms around me. "Woman, just tell me you love me too. You're making me tense with all of these questions."

"Of course I love you, you silly man," I replied. More tears dripped onto Ace's chest, staining his white shirt with dark mascara-filled droplets. "I love you so much that it hurts."

"I hope it's a good hurt." He chuckled.

"Oh, shhh. Yes," I said, pulling away and smiling at him through my tears. "But…I…things are different now."

He took both of my hands into his own and squeezed them. "Because you're expecting?" he asked mischievously.

I gasped.

"How do you know about that?" I could feel the blood draining from my face. Goosebumps covered every inch of my skin. "Is it that obvious?"

"Damon."

"Damon? I'm going to *kill* him," I joked, but not really.

"He isn't good at keeping secrets, apparently." He chortled. "Runs in the family, I guess."

"I guess."

He leaned forward, kissed me, and simultaneously placed his hand on my lower abdomen. "He's nearly as excited as I am about meeting this little one."

"I'm so glad you're not upset. This whole mess is my fault. I told you not to worry about not having protection."

"How could I be upset? First, it takes two to tango. Second, this is a dream come true. I've always wanted a child of my own, well, maybe not while everything was still hanging in the balance, but I couldn't possibly have chosen a better mother for that child. Stella, I don't just want to be a part of this kid's life. I want to be a part of yours too. Please, let me be the man you deserve. Let me take care of you. Let me love you." He leaned forward and kissed me on my tear-logged lips. "Now, please stop crying. We have something to celebrate."

"Just as long as you weren't hoping to have a glass of champagne." I giggled. "Because that's off the table for me now."

It felt like a boulder had been rolled off me. The heavy feeling I'd been carrying around in my chest since I'd first seen that fateful positive turned into a beam of sunshine that warmed my heart and healed its bruises.

"I'll have a glass for both of us," he said, grinning. He wrapped his arms around my waist and pressed his lips against mine. "At least now I don't have to worry about getting you pregnant right away," he said as he opened my bra's clasp under my shirt.

"Oh, Ace." I laughed as his tongue slipped into my mouth, and my clothes fell to the floor like a downpour of fabrics around us.

He kissed me again, more passionately this time, and unbuttoned his jeans. Then, he lifted me up. How strong he was! I slung my arms and legs around him.

"I wanted to go insane when I thought there was a chance I might never get to do this again," he groaned as he positioned himself, his hands firm on my bottom. When his hips finally met my center, he pushed inside me deeply.

Ahhh. We moved like dance partners, executing a well-practiced routine, and I bit his neck and dug my nails into his back as the dance's rhythm increased.

"I dreamed about you...every night...since the last time I saw you," I whispered in his ear as a wave of pleasure washed over me.

He strained and groaned, spilling inside of me.

"They were dreams like this?" he asked a few seconds later, breathless.

"Yeah."

Still inside of me, with my legs still firmly wrapped around him, he locked eyes with me. "I love you."

"I love you too," I said, feeling happier than I'd ever been in my entire life. I closed my eyes when he laid us onto the couch and snuggled up against his inked chest, hugging him closer, and then bolted upright again. "Oh, crap! My éclairs!"

## 50

## ACE

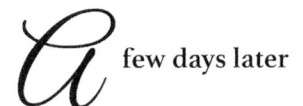

*A* few days later

Tilly brought Stella into the biggest embrace as soon as we entered my apartment. "Congratulations on your pregnancy! There's a great new doc in town—he's *so* hot! He's working in a brand-new joint clinic with a few other doctors. You should go see him."

It was hilarious to me that my sister jumped right into the baby business. As a fellow mom, I guessed it was only natural. Sometimes I suspected that Tilly had deliberately chosen a man who would never take responsibility to be the father of her child. It was a strange idea for me, but totally okay. Tilly had wanted and had had a child, in an uncomplicated way, and she loved Teddy dearly. He would never lack for anything.

"How old is he?" Stella asked.

"Great question. I only saw him once as a replacement when my doctor wasn't in. Pure luck, I'm telling you. Maybe thirty-ish? He's the most handsome man I've *ever* met." She made swoony eyes.

"Sounds great." Stella smiled, glancing at me.

"And according to the papers, he bought the penthouse in the Sky Gold Tower, isn't that right, Ace? As an investment. You know what that means? He's a freaking *billionaire*, I think." She spread her fingers and made jazz hands. She'd fallen in love with some cheerleading movie made back in 2000, and ever since, "jazz hands" had become a thing.

"Oh, wow," Stella said.

"If I wasn't seeing someone, I would totally grab his number. He's not the typical douchey, grumpy billionaire though. Down-to-earth. Respected, confident, and real. Rides a motorcycle—I mean, that says it all, doesn't it, Ace?"

"How do you know he rides a motorcycle?" I grumbled while working around the bar.

"I saw his helmet. Duh. By accident, not because I was stalking him. Also, because he has a smattering of tattoos. He keeps them well-hidden due to his work, but I saw his *sleeve* by accident when he rolled up his shirt sleeve a bit to look at his watch. Hot. He probably has tattoos *everywhere*. If you know what I mean." She closed her eye into an exaggerated wink, shaping her lips into a hilarious grin.

"For fuck's sake, Tilly, can you stop?" I said, preparing our milkshakes. "I'm right here."

"No, I mean, I'm just saying, he's something for the eye, ya know, eye-candy, *besides* being highly professional and the best in his field. They say he's got a great...tool. I mean, an arsenal of *mesmerizing, breathtaking, incredible* tools."

"Tilly, I'm not going to repeat myself," I growled.

"What? You do want the very best for your girlfriend, medically, *don't you*?"

"Of course I do. But keep the dick talk down, will you?"

"Who was talking about dicks?"

"Okay. That's it."

"Relax, Tiger." Tilly laughed, looking at me. "I bet he's taken. Men like him are never single. Besides, your girl only has eyes for you. Right, Stella?"

"Of course," Stella said. "I *do* need a good doctor. But I'm not sure if I want a good-looking one."

"Exactly. You don't," I agreed.

"Wait, where did I put his number?" Tilly went to grab her huge bag, and after half an eternity of shuffling inside of it, she retrieved a business card. It was slightly crumpled. "Here you go. You can keep it. Or would you like me to make the appointment?"

She placed the card on the marble countertop, close enough for me to see. A neat black font on a bright thick paper read, "Dr. Dillan Maxwell." It was followed by his phone number, email address, and clinic's location.

Tilly gave Stella an encouraging nod and glanced at me.

I grumbled something like "Women," and Tilly and Stella looked at each other. Stella took the card and put it in her pocket.

They would be best friends, no doubt.

~

Three weeks later

In the late afternoon, we had one of our last meetings with Humphries Properties' lawyers before the merger. The agenda was to discuss the purchase agreement so we could close the deal and begin integration. It went well, just like the meetings leading up to it had. Now, it was only a matter of time before an eight-figure amount rolled into my bank account.

The day we signed the papers, all calls from Ecclestone stopped.

To me, it proved my little theory had been right—but ultimately, I would never know. The "construction shark" never had a chance to begin with. Just as I would never be able to prove he'd had his fingers in my previous assistant's spying. Unless Harris found hard evidence, I had better shit to do than waste time fighting a shady war. If someone was throwing shit, you didn't waltz into their line of fire.

It didn't mean we wouldn't be vigilant and ready to kick ass if needed. Because kick ass, we would. In future price battles, due to our size, we'd win against him or any other competitor, fair and square.

To me, there couldn't be a bigger win.

I told Mrs. Mills she could go home directly after the lawyers left—

she deserved a day off, and I would surprise her with a raise in the next payroll. Stella, though back as my assistant, I had other plans for. I asked her to meet me in my office for dinner.

She knocked on my office door in a confident way and opened it.

"I'm here," she declared.

Stella emerged from the doorway like a vision. She was sporting a dazzling smile, strawberry-red lipstick, and a formal form-fitting beige dress. Those weren't her most impressive features though. That honor went to the tiny bump that was forming just under her navel. If you didn't know it was there, it would be hard to notice, but I'd spent enough time staring at it to notice it every time she walked into the room. Seeing it filled me with an odd sense of pride I couldn't eloquently explain even if I tried.

"What are we eating today?" she asked. "Are you in the mood for Italian? Bonnie and I love this quaint little pasta place just a few blocks from here. We could walk, it's beautiful outside."

I pushed my chair back from my desk and got to my feet. "You shouldn't be walking around too much in your current state."

"Dr. Maxwell said a little exercise here and there won't hurt, and he recommended at least thirty minutes of moderate-intensity exercise on most days. Besides, walking a few blocks hardly counts as exercise. It'll be fun." The smile on her face widened. "Or are you in the mood for something else?"

"Something else entirely." I chuckled, stalking toward her like a creature slinking toward its prey.

"I hope whatever you have in mind has comfortable seating." She slipped past me, pretending not to notice the way I approached her. I knew she was teasing me. She sat down on one of the chairs next to my desk and took off one of her brown stilettos. "Don't get me wrong, I love walking, and I'd still love to walk to that Italian place, but these shoes are *killing* me. I swear my feet are swelling up already." She rubbed her heel and shook her head. "Will you still love me when I have Hobbit feet?"

"I'd love you even if you were a Hobbit."

I crouched down in front of her.

Her eyes widened.

"What are you up to?" she asked, raising one of her eyebrows and quickly slipping her swollen foot back into her shoe. "You'll give me a heart attack, getting down like that, almost like getting on one knee."

"I just want to look at you."

"Are...you sure?"

"I'm sure, baby." I smiled at her, took her hands in mine, and kissed each in turn. "Besides, would it be that bad if I really was getting down on one knee? I mean, you're looking at a man who is substantially richer than he was yesterday. This man could get you a pretty big diamond."

"Do I look like the kind of woman who is worried about the size of a diamond?" She playfully scoffed, leaning forward and brushing the tip of her nose against mine. "Don't answer that."

I kissed her forehead.

"Wait, let me help you." She laughed. "Maybe you could—"

I didn't let her finish her sentence before I pressed my lips against hers. Hooking up in my office during late office hours had become somewhat of a habit, and I didn't see why such a proud tradition should be interrupted. Apparently, she felt the same way, because she kissed me back like she'd never kissed me before. There was always something urgent and burning about the way her tongue met mine, and it drove me to absolute insanity.

"Oh, Mr. Windsor. What are you doing?" she jokingly cooed, pulling away from our kiss just long enough to say it.

"I'm about to give my assistant a pretty hard task."

She grinned. "Are you now?"

I stood and scooped her up in my arms. Her long mahogany hair hung over one arm and her shapely legs hung from the other.

"Are we going to erect another project somewhere, Mr. Windsor?"

With a chuckle, I carried her over to my desk, swiped some papers off it, and set her down. I positioned myself between her legs. Her dress's zipper slid down with a satisfying *whirr*. "The project has already been raised, *Mrs.* Windsor. We just need to see it through to its pinnacle," I added as I wriggled her dress off her.

"You called me Mrs. Windsor again." She blushed as she undid my belt buckle.

"I'm just practicing," I growled.

I nudged her legs farther apart. Our hips met like a supernova imploding on itself. We kissed each other to muffle our moans. I nestled one hand in her curly hair while my other hand ran down from her neck, over her chest, to the small of her back. With one jerk, I pulled her closer to me, pushing myself in fully. *Fuck.* She threw her head back and loudly groaned, "Ohhhh! Ace...it feels amazing..."

"Yeah, baby...yeah." I thrust into her and pulled her face toward me, pressing her lips against mine.

*Knock. Knock. Knock.*

We both froze. Someone cleared their throat behind my office door.

"Hm-hm. Are you okay in there, Mr. Windsor?" Mrs. Mills asked from the other side.

"Yes, I'm okay. Don't come in. I'm just...exercising."

"*Exercising?*"

Stella laughed a little and whispered, "Tell her you're doing push-ups."

"I'm doing some push-ups."

"Push-ups?!"

Stella whispered, "Tell her your doctor suggested thirty minutes of intense exercise."

I chuckled. "Didn't I tell you that you could go home?"

"You did," Mrs. Mills said from behind the door, "but I had some filing to do, sir."

"Very well. Good night."

"You don't need me to come in to help with anything?"

"No, thank you."

Stella whispered, "Tell her you're exercising in your underwear."

I shook my head, chuckling, trying to sound grumpy and serious. "Good night, Mrs. Mills."

"Alrighty then! Have it your way," Mrs. Mills said brightly. "Although it's such a pity you don't need my help with anything...being the dashing young man you are. Cheriooo." She cackled as she left.

I waited until the sound of her footsteps disappeared down the hallway and then turned my attention back to Stella's face. She grinned at me impudently. I pulled out and pushed back in. Hard.

"Ahhh," she moaned. "That was close."

I kissed her collarbone, thrusting harder. "Oh, she knew," I rumbled, eyes on the place we were joined.

She gasped, throwing her head back and squirming beneath me. The smell of her fruity-scented perfume consumed me as time stopped.

## 51

## STELLA

Despite the huge portion of delicious *tagliatelle al ragù alla Bolognese* I'd eaten during lunch at Giovanni's when Ace picked me up from my doctor's appointment, I was already starving. Ace had said he couldn't deny the most beautiful woman on the planet anything. And yes, Dr. Maxwell was a wonderful doctor, and possibly even hotter than Tilly had described him, but me—of course—I only had eyes for Ace. We were going to have dinner at his place. In fact, he'd offered to cook—something I was particularly taken aback by because I'd had *no* idea he could cook.

The drive to the Upper East Side was like stepping into a different dimension. I was in awe of the stark contrast between my neighborhood and his every time I made the trip.

"It'll rain later," I commented, staring out of the Aventador's passenger-side window as we raced toward his home.

He put his hand on my leg and squeezed. "How do you know?"

"The birds are roosting in the trees earlier than they usually do." I wrinkled my nose at him and adjusted my glasses. I had become perfectly comfortable wearing them around him, especially now that my eyes felt drier than usual.

He laughed. It was a noise that resembled what I imagined an avalanche would sound like. "What makes you say that?"

"I read a lot," I replied, shifting to look at him. "And not just detective books. Sometimes I throw a little baking book or a nature guide in there, you know, as a palette cleanser."

"Huh. Palette cleanser. I like that." He chortled. He looked like a sculpture made of pure gold in the late-afternoon sun. His wheat-colored hair partially concealed one of his icy-blue eyes. "Did you know I read several Miss Marple novels in my last year of college just because I knew you liked them?"

"Shut up. You did *not*," I gasped, playfully slapping his chest. "Don't lie."

"I'm not. I really did," he admitted, giving me the cutest smirk.

"There's only one way to know if you're being honest. Which ones did you read?"

"Not trusting me, huh?" he teased. "Let's see. *The Body in the Library. Sleeping Murder*, and my personal favorite, *4.50 from Paddington*." He smiled, triumph coloring his expression.

Oh, my gosh. "Who was the murderer in *4.50 from Paddington*?"

He whispered the answer into my ear, and I thought it was so cute—there was nobody here—but, spoiler alert: His answer was correct! "All right! I'm impressed. Did you know the author, Agatha Christie, wrote sixty-six detective novels?"

"That's a good number of murder cases."

We pulled into his apartment building's underground parking lot. "Right? I've read all her books. She cast a spell on me when I was young, and it never let me go."

Ace grinned. He parked the car in his designated spot, got out, and walked around to open my door for me while I gathered my stuff. "I can relate. Just like you, because you've already bewitched me." He extended his hand to help me out of the car. I took it and smiled up at him.

"You're way too smooth," I said. "If anyone is casting spells, it's you." Hand in hand, he led me to the elevator.

"It's easy to be smooth when the person you're flirting with is perfect," he said sincerely and summoned the elevator. I looked down and noticed a handful of red rose petals on the floor.

"Someone had a fight. Look at the ruined flowers—they ripped them apart," I commented, pointing at them. "Isn't that sad? But this looks just like a perfect murder plot set up for a novel, doesn't it? I hope whoever it was is fine."

He kinda chuckled but didn't say anything.

Strange. He had always been the quieter type, but now he seemed abnormally quiet.

"Am I going to see your sister and the baby?" I asked while we waited for the elevator to arrive.

"Not tonight. My sister met someone. A woman, actually. She's a single mom, and they've been dating for several weeks now. They're spending the weekend together."

"That's wonderful. I'm happy for her."

"Yeah. Me too. Me too."

"I didn't know your sister was into girls."

"Neither did I. I'm glad to see her happy."

The elevator doors slid open, and he led me inside.

"Oh, look, there's more here," I said, pointing at the red petals on the floor. "The poor flowers." We turned around, and he pressed the button to his floor. The elevator slowly started ascending.

He squeezed my hand and gave me a wink. "You're funny."

"Thanks! Wait, why?" I asked.

He didn't reply.

His living room was darker than usual. I blinked and noticed it was entirely lit by hundreds of little white candles. Bach was softly playing from a vinyl record player under his television. Candles lined the coffee table in the center of the room and marked out a path on the floor. It led to the balcony's glass double doors.

Ace tugged at my hand to encourage me to follow him. Looking down, I realized the floor was littered with hundreds of red rose petals too.

Oh. I was *such* a goof.

This wasn't a murder set-up. Duh. There hadn't been a fight. Nobody had been killed.

Those rose petals had been placed there on purpose. They had been placed there for *me*.

"Ace?" I asked shakily as we stepped onto the balcony.

The warm summerish breeze tugged at my hair like a playful child. New York City sparkled around us like an ocean of diamonds. It was enough to take anyone's breath away. I tucked a flailing strand of hair behind my ear and waited for his reply.

He didn't say anything. Instead, he took hold of both of my hands and got down on one knee.

Oh, my God. Oh, my God.

"I'm sorry if I've been acting a bit odd today," he finally replied, staring up at me. His eyes sparkled far more brightly than any of the lights around us. "I was planning this...surprise. To be honest, I've been planning it for a while."

He stuck his hand in his pants' pocket and withdrew a small black box.

My hand landed on my mouth.

This was really happening. My heart!

This time, I was the one who didn't say anything. I didn't know what to say. For a brief moment, the entire universe rotated around us, and the stars shone just to illuminate the occasion. My heart was beating like a drum, and my pulse was almost deafening.

He opened the box.

I had to blink several times.

It contained a small silver key, resting on shiny velvet lining.

Ace took the key from it and held it toward me. "This is the key to my front door. The elevator code is 1891. I'll write it down for you. You don't have to move in with me right away, but I want you to know that the second you're ready, you're free to—and by that, I mean you better move in tomorrow." He laughed, and so did I as he continued, "You can just walk right in and start calling this your home." He placed the key on the palm of my right hand, closed my fingers around it, and kissed my fist.

"There's enough room in my apartment, and we'll be a big happy family."

"Oh, Ace," I sniffed. "You silly man. Of course I want to move in with you. It'll probably be a while. I need to give my landlord notice, and I can't just move out and keep paying rent for the place."

"Do it," he insisted. "I'll pay whatever rent you still need to pay."

"You know I don't like feeling like a charity case, you already got me a car, and—"

"That's not what this is. What's mine is yours now, and that brings me to my next point."

He reached into the box and removed the velvet lining.

A diamond ring was nestled inside the bottom of the box.

I gasped.

He took out the golden ring. The square diamond mounted on it glistened in the starlight. It was huge! He took my trembling left hand and slid it onto my ring finger.

"You fooled me! Ace! You did that on purpose." Tears started to roll down my face.

He laughed. "Of course I did." He paused and looked up at me. "Stella. Will you marry me?"

I knew it was coming, but somehow it still caught me by surprise. I rocked back on my heels and stepped backward. His eyes grew large as he realized I was putting distance between us.

"No, no. Don't do that, baby," he said, his mouth agape. "You're supposed to be happy. Don't go..."

I took another step back, inhaled deeply, and rushed at him. We tumbled to the floor together, rolling around on the marble tiles that covered the balcony's floor. "I *am* happy. I'm happier than I've *ever* been," I said, peppering his face with kisses.

"Jesus Christ, woman, you almost gave me a heart attack," he rumbled, kissing me back. He wrapped his arms around me and pulled me on top of him.

"It would have been well deserved!"

"So that's a yes?"

"Yes. It's a yes! A million times yes," I squealed. I nestled my face in the nape of his neck and kissed his shoulder.

"I can finally call you Mrs. Windsor without having you laugh at me," he announced, stroking my curly hair.

"Soon," I replied, kissing his stubbly chin. I leaned back and put a hand on his muscular chest and smiled at him innocently. "Mrs. Windsor sounds good. I almost think a Mrs. Windsor has boss qualities."

Ace grinned. "Definitely."

I waited. It wasn't like him to unreservedly agree with me on the question, "Who's the boss here?"

"However, I'm pretty sure we'll both have a very small and very demanding boss to keep us busy for the foreseeable future."

## 52

## ACE

*R*ing. Riiiing.

I picked up my cell. "Yes," I barked. It had been ringing nonstop ever since the news of the acquisition had gone public and made headlines in the *New York Times*.

> *Construction World in Turmoil*
> *Over Biggest Merger of the Century*

"Edmond Ecclestone. Hello, Mr. Windsor," a deep, rusty voice sounded, a slight French accent coloring the words.

For a second, I was baffled. But it wasn't hard to guess where he'd gotten my private number from.

"Mr. Ecclestone," I said.

"Congratulations on the merger."

"You're congratulating me on the merger that you tried to prevent?"

I heard a soft chuckle. "I don't know what you're talking about."

"Then let me make myself absolutely clear to you," I said, trying to leave the emotion out of my voice. "The stunt you pulled by having somebody infiltrate my company failed. It failed in every aspect. Did you really think that causing disarray and making me the laughingstock in my own company would weaken my overall standing? And just out of curiosity, what did you intend on doing next? Sweep in as the knight in shining armor, saving the place from ruin like Sodom and Gomorrah? Was that your plan?"

Another chuckle. "Mr. Windsor, s'il vous plaît. Please. I don't know what you're talking about." It wasn't hard to detect the hint of mockery in his tone. He knew damn well what I was referring to. But he also knew I had no proof, and he wouldn't make the mistake of incriminating himself.

"In that case, our conversation is over. Goodbye." I'd heard all I needed to hear. Any more words would be a waste of breath.

"Wait, Mr. Windsor. Un moment," he said, just as I was about to end the call. "We were just having fun. Let's talk over a nice glass of Cheval Blanc. I hear it's your favorite."

I chuckled and hung up.

~

Days later, I picked up a paper.

*Scandal Pulls the Plug on Construction Shark*

People claimed there was no justice. Ecclestone, "Mr. Après moi, le deluge," had gotten slapped in a different way: karma style. According to the article, he'd been jailed for money laundering and tax evasion. All of his properties and assets had been seized by the IRS, and there was an ongoing investigation by the FBI. By the looks of things, his lawyers' hands were tied.

He'd be back. Men like him always came back. But it might be a while.

~

A few weeks later
We found out we were having a boy on a rainy Thursday.

I'd gone with Stella to her twelve-week checkup at noon. The traffic on the drive there was bad, but we were too excited to care. Neither of us expected the ultrasound technician to be able to tell the baby's gender so soon, but Lady Luck was on our side. We both cheered when she said we were having a boy. We would've cheered had it been a girl too. It was just that knowing something about the little life growing in Stella somehow made it feel more real to both of us.

Dr. Maxwell peeked in quickly to congratulate us. We discussed babies, tattoos, and motorcycles. In that exact order.

By Friday morning, we'd decided on a name: Jack. Stella thought it'd be witty to stick to a card-playing theme.

"You'll be the Ace," she said. "He'll be the Jack, and I—"

I finished the sentence for her before pulling her into a kiss. "You'll be my Queen of Hearts."

# EPILOGUE: STELLA

**Great Hair Days Are a Thing**

"How was your honeymoon, by the way?" Oliver asked. "We've seen photos and videos on social media. It looks like you did more than a bit of traveling."

"We did," I said proudly, cuddling little Jack in my arms.

"The article in the paper was hilarious," Miles laughed at Ace. "Good job, bro."

Ace and I had gotten married shortly after our engagement (mainly because I didn't want to be heavily pregnant at our wedding), and we'd jetted off on our honeymoon directly thereafter. We landed in "Paris, la ville de l'amour," the most romantic place on Earth, the so-called City of Love. Trust me, it was. On the top of the Eiffel tower, Ace had whipped out a megaphone and declared his love to me. End result: a photo of him —bullhorn in front of his face—and me—slack jawed and speechless— spread like wildfire.

It was everywhere, including front and center of the *New York Times*:

*The Whole World Watches as Billionaire Ace Windsor*
*Confesses Everlasting Love to His Assistant*

## Epilogue: Stella

When I'd presented the article to Ace (and my goofy face on the photo), his smile could have replaced the sun.

I know. I married a silly man. *And I couldn't be happier.*

"We continued our vacation with a visit to his parents in France." I carried on retelling our "adventures." "They live in the quaintest little town. It was like stepping into a fairytale. His mom taught me how to make the most amazing éclairs. Then we flew to England and met up with Jay and his hubby." The two men raised their glasses at me. "We spent a few days with them in beautiful, vibrant London. Then Ace surprised me with a trip to Torquay, a seaside town on the English Channel in the Southwest of the United Kingdom. You know why?"

"Why?" Miles asked.

"It's the birthplace of Agatha Christie! We stayed in The Grand Hotel, which has its own Agatha Christie Suite where she spent her honeymoon. So *romantic*. We visited her international annual festival at Torre Abbey, with tons of talks and performances in honor of her, and then we went on a self-guided walk that takes you to several key spots in her life. It was amazing and eye-opening, and I love her even more. I gained so much more appreciation for her work."

"Sounds like a dream come true for you, Pancake," Damon said, smiling. "Happy for you guys. Hey, Ace, did Stella dress up like Miss Marple and take you on a real mystery adventure?" He chuckled.

"She didn't have to," Ace said. "I've already witnessed her 'Miss Marple routine,' and I loved it." I smiled as he pulled me in for a kiss.

"Touché." Damon shook his head. "Seriously, man, you couldn't have taken her on a better honeymoon."

Ace nodded. "Thanks, bro. We had a great time. I wouldn't have had it any other way."

"We love you, D," I told my brother. Damon was being silly about my "Miss Marple" routine, and he knew all had been forgiven. We were all blissfully happy. Even my broody big brother. It made sense he and Ace were best friends.

We were standing at the punch bowl, filling our glasses. The orange liquid sparkled almost joyfully in the mid-afternoon sun. We'd posi-

## Epilogue: Stella

tioned the beverage table in front of vining jasmine that grew up the wall, and a lazy bee buzzed around.

"And that wasn't the end. Then we jetted off to the Cayman Islands and spent some time living in a property Ace bought there. He designed the house himself. So beautiful! With a pool. Oh, and another great perk? Good hair days are a thing there. Who knew?"

That earned a chuckle from Bonnie first. She understood me and knew the struggle was *real*. Then everyone else joined in. It was no secret that I constantly had trouble taming my mane of curls.

"I love your hair," Ace said, tucking a stray strand behind my ear. Then he leaned in and whispered so only I could hear, "Especially when you're on top." I slapped his arm playfully, but, dear Lord, how I loved this man. He'd given me everything I wanted and then some. It was as if he'd been created specifically for me, and when the stars were perfectly aligned, we had found each other again.

After all the laughter subsided, Miles cleared his throat. "Who were you trying to impress with all of this?" Miles asked Ace, nudging him with his elbow. "You know she'd already married you at that point, right?"

Ace shrugged. "What can I say? I had those drafts and contracts locked up in my desk for a long time. I'd do anything for her."

"Plus, he owed me," I said. "I was in labor for twenty-two hours."

"I did get her a clawfoot bathtub for that." Ace chuckled. He wrapped his arm around my waist and squeezed.

"I love it." I beamed. "I feel like a duchess."

"And even that probably won't be enough. I could never repay you for giving me Jack."

I kissed Jack's little mushroom nose and nodded. "Don't worry, you've got the rest of your life to spoil me."

We were madly in love.

We weren't the only ones. Bonnie had snatched a spot in Ace's heart *the second* I'd told him she had been the one who'd helped find the twenty boxes. Bonnie had warmed up to Ace *the second* I'd told her that he thought that made her the smartest operations agent *and* best friend there was. She

*Epilogue: Stella*

lit up so hard, she even forgot he was driving a Lambo. Part of that might have been because her date, Benjamin, was a tall and handsome Lambo enthusiast. Benjamin was one of the instructors at my yoga class, and when Bonnie had finally taken up my invite (even though she'd always claimed that yoga wasn't her thing), sparks had flown. She and "Benji" had started dating a week after I'd introduced them, and now they were inseparable—and too busy raiding the snack table to join the throng of onlookers.

"Ready for your surprise? Please join me," Ace said, gesturing to his side. He tapped a teaspoon against his champagne glass and cleared his throat. The small group of people gathered on our lawn fell quiet. He grabbed a microphone and tapped on it. "I'd like to make an announcement," his loud voice boomed.

An announcement? Over the microphone? What? I handed the baby to my brother, hoping no one would notice my nervousness. What was he going to say?

Ace took my hand and pulled me to his side, grinning at the group of people in front of us. Miles, Oliver, Damon, Jay, and their significant others smiled back at us. Tilly's date was a young single mother named Kate, a schoolteacher she'd met waiting in the doctor's waiting room.

"You guys *have* to try these," Bonnie praised from the nearby snack table as Benjamin shoved an éclair into her mouth and then took a bite from the other side. Hand in hand, they beelined over to us. I was so happy to have finally managed to make a good batch, thanks to Ace's mom. And even more than that, I was glad I'd been able to make a good match—Bonnie and Benjamin seemed truly perfect for each other.

"I just want to thank everyone for coming today." Ace raised one of his hands like a monarch about to lay down a decree and said, "Stella and I have been looking forward to this housewarming party since we decided to buy this place. It means a lot to us that all of you are here to celebrate the day with us."

"Hear, hear!" Miles shouted in response. "It sure was about time."

"Yeah, any longer on the Cayman Islands, and we'd have had trouble remembering your names, guys," Jay joked.

"I agree," Damon said. He and his significant other, Aria, were

## Epilogue: Stella

taking turns cradling baby Jack in their arms. The little man was wrapped in a thin pastel-blue blanket. The only thing protruding from it was his chubby little face and a shock of white-blond hair. As Ace had predicted, not only did he keep us busy, but everyone else too. He wasn't a fussy baby, oh no, but one look from his blue eyes—which Ace had given him, and heavens, how happy I was about that—or a majestic wave of that chubby little fist, and everyone rushed to see what Jack wanted.

"If you keep heckling me, you'll all be stuck on permanent babysitting duty," Ace teased, making the crowd laugh.

"Bring it on, bro," Miles challenged.

Ace surveyed the chuckling people in front of us and continued. "I'll get to the point," he rumbled, reaching over to an elegant gift box sitting on a nearby chair. He held it out to me. "The person I want to thank the most is my beautiful wife, Stella, who has been there for me through thick and thin. As most of you know, she isn't only a catch, the most mesmerizing beauty, *and* an outstanding detective—" He paused for dramatic effect.

"Ace!"

Laughter filled the room.

"—but she's an even more amazing woman and mother. You really are, baby." He leaned into the microphone. "More than that. The greatest thing about you is that you don't know how amazing you are. You make me the happiest I've ever been. You make me the man I always wanted to be. You make me feel like I can take on the world if need be. You're my everything." His hand cradled my cheek. "I love you."

"Ace...I love you too," I choked, tears filling my eyes.

He handed the box to me and grinned. "I got you this as an expression of my gratitude. Please open it." He winked at me.

With trembling fingers, I took the box from him and ripped the red wrapping paper off of it. Ace put the microphone down. It was dead silent. All eyes were on me. The box itself was non-descript, not too small, not too big, not very heavy—and I realized I'd have to open it to find out what exactly my husband had decided to gift me as an "expression of his gratitude."

*Epilogue: Stella*

Nervous curiosity had my mind going in a thousand different directions.

With a shaky breath, I opened it.

It was a white bikini.

The End

Thank you for reading my novel.

If you liked "Assistant to the Billionaire CEO," you will LOVE "Blind Date with the Billionaire Doc." You get to meet Dr. Maxwell, the oh-so-respectable (and dangerously hot) character you've caught glimpses of in this and some of my other books.

I've included a sneak peek on the next pages.

# BLIND DATE WITH THE BILLIONAIRE DOC SNEAK PEEK

**First, Dr. Jerk ghosted me.**
**Now, I'm pregnant, and he's the daddy.**
**Skip ahead 9 months, and surprise! Guess who's delivering our baby?**

It's supposed to be a normal blind date–awkward, nerve-wracking, uneventful.
But I walk up to the wrong guy:
The hottest, sexiest, richest doctor in all of New York:
Dr. Dillan Maxwell.
My first crush and first kiss.
Hours later, the doctor is in! (Talk about opening wide and saying, "ahhh.")
Then, he's gone. For him, it was just a one-time thing—a wham, bam, thank you ma'am.
Not that a broke exotic dancer and a well-respected doctor ever had a chance.
But he left me with a parting gift: a pregnancy.
Nine months later, it's time to deliver my bundle of joy, and my contractions are getting closer together.

*Blind Date with the Billionaire Doc Sneak Peek*

Who walks in as my OBGYN?
Oh, hi, Dr. Maxwell. Do I have a surprise for you.

Grab "Blind Date with the Billionaire Doc" on Amazon.

# BILLIONAIRE BOSS: SECRET BABY SNEAK PEEK

"How about another drink?"

The deep voice sent a shiver down my spine, and I glanced to my left to see who'd spoken.

*Holy smokes.*

I was face-to-face with the most gorgeous man I'd ever seen. He was tall enough to tower over me, even while I sat on a high bar stool, and his broad shoulders strained against the form-fitting sports jacket he was wearing.

Thick black hair was slicked back from his face, giving me a full view of his dark-blue eyes. They observed me with an intensity I'd never known before, and I immediately found myself drawn to him.

I toyed with the rim of my empty glass. "And ... what would it cost me?"

His smirk widened. He took a seat on the stool next to mine, leaning in close. "Time." He paused, tilting his head. "And sleep."

"Sleep?" I rose a questioning brow at that.

"Well, we won't be getting much sleep tonight, so you're probably going to be tired in the morning."

I couldn't help but blush.

Normally, a blunt come-on line like that would have been a major turnoff, and I'd have headed for the door without a backward glance. I'd been hit on before, and I was *definitely* no stranger to men with large ... egos, but his confidence seemed well-earned. I could sense there was something ... breathtaking about him.

The bartender slid a full glass in front of me before removing the empty one.

Hooking up with a strange man was *not* something I'd planned to do tonight, in fact, not something I'd *ever* done before or had ever even intended to do. I could feel the refusal I'd prepared dying in my throat. I'd been working so hard for Christ's sake! I deserved to blow off a little steam and have some fun for a change.

"Convince me." I accepted the drink and felt rather daring—like a bit of a *femme fatale*.

He raised his eyebrow in amusement and gave me an "I would think looking at me would be enough" gesture.

"Well, you *are* attractive," I admitted. "And you seem nice enough so far, but I don't know you."

"What better way to get to know someone than by getting naked and exploring each other?"

"Maybe, I don't know ... a name *first*?"

He laughed, his rich baritone sending a ripple of desire through me. Those deep eyes sparkled as he leaned in closer. "Jonah."

"Hi, Jonah. I'm Naomi."

Jonah's eyes softened, and he reached out to take my hand. "It's nice to meet you, Naomi." The way his mouth wrapped around my name made my entire body feel flushed. "There, now we know each other. So, we're going to finish our drinks, leave together, and spend several pleasurable hours discovering each other."

I had to admit, all of it sounded amazing. When the collar of his jacket moved, I could see the hint of a tattoo on his neck, trailing away under his neatly pressed shirt. It surprised me. He didn't seem like the type—then again, what did I know? The one thing I was sure of was that I desperately wanted to see just how far down that tattoo went.

And, then I remembered ... Oh, *no*! Well, damn it! Today, of all days, why was I wearing the Halloween monster underwear that Lily had given me as a gag gift? To be fair, they were pretty comfy (so comfy, in fact, I wore them on days to cheer me up, or when I wanted to be reminded of Lily's unwavering self-confidence), but that wasn't going to stop me from killing her later. And—double damn—the reason she'd given them to me in the first place was now more hilarious than before. She'd presented them to me, saying, "There you go. For the only virgin left in our circle over the age of twenty-one! They'll keep your mind *below* your waist for a while." She'd laughed hysterically at her own joke, and at the time, I'd laughed along with her.

Finally, finally, there was this hunk of a man, seemingly hell-bent on deflowering me ... having him see me in these panties would beat all awkward moments I had *ever* been in (and trust me, there had been quite a few). I imagined his face dropping as he undressed me, and instead of finding some sweet hot lingerie, he discovered orange panties with an ogre staring back at him.

"There's just one little problem." I could hear the evasiveness croaking in my voice.

"What's that?"

"I—I really wasn't expecting to meet anyone tonight..."

"I guess we both got lucky then," he murmured.

"I'm a virgin," I blurted out. *I know. Completely out of place.* But somehow this seemed a *slightly* better confession than telling him about Shrek. *So much for femme fatale!* I wanted to crawl under the bar stool and hide. I regretted my words as soon as they fell out of my mouth. If that didn't put him off, nothing would. To my surprise, it didn't.

Jonah showed no signs of surprise, only curiosity. "Why would that be a problem?"

"Well..."

"Is it a problem for you?"

"What do you mean?" *I couldn't even think straight.*

"I mean," Jonah leaned in so close, our thighs touched—the solid heat of it drawing my attention, "is your virginity a conscious decision, or are you using it as an excuse not to get close to anybody?"

"I think maybe a little bit of both?"

Jonah studied me carefully, his gaze drifting from my eyes down to my lips and then back up again. "What are you afraid of?"

That was a loaded question. *If you only knew.* But seriously, with everything going on in my life, romantic relationships were very low on my list. And I mean *very*. Those panties were proof enough of that. I had my parents to worry about, which meant I never had time to get close to anyone. If I did, my virginity was always something I could use to push them away when things became too serious. Mostly, I just didn't want a relationship or the emotional ties that went along with it.

I probably would have done the same thing tonight if another man had shown up, but, now, in Jonah's presence, it seemed I was throwing caution to the wind—my usual excuses were flying out the window at record speed. I mean, it wasn't like I planned on staying a virgin forever. And this guy, well, he was freaking hot. And his pick-up lines didn't make me want to run for the hills. So, why not give him a shot? What was the worst that could happen?

Right. I could lose my virginity in Halloween underoos. Maybe I should just play it cool and see how it goes.

"There are a lot of things to be afraid of."

Jonah gave a nod of agreement. "But if you're always afraid, you're never gonna live."

"A nice sentiment, I could *almost* believe it, if I didn't think you were just saying it to get in my pants."

"I wouldn't say it if I didn't believe it." Jonah gave me a mischievous smile. "Besides, I don't need to resort to cheap lines to get *anyone* in my bed."

"I'm sure you don't." I took a sip of my drink as he took one of his, and our eyes locked.

We wound up in an expensive hotel across the road from the bar. When I heard the price of the room, I almost fainted, but Jonah paid it without batting an eye. His expensive clothes and Rolex had already tipped me off to his wealth, but seeing him drop hundreds of dollars for one night made me feel a little uncomfortable.

I didn't have time to dwell on it. The second we slipped inside the room, he shoved me against the door and kissed me. He tasted like

## Billionaire BOSS: Secret Baby Sneak Peek

expensive whiskey and smelled like laundry detergent, soap, and musk. It was an intoxicating combination of scents and tastes, and I quickly became addicted. I melted against him, grabbing his jacket to pull him closer.

"Let me know if it's too much and I'll stop," he whispered into my ear as he nipped at the lobe. His tongue lapped at the spot his teeth had grazed, before he traveled down to feast on my neck.

"Don't you dare."

Hands groped at my clothes, pulling and tugging to remove them. I did the same to him, eager to feel his hot skin against mine. By the time his hands were removing my skirt, I really didn't care about the "panty problem" anymore. Now, they were just a small barrier between me and my fabulous and pleasurable destiny.

I felt him hesitate, and then a smirk crossed his face. "Why, Naomi, you make me sorry my *Three Little Pigs* undies are in the wash!"

"I'll forgive you as long as you brought the Big Bad Wolf." I actually heard him snicker like a schoolboy.

The rest of the night was a blur of new feelings and sensations. We did so much and touched each other for so long, I lost all sense of time.

He was dominant and rough, but never with malice. I matched his roughness with my own eagerness, and when we finally collapsed, spent and satisfied, I was changed forever.

"What are you thinking about?" he asked as we lay face-to-face with him stroking my hair, and me, lying against his chest.

"Nothing," I said with relief. "For the first time in years … I'm not thinking about anything. Just this moment. Just us."

Jonah cupped my cheek, bringing me into a surprisingly tender kiss. "Nice."

I tucked my head under his chin, listening to the steady drumming of his heartbeat. My fingers traced the tattoos etched into his skin, and I followed the black lines until my eyes began to droop.

I dozed off before I could stop myself.

With a sleepy groan and the beginnings of a hangover, I returned to some semblance of consciousness hours later. My surroundings were unfamiliar, and it took me a good thirty seconds to remember where I was. Memories of firm hands and a distracting mouth flooded my muddled brain, and I smiled at the naughty images. I'd never anticipated that sex could be *that* intense. Sure, I had read my fair share of romance novels and heard my friends go on and on about their sex lives, but I'd always assumed the stories had been greatly exaggerated.

Pushing my messy hair out of my face, I rolled over, reaching for my, well, Jonah, only to touch cold sheets. My heart sank. I sat up and looked around the room. The only source of light came from the bustling city outside the large window.

Had he left a note? *No.*

A business card on the pillow? *Nope.*

A message on the bathroom mirror? I kicked off the blankets, went and checked. *Nada.*

Frustrated, I let myself fall back onto the bed. I should have known he wouldn't stick around. He'd been way out of my league. Rich, muscular, hot, tattooed, *and* mesmerizing? I *knew* it was too good to be true. I'd acted out of character and, sure, I definitely enjoyed it, but there wasn't going to be a fairy tale ending. *No, that's not me, I'll never be prom queen* lyrics sounded in my mind.

I could feel myself starting to become self-conscious and a little guilty. I pushed it away. Why should *I* feel bad? Why should *I* let him have that power over me? It wasn't as if I'd fallen in love. Me? Never. Not with him. *Please, Naomi,* I scolded myself, *you can't be in love with someone you just met.*

I decided that what I felt for him was "first sex affection." A simple mixture of lust and gratitude! Angry, I stood from the bed. The room was paid through the night, but there was no way I was going to stick around. If he could bang and leave, then so could I.

I got dressed as quickly as possible, and despite my disappointment and determination, I couldn't help but feel ashamed. I hadn't expected us to exchange numbers or anything (I had), but, I at least deserved a goodbye.

Before I left, I took a moment to calm myself. *What's done is done,* I thought. *It was fun and now it's over. Once you leave, put him out of your mind and move on.*

That's exactly what I did.
At least, I tried. I really, really tried.
...
*End of the sneak peek.*
Grab "Billionaire BOSS: Secret Baby" on Amazon.

# ALSO BY JOLIE DAY

### *Kiss a Billionaire* Series

In this steamy-hot series, alpha billionaires working in the same company will catch your eye and drive you wild. This series follows a group of friends. Just some good old fashioned romance, comedy goodness, and sexy fun. *All novels can be read as single books.*

Crushing on my Billionaire Best Friend

She's my best friend. Of course, I'd never think about touching Laney. Not today. Not tomorrow. Not ever. Then she moves into my penthouse.

(Laney and Oliver)

Faking It with the Billionaire Next Door

He's my next-door neighbor. My mortal enemy. Cocky. Infuriatingly hot. The biggest jerk I've ever met. Imagine my jaw drop when he asks me to be his fake fiancée. Imagine his jaw drop when I agree.

(Rose and Miles)

Charming My Broody Billionaire Boss

He's the devil himself: Damon Copeland (he practically carries a pitchfork). He's the top dog at my father's company and my brother's best friend. Oh, and someone I *accidentally* slept with.

(Aria and Damon)

Assistant to the Billionaire CEO

I was madly in love with my brother's best friend.

Until he broke my heart. Now he's my new boss: Ace Windsor. Tall. Difficult. Insanely gorgeous. And insanely strict. *Never run in the hallway. Never loiter. Never be late.* He fired his last assistant over nothing, but your girl needs this job.

(Stella and Ace)

Blind Date with the Billionaire Doc

First, Dr. Jerk ghosted me.

Now, I'm pregnant, and he's the daddy.

Skip ahead 9 months, and surprise! Guess who's delivering our baby?

(Lizzie and Dillan)

∽

### Oh Billionaires! Series

The plots are set in New York City—the Big Apple (I hope you're ready for a juicy bite). If you love a man in a business suit during the day and biker gear by night, this series is for you. *All novels can be read as single books.*

Billionaire BOSS: Secret Baby

I hate him—the man who'd taken my v-card. Now, I'm supposed to work with him–*for* him. What's worse, he doesn't even recognize me! What if he finds out that I have a son…his son?

SOLD: Highest Bidder

I bought her at an auction. My best friend's sister.

Billionaire Baby DADDY

OMG…I'm pregnant with a billionaire's baby!

Billionaire CEO: Fake Girlfriend

He's my worst enemy. He's about to acquire my family business. But, he's got a solution for me: My company in exchange for an *arrangement*. He needs a fake girlfriend, and I fit the bill. Fine, I'll pose as his girlfriend. Problem is–What if I don't want to stop pretending?

BOSS: The Wolf

You ever wake up completely naked next to your boss? Alpha AF Joel Embry isn't exactly Prince Charming. In fact, they call him The Wolf. A sharp suit by day—a tight T-shirt and jeans roaring the streets by night. Get in line for the hottest night of your live.

# CONNECT WITH JOLIE DAY

From a sexy bad-boy hero and laugh-out-loud moments to the happily-ever-after. If you stay up way too late reading sizzling hot romance novels, you've come to the right place.

Do you want to read about the knight in shining armor—specifically, the man in a business suit during the day and biker gear by night—willing to do anything to protect his woman?

Then Jolie Day's books are for you.

Read More from Jolie Day on
Jolie Day's Website:
www.joliedayauthor.com

amazon.com/author/jolieday

Printed in Great Britain
by Amazon